Force of the Immortals

BOOK ONE OF THE DRAGONS OF DESTINY TRILOGY

REBECCA JOSE

FREE DOWNLOAD!

OTHER BOOKS BY REBECCA JOSE

THE NETHER SOULS (BOOK ONE OF THE NETHER SOULS SERIES)

TIME AND TIME AGAIN (BOOK TWO OF THE NETHER SOULS SERIES)

THE LAND IN BETWEEN (BOOK THREE OF THE NETHER SOULS SERIES) ***** COMING SOON *****

FOR THE LOVE OF DAWN (BOOK ONE OF THE PRODIGIUM MORTEM SERIES)

SHARDS OF DUSK (BOOK TWO OF THE PRODIGIUM MORTEM SERIES) ******COMING SOON*****

WITCHBALL

WITHCBALL II ***** COMING SOON *****

SHATTERED APPARITIONS

This is a work of fiction. All the characters, creatures, organizations, and events portrayed in this novel are either products of the author's imagination or are used fictitiously. Any resemblance to persons or other forms of being, living or dead, is purely coincidental.

THIS BOOK CONTAINS GRAPHIC SCENES CONTAINING VIOLENCE, FOUL LANGUAGE, AND SEXUAL CONTENT AND MAY NOT BE SUITABLE FOR CHILDREN UNDER THE AGE OF EIGHTEEN. PARENTAL DISCRETION IS ADVISED.

ACKNOWLEDGMENTS

I dedicate this book to my wonderful fans. I am so happy that you are enjoying my stories, and I hope that you continue to do so for years to come. I hope to meet you in person one day so I can see your shining, smiling faces and sign a book for you! All of you make it possible for me to write more books, and I thank you from the bottom of my heart!

MUCH LOVE,

Rebecca Jose

Author of steamy fantasy adventure romance

CONTENTS

x

CHAPTER 1: THE SEER

I looked around at the destruction surrounding me and wailed in despair. There was nothing left. There was no one left. Everything was gone. The ground was black and burned as far as the eye could see. There was no grass, no trees, no people; there was nothing. The sky was dark and gray through the haze of smoke and ash. There was no sun, no blue sky, no clouds…

There was nothing.

I had done this. This was all my fault.

Everyone told me I needed to learn discipline and control, but I did not listen. I was reckless, arrogantly thinking I had it under control, but my emotions had gotten the better of me, just as everyone had said they would.

I had a moment of confusion as I thought about this. The fact that I had lost control made no sense to me. Despite my low energy reserves, I could shift forms when I wanted to, and none of the others could accomplish that. I could pull in energy from my environment to control my shifts, unlike any of the others of my kind.

The others of my kind depended on their energy reserves, their shifts controlled by how much energy they had stored away. Intense, uncontrolled emotion could also bring on the shift. The shifter had no control over their beast form when this happened, which was sort of what had just happened to me.

But I could control my shifts; they did not control me. I had never lost control like that before. I had impeccable control, even during times of emotional overload, so I did not understand how this had happened.

The only conclusion I could come up with was that the third form had somehow taken control of me. I had two forms, just as every shifter did, but I had not known that a third was hidden inside me. I did not know it was even possible to have a third form.

I had been arrogant and ignorant.

I ignored Tenebris, my teacher and the person helping me control my magic. I had thought I knew better than he did. It was my magic, after all. How could he know more about it than me?

I ignored the warnings from my friends and family. They told me to be cautious, pay attention to my training, and learn to control myself. I had thought myself above their advice and warnings because I had thought I knew better than them.

And now they were all gone.

I had killed them.

I had momentarily lost control of my emotions, and the third form had overtaken me. I had no control over what I was doing when it unleashed a reign of destruction and havoc throughout the city, worse than any dragon, dark or light. This third form had been powerfully destructive, and my anger had only fueled its strength as it had lain waste to everything that I had held dear.

I had no clue what it was. It had not been angel or demon, nor had it been dragon. I could not explain it fully, but it was like a mixture of all three. It had been hideous, and I had no control over the foul beast.

After shifting back to my bipedal form, I stood naked to the elements, the smoke and ash coating my skin with a sickly, gray sheen. My lungs ached from inhaling too much smoke as the last of the houses burned away. Tears slid down my cheeks, leaving salty streaks trailing down the sides of my face.

I fell to my hands and knees as the smoke filled my lungs, making it impossible for me to breathe. Spots danced in the corners of my vision, and I knew it was only a matter of time before I died. There was no clean air left to breathe.

My thoughts turned to my mother as my oxygen-depleted lungs sucked in the smoke-filled air. Her chocolate brown hair, fair skin, jade green eyes, and beautiful soft features filled my mind's eye.

I could hear her harsh words, fussing at me for not paying attention in my classes. I could see the tiredness in her eyes as she lectured me on controlling myself whenever we would argue, and I would get angry and start yelling. I could feel the pressure of my heart breaking again because I felt as if she were tired of me and no longer cared.

If only she could have loved me despite my grumpiness, I thought. If only I could have come to her and trusted her with my overwhelming adolescent emotions, then maybe I could have talked to her and relieved my heartache.

I could have told her my grievances and had her hold me as I cried on her shoulder. I could have held her and told her how much I loved and appreciated her. I wanted…no…needed her approval to feel important, but all I had gotten was admonishment.

I had not been important. If only she could have made me feel important to her.

I had not been important to the person who had broken my heart either.

These were my last thoughts as I fell to my side, tears streaming down my soot-covered face, as I took my last breath.

Celia jerked her wrists back from the woman's grip. Her hands were shaking uncontrollably, and she was not sure if she would have the strength to pull her hands away. However, the frightened woman released her of her own accord, and Celia almost fell out of her seat as she jerked back.

Celia's breathing was ragged and shallow, and her heart beat fast and hard in her chest. Her palms were sweaty, and her nerves were shaken to their limit.

The vision she had just experienced had been horrible. She had been inside someone's mind, and the experience had felt so real that she thought she could still feel her lungs burning inside her chest.

She could still smell the smoke, still feel the heat from the burning houses, and the memory of a mother she did not even know still danced inside her mind's eye. The face of the mother had been the face of the woman that sat across from her now, staring at her with horror-filled, jade-green eyes.

She had a soft, round face, a small nose, and full lips. She had pulled her chocolate brown hair back from her face and wound it into a tight bun, covering the style with a sheer, gauzy head wrap. This was the traditional style for women of her position if they were not wearing the traditional habit.

She was a beautiful woman, but the terrified look on her face failed to accentuate her soft features. Her green eyes were too wide, showing too much white, and her full lips were slightly open and thinned out over her teeth. Her eyebrows were so high on her head that Celia thought they might disappear into her hairline.

"What happened? What did you see?" the woman asked in a tremulous voice.

Celia raised a hand, gesturing for silence as she replied, "Please, Sister Maldia, give me a moment."

The woman gave a nod and fell silent.

Celia could see Maldia trembling visibly as she sat across from her at the small round table where Celia performed her readings. Celia took a deep breath and turned away from Maldia. She scanned the folding chairs where people usually sat and waited for their turn at the reading table.

No one sat there today because the High Priestess of Palace Solaris had requested that this reading be private. Celia was glad of that request because it would take her time to get through this vision.

Vision…

Celia had never had a vision before. The closest she had ever come to having a 'vision' was the pictures that floated around in her crystal ball or the pictures that floated around in her mind from the time strands that were permanently placed in her subconscious mind.

She needed time to process what had just happened to her.

Celia placed her hands flat on the table and leaned slightly forward, taking deep gulps of fresh air to calm her pounding heart. She opened her eyes and stared into the crystal ball on the table before her. She saw her startled face reflected off the glass surface, and then she understood why Maldia had been so scared of her a moment ago.

Celia's dark brown eyes held a haunted look, almost as if she had just witnessed a horrible sight, which she had. Her brown skin was smooth, which belied her age of forty years, but there were worry wrinkles in her forehead and the corners of her round eyes.

Her jet-black hair was braided into small braids all over her head, and a few of the braids had fallen over her shoulders. They framed her oval-shaped face with colorful beads tied at the braids' ends. The nostrils of her wide nose flared as she breathed in slowly, trying to calm herself. She pressed her large, full lips together nervously, then ran her tongue over them to relieve the dryness.

She had experienced a vision like the great prophets of old, like the Three Great Oracles.

Celia was not sure what this could mean. Maybe her powers were growing stronger. That sometimes happened, especially to seers. The older the seer, the stronger their scrying powers. Celia decided that she would speak with Tenebris about this later.

For now, however, she needed to translate this vision for Maldia.

Maldia was training to be the High Priestess under Celia's friend, Hestia, who was the current High Priestess. While Celia did not know the mechanics of being a High Priestess or what that station involved, she knew that the holy women, no matter their station, were supposed to remain celibate.

Celia's vision had implied that Maldia would go back on her vows. Otherwise, there was no way she would ever have a child. Was this the reason for the secrecy? Did Hestia suspect Maldia would possibly commit adultery and had therefore sent her to Celia for confirmation?

Celia really did not want to tell Maldia that she could possibly go back on her vows and have a child, but she had to be truthful with her predictions. Celia was not the type of seer to tell her clients only what they wanted to hear. She told people the truth, even if it was not in their favor.

Besides, the future was not always set in stone. With the right actions and choices, one could change their future for the better if they chose. Celia hoped that Maldia would choose wisely.

Maldia sat across from Celia, gazing expectantly at her over the crystal ball in the table's center. Celia could tell that she had calmed since the terrifying reading. Maldia's features did not look as haunted as before, and she even slightly smiled as she waited for Celia to speak.

Celia cleared her throat and took a deep breath. "Sister Maldia, my vision was not a good one. First, it seems as if you might stray from your vows and have a child. Second, the child will be dangerous if she is not properly loved."

Maldia laughed nervously. "Surely, you must be mistaken."

Celia's stare did not waver. She did not back down or cower. Instead, she held her chin up proudly and spoke in a clear, steady tone. "I assure you, I am not. This was not a regular reading. I did not see the future in my crystal ball or translate this prophecy from my runes or cards. I had a vision, Sister Maldia. I have never had a vision before.

"I was in the body of your future child. I felt her emotions and thoughts as if they were my own. She was stubborn and prideful, hurt beyond repair because you failed to validate her, and she made an egregious error.

"Someone broke her heart, Sister. Someone made her feel so unimportant that she made a terrible mistake. One horrid mistake that cost the lives of everyone and everything she loved because she felt she could not come to you for guidance. She felt as if her mother, YOU, did not love her. You were too hard on her."

Celia had not meant for her voice to rise to almost a yell, but her emotions were still shaky from the vision. By the end of her tirade, her voice had raised several octaves, and Celia had to stop and take a few deep breaths.

Maldia stared at Celia with wide eyes that held traces of unshed tears. Her lips trembled, and her voice wavered as she responded, "I will always love my child. There is no reason the child will ever doubt that."

Celia's voice was calmer as she responded, "Are you sure you would not hold a grudge against the child subconsciously? Would you, perhaps, feel guilty for forsaking your vows and maybe, unintentionally, take out your guilt on the child?"

Maldia blinked several times, her eyes widening in disbelief at Celia's words. She cleared her throat before she responded mildly, "I assure you, seer, that I will not forsake any vows to give birth to this child. I am still pure, and I will remain so. My child is the chosen one, born of a virgin priestess."

Celia sat bolt upright in her seat. She tried to keep her gaze neutral but could not help the slight widening of her chocolate brown eyes. She brushed the braids back from her face with a sweep of her hands in a hurried gesture.

She managed to keep her voice calm and her tone neutral as she asked, "Are you talking about the ancient prophecy?"

"Well, yes. It is time for the prophecy to begin. The beacon shines in the sky every night, but this is not the only reason we know. I am already pregnant and have never known the touch of a man." Maldia sat back in her chair and patted her still-flat stomach with a soft smile.

Celia swallowed back the nervous tension that spread throughout her entire body. That explained why Hestia had sent Maldia to her and why she had wanted privacy.

Celia was the last living descendant of The Great Oracles, an ancient set of triplets that had been the most powerful seers ever to walk the planet Mikka. Every prophecy they had ever told had come to pass except one, a prophecy that was now ancient and the stuff of legends. They were recorded into an old tome, which was well protected by Celia. There were also two ancient scrolls, an angel scroll and a demon scroll. These were the original translations of the prophecy.

Celia had never doubted that the scroll's words would someday come to pass, even though she never believed it would happen in her lifetime. She had not read the scrolls in quite a while, so she needed a refresher, and Celia wondered if anyone had taught Maldia the words of the prophecy.

She knew that the High Priestess taught her protégé everything, including the scrolls, but she was unsure how far in her training Maldia was.

Celia stood slowly and excused herself, brushing her ankle-length skirt aside so that she could safely stroll toward the back of the room. The light, silky material of the flowing skirt swirled around her bare feet with the motion, and it trailed behind her as she walked.

Her long, flowing sleeves billowed around her arms as she lifted her hands to push back the beaded curtain that separated the front room from the back. The beads clanked together, echoing in the silence, as they closed around her when she walked into the back of the room.

Celia gazed along the rows of shelves set into the back wall, her brown eyes searching for the tome. It was an ancient-looking tome, but it was a fake. This was simply the switch to the secret hole in the wall that hid the safe. She pulled the book from its top as if she meant to pull it from the shelf, but it did not come off. Instead, a clicking sound filled the silent room, and the book sprang back to its original position on the shelf.

A hidden panel slid back on the wall beside the bookshelves, revealing the safe's front, secured with a combination lock. Celia put in the combination and opened the safe. She then pulled out the ancient tome that contained the translation of the prophecy as told by the Great Oracles.

This one was also a fake decoy to throw off anyone who wanted to steal the genuine tome of the Great Oracles. It was as old as it looked, but there were not as many pages in this book. It contained information about the scrolls and not much else. The critical and secret information about the Great Oracles and the original prophecy was safely stored in the original Oracle Tome.

Celia lifted the decoy tome from the safe gently, dusting off the layers of dust that had collected on its surface. She adjusted the filmy material of her dress once more, then made her way carefully to the table where Maldia still sat waiting patiently.

Maldia glanced up at Celia questioningly as she pushed the crystal ball to one side and gently placed the tome on the table. Celia opened the tome carefully, minding the old pages, and the leather binding creaked in protest. She flipped the pages carefully several times before stopping at a page and then scanned her finger down the page as her eyes narrowed in concentration.

After a few minutes, she glanced up from the ancient book and gave Maldia a questioning gaze. "Have you read the entire prophecy, Lady Maldia?"

Maldia straightened in her seat and peered at Celia with disdain. "I am a training high priestess, so of course I have. High Priestess Hestia has tasked me with memorizing it as part of my training."

Celia quirked an eyebrow at Maldia's sudden shift in mood. Celia raised her head and lifted her chin, matching Maldia's disdainful look and tone as she replied, "So, you know about the demon scroll?"

Maldia's green eyes narrowed. "The what?"

"The demon scroll," Celia answered matter-of-factly. "There is a demon scroll and an angel scroll. They both tell of two futures, depending on which chosen one wins."

Maldia's proud look faltered, and her eyebrows rose in curiosity. "I have been told of the demon scroll and the demon dragons' chosen one, but I have not yet read their scroll."

Celia lowered her head, softening her eyes and tone as she responded, "Then you have not read the entire prophecy. It would be safe to say that you need to know the whole prophecy if my vision is any indication."

Maldia placed a protective hand over her lower stomach as she said, "Are you saying that my child is in danger of failure?"

"According to the demon scroll, yes," Celia answered softly.

Maldia deflated, curling in on herself in her seat. She placed her other hand over her stomach on top of the first and stared helplessly at Celia. She looked defeated, slumped down in her seat, and her tone trembled slightly as she responded, "I have only read the angel scroll."

Celia nodded. "Yes, the palace only has the original angel scroll, so that is usually the scroll that is taught first. The demon dragons protect the original demon scroll, but the palace possesses a replica of the demon scroll for teaching purposes."

Maldia paused momentarily, gesturing toward the ancient tome on the table before continuing. "This book is a replica of the ancient Oracle Tome, but it is not an exact replica. This replica has information on both scrolls, along with a brief synopsis of each prophecy. I can go over the demon scroll synopsis for you now.

"The original tomes held records of all the Great Oracles' prophecies, including the angel and demon scrolls. It held a plethora of information on The Oracles and their lineage. Each generation would add to it before passing it down to the next generation. I am now the keeper of the original tome."

Maldia's eyebrows rose in surprise. "You are a descendant of The Great Oracles?"

Celia chuckled. "Well, do not look so surprised. Why do you think Priestess Hestia sent you my way?"

Maldia shifted in her seat, confusion causing her eyes to wrinkle slightly in the corners, and her lips thinned out over her teeth. "I was not aware that you knew the Priestess."

"Why? Because I live here in Terrien and not in Solaris?" Celia quirked an eyebrow resentfully.

Maldia flinched, her eyes widening and her hands flying up in a gesture of denial. "No! No, Lady Seer, I meant no offense! Please, do not take it that way." She lowered her gaze guiltily and settled her hands back into her lap before continuing, "I only meant that Priestess Hestia rarely leaves Solaris or even the palace, so I did not think she had ever ventured to Terrien to visit this shop."

Celia smiled in understanding. "Ah, yes, well, High Priestess Hestia was not always a high priestess, you know. She was a teenager once, too. We went to the academy together, so she knows my heritage and abilities. It is one reason that I hold the title of Palace Seer."

Maldia's confused look increased as she replied, "You went to the academy?"

Celia huffed. "And why does that surprise you?"

Maldia wrung her hands nervously. Her gaze darted side to side in rapid succession before centering on Celia. "I assumed that everyone from the academy lived in Solaris."

Celia crossed her arms over her chest and shook her head in disappointment. She scrutinized Maldia as she replied, "Not everyone has the luxury of living in Solaris, nor does everyone have access. Anyone can enter Terrien."

She paused, but upon Maldia's confused expression, Celia huffed in exasperation and explained further. "The Great Oracles were not discriminatory on who they helped. I am carrying on their traditions in this way. Therefore, I choose to live here in Terrien, where everyone can access my services. If I lived in Solaris, only certain people could seek my help. Before I agreed to serve as the Palace Seer, I beseeched the queen to allow me to live here and share my services with the rest of Mikka. The queen agreed, and here I am."

Understanding crossed over Maldia's features. She glanced apologetically at Celia and said, "Oh, I see. That is very noble of you. I apologize for making assumptions, truly."

Celia waved her hand dismissively. "It is fine. Can we get back to the prophecy?"

"Yes, of course," Answered Maldia. "Tell me about the demon scroll."

Celia leaned forward once more, concentrating on the ancient tome. She ran a finger down a few lines on the page she had turned to before speaking.

"Ok, so the synopsis says the demon scroll speaks of a child born from a worldly woman in a land of smoke and fire. This child will be born when the sun darkens over the land. He will later kill the light and allow the darkness to rule the planet.

"However, the demon scroll also warns of this light. The prophecy tells of a child who can purify the chosen one and lead him away from the darkness. The demon's chosen one must darken light's heart to prevent this from happening."

When Celia was finished, she carefully closed the book and leaned her arms on top of it as she regarded Maldia thoughtfully.

"Now, do you understand? Do you see how dangerous it can be for your child to allow darkness into her heart?"

Maldia shuddered as she said, "I understand. I vow this very day that I will try my best to be the best mother I can be. Do you have any suggestions for me, seer?"

"Indeed," Celia answered. "I believe my vision was a warning for you. Make sure you show your child understanding, validation, and, most of all, love. Teach her discipline, respect for authority, and humility, but do this gently. This is a delicate and difficult balance, especially for a teenager going through adolescence."

Maldia regarded Celia thoughtfully for a moment before responding, "I must confess that I am pretty frightened about this whole thing. When I first began to exhibit symptoms of pregnancy, Priestess Hestia took me to the palace doctors right away. They confirmed the pregnancy and my virgin status, and things have gone from there.

"I have not even had time to absorb all this information. I do not know the first thing about caring for a child, but I am determined to do this.

"The entire planet depends on me. It is a challenging weight to carry on my shoulders."

Celia reached over the table, careful not to knock over her crystal ball, and patted Maldia's arm. "I will help you through this, Sister. Feel free to consult with me as often as you wish. For now, however, I am afraid that our time has ended for this session."

Maldia smiled at Celia kindly as she rose from her seat. "Thank you for everything, Lady Seer. Your vision was beneficial."

"That is what I am here for," Celia responded as she walked Maldia to her shop door. "Again, do not hesitate to return to me if you need more advice or any help that I can give. And please call me Celia."

"Alright, Celia. You may call me Maldia. Sister is so formal, don't you agree?"

Celia chuckled and nodded as she said, "Yes, I do. We do not need to be formal here."

Maldia smiled, and Celia noticed how it lit up her face and made her beautiful.

"Goodbye for now," Maldia said, and then she turned and ducked out of the shop door.

Celia stood in the open door and watched Maldia disappear into a waiting pod that would take her back to the palace. Celia sighed and returned to the interior of her shop, closing the door behind her. She returned to her table and sat back in her seat to await her next clients.

She considered closing shop early and going home to soak in a hot bath. It had been a trying day and the haunting memory of that vision she had had still danced in her mind. She had no bosses to answer to since she owned the shop and had no more clients scheduled for the rest of the day. Nothing prevented her from going home early.

Celia had a pleasant home in the urban section of Terrien, and her small shop sat in a busy section of the main commerce area of the city. Most of the shops here were tents made from cheap leather or shops made from cheap wood and mud. Some vendors had only a table in the open air, with no roof or covering. But Celia had her shop constructed with sturdy stones and concrete because she wanted to be sure that her shop stood for a while. Since Terrine's weather was mild, Celia was confident it would last for years.

The wards and spells that she had paid witches to put around her shop to avoid robberies and uninvited guests had cost a fortune. Celia considered the spells an excellent investment in this bustling part of Terrien, and she was happy to pay the price. She had been doing business here for over five years and had no problems yet, but one never knew.

Better safe than sorry.

The familiar buzzing of energy that went through her when someone attempted to enter her shop interrupted Celia's thoughts. The small zap of energy was slight and quick, telling Celia that whoever it was meant no harm.

If someone were attempting to enter with malicious intent, the buzz of energy would have been more like a surge of warning that caused the tiny hairs on Celia's neck to stand on end. She had never felt the sensation, but the witch who placed the spell told her what to expect.

Celia straightened in her seat and put on her best smile, preparing to greet her guest. A cloaked figure entered through the shop door with the hood up over a bent head. The person's face was hidden, but Celia could tell it was a woman by their gait and the shape of breasts on the upper part of their cloak.

The woman swayed over to the table where Celia sat, and Celia rose from her seat to greet the mysterious stranger.

"Hello. I am Celia, the seer. How may I help you?" Celia said in her friendliest voice.

The voice that responded was surprisingly masculine, but Celia could still detect the female overtones as if the woman were trying to disguise her voice.

"Tread lightly on the path you are taking. It will only lead to destruction."

Celia's smile faded, and she dropped the hand she had offered in welcome. She frowned in confusion as she asked, "Are you a seer too?"

The chuckle that rumbled from underneath the cloak hood sounded malicious, causing icy fingers to slide along Celia's spine.

"I am no seer. I am a procurer of ancient relics."

Celia took a step back and scrutinized the woman carefully. "I am afraid I do not understand. I have nothing here."

"Oh, I believe you know exactly what I am talking about," the mysterious woman said, slanting her eyes down toward the tome that still sat on the table before Celia. "If you continue on this path, you will only encounter death. Allow me to take that from you and save you from this."

The warning energy from her security spell flashed through Celia in a chilling rush, and Celia took another step back, away from the cloaked visitor. She snatched up the tome and held it close to her chest.

"I think I will keep it, thank you," Celia said in a shaky voice.

The witch had not been kidding when she had told Celia that the security spell would cause a frightening sensation, warning Celia of danger. Every hair on her body stood on end as the energy shot through her, and she backed away even further from the cloaked figure.

Celia felt another rush from the spell, and the bell over her shop door rang again. She locked her gaze firmly on the woman in front of her while using her peripheral vision to check the shop door.

Two more cloaked figures entered the shop, both male, judging from their size and stature. They strolled casually across the floor toward the woman, and the energy flowing through Celia began to burn along every vein in her body. The witch had warned her about this sensation.

Celia threw herself to the ground, still clutching the tome to her chest as she prepared for what would come next. The witch had told her what the security system did when the threat stayed too long inside the shop, so Celia was prepared for the Bolts of fire that shot through the air over her head.

Celia heard screams echo over the flames, but she did not dare look up. The flames and screams continued for what seemed like an eternity. The smell of burning hair and flesh made Celia retch, but she stayed plastered to the ground with the screams assaulting her ears.

Finally, the screams quieted, and the heat from the flames receded. The burning smell hung in the hot, dry air, but it was more bearable now. Slowly, Celia picked herself up off the floor and surveyed the damage.

Three burned bodies lay on the ground just inside the shop door. The woman had attempted to flee, but the torrent of fire had caught her along with the two men. The cloaks had burned away, leaving three masses of melted flesh and charred, blackened bone. Celia could not have identified them even if she had known them.

The round table that had held the tome was burned beyond repair; the crystal ball shattered on the floor beside it. Celia sighed in relief that she had grabbed the book from the table before throwing herself to the floor.

Celia's gaze flicked up to the tattered remains of her door. It lay in black, ashy ruin around the bodies, and the walls beside the door were black and charred. Her beautiful wood floors, which had cost Celia a small fortune, were streaked with burn marks and ash, and layers of smoke hung heavy in the air.

The smell of burning wood and flesh permeated the shop, and Celia sighed as she thought how expensive it would be just to get rid of the smell. Thankfully, the cost of the security spell had included repairs and cleanup, so the money would not come out of Celia's pocket.

Celia only hoped that the cleanup crew that was included in her security spell was a decent one. Would they put her beautiful wooden floors back the way they had been? Celia hoped so, and she hoped that it would not take too long. She had many clients that depended on her.

Celia closed her eyes and took a deep breath, blowing it out slowly as she sagged down into the soot-covered chair and waited. All security spells were linked into the magical webbed network and monitored by the law. Celia had registered hers the day the witch had put it on the shop. Therefore, Celia knew the authorities were coming soon.

They had set her spell off, so the magical signatures would send a signal to the network, through the web, and into the local precinct. The monitor on duty would see the location of the signal on the precinct's web board, and they would send the authorities to the proper address.

Security spells could be set to trap or immobilize the intruders until authorities could arrive, which was the standard type of spell sold. However, Celia paid extra for her protection spells. She did not have the luxury of taking the chance of being overwhelmed.

Celia was a seer and had never had any fighting training. She could not defend herself magically or physically. Therefore, her spell was a less common type of security spell. It dealt with intruders in a way that they could not escape, but Celia had not thought of the implications of that until now.

It was perfectly legal, albeit violent and messy. It was considered self-defense by the authorities. But three people were dead in her shop. The woman had been someone's sister, daughter, or possibly even mother. The men had been someone's son, brother, or possibly even father. Celia had no clue who they were.

She only knew that they had been after the tome, and it was the last mistake they would ever make.

Add to that, a priestess of Solaris, a virgin priestess, was pregnant, indicating that the prophecies in the tome were coming to pass. Something strange was happening here, and Celia was afraid she was getting caught in the crossfire.

Frowning, Celia thought about the mysterious (now dead) woman in the cloak and her enigmatic words of warning.

"Tread lightly on the path you are taking. It will only lead to destruction."

Had the woman known something that Celia did not? Celia searched the strands in her mind, testing for any that might have changed or show trouble for her. She could see nothing right away, so she turned to her table, intending to glance inside her glass ball.

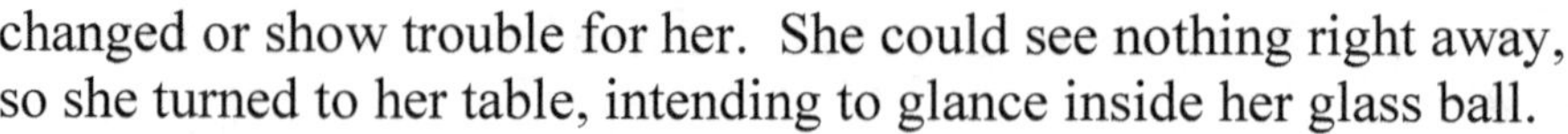

Celia sighed. She had forgotten that it had gotten broken during the incident. She wondered if that cost would be covered by her spell as well. If not, Celia would need another crystal ball; the sooner, the better.

Celia sighed again. Such was the life of a seer, especially one descended from The Great Oracles.

CHAPTER 2: THE PROSTITUTE

Raina pulled the hood up over her head more securely. It was raining, but Raina did not mind so much. She did not want to be recognized, so she welcomed any excuse to pull up her hood and hide her face without attracting too much attention.

However, she would have liked to feel the cooling rain on her skin. Especially after the heat she had gone through from flying over the lava-filled Lake Divere.

A spell gone wrong during the last great war had created the massive lake of lava that had cracked open the entire middle of the planet. Now, the planet was divided into two great hemispheres.

The northern hemisphere was home to most of the angel dragons, though this did not insinuate that all the citizens of the northern hemisphere were kind. The north was well-guarded by soldiers and law enforcement officers that mostly kept the peace, but some people were always determined to cause trouble.

The southern hemisphere was a different story, however. The southern hemisphere was home to most of the demon dragons. Most of the southern hemisphere's cities were lawless and rough, so only the thickest-skinned creatures lived there. However, there were some peaceful places, such as the capital city of Asgorath, the palace, and some of the smaller cities surrounding Asgorath.

Raina and her mother had been thick-skinned enough to survive no matter which part they lived in, but Raina had a good reason to want a new, more peaceful life now. She placed a hand on her massively protruding stomach as she felt the kick from her unborn child and smiled softly.

She hoped she had not hurt the baby

from her ride on the dragon or from breathing in the sulfur and smoke that had risen from the immensely vast lava lake. She had kept the attached cloth from the cloak firmly around her face as a sort of filter, but she could still smell the remnants of brimstone on her skin.

The lake had been extra ashy as of late.

Typically, the clouds of ash and smoke stretched straight up as far as the eye could see, almost as if an invisible barrier prevented it from spilling out over the land.

No dragon had ever flown high enough to escape the cloud of ash that filled the entire sky on top of Lake Divere, and no one knew how far up the smoke went. No one knew much about this phenomenon or how it had happened.

However, for the past nine months, the smoke had escaped into the sky of the southern lands. Strangely, it had never settled onto the ground but only hovered above the southern hemisphere's capital city.

Today had been the worst day forAsgorath and the palace. The smoke and ash had been so thick over the palace that it had partially blocked out the sun, causing today to be one of the darkest days in recorded history for Asgorath.

That had been just fine with Raina. It had made it easier for her to escape. Since the land was darker than usual, it had been easy for her to slip past the guards and meet with her ride in a neighboring city at a designated hidden spot without being seen.

Even after traveling across the lake, it would still be hours before the sun traveled across the southern hemisphere and lit up the north, so the entire trip would be nighttime.

However, the fact that Raina's trip to the northern hemisphere was not exactly a pleasure vacation made Raina jumpy. She was running, almost positive that the entire planet was looking for her. Her I.D. and paperwork were fake, giving her hope that she would not get caught and dragged back to the palace.

Some dragons would smuggle people over and provide fake paperwork for a hefty price. This service was primarily used by criminals and people that could pay exorbitant prices, but for Raina, the ride across the lake and her paperwork had cost her nothing.

Raina's mother had a client that she had 'serviced' for years, and he had always been kind to Raina and her mother's favorite. Fortunately, Tanner was also one of the biggest smuggling bosses in the southern hemisphere. Tanner offered his services to Raina, and soon arrived with fake documents that would be sure to fool the most vigilant of law enforcement. He even agreed to smuggle her over personally.

He had flown Raina over Lake Divere to a remote location where few people ever landed due to the rough terrain. This is where most of his mob smuggled the criminals, especially the drug bosses featured on the most wanted lists.

"There will be less of a chance of you being recognized here," Tanner said to her after dropping her off and returning to his human form. "Most dragons never land here, so the crowd crossing the border will be limited."

"I will be fine," Raina had told him, ignoring his after-shift nakedness. It was not the first time that she had seen Tanner naked.

Her mother was a prostitute, and Tanner was her favorite client. Many mornings, Raina would wake up and find him strolling naked around their house. Nakedness was not a big deal for a shifter, so Tanner never seemed ashamed, so Raina became used to casual nudity. She only ignored it, as she was doing now.

"You need to get back and make sure my mother got out of the palace. If something happens to her, I will never forgive myself for escaping and leaving her there."

Raina had followed in her mother's footsteps from the moment of her first blood cycle. They considered her a beauty among the women of Nokhe, the neighboring city of Asgorath and the city she had grown up in.

Men began offering high prices for a chance at Raina's bed when she had grown into an alluringly gorgeous young woman. So, she turned to the same path as her mother to help make ends meet and keep food on the table, despite her mother's objections.

However, when she captured the notice of the prince of the demon dragons, she neglected her duties to spend time with him. The prince compensated her well, and Raina and her mother enjoyed comfort for a time. Then the prince made Raina an offer.

He asked her to come to the palace and become a member of his harem. They would give her a living space where her mother could live with her. She could have a prince in her bed without worrying about unwanted pregnancies since they gave the harem ladies a special anti-pregnancy tea daily. How could Raina refuse?

However, the tea had not worked for Raina.

Tanner responded to her earlier statement, pulling Raina from her thoughts. "My men have already taken your mother to a safe house.

My focus is on you. If something happens to you, your mother will never forgive me."

Raina smiled at his attempt to appease her, but she did not let him off the hook that easily. "Just please, promise me you will not let anything happen to her."

Tanner sighed and ran a hand through his black hair. "Look, Raina, do not worry. Have I ever let anything happen to you or your mother? Mary will be fine. I will stay with her until you find your estranged sister in Terrien, and then I will send your mother to you with her own set of fake paperwork."

Raina took in a calming breath as she nodded her head. "Alright. I trust you, Tanner."

Tanner smiled, causing his hazel eyes to crinkle in the corners. His smile lit up his handsome face, but it quickly vanished as he scanned their surroundings.

"Are you sure you will be safe in the north when the palace finds out you are gone?"

Raina shrugged as her eyes followed Tanner's, scanning the land around the ledge where they had landed. She did not know how to answer Tanner's question without causing him to worry. Raina knew that Palace Asgorath would search relentlessly for her and would not give up easily. She was pregnant with a prince's child, but there was more to it than that.

When Raina showed signs of sickness, they took her to the palace doctor. The doctor informed Raina of her condition and then announced her pregnancy to the prince and the king. Strangely, instead of becoming enraged at the news, the king gave Raina a room with the prince and was told she would now be his princess.

This confused Raina until they sent her to Asgorath's seer in the third month of her pregnancy. Raina had asked many questions, hounding the old seer until she had finally told Raina of the prophecy and the scrolls. It horrified Raina to learn that they planned to raise her son to be an evil thing, killing the light and allowing the chaos-seeking demon dragons to rule the land.

Tanner cleared his throat loudly, pulling Raina from her thoughts once more. Raina shook her head to clear it and focused on her surroundings.

"Look," Raina said, pointing to a small group of people that had just gotten off a gigantic dragon's back. "There is a group that has just arrived. I will travel to the landing station with them as if I were part of the group and be safe."

Tanner glanced up at the group. "What if one of them recognizes you?" He had asked.

That was when it first started to rain. Raina smiled up at Tanner as she lifted the hood over her head. "See? Luck is on my side. I can wear my hood, and no one will be the wiser."

"I am not talking about just this group," Tanner said sternly. "I am talking about once you reach the cities. If anyone recognizes you, it could go bad for you and your mother."

"I have the papers you gave me to prove that I am not Raina Beals," Raina said. "I am Amelia Cass. I have my disguise in my bag, and I can keep my hood up for now."

Tanner smiled a wicked little smile. "I had my best man on that paperwork. It should be foolproof."

"See, you have nothing to worry about," Raina said, returning his smile.

Tanner's smile faded as he took Raina's hand and brought it to his lips. "I love you as if you were my daughter, and I love your mother. You know that, right?"

Raina swallowed a lump that had formed in her throat as she took her hand back from Tanner, tears threatening to form in her eyes. She blinked them away, straightening her back with determination.

Her voice showed no sign of her emotion as she said, "I will be careful, Tanner. I promise. Please, just focus on keeping my mother safe. I love you too."

Tanner sighed and nodded, giving Raina a fierce goodbye hug and a quick peck on the cheek. "Do you still have my contact info?" He asked as she pulled away from him.

Raina nodded, pointing to the side of her head to indicate that she had memorized it. "I have your number here and the burner phone you gave me in my bag."

Tanner chuckled and said, "Good girl. Call me when you have settled, and you can check on your mother then."

Raina nodded again and smiled. "Thank you for everything, Tanner."

Tanner gave Raina a slight nod and then shifted back to his massive black dragon. His golden dragon eyes took one last look at Raina before launching into the sky, ruffling the edges of Raina's hood with the wind from his wings. His shiny midnight scales caught a glint from the bright moonlight on the northern border as he disappeared into the smoke and ash over the lava lake.

Raina took a calming breath as she sashayed into the group of the more recent immigrants to the northern hemisphere with her bag slung over her shoulder. She acted casually as if she had arrived with them and belonged in the group. No one in the group noticed her stealthy arrival, and they all flowed around her as they moved as if she had been in their midst all along.

The rain had stopped, but Raina was not in a hurry to remove her hood. She did not know if the palace would be looking for her this soon or not, and she did not want to be so close to her destination only to be dragged back to the capital. She would not let her son grow up to be evil.

She had no special powers like the witches and wizards, no shifting abilities like the dragons and other shifters, and could not tell the future like the seers. Raina could not fight, could not wield any weapons, and did not know the first thing about defending herself. She had never had to. Raina had been a prostitute; she was a lover, not a fighter.

She had no other choice but to run away.

Like all the other surviving pure angels, her mother was a pure angel who had lost her wings in the war. The rest had been killed in the war. Her father had been a powerful, pure demon who had lost his life in the war, leaving Raina's mother to raise her and her newborn sister alone.

Her mother sold all their possessions to keep a roof over their heads, but it was not enough. She regretfully gave up her baby for adoption, but only on the condition that she be adopted by someone in the northern hemisphere.

Mary did not have the heart to part with Raina.

She resorted to selling the one thing she had left to make ends meet and to keep one of her children.

Her body.

And Raina had followed in her mother's footsteps, which had put her in the situation she was in now.

Raina shook herself from her reverie when she noticed the group around her slowing to a crawling pace. The group traipsed across the uneven earth toward a single tower that overlooked a massive wall stretched as far as Raina could see on both sides. She could see guards at the top of the tower holding large weapons, scanning the sky for trouble-causing dragons.

There was an opening in the wall, closed off by an enormous gate, and two guards were stationed on either side of the gate. One guard stood in front of the gate with a stern expression, holding a pen and clipboard at the ready. He was gesturing for the group to slow down.

"Please, make a line here. I will need to check your passports before you go through the gate," the officer said sternly as the group drew closer.

They formed a line, and Raina slipped toward the back. She was not yet ready to reveal her face. The officer began checking each person as they stepped up. He would check their I.D. thoroughly, then motioned them toward a bus waiting to take them through the gate and to the nearest town.

Raina stepped up as the line moved forward. The closer she got to the officer in front of the line, the more nervous she became. She clutched the documents with her fake identity and kept her head down.

It would raise suspicion if she stayed hidden under her hood for much longer. Raina prayed for more rain. The line moved again, and Raina was third in line now. She turned to move further back in the line, but one soldier caught her in his gaze, and she froze. She did not want to look suspicious, so she took a deep, calming breath and removed her hood but turned her head so the guards could not see her face.

She heard someone make an appreciative noise behind her, and she glanced over her shoulder questioningly. A dark-haired male stared at her with a smug smile that lit up his bright blue eyes. She could tell he was a dragon shifter by the glow of his skin, but she could not tell if he was an angel or a demon. He had to be one or the other since all pure dragons were extinct. However, his ancestry could not be determined until he shifted.

Raina huffed and turned around, not caring if the guards saw her now. Raina knew that look all too well, but she had no time for it.

Being pregnant had done nothing to tone down the attention she had always received from men. Her wavy black tresses, her bright green eyes, and her full rosy lips seemed to only be amplified by her pregnancy. Her voluptuous hips, large breasts, and ample buttocks received many stares from men, and envious ones from women, despite the largeness of her belly.

She could feel the eyes of the man behind her on her buttocks now, but she ignored him. She huffed in exasperation. That said much about his nature if a man was willing to flirt with an apparently pregnant woman.

He must be a demon dragon.

A pain shot through her abdomen suddenly, and she clutched her stomach and grunted low in her throat. She was next in line, so she gritted her teeth against the pain and breathed slowly. The officer waved the person in front of her away to the bus and then motioned for Raina to step forward.

'*Not now,*' she thought to herself. *'I must make it across the border before my labor starts.'*

Raina stepped forward slowly and handed the officer her documents as she smiled at his stern face. He paid her no heed and only scanned the documents thoroughly before glancing down at her and scanning her just as thoroughly. Raina fidgeted under his gaze, but she kept the innocent smile on her face as the officer continued to look her up and down.

He noted her pregnant state as another wave of pain washed over Raina's stomach, and her eyes narrowed as she tried to keep the pain from her features.

"Where are you headed, Miss Crass?" Raina was confused for a split second before remembering that Crass was the name on her fake documents.

She recovered quickly, sweetening her smile as she answered, "I am headed to Terrien. I have a sister there willing to take me in and help raise the babe." Raina glanced down at her stomach and ran a hand over it lovingly.

Another wave hit her, and this time she could not help the moan of pain that escaped her throat. She could not prevent the anguish from washing over her features as she grasped her belly and almost doubled over in agony.

"Miss Crass," the officer stated, seemingly unaware of Raina's pain. "You cannot have your baby here."

Raina jerked her gaze up to the officer. "Why not? I do not want my baby raised in the lawlessness of the southern hemisphere," Raina said through gritted teeth. "I want my baby born in the north."

"No, I mean you cannot have your baby here, at this entry station. Miss Crass, you have an hour's bus ride before you even get to the first city here. I cannot have a woman in labor riding on the bus."

Raina breathed slowly as the pain receded somewhat.

"What can I do?" Raina asked, her voice trembling with panic and pain as another contraction hit.

"I suggest you go back to the south to have your baby," the officer answered, and he seemed almost annoyed. "There are hospitals nearer to the border on the south side, or you can take your chances elsewhere. You may return after the babe is born and you both have recovered. Whatever you decide, it must be quick. People are waiting behind you."

The dark-haired demon dragon standing behind Raina stepped up to her side. "Officer, let me take her to the side. I think I can help her. I am a doctor."

Raina turned to him. "Why would you…" Her words were cut off by a wail of agony as another contraction hit, and she doubled over in pain. Raina felt like someone was trying to rip her stomach apart from the inside, and a painful pressure was beginning to build inside her womanly walls. Her bag slipped to the ground.

"Come with me, please. I will help you," the man said urgently.

Raina took in gulps of air as she tried to breathe around the pain. "I do not even know you," she wailed from her bent-over position.

"My name is Tenebris Fray. I am a doctor," He paused to lean over close to her ear and whisper, "I can shift. I can take you somewhere private to have your baby, somewhere close, and then fly you to Terrien to your sister with the babe. You won't even have to come back to the border."

Raina stood and looked up into the shifter's eyes. It surprised her to see serious concern in those icy blue depths. Earlier, he had been ogling her like a love-sick schoolboy, and now he looked every bit the part of a concerned doctor. Another contraction hit, and Raina doubled over in agony once more.

"Alright, I agree. Just make it stop," Raina wailed miserably.

"I am afraid I cannot control the pain, dear. But I can teach you to manage it. First, we need to get out of here, though."

Tenebris snatched up her bag and draped it around his own shoulder. Then, He grabbed Raina around her waist, threw her arm over his other shoulder, and helped her hobble away from the gate and border wall.

He was surprisingly strong, and Raina could walk fine with his muscular arm around her waist. He led her closer to the path back toward the lava lake, where she had landed on Tanner's back earlier.

"Where are you taking me?" Raina asked in a panicked voice.

"Somewhere where no one will see or find us," Tenebris answered soothingly. "I promise it will be fine. I am going to shift so you can hop on my back."

"I do not know if I will be able to climb onto a dragon while I am in this much pain," Raina said, tightening her arm on his broad shoulder.

"You will not have to climb," Tenebris said with a smirk. "I am a small dragon, about the size of a small horse. You can hop on quite easily if I kneel for you."

Raina turned her head to give Tenebris a surprised glance. "Well, that is surely convenient."

Tenebris chuckled as he nodded his head in agreement.

When they were far enough away, Tenebris glanced around for any signs that they were being watched. When he was satisfied that they were alone, he released his hold on Raina and her bag and shifted.

Raina gasped as another contraction hit, and this one was much stronger than the others had been. She did not even have time to admire the beautiful, jade-colored dragon with the copper-colored eyes before she descended onto her hands and knees in torment.

The dragon brushed one of its wings over her as if it were comforting her, and she raised her head to look up at it. As promised, Tenebris was a tiny dragon with small black horns protruding from either side of his head and tiny horn buds on his snout.

Raina had been right. He was a demon dragon with those black horns, although he could almost pass for an angel dragon with the copper eyes. Furthermore, most demon dragons towered in height, standing easily taller than the tallest buildings in the city. There were smaller dragons, but Raina had never seen a demon dragon as small as Tenebris. It led her to wonder if he really was a demon dragon.

Raina reached a hand toward the dragon in a silent plea for help, and the dragon lowered itself to the ground, dragging its belly along the dirt as it scooted toward her.

Its head reached her outstretched hand, and the dragon nuzzled her hand with its nose. The scales of the dragon were soft and somewhat rubbery. She grasped at a spot between two scales on the top of the dragon's nose and found a small handhold. She grasped it gently, not wanting to hurt the dragon, but the dragon did not seem to mind. It pulled firmly as she held on, and she pulled herself up with the dragon's help. Pain shot up her legs and stomach as she tried to stand, and she gritted her teeth against the agony.

She let out a cry of determination as she rose up through the pain. When she stood and released her hold on the dragon's face, the dragon scooted around until its back was within Raina's reach. She found a handhold on the dragon's neck, as she had on his head. With another scream of agonized fortitude, she pulled herself onto Tenebris's back by placing her fingers in the space between his scales.

The dragon picked up Raina's bag in its mouth and then took to the sky. Raina held on for dear life as they rose into the air. Tenebris flew toward the lava lake, and Raina panicked as they neared it. Where was this stranger taking her?

They arrived at the lava lake, and the dragon flew straight toward the burning lava. The dragon hovered dangerously close to the lava's surface as it swung its head as if searching for something. Raina's bag swung from the dragon's mouth, and Raina was sure it would catch fire.

Raina did not know how the dragon could see through the thick smoke or how it kept from burning the scales of its underbelly this close to the fiery surface of the lake. However, the dragon seemed unscathed, and even her precariously dangling bag remained untouched by flames.

The heat did not scorch her skin from atop the dragon's back, but the smoke burned into her lungs as she tried to breathe. Raina screamed when the dragon dipped even closer toward the lake, thinking that the dragon meant to fly with her into the fiery lava below. Instead, the dragon landed on a ledge just above the bubbling lava, high enough that the lava did not touch it.

Raina could feel the intense heat from the lava, but it still did not burn her as she slid to the side of the dragon's back. The smell of sulfur almost overwhelmed her as she climbed off, and she immediately collapsed to her hands and knees on the dirt-packed floor of the ledge. Smoke rose from the lake and surrounded them, and Raina coughed with the effort to breathe. Her lungs felt like they would burst inside her chest, and the pain of contractions ripped through her abdomen and radiated down her legs.

Raina lifted her head to see the dragon open its mouth and drop her bag to the ground. Raina saw a light deep down in the dragon's throat flare. The dragon roared, and the light shot from its mouth and surrounded the ledge, immediately cooling the air and dissipating the smoke. It formed a bubble around the ledge, feigning off the smoke and ash and filling the inside with cool, oxygen-rich air.

The surface of the protective bubble crackled and sparked with electricity, and Raina's eyes widened in surprise. Not only was he the most miniature demon dragon Raina knew of, but he blew electric energy from his gut, one of the rarest dragon breath magics.

The bubble of electric energy surrounded Raina as she took in huge gulps of the fresh air. She nodded to the tiny jade dragon in gratitude, but the dragon did not respond and only flew off, leaving Raina alone on the ledge.

She panicked, wondering if the dragon had left her there to die alone and in pain. She was in labor. Her child would die along with her. If not from heat and exhaustion, then from dehydration and starvation. Her mind scrambled for a solution as panic set in, but another contraction seared through her, and she could think of nothing but the pain.

The agony raged through her for what seemed like an eternity, but her panic was short-lived. The dragon returned shortly after, shifting back to his bipedal form as he strolled over to where Raina kneeled on the ground. He was completely naked after his shift, but Raina was used to nudity. However, this man's muscled form had Raina wishing she was in a better position to admire him.

His chest was nicely cut but not too large. His biceps rippled with power but were not too bulging. His stomach sported a six-pack, and his sleek muscular legs carried his form gracefully. And his groin…

Raina turned her eyes away from that spot. That was what had gotten her into this position in the first place. However, this man's impressive member was much larger than the prince's, and Tenebris's grace and posture implied that he had the knowledge to use that member to bring immense pleasure.

Raina sucked in a breath as another contraction hit, and thoughts of Tenebris striding toward her slipped from her mind as she closed her eyes in anguish.

He kneeled beside her and removed her cloak. He spread it onto the ground and then placed a comforting hand on her shoulder.

"Lie down and get comfortable. I will remove your undergarments so the babe can be born." His voice was soothing as he spoke, and Raina relaxed under his touch as much as she could.

She lay back with Tenebris's help and took calming breaths as she felt him tug her pants and panties off. He folded her pants tightly and tucked them under her neck for a makeshift pillow, then pushed the hem of her shirt over her belly.

"I am going to be right here with you," Tenebris said.

Raina only nodded as she continued to take deep breaths, and her muscles tensed instinctively as she felt another contraction take her.

Tenebris sat on the ground at Raina's feet and turned his gaze to her face. "It may be a while before you are ready to push, and the pain will only get worse. I will show you how to deal with the pain so you can follow the cues from your body. You will feel the overwhelming need to push when it is time. Listen to your body."

Raina groaned. She was already in agonizing pain with each contraction. How much longer would she have to endure this pain, and how much worse would it get? Raina wished she had not asked that question when the next contraction hit. She screamed in agony as the contraction roiled through her, and Tenebris moved to hold her legs as her upper body thrashed with the pain.

He coaxed her to breathe in through her nose and blow it slowly out of her mouth. He coaxed her until she got the exercise right and then instructed her to relax if she could. Raina tried, and she found that the breathing actually helped somewhat. However, when the contractions became even stronger, the breathing no longer helped.

The loud thundering of the rolling lava beneath them drowned out her screams, and the smoke and ash that rose from the lake's surface hid them from view behind Tenebris's protective bubble of magic. Raina's screams filled the air around them as her labor increased in intensity, and soon the contractions were coming one right after the other with no breaks in between.

When she finally felt the overwhelming need to push, coupled with the unbearable pain, she was tired and spent. She had no idea how she would find the strength to push her child into the world, but somehow she did.

Following Tenebris's instructions, Raina pushed with each contraction. She struggled to pull the energy to do it again and again, using thoughts of her baby and what a wonderful mother she was going to be to fuel her next push.

Her body grew shaky and weak, but Raina focused on Tenebris's calming words of encouragement as she pushed again. Finally, after the next desperate bout of pushing when she thought she could do no more, she felt the release of the pressure from her lower body and heard the cries of her newborn baby boy. That and Tenebris's happy cries of congratulations were music to Raina's ears.

Raina named the babe after her dead father and the doctor who helped bring him into the world. And so it was that Ethan Tenebris was born surrounded by smoke and fire at the exact moment that the ash from Lake Divere completely blotted out the light of the moon and sun, leaving the land of Asgorath in utter darkness.

CHAPTER 3: THE VIRGIN

Miles away in the palace of Solaris, the sun sank low on the horizon as a star lit up brightly in the sky above the palace, brighter than any star had ever shone before.

It was almost as if three full moons were in the sky until the star lit up so brightly that it even blotted out the light from the moons. Then, it was as if there were a sun in the sky in the middle of the night, lighting up the land of Solaris as if it were daytime.

The palace was full of chatter about the strange occurrence, but the queen understood its significance. It was part of the prophecy of the angel scroll.

Maldia climbed into her comfortable bed to prepare for her labor. She was surrounded by handmaidens, the palace cleric, the palace doctor, and a midwife. The queen had assigned them to her personally.

Maldia had felt the beginnings of contractions earlier that day, and Hestia had hurried to make all the arrangements necessary to ensure Maldia's comfort. She had been undressed and bathed, and her bed prepared for the mess of birth. The doctor had given her tea for pain, and the palace cleric had placed a spell of comfort over her entire body. The doctor and the midwife checked the progression of her contractions periodically, and the handmaidens saw to Maldia's every need.

Maldia was resting peacefully as she went through her labor and she only felt a slight pressure from her contractions.

It gave Maldia plenty of time to rest, but she was too nervous and excited to sleep. Instead, Maldia lay in bed wide awake with her mind wandering wildly.

Maldia thought back to her first reading with Celia during her earlier term of pregnancy. Celia had had a most distressful vision of her future daughter, which had scared Maldia into buying many books on child care and parenting. She wanted to be the best parent she could be, which meant learning everything she could.

Maldia's reminiscing took her back to her childhood and the person who had raised her. Maldia had been raised by her aunt, her mother's sister, in the capital city of Solaris. Maldia's mother had died when she was very young. She remembered little of her mother and often asked her aunt Gabriella what happened to her, but Gabby would not tell Maldia much. She only said that Maldia's mother had died unexpectedly, and the authorities had sent Maldia to Gabby since she had been the only living relative.

It had never been enough for Maldia. She tried hard to remember more of her mother, but the memories would never come. It left her feeling empty like a piece of her soul was missing. She needed closure, but her aunt refused to give it to her…refused to tell her what had happened to her mother.

Maldia vowed that her child would never experience that feeling of emptiness. Maldia would always be there for her child to love and guide her through her entire life, even if she died unexpectedly like her mother had. She had already prepared a letter and a video for her daughter if that occurred. She had also assigned someone to take custody of her daughter and give her any information she needed.

Maldia's thoughts were distracted by the pressure building in her abdomen, and she placed a hand over her stomach. When the pressure began to build to an uncomfortable level, Maldia squirmed on the bed.

"Chandra," Maldia said worriedly, addressing the midwife. "I think the tea is wearing off. It is beginning to hurt."

Chandra glanced up from the book she had been reading, rocking softly back and forth in the wooden rocking chair by Maldia's bed.

"Does it actually hurt, or is it just tightening pressure?" Chandra asked.

"There is tightening and pressure, but it is painful. It is hurting my…umm…," Maldia struggled to complete her sentence as her face flamed with embarrassment.

Chandra quirked one eyebrow. "Your vagina? Is that what you are trying to say?"

Maldia swallowed hard and nodded.

"Is it a constant pain, or does it come and go?"

"It comes and goes," Maldia answered. "It is about every five minutes."

Chandra nodded knowingly and replied, "That is normal. We need to monitor the pain, so no more tea for now. Let me know when the sensations flow closer together."

Maldia nodded and settled into a more comfortable position as Chandra read from her book. Maldia cringed inwardly as she felt another twinge of pain but did not complain again.

As if Chandra could sense Maldia's discomfort, Chandra reached one hand up and gripped Maldia's hand, giving it a slight squeeze. She smiled up at Maldia comfortingly.

"You got this," Chandra whispered, giving Maldia a wink.

Maldia smiled. She was glad that the queen had assigned Chandra as her midwife. She had always been close to Chandra since they had a bit in common. They were both orphans.

Chandra's heritage was unknown, but she had many angelic-like powers, leading Chandra to believe she had angel heritage. Her adoptive parents were shifters, and Chandra never shifted when she reached maturity, leading Chandra to question things.

Her adoptive parents explained to Chandra that her mother had given her up not long after birth. But, like Maldia's aunt, Chandra's adoptive parents refused to give Chandra many details about her mother or the reasons she had given Chandra up. Chandra had that same emptiness inside her, the same compulsion to have closure.

Maldia was thankful she had someone to talk to about the pain and emptiness, but she often felt envious of Chandra's position. Chandra's mother had not died. She may have the chance to gain closure from her mother someday if her mother ever came looking for her.

It would be easy to find her. Chandra's adoptive mother had never changed her name. She had the same name that her birth mother had given her, although she had changed Chandra's last name.

"Maldia, are you feeling alright?" Chandra's worried voice asked, breaking through Maldia's thoughts. "You have gone pale suddenly."

Maldia smiled at her friend. "Yes, I am just in a bit of pain. I was just thinking of other things to keep my mind busy."

Chandra smiled and nodded. "Yes, that is an excellent strategy. Keep that up. It should not be long now."

Maldia shifted as another pang hit, and she breathed through the pain and let her mind wander.

They had sent Maldia to the palace school shortly after she had settled into her new home with her aunt. She excelled in all her classes in the first semester. She was kind to everyone she encountered and very curious about spiritual beliefs and practices.

At the beginning of the second semester, Hestia, the High Priestess of Queen Damaphur, handpicked her for the special classes. These classes were held for the students who would be initiated into The Brothers of Typhon or the Sisters of Echidna, Solaris's priests and priestesses of the angel dragon's Goddess, Tiamat.

Hestia took a particular interest in Maldia, and Maldia soon became one of three front-runners to become High Priestess in training under the direct tutelage of Hestia. After graduation, the three front-runners were given many tests and trials, and Maldia excelled in them all.

She had met Chandra during this time. Chandra had been training in the warrior classes for the Sisters of Echidna and had quickly befriended Maldia. She had been so proud of Maldia and her accomplishments. Chandra quickly became Maldia's number-one supporter throughout the entire experience, and Maldia supported Chandra's accomplishments just as fiercely.

The pressure building inside Maldia became even more painful, drawing Maldia once more from her ruminations. She groaned in discomfort when a powerful contraction shot tiny rivulets of pain through her most secret place.

Chandra clamped down firmly on Maldia's hand as she asked, "Maldia, is the pain worsening?"

Maldia returned Chandra's tight squeeze on her hand as she held her breath. The contraction pressed her longer than before until finally releasing her, and she let out a shaky breath as her muscles trembled with relief.

She answered in a shuddering voice, "Yes, it is becoming painful and closer together."

Chandra placed her book, still open on the page she was reading, upside down on the table and stood. Her hand still gripped Maldia's firmly as she moved closer to the bedside.

She stroked Maldia's hair softly as she said, "It has been a while. Do you feel as if you are ready to push?"

The palace doctor and the cleric glanced up from the chess game they had been playing across the room when Chandra rose from her seat. They abandoned the game as they heard Maldia's shaky answer.

"Yes, it is an almost overwhelming need."

"Listen to your body," Chandra said softly. "It knows what it is doing. Go with your instincts."

"Is there a problem?" The doctor asked as he came up beside Chandra.

Chandra shook her head. "No, nothing abnormal. Maldia says she is ready to push and in a lot of pain."

"Perhaps I should cast another spell to nullify the pain," the cleric suggested, coming up beside the doctor.

"No, do not numb her," stated the doctor. "She needs to have some feeling so she can effectively push. Perhaps dull the pain a bit."

The cleric nodded his understanding as he stood and came to Maldia's bedside. He placed his hand over Maldia's stomach, and Maldia felt warmth pool into her from his hovering extremity. The warmth dulled the shooting rivulets of pain, but the pressure still seized her muscles in its tightening grip.

Maldia breathed out in relief, but the tightness returned almost immediately. She gritted her teeth in discomfort as a rough whimper escaped her throat.

"Just relax," Chandra said in a calming tone and then nodded to the doctor and the cleric.

"It is time," she announced to them and then turned to the handmaiden. "Go fetch Hestia."

The handmaiden dipped her head in a quick, acknowledging bow and fled the room.

Maldia trembled with nervousness and building adrenaline. Sweat beaded on her forehead as the trio caring for her propped her knees up and pulled her hips down until Maldia's back was lying flat on the bed. Her heart thundered in her chest, and her breathing grew rapid and shallow. The doctor told Maldia to slow her breathing and to begin pushing when she felt the pressure again.

Chandra stroked Maldia's hair as she washed the sweat from her forehead with a soft, dry towel. "Just stay calm, Maldia. Everything is going to be fine."

"I am scared," Maldia said weakly. "What if I cannot push out the baby?"

Chandra chuckled. "You will do fine. You have had plenty of rest, and you are strong. Do not waste your energy worrying."

"When you feel the pressure increase, just nod your head," instructed the doctor. "We will tell you what to do from there."

Maldia took a deep, calming breath and lay back on the bed. She slowed her breathing as the doctor had instructed and then concentrated on the feel of pressure below her belly. She waited for it to increase its intensity, and when she felt the pressure tightening, she nodded.

Chandra placed her hand under Maldia's neck and said, "When I raise you up, take a deep breath and push hard. Keep pushing until I finish counting to ten. Can you do that?"

Maldia swallowed hard and nodded. She took a deep breath and felt Chandra's hand raise her up almost to sit. She felt the doctor, positioned at her raised knees, grasp her knees and raise them even higher just before she pushed.

She pushed as hard as she could, listening to Chandra count slowly to ten. Chandra lowered Maldia's head back down, and Maldia took in a deep breath of blessed air.

"See, that was not so bad," Chandra said as she smiled at Maldia.

She was right, Maldia thought. It had not been that bad, although she could not breathe while pushing. Moreover, the pushing was hard, especially when the doctor urged her to push even more forcefully.

Maldia discovered just how difficult it was after about the fifth round of pushing, and it became harder and harder to push for the entire count of ten. Her body was wearing down, and she trembled all over with fatigue. Sweat beaded all over her body, and tears ran down her face when Chandra told her to push again.

"I cannot push any longer," Maldia said weakly. "I feel as if I will pass out from exhaustion."

Chandra patted her hand gently. "Do not think that way. You are strong, and you can do this. If not for yourself, do it for your child. You are almost done."

Maldia gathered every last bit of strength she had. She had to do this for her daughter. This was her first task of being a mother, and if she failed, she would fail in every aspect of motherhood.

This was the ultimate test.

Maldia gathered herself and rose up with Chandra's help, pushing with everything she had. The thought of her sweet babe finally being laid safely in her arms kept her going through three more rounds of pushing.

Finally, it was over, and Maldia heard the sweet cries of her newborn daughter. The doctor wrapped the babe in a soft blanket and gave her to Maldia. Chandra instructed Maldia to feed the baby from her breast, and the sweet angel baby drank its first meal comfortably wrapped in its mother's arms.

Maldia named the baby Destiny Faith because she had a tremendous and vital destiny ahead of her, and Maldia had faith that she would succeed.

And so it was that Destiny Faith, the child born of a virgin in a city of wealth and comfort, was born the exact second that Ethan Tenebris, born of a prostitute in a land of smoke and fire, came into the world.

The bright star that was shining as bright as the sun suddenly flared. Its light became brighter than even the sun as the land of Solaris experienced the brightest day in recorded history.

Celia returned home after a long and trying day. The repairs on her shop had taken longer than expected, but they were finally done. Thankfully, the clean-up crew had allowed Celia to run her shop and do readings while they worked, so Celia had not had to close the shop during the repairs.

Celia had not renewed the security spell. Instead, she had paid for a different spell that would not be fatal. Celia had felt horrible for the deaths of the three mysterious strangers, even if they had meant her harm. Celia was not a killer, nor did she want to be, even if she could.

She had commissioned the builders to replace the ruined storefront with a more secure entrance with a plain old-fashioned lock. She had even installed a modern, non-magical security system along with the magical one to be safe. Those repairs had to be paid out-of-pocket, but Celia felt it would be worth it. The clean-up crew had taken care of the rest of the repairs covered under the original spell's cost.

Memories of that night still plagued her, and she had trouble sleeping lately. Her dreams had been invaded with images of the mysterious intruders, and the cloaked woman's words rang in her ears every morning upon awakening.

"Tread lightly on the path you are taking. It will only lead to destruction."

Celia still did not know what she had meant by those enigmatic words. The thief had probably only been trying to scare Celia, and it had worked.

After weeks of reading tarot cards and tea leaves, pondering, and worrying, Celia had still not found why the intruders wanted the tome. The scrolls were far more valuable since they were the original documents of the prophecy, but Celia had heard nothing from the palace about anyone trying to steal the scrolls.

Not that it was even possible.

The scrolls were much better protected than Celia's fake tome, hidden in a measly little safe in a spell-protected shop. Nevertheless, it had been the last mistake of the three mysterious thieves.

Celia sighed and sank into the hot bath water she had prepared, allowing the steam and wetness to wash away her worries and concerns. She laid her head back onto the side of the tub and relaxed into the steaming water, sighing with relief as she felt the warmth seep into her skin and loosen her muscles. She closed her eyes and let her mind drift to more pleasant thoughts.

Celia thought about Maldia and wondered how she was faring in her pregnancy. Celia figured that it must be about time for her to deliver. The last time she had seen Maldia was about a week ago at the palace.

The queen summoned Celia to read for Maldia at the palace since her shop was no longer private because of the renovations. It had been the best reading Celia had done for Maldia so far.

The many readings she had done for Maldia during her pregnancy had been good, other than that first really bad one. Something had shifted since that first reading. She had seen the child growing strong in power and kinder in heart inside the crystal ball. The cards had shown promising results as well, predicting a few bad decisions and mistakes, but nothing as bad as that first vision that Celia had had.

If Celia's readings continued on this path, she was confident that the future would improve. The future could always change and was constantly changing, and Celia liked it when the change was good.

CHAPTER 4: THE CHILD OF DARKNESS

Ethan Tenebris was nestled in his mother's arms, having been fed from Raina's breast with help from Doctor Tenebris. During the feeding, Tenebris parted little Ethan from the umbilical cord and covered him with Raina's cloak. He was sleeping soundly now as Tenebris smiled down at him, wrapped in Raina's arms.

"He certainly is handsome," he said as he bent down and played with one of Ethan's tiny hands.

The tenderness in Tenebris's tone surprised Raina. "Yes, he is," Raina said, smiling proudly at her son.

"Are you ready for me to take you to your sister's?" Tenebris asked.

Raina fidgeted guiltily and cast her gaze away from Tenebris's piercing stare. "Well…see the thing is…umm…"

"There is no sister, is there?" Tenebris asked, interrupting Raina's stuttering. His tone was not angry or accusing but still had that tender concern laced into it.

Raina's emerald eyes turned back to Tenebris. "There is a sister. I just don't know who or where she is."

Tenebris frowned in confusion. "What do you mean? How can you not know who or where your own sister is?"

Raina sighed. "My mother gave my sister up for adoption when she was a baby. I was very young, so I don't remember her. I was going to try to find her."

Tenebris ran a hand over Ethan's tiny head, stroking the soft downy hair.

"What did you plan on doing until then?" Tenebris asked in concern. "Were you just going to live on the street with a baby until you found her?"

"I was going to find a room in an inn until I could get a job and housing. I should have had another couple of weeks, at least. This little guy came too early." Raina smiled and looked down at the baby, still asleep in her arms. She tucked her cloak more securely around him as Tenebris continued to stroke his hair gently.

"So, you have a bit of coin, then?" Tenebris asked. "To pay for a room, I mean."

Raina nodded and responded, "I have a bit of coin. It isn't much, but I hope it will not take me too long to find a job and babysitter or find my sister."

"How do you plan on doing that?" Tenebris asked. "Do you know her name or who adopted her?"

Raina looked up suddenly, suspicion clouding her gaze. "Why are you asking so many questions?"

Tenebris's tone never changed. He answered with the same tender concern he had been using, "because I am worried for you and your baby. I just delivered your baby beside a lake of lava, used much of my magic to create an electric shield to keep out the ash and cleanse the air, and gave you aftercare without any equipment. Thankfully, you did not tear and therefore need stitches. I am trying to say that I am emotionally invested now, and I want to ensure that my patients are cared for."

Raina's eyes narrowed. "So, we are your patients now? That is the reason you want to know so much?"

Tenebris smirked and said, "I may have other reasons."

He paused before continuing, "I have a friend that could help you, give you a place to stay while you search for your sister. I want to know that I can see you and Mr. handsome more."

Raina raised questioning eyebrows at him, suspicion still prevalent in her emerald gaze. "Why? You do not even know me."

"I would like to remedy that," Tenebris said, the seductive smirk still on his face.

Raina rolled her eyes. "Yeah, sure. So would a thousand other males."

"I am different," he said.

"And how are you different?" She asked sarcastically.

"Because I know who you are and am still willing to help," Tenebris said softly, the smirk vanishing to be replaced with a knowing look.

Raina's heart fluttered in panic. She swallowed hard and tightened her grip on her son, pulling him away from the man looming over her. "What do you mean, you know who I am?"

"Well, you certainly are not Miss Crass," Tenebris said with a chuckle as he straightened. "Do not worry, Raina. Your secret is safe with me. I will not even tell Celia who you are."

Raina had not told Tenebris her real name. Her tender stomach tightened with dread. Was he going to drag her back to the palace now? Had this whole thing been a charade to coax her to a sense of safety so she could give birth to the chosen one before taking her back?

Sensing her fright and mistrust, Tenebris kneeled beside her and gazed into Raina's emerald eyes. "Raina, do not worry. I have no intention of taking you back or exposing your identity to anyone. I want you to escape, and I want you and the babe safe."

Raina returned his concerned gaze with a wary look. "Why are you helping me?" She asked with a trembling voice.

"Because Mikka will be destroyed if the demon dragons take over. If I help you escape with their chosen one, then they cannot take over the world," Tenebris said as he gazed down at the babe in Raina's arms.

"But you are a demon dragon," Raina said in confusion as she stared into Tenebris's icy blue gaze.

His stare darkened as he answered, "That does not mean I do not care about the planet. I would rather see peace than war, and I am not the only demon dragon that feels this way."

Raina responded quickly. "I know. I have friends that feel the same way."

Tenebris smiled. "Then why are you giving me such a hard time?"

"Because I do not know you, I do not trust you as a friend."

Tenebris's light-hearted visage disappeared and became serious. His tone reflected the change as he responded, "Good. You should not trust anyone, but that does not mean you should not accept help where you can get it. I may have selfish reasons for helping you, but it is help nonetheless."

Raina raised a questioning brow as she asked, "What kind of help are you offering?"

Tenebris answered, "To get you into the north and keep you safe and hidden until Palace Asgorath gives up its search for you. I can keep an eye on the search and tell you when it is safe to come out of hiding."

Raina swallowed. It would be wonderful to have eyes on Asgorath and to know when they stopped searching for her. Once the search ended, Raina could find her sister and raise her son how she wanted. So what if she had to accept help from a stranger to accomplish these things?

But she still had to be careful. She could not just blindly trust strangers, especially when that stranger knew her secrets. She had to know more about what he was offering and his motives for helping.

"So, let's say I accept your offer. What's the next move?" Raina asked.

Tenebris smiled victoriously. "I will take you to my friend's home. She will provide housing for you until you find your sister, or she could help you find work and a home of your own."

"And, what's in it for you?" Raina asked suspiciously.

Tenebris shrugged. "I already told you, Raina. I want the angel dragons to win the war."

The suspicion still showed on Raina's features as she asked, "so, how will helping me help you accomplish that?"

The triumphant smile on Tenebris's face widened as he answered, "I can ensure that Ethan comes to know the angel dragon's chosen one."

Raina raised her eyebrows in surprise. "You know the angel dragon's chosen one?"

Tenebris chuckled. "I have not yet had the pleasure of meeting the little angel. Last I saw Maldia, she still had not given birth, but if the prophecy is true, then the baby should have been born at the exact time as little Ethan here."

Raina scoffed humorously as she responded, "Of course you have not met the baby yet. You knew what I was asking."

Tenebris laughed and answered, "Yes, I knew what you were asking,"

Tenebris paused, his tone and visage growing more serious. "And yes, I know Maldia personally. I can ensure that Ethan comes to know his counterpart."

"It would be a good thing for Ethan to know her," Raina said with a shrug. "So, I accept those terms."

Tenebris's eyebrow quirked with a rakish smirk. He gave Raina a wink and added, "There is one more thing I would like from you in exchange for my help."

Raina's face fell, and she sighed. She knew it was too good to be true.

Raina's tone was dull as she said, "Fine. I knew there would be something else you wanted. What do you want in exchange for your services?"

Tenebris's rakish grin never faltered as he winked and answered, "I would like permission to visit you and little Tenebris as often as I like."

Raina scoffed, but a slight smile lifted the corners of her lips. She had not expected that answer, and it had surprised her. But Raina had to admit that, despite her mistrust, she liked the idea of Tenebris checking up on her. Plus, she did want to get to know this handsome stranger, especially since she had impulsively named her son after him.

However, doubt and fear still nagged Raina, tickling the back of her mind as she asked, "Why would this friend of yours help me?"

Tenebris shrugged. "That's just her nature. She helps people."

"Just like that?" Raina asked with raised eyebrows.

Tenebris smiled as he nodded and answered, "Yes, just like that."

Raina took in a deep breath and said, "Okay, then. Take me to meet this friend of yours. I will stay with your friend until I can find my sister."

Tenebris's smile faltered. "It will be difficult to find her, you know. There are many orphans from the war in the north."

Raina shrugged, but the sadness remained in her eyes as she said, "I'll do the best I can. But even if I do not find my sister, I am determined to make a living in the North. The demon dragons want to turn my child into a monster, and I will not allow it."

Tenebris nodded his approval and said, "Good. Now, let us get off of this ledge and get you and the baby to safety."

Tenebris shifted back into his beautiful jade dragon form with bright golden eyes and flew Raina and the babe to the private home of Celia, the seer. If anyone could help Raina, it would be Celia.

Celia was one of the war orphans Tenebris had mentioned, and Tenebris had adopted and raised Celia himself. But that was not the reason for taking Raina to Celia. He knew Celia was not Raina's sister.

Celia was an exquisite ebony woman, while Raina was a porcelain beauty. Celia couldn't be Raina's estranged sister unless they had different fathers. Besides, Tenebris knew for a fact that Celia's parents were dead.

However, Tenebris would trust no one else with the chosen one's safety, and he was confident that Celia could help Raina and the child born in smoke and fire.

Celia moaned in disappointment as she noticed the steaming hot bath had changed to mildly lukewarm. She did not want to leave the comfort of the water, but now that she noticed the heat was gone, it began to chill her skin and seep into her bones. She stretched languidly as far as the confines of her bathtub would allow, rose from the water, and reached for her towel.

The chime of her doorbell startled Celia, and she almost slipped in the tub. She recovered quickly, however, and stepped safely out onto the bathmat, holding her chest to stop the startled fluttering of her heart.

"Who could that be?" Celia mumbled as she grabbed the robe always hanging by her in-suite bathroom door.

She donned the robe as she walked through her bedroom, fastening the tie around her waist as she walked out of the bedroom and down the hallway toward her front door.

She hesitated just beyond the entryway of her home. Images of the dark, cloaked figures infiltrating her shop danced in her memory as she approached her front door.

What if this was a repeat of that frightening night? What if the "procurers" had found out where she lived and had decided to try her home for more artifacts? Celia shook her head, clearing it of such irrational fears. Those people were dead.

Even so, Celia needed to be cautious. She had a few protection spells bound to her home, but nothing like the one she had on her shop. The one on her home would not protect her if someone meant her harm. It would alert the authorities, but who knew if they would get to her in time.

She clutched her robe's edges, holding it to her body like a lifeline. She took a deep, calming breath and yelled, "Who is there?"

"Don't be frightened, Celia. It's only me," a familiar male voice answered.

Celia frowned in concentration as her mind whirled to place the voice to a face. Images of the doctor that had cared for her as a child, had become her teacher when her powers manifested, and then had been her closest confidant throughout her adult life floated through her mind.

She had been present for the death of her parents in a horrible accident. They had slipped from a dragon's back over Lake Divere while attempting to travel to the northern hemisphere with her in tow. She had lived, clinging to the dragon's back as she watched her mother and father fall into the lake.

She arrived alone, terrified, talking about the nightmare she had gone through. The terrified and extremely guilty young dragon had taken the girl to a hospital, where she had been placed under the care of Doctor Tenebris.

Tenebris was a doctor of many talents. He had certifications in general medicine, surgical procedures, and mental health. He worked at the Solaris Hospital during the winter and trained new interns at Asgorath Hospital during the summer. However, his specialization was unique to Tenebris alone.

He was the paranormal doctor specializing in helping children deal with and control innate powers and the only one in existence. He could imprint on a child's power, soaking it into himself and controlling it until the child was disciplined enough to control it independently.

Tenebris felt Celia's impending powers the moment she entered the examination room. He immediately took custody of Celia when he found out about the accident.

When her powers came to her, he put his stamp on Celia's power and enrolled her into the University at Palace Solaris. Tenebris helped Celia hone her gifts while she attended the university.

"Celia, are you okay in there?" Tenebris's voice rang out, and Celia mentally shook herself as she realized she had zoned out of reality for a moment.

"Yes! I'm coming Tenebris!" She called out as she hurried to open the front door.

Tenebris looked casually perfect as always in his short-sleeve button-up shirt, dark blue jeans, and loafers with no socks. He had a bag draped over one shoulder. His dark brown hair was cut in a crop style that was slightly longer on top. His large, round, bright blue eyes sparkled with a light that made his entire face seem to glow. His light skin was so white that he almost looked like a vampire instead of a dragon shifter, and it sharply contrasted with his dark hair. He had a straight nose, full lips, and a strong jawline.

Her adopted father's handsomeness elicited Celia's sense of pride, as it always did when she saw him. But then her eyes landed on the woman beside him. She appeared frightened and nervous, and Celia could tell by how she wobbled slightly that she was in pain. Despite how often Celia wished Tenebris would bring a woman home and finally settle down, Celia did not think this was a social visit.

The terrified woman held a cloth-wrapped bundle tightly to her chest as she stared at Celia with wide, emerald-green eyes. Her raven black hair was tousled and frizzed, and she had dirt smudged across her pretty, round face. Blood soaked through her jeans along her crotch area; some dripped from her pant leg, down her shoes, and pooled on the ground.

Celia darted a questioning look toward Tenebris, and the worry and concern in his eyes told Celia that this woman probably needed help. The squeal of a newborn babe's cry came from the bundle, and Celia's eyes widened in shock. Had this woman just given birth?

Celia ushered the trio inside with a wave of her hand as she said, "Come on, get in here and get her and the babe cleaned up. I have fresh clothing and supplies in the supply room. You know the way, Tenebris."

The woman did not speak, but the nod of gratitude and relief in her eyes as she passed Celia in the doorway spoke volumes. The woman's eyes were striking, a piercing emerald green that seemed to hold a world of secrets behind them, even though she looked worn out.

Celia wondered what had happened to this girl to have put her in this situation and why Tenebris was helping her. She tried to read the situation, reaching for the strands of time in her mind for a hint of change, but nothing came to her. She watched Tenebris lead the girl down the hallway toward the supply room before turning toward the left and entering the kitchen through the open, arched doorway.

She rummaged through the various cabinets until she had the pots and pans she needed to cook a meal, then gathered the ingredients. Once she had the food prepared and on the stove, she dashed into her bedroom and quickly slipped out of her robe and into a pair of sleep pants and a t-shirt. She then returned to the kitchen to tend the food.

The food was on the stove and simmering nicely, filling the kitchen with the aroma of various spices when Tenebris entered the kitchen alone.

"Something smells wonderful," he said, leaning onto the island bar beside the stove.

Celia chuckled as she raised her eyes from the pot she was stirring. Celia glanced around and then back to Tenebris with raised, questioning brows.

"I got the bleeding stopped, and she is washing up in the bathroom. The babe is with her," he said in answer to her inquisitive look. "We found a basket and stuffed it with blankets, cleaned up the baby, and then wrapped him up and placed him in the basket. The babe is sleeping in its makeshift bed while mom cleans up. I brought her here, hoping you could help her."

Celia pulled her attention to the stove, stirring the contents of the pot on the front burner as she replied, "What is her situation?"

Tenebris cleared his throat. Celia knew that sound. It was a clear sign that she would not like the answer. "She is probably being hunted by the southern hemisphere's palace and needs a place to lie low for a while. Her paperwork is fake, but it looks like the real thing. It even fooled the border guards. Her real name is Raina."

Celia laid the spoon down on the spoon holder next to the stove and turned to Tenebris grimly. "Tenebris, how could you? If I get caught harboring a fugitive, it could harm my business. Furthermore, my station as palace seer could be compromised if the queen gets wind of it."

Tenebris sighed and pinched the bridge of his nose between his fingers. "I know that, but I was hoping that you, of all people, would understand. Besides, she is not technically a fugitive. She has done nothing wrong."

"Then why would the palace be looking for her?" Celia asked, placing a hand on her hip.

"Because she was part of the prince's harem. She wants to leave that life and raise her child in a better atmosphere. She says she has a sister that lives here, but her sister was orphaned when Raina was small, and she doesn't remember anything about her."

Celia's breath hitched, and her heart squeezed. She had always had a soft spot for orphans; Tenebris knew it, the clever bastard. How could she deny this woman the freedom to raise her baby away from the lawlessness of the Asgorath Palace and be reunited with her orphaned sister?

Celia sighed in defeat as she turned toward the island counter. She lowered her head and placed her hands on the counter. "Fine, she can stay. But we must disguise her before she can go out in public."

Tenebris smiled in gratitude, and that gratitude carried in his tone as he replied, "Yes, I will ensure that she complies. Thank you, Celia. You have no idea how much this means to me."

Celia shrugged. "It is the least I can do after everything you have done for me."

Tenebris moved closer to Celia's position. The island counter sat between their bodies, but Tenebris leaned over it to place his finger under Celia's chin. He lifted her head until Celia was gazing into his eyes.

"I would do it all again for you, love," he whispered, and his father-like adoration for her shone through his ice-blue eyes.

Celia's dark brown eyes locked with Tenebris's gaze. "I never understood why you helped me, but I am thankful daily for you."

Tenebris smiled, and the admiration of his tone could not be denied. "The spark I saw in you was like nothing I had ever seen. You have an aura about you that cannot be ignored. Surely, you see your own worth, Celia."

Celia pulled away from Tenebris's touch, but she smiled as she responded, "Careful, doc, before you give me a bigger head than I already have."

Tenebris's baritone laugh rang sharp and clear through the kitchen, and Celia could not help but join in. Her crystal tones melded with his as she returned to the stove to finish her task.

Celia's laughter died when she noticed a figure entering the kitchen behind Tenebris. Tenebris turned upon seeing Celia's eyes fixate on something behind him, and he sprang upright when he saw Raina enter the kitchen carrying the baby.

Her hair was still damp and hung in plastered waves past her shoulders and down her back. She wore a blue flannel gown that Tenebris must have found in the storage room. She had a pair of matching blue fuzzy slippers on her feet that made shuffling sounds as she walked.

The baby was wrapped in a small, blue fuzzy blanket, and it must have been asleep because no sound or movement was coming from the bundle. Raina clutched the bundle as if it was the most crucial thing in the world, and to Raina, it probably was.

Raina's large, emerald-green eyes, rimmed with long, black lashes, were wide with curiosity as she gazed around the room. Her pale skin glowed with freshly scrubbed exuberance, and Celia thought about how beautiful she looked despite having no makeup or fancy clothes. It was no wonder that the prince had wanted her for his harem.

Celia came around the island counter to stand in front of Raina, giving her plenty of room so as not to frighten her. "Hello, I am Celia. Tenebris here tells me you need a place to stay."

Raina lifted her head and fixed her gaze on Celia. Her eyes narrowed suspiciously as she said, "It would do me no good to lie and say that I did not need help, but I have already spoken my suspicions to Tenebris."

Celia turned to Tenebris questioningly.

Tenebris shrugged and said, "She does not understand why we would help a stranger."

Celia turned back to Raina with a warm smile. "I would not be the person I am today had I not accepted help from strangers."

"I did not say I would not accept," Raina responded. "I only said that I did not understand it."

"At least you are honest," Celia stated with a humorous smile and a quirk of her eyebrows. "If you would like to stay here, you are more than welcome, despite your misgivings."

The relieved slump of Raina's shoulders was evident, even though her distrustful visage remained.

Celia turned her gaze to Tenebris and said, "You need to speak with Raina about the conditions of her stay."

Raina turned to Tenebris, and her suspicious look deepened. "You told her my real name? And what conditions?"

Tenebris cleared his throat. "Well, I have explained to Celia why you are hiding from Asgorath Palace…"

Raina noticed the pointed look Tenebris gave her before he continued, "You wish to leave the prince's harem and raise your baby in a more favorable environment, so I figured it wise to tell her your true name."

Raina nodded subtly as she took the hint. He had not told Celia of her child being the chosen one of the demon dragons, and for that, she was thankful. The fewer people that knew of that, the better.

Taking up the ruse, Raina put on her most serious face as she turned to Celia and responded, "Yes, that is correct, so I would appreciate you not using my real name in public."

Celia nodded her head in approval.

Raina continued. "My mother raised me in the south, alone. My father was killed in the war when I was young, and my sister was a newborn. My mother could only keep one of us, so she sent my sister here to be adopted."

"Hmm," Celia said. "Do you know your sister's name?"

"Her name was Chan Dionra Beals, but I do not know if the people that adopted her kept her name." Raina lowered her head with a sad look on her face.

Celia responded comfortingly, "Do not worry. We will find her somehow. But, in the meantime, you must be careful to keep yourself hidden. I take it that the babe is the prince's child?"

Raina nodded somberly.

"Then they will most definitely be looking for you when they discover your absence," Celia said.

Tenebris stepped forward and placed a hand on Raina's shoulder. "That is why Celia and I thought it best that you lie low for a while. If you go out in public, you must wear a disguise and use your fake name and I.D."

"I have a disguise in my bag that you were so kind to help me bring," Raina told Tenebris.

"Perfect," Tenebris responded. "After a time, I will scope out the situation in Palace Asgorath and report back. If the search for you has died down, then we can work on finding your sister."

Tenebris lowered his hand from Raina's shoulder, and Raina's hopeful gaze landed on Celia. Celia's heart lurched with compassion. She remembered having that look on her own face. She gave Raina a comforting smile with a slight nod of her head.

Raina's return smile was filled with hope and gratitude as she said, "I will gladly accept those terms."

Celia stepped forward, the smile never leaving her face, and grasped Raina's shoulders gently, much as Tenebris had done.

"Then it is settled. I will have Tenebris go into the market tomorrow and purchase a bed for the babe. I will set you both up in the guest bedroom. For tonight, however, we can put the baby in the basket that Tenebris prepared for you earlier."

Raina's smile brightened. "That sounds fine. I cannot thank you enough for your help and kindness."

Celia dropped her hands and shrugged. "You do not have to thank me. I would not be where I am today had others not helped me. Seeing you and your child thrive will be all the thanks I need."

"Come," Tenebris said, gesturing toward Raina. "I will see you settled before I take my leave."

"Won't you stay for dinner?" Celia asked as she stepped around the island counter and back toward the stove.

Tenebris turned back to Celia. "I think I will let you ladies eat alone so you can get to know one another. I can grab something at one of the all-night cafes in town."

Celia shrugged. "Suit yourself. You know you will regret missing my spiced dragon soup."

Tenebris's mouth watered. It was Tenebris's favorite dish. It was not, technically, dragon meat. The dragon shifters were not that barbaric. It was primarily made from wild game meat. It was called "spiced dragon" because it made dragons "spicy" for more.

Tenebris did not know one dragon shifter that did not like spiced dragon soup, and Celia made the best spiced dragon soup in the northern hemisphere. He glanced at Raina, who stood swaying the babe gently back and forth.

Tenebris grinned and shuffled his feet as he said, "Well, maybe I can stay a bit longer and have some soup."

Celia chuckled knowingly. She had caught the look he had given Raina. Maybe she was wrong before to have assumed that Raina was not the one that would capture Tenebris's heart.

"Take Raina to the guest room so she will know where she is sleeping tonight, and then you both can come have some soup," Celia said.

Tenebris gave a low, exaggerated bow as he replied, "As my lady commands."

Celia only smiled at Tenebris's goofiness and shook her head, returning to the stove to stir her soup.

Tenebris turned to Raina, giving her his arm as he said, "Come, my lady. Allow me to show you to your room."

Raina smiled humorously at the show as she arranged the babe so she could hold him in one arm and slip the other arm into Tenebris's.

Tenebris's arm tingled where she touched him, and he sent a silent thank you to the Goddess that he had not carried out his original plan.

Tenebris's silly behavior was a front to the sickness he felt roiling around in his gut over what he had almost accomplished.

Raina had been right not to trust him.

The Asgorath Palace had commissioned Tenebris to help the babe develop and control his powers when he became ready. He was supposed to have kept himself a secret from Raina until it was time to magically stamp her son with Tenebris's signature, but Tenebris had never intended for the chosen one to be born.

He intended to get to know Raina somehow, gain her trust, and dispose of her and the babe mercifully while she was still pregnant. Maybe he would give her a quick-acting, non-traceable toxin that would allow her to pass peacefully in her sleep. No one would be the wiser.

He made several attempts to approach her and introduce himself. But he had chickened out every time, procrastinating and coming up with excuses until it had been too late. As Raina's belly swelled with pregnancy, she became even more enchanting, navigating every obstacle with elegance and charm, searing herself into Tenebris's heart as he watched from afar.

It had devastated him when she had run away.

Tenebris followed the guards that had been sent to look for her. He sniffed around every landing port in the northern hemisphere, searching for the woman that had captured his attention so completely. When he finally found her with the mob boss, he followed her over the lake discreetly, hitching a ride on the back of another dragon.

He watched her from afar as he had for the past nine months. She was sensational. Her beauty lit a fire in Tenebris's very soul. Her strength and courage gripped his heart. Her fierce determination to give her child a better life blossomed respect for Raina in Tenebris's gut. She set his entire world ablaze, and Tenebris wanted her in a way he had never wanted a woman before.

His plan to get rid of her would be next to impossible.

He had shaken off the feeling and had strengthened his resolve to carry out his plan. He had no time to garner her trust, but her going into labor early provided the perfect opportunity. He could offer to help, take her somewhere private, and then throw her into Lake Divere. It would not be merciful, but he would be done with it once and for all.

When she reached for him, the pleading look in her emerald eyes caused him to hesitate, but he allowed her to climb onto his back anyway. He flew over the lake, determined to follow his plan, but the feel of her clinging tightly to his back caused him to hesitate at the last second. He wanted nothing more than to have her hold him that tightly in his human form as he made mad, passionate love to her.

Then he had dumped her on the ledge, and it crossed his mind to let her choke to death on the ash from the lake as she lay gasping and coughing. But his resolve failed him again when his heart crumpled at the sight of her lips turning blue from lack of oxygen.

He put up the shield to help her breathe, praying the baby was still alright. The sight of her writhing and screaming out in pain had been his downfall.

He would not be getting rid of her or the baby.

Instead, he helped her through her labor, forgetting his plan and developing a new one. It was one thing to kill a pregnant woman mercifully but quite another to kill a baby, humanely or not. He would have to find her help of some kind.

As if it was not enough that she had unknowingly touched his heart and lit his soul with passionate want, she upped the stakes and named the babe after him! Curse it all, but he could not kill her or the child now. That was when he decided to bring her to Celia.

His boss was not going to be happy when he found out. He had to keep her and the babe hidden until he could figure something else out. If anyone could help him save Raina, it would be Celia.

Celia would know how to handle his boss.

Once she met him anyway.

Tenebris sighed and ran a hand through his hair as he shook himself from his thoughts and led Raina down the hallway to Celia's guest bedroom. He ushered her inside and then stood in the doorway, watching her as she took in the room with the baby in her arms.

"This is certainly a pleasant house. I am sure I will be comfortable here after I get to know Celia better," Raina said softly as she turned to Tenebris.

Tenebris's grim expression took in Raina's uncertain features. Her green eyes were rimmed with red and swollen. Of course, she had been crying from intense pain during the labor. He could see the pockets of sleeplessness forming under her eyes, and her movements were stilted and strained. She was probably still in pain, but she was hiding it well.

Raina frowned up at Tenebris and asked, "Is something wrong? You look angry."

Tenebris shook his head and gave her a tight smile. "I am fine. I am worried about you, is all."

Raina's frown remained as she responded, "Why? I still do not understand. Why did you help me, and why are you so worried about my safety?"

"I am asking myself those questions as we speak," Tenebris answered gruffly. "When I discover the answer, you will be the first to know."

Raina chuckled. "Well, whatever it is, I am grateful."

Her chuckle made Tenebris smile despite himself, and he moved toward her into the room. Her eyes widened as he gently grabbed her by the shoulders and kissed her forehead.

He smiled softly as he gazed into her bewildered eyes and responded, "So am I."

CHAPTER 5: THE CHILD OF LIGHT

Tenebris gazed down into the tiny bed where the small baby girl lay. Her bright blue eyes were open and fixated on the plastic mobile above the bassinet. Her fine baby hair was sparse, but what she had was a light, golden blond color. She had the chubbiness and innocence of a babe, but there was a look about her eyes as if they had seen many lifetimes before.

Tenebris reached into the bassinet and stroked the baby's head softly. The baby let out a cooing sound, causing Tenebris to grin.

"What did you name her?" Tenebris asked as he looked up at the baby's mother.

Maldia sat in bed beside the bassinet with the blankets pulled up to her waist. She wore a loose button-up shirt with the top two buttons open, and Tenebris could see the straps of her nursing bra through the gap. Her jade green eyes were bright and shining with pride as she gazed down into the bassinet at her babe, and her round face showed no signs of tiredness.

"We named her Destiny Faith. It seemed an appropriate name." Maldia answered, and her tone was smooth and clear.

"Indeed it is," Tenebris replied. "You seem well rested."

Maldia shrugged her shoulders. "I feel fine. The birth was not that painful thanks to the palace cleric's tea, and afterward, he healed everything back up."

"Lucky you," Tenebris replied. He had not meant for his tone to sound so sardonic, but the image of Raina's horrible suffering during her birthing process ran through his mind.

Even after he had gotten Raina to Celia's, she was still bleeding heavily.

She had turned pale as death,

and if Tenebris had not been a doctor and knew this was normal after birth, he would have been worried that she might die.

As it were, he had explained to her that the bleeding would continue for a time, shown her how to fashion a cloth to catch the blood, and then helped her to the bathroom so she could clean up. Afterward, Raina had been so drained that she had barely made it through dinner. Tenebris remembered the vision of her sipping her soup tentatively as he had watched her with worried eyes.

Tenebris had tucked her in before leaving Celia's house, and she had practically been asleep before her head had even hit the pillow. Mercifully, little Ethan had been asleep.

Even now, three weeks later, Raina still had a small amount of bleeding and more internal healing to do. She would not be healed entirely for at least three more weeks.

Maldia's voice pulled Tenebris from his sour thoughts.

Thankfully, Maldia seemed not to notice the condescending tone in Tenebris's voice because her tone was normal as she replied, "yes, I suppose I am quite lucky to be the mother of the chosen one."

Tenebris did not respond. He had come here to do a job, and he would do that job quickly so that he could make his way back to Raina. He did not need all the small talk delaying him.

He reached into the bassinet and placed his hand over the baby's tiny chest. He did not have large hands, but the baby's body was so tiny that his hand covered her from her neck to her hips. He bore down with slight pressure, not enough to hurt the babe, but enough so that he could feel the hum and buzz of the energy that coursed through her body.

He closed his eyes in concentration as he connected with that energy. He pulled it into himself ever so slightly, churning it around in his hand and arm, and read the signatures in the line of magic from the babe.

Huge bolts of sensation flew up his arm, and Tenebris winced with the effort to keep his hand and arm still. He had never felt energy this powerful from one so young! He was expecting a strong stream but nothing of this level.

He let the energy flow through him for the tiniest hair of a second before stamping his signature into the coalescing strands. He released his hold on it suddenly, and it flew back down into the baby like a rubber band snapping back after being stretched and released.

The baby did not so much as flinch as the energy settled back into her tiny body, and Tenebris raised his hand back from the baby's chest.

It was done. Tenebris had successfully stamped his energy signature with hers, allowing him to control her magic when it bloomed into awareness inside of her. This way, he could help her control, manipulate, and become one with it.

Most creatures learned to do this independently, or it was inherently ingrained into their knowledge base at birth. But with creatures that held tremendously powerful magic, it could be disastrous if their powers went unchecked. This was the essence of his job, and he was the only one in existence that could do this. It was the reason his services were sought after in both hemispheres.

"It is done," Tenebris said to Maldia as he rose back up from his bent position over the bassinet. "I will help her control her powers when they awaken."

Maldia breathed a sigh of relief. "Good. I have been so worried since that first reading with Celia. Even though the other readings have improved slightly, I did not want to take any chances that she might lose control of her powers. I hope you can control them."

Tenebris chuckled. "I have not yet met anyone with powers beyond my control."

Their conversation was interrupted by the baby fussing in her bassinet. Maldia sat up straighter as Faith let out a keening wail, and almost instantly, a handmaid burst into the room as if she had only been waiting for the baby's cry. She flew to the side of the bassinet, shoving Tenebris aside, and tenderly picked the baby up into her arms. She carried the baby to Maldia, who already had her shirt unbuttoned and her breast ready. She took the baby from the handmaid and put it to her breast, and the baby instantly suckled the life-giving breast milk into her mouth.

The handmaid momentarily gazed down lovingly at the babe before turning and leaving the room. Tenebris stood for a moment in stunned silence at the scene. He knew that the palace would probably care for Maldia and the babe, but he had not imagined that they would have catered to their every need. If they continued catering to Maldia and the baby's every need, the baby would grow an attitude of entitlement.

This would not do at all.

Tenebris's gaze darkened with agitation as he said, "You need to see Celia for the babe's first reading soon."

Maldia glanced up from the baby in her arms and darted a surprised look at Tenebris. "I have an appointment next week. Why do you seem upset?"

Tenebris shook his head and turned away from Maldia. "It is nothing. I will check in on you after the child has had her reading."

Tenebris did not say another word. He strolled out of the room and down the long corridor leading to the main chamber of the palace's west wing. He stormed past the chamber and down the hallway to the throne room.

From there, he plodded through the large waiting room, through the entry room, and out the palace doors. He walked hurriedly through the courtyard, determined to be away from the palace grounds before anyone could see the look of disappointment and disgust on his face.

This was no way to raise the chosen one. This child needed to be raised to be independent and strong, not slothful and reliant. He would speak with Celia on this matter. Perhaps Celia could make Maldia see reason. It was alright to receive help with the baby, but to have Maldia lying comfortably in a bed while others tended to her and the babe's every need…

It was abhorrent.

Tenebris finally made it out of the palace grounds and turned left down the lane toward the city. He needed to visit the market in Solaris to purchase a crib for the other chosen one living at Celia's house in Terrien.

He had not yet connected himself to that one, but he would do that soon. With powers as strong as the chosen ones, their energies would awaken earlier than most children. Typically, he was recalled to a child when they reached around ten years of age, but he figured they would recall him to this one around five years. Who knew how long it would be for Ethan.

Tenebris's anger grew as he thought about Palace Asgorath and how they had manipulated Raina. He knew how they had schemed to have the chosen one born at the palace and have the prince be the father.

The king cleaned the streets of all prostitutes in the southern hemisphere, assigning them to the prince's harem in small groups at a time. That had been the simple part. There was not a prostitute in the land that would turn down a chance at a better life in the palace.

The hard part had been the special tea. The prince had given his entire harem a special anti-pregnancy tea that the palace wizard and seer had made. Combining the wizard's magic with the seer's visions of the prophecy, the resulting potion would prevent any woman from ovulating except the woman prophesied to be the mother of the chosen one.

If the group's women failed to become pregnant after a couple of months, they would release them from duty and bring in another group of prostitutes. This continued until one of them became pregnant despite having drunk the tea.

When Raina became pregnant, the king was ecstatic. He had lavished her with kindness, status, and anything and everything he thought the beautiful Raina would want. The king was thrilled that the most gorgeous prostitute in the harems had been the woman chosen to birth the unique child.

Tenebris screwed up his face in anger as he made his way down the streets of Solaris. He balled his hands into fists as he stalked down the sidewalk, and Tenebris noticed people shrinking away from him as he passed by.

Tenebris stopped and sighed, running a hand through his black hair as he took deep, calming breaths. He needed to calm down. He had worked himself into a frenzy over thoughts of the beautiful Raina and her son. His protectiveness of them knew no bounds, and Tenebris wondered once again why the beautiful former prostitute had gotten so far under his skin.

"I think you should let her wear the white one," Chandra said as she gazed down at the tiny dresses spread along the bed. Her chin was propped on her finger in a discerning stance. Her long, luxurious light brown hair swished around as she looked back and forth between the dresses. Her large, bright green eyes darted back and forth with the movement of her head.

"I really like the pink one, though," argued Maldia as she stood beside Chandra. She wore her chocolate brown hair in its usual tight bun, and her white holy robes hung straight and loose down to her ankles. "I have no choice but to wear white, so I would like Faith to have some color."

Chandra shrugged and began gathering the dresses into a pile. "Fine. I'll just put the rest away."

Maldia moved to help, but Chandra waved her away. "I can do this. Get Faith ready."

Maldia refused to move away. "Chandra, you must stop doting on me and sending handmaids to cater to my every whim. I let you by with it for the first four weeks, but I need to learn to care for my baby on my own. What kind of example would it set for her if she and I were being catered to?"

Chandra huffed in irritation and backed away from the dresses, crossing her arms over her chest. "Alright, have it your way. I only wanted to help my best friend and get to know my goddaughter. Besides, the queen appointed me to you for Faith's first year, so you need to give me something to do."

Maldia began folding the dresses neatly into a pile as she smiled at her friend.

"If you cannot find something to occupy your time alone, then that is not my fault," she said jokingly.

She saw the hurt come over Chandra's face and added quickly, "Oh, Chandra, I was only joking. Besides, you have other duties in the palace that you can see to. Take a break from us until we return from Celia's shop. Look in on your troops and workers. You are still the captain of the queen's guards, so surely some matter will occupy your time. I promise I will let you have time with Faith upon our return."

Chandra let out another huff, but a small smile was on her face. "Fine. I will go see if Sage needs my help. I left him in charge of my troops while I was assigned to you. Apparently, Sage is not only an advisor but also an army general."

Maldia's eyebrows rose. "Impressive. How did you find that out?"

Chandra shrugged. "Tenebris told me. He is the one who introduced him to Queen Damaphur after her previous advisor fell ill and passed away."

Maldia sighed and gave Chandra a somber look. "Ah, yes. I remember Malcom. He was very kind."

Chandra nodded in agreement. "Yes, he was. He kept to himself a lot, though."

Chandra paused momentarily as she watched Maldia fold the dresses. Then, she turned for the door, looked over her shoulder, and said, "Come and find me when you return."

Maldia chuckled and said, "I will, Chandra, do not worry."

Chandra left the room as Maldia returned the folded dresses to the dresser. Maldia picked up the pink dress she had left on the bed and walked over to the bassinet, where Faith lay cooing on top of her fuzzy blanket.

Maldia had seen the looks that Doctor Tenebris had given her during his visit to Faith. She knew what he must think of her, lying in bed lazily while Chandra's chosen handmaid had run into the room when Faith had started crying. It was true that Maldia had allowed Chandra to tend to her and Faith during the first four weeks, but it was custom in the palace for the mother to rest for a month after the trial of giving birth.

Maldia had felt guilty enough for that, especially since her birthing process had been considerably eased from the normal, but Maldia was a woman of tradition. She had been practically jumping from her skin and ready to take on the world by the time the weeks had passed.

Maldia had never been a languid person and certainly did not intend to take up bad habits. She would care for her child like any mother should, and she would not be coerced into letting others do her work. Perhaps she would explain that to the good doctor when he visited again to ease his mind.

Tenebris had no way of knowing about palace tradition, so she did not blame him for his judgments that day. However, she would not allow him to continue to think badly of her or worry that her child was raised by an idle mother.

Maldia smiled as she picked up the squirmy baby from its bassinet and laid her on the bed. She gently undressed Faith from her bunting wrap and changed her diaper. She slipped the frilly dress onto Faith's chubby form and then put on the matching diaper cover. She placed pink frilly booties on her feet and stepped back to admire the adorable ensemble.

Faith's pale baby skin seemed to glow, accentuating her bright, sky-blue eyes and chubby, pink lips. Her tiny nose was slightly upturned, and her cheeks held that natural baby rosiness. The fuzz of hair on her head was a very light golden blonde, and Maldia wondered if it would darken like most newborns' hair did.

Faith's coloring was so unlike hers, and Maldia had no father to compare it to. Maldia would just have to wait and watch as her baby grew to see her final coloring.

Faith started to fuss, her chubby little arms and legs waving in the air, and Maldia scooped her up and held her close to her chest. She

knew the baby was probably sleepy since she had just eaten before
Maldia and Chandra started fussing over the dresses.

She swayed the baby back and forth in her arms as she gazed down
lovingly into Faith's perfect features, smiling softly as she envisioned
the beautiful young lady she would grow into. Faith's eyes closed
slowly, and she slept soundly in her mother's protective arms within
minutes.

My chest hurt. My eyes burned with tears as the pain and shame of
his betrayal swirled through me. The pain was not only mental but
physical as well. My chest ached intently.

I touched the ache and pressed, trying to relieve the pain as much as
possible. I inhaled a gulp of air as my lungs burned for much-needed
oxygen, and a sob escaped my throat as I exhaled.

It was too much. I could not control the pain in my chest or the
anger that seethed in my gut. He had betrayed me. He had promised
to never hurt me, and he had broken his promise. He said it was not
what it looked like, but wasn't that what they all said? He begged me
to wait, stay and listen to his explanation, but I did not want to. I did
not want to look like more of a fool than I already did.

I breathed another great gulp of air as a burning sensation flowed
over my skin. My shift was trying to burst forth, but I pushed it down.
I controlled my shifts. They did not control me. I differed from most
shifters in that way. However, this felt different from my usual shift.
This shift was more assertive, more dominant, and harder to control. I
breathed in deeply and out slowly the way they taught me to do to
keep the shift at bay, but it continued to persist.

I reached into my gut for that stamp that lived inside me, the stamp
of my paranormal doctor, Tenebris. He could help me. I felt around
for that strand of his energy as my blood boiled and the shift
threatened to come.

My heart pounded with dread as I frantically scrambled to connect
with Doctor Tenebris, and suddenly it worked. He was there, holding
the shift back and pulling me back into myself. I felt his presence as if
he were standing right there before me, even though I knew he was in
Asgorath and could not be here.

He may not be here physically, but that was not what I needed right now. He was here where it counted, pulling back the shift and controlling the flow of my magic. I smiled and breathed a sigh of relief as I felt his control, and I paid close attention to the procedure so I could repeat it for myself when needed.

The burning dissipated and coiled back into my center, and my heart, which had been beating rapidly, slowed to a more normal pace. I would have to ask Tenebris about this unfamiliar sensation. He would know why this shift had felt different. He could help me with my magic from halfway around the world, but he could not speak to me in my mind. I would have to wait and speak with him about it when I saw him physically, which would be in two more weeks.

For now, however, I must face the hurt and betrayal in front of me. I will handle this with kindness and grace the way my mother would. My mother is a shining beacon for this city, and with her influence, I will become a loving person like her. I would forgive him for his betrayal and handle him gracefully, but I would not trust him again so easily.

He would have to earn that.

I looked into the face of the boy in front of me as he begged and pleaded with me to listen to his side of the story, and I smiled softly. Upon seeing my smile, a look of relief came over his face, and his shoulders relaxed.

His face lit up with relief, and he immediately launched into an animated explanation.

I had made the right decision.

My mother would be most proud of me.

However, this boy would work hard for a while if he wanted to re-earn my trust.

Celia was smiling as she removed her hand from the glassy surface of her crystal ball. Faith had slept soundly through the entire reading, and Celia was glad. It had been another of those visions where she had been inside the person instead of an outside observer. She had been staring into her crystal ball when the vision sucked her in.

Faith had handled herself nicely in this vision despite her pain and hurt, and Celia wondered who the boy was that had betrayed her. He had looked strangely familiar to Celia. He would be just a baby right now, but the shape of his eyes and lips were ones that Celia knew from somewhere.

She had read many babies lately, so there were many possibilities of who this boy might be. The more important point of the vision was the significant change in Faith's attitude.

This time had been entirely different and much more positive. Future Faith had taken the help of her teacher and taken control, and she had followed her mother's influence to handle the situation with grace. Celia was delighted with the reading.

It did not satisfy Celia that her powers were changing, and she did not know why. She would have to talk with Tenebris about this before this happened with someone else. Celia did not want to have first-hand experience of some poor soul's horrifying death while doing a reading.

"The look on your face tells me something is bothering you," Maldia commented. "Are the readings becoming bad again?"

Celia glanced up at Maldia. She sat in the chair where she always sat during their meetings, with Faith nestled in her lap. She looked over the crystal ball at Celia with a worried look.

Celia smiled and answered, "No, no. nothing like that. As a matter of fact, this reading was perfect."

Maldia's frown deepened. "Then, what is wrong?"

Celia answered Maldia with a sigh. "I was in your teenage daughter's body yet again. I do not understand why my visions are changing where Faith is concerned. What if this happens to me with someone else?"

Maldia shifted Faith in her arms and swiveled in her seat. She rose and came around the table to stand in front of Celia. She shifted faith into one arm and placed her other hand on Celia's shoulder in a comforting gesture.

"Maybe it is not you. Maybe it is simply that Faith is more powerful than other people that you read, so it makes the visions different."

Celia smiled up at Maldia and patted Maldia's hand that still sat resting on her shoulder. "Maybe you are right. However, I will consult with Tenebris just to be sure. Speaking of that, he was on your daughter's mind during my vision. It was his help that calmed her shift, and your influence tamped her anger."

Maldia's eyes rose in surprise. "Really? How do you know that from just a vision?"

Celia's smile widened. "Like I said, I was inside your daughter's body. It was as if I had possessed her. I could feel what she felt and thought what she thought. I was her for that moment in time. She will grow up to love you and look up to you."

Maldia glanced over at the baby sleeping in the crook of her arm and smiled brilliantly. "I know, and I hope she grows to love you as well." Maldia removed her hand from Celia's shoulder and twisted Faith to her front.

"Would you like to hold her?" She asked, smiling down at Celia.

Celia looked up at the tiny bundle in Maldia's arms, and her arms itched to have the baby nestled there. She had held Ethan, Raina's baby, many times over the past month that she had been in Celia's home, but Celia had not felt as connected to him as she did to Faith.

Although she had only visited baby Faith a few times, she already felt strongly attached to the newborn. She guessed it was from being inside Faith's future self during that first reading with Maldia.

She raised her arms in a gesture for Maldia to place the baby there, and Maldia carefully lowered the baby into Celia's arms. The tiny bundle was heavier than Celia remembered. She wrapped her arms around the baby, carefully supporting her tiny head, and gazed down into the opening of the blanket.

Miniscule eyes opened and stared up into Celia's face. The piercing blue color surprised Celia as it had the first few times she had held Faith, but not as much as the wisdom that flashed deep inside of those crystal blue orbs. This was not the innocent look of a tiny baby but the wizened look of an older, more powerful being.

The look vanished as quickly as it had come, leaving Celia to wonder if it had only been a trick of her mind. The innocence of a baby shone from the clear blue irises that stared up at Celia, and the corners of her teensy mouth curled and puckered into a tiny O shape. Her chubby cheeks puffed out, and a small coo escaped the tiny lips, causing Celia to chuckle and return the baby's coos.

Celia giggled as a small, dribbling smile crossed that tiny angel's lips. Maldia jumped, clapping her hands excitedly as she bounced on her toes.

"Oh, my goodness! That was her first smile!" she exclaimed.

"It was?" Celia asked in surprise.

"Yes," Maldia answered laughingly. "I knew she would love you."

Celia did not respond. She stared down in wonder at the baby in her arms, smiling into its face lovingly. A fierce protectiveness settled inside of her, for the tiny baby swaddled in the crook of her arm. She thought about Ethan, the tiny babe living in her home with his mother, and knew she would probably grow attached to him as well.

Maldia's smile remained as she stood and watched Celia with her daughter. After a moment, she reached out her arms for Faith.

Her voice was tinged with regret as she said, "I am afraid I must be going now. The pod is here to take us back to the palace."

A flare of sadness lit inside Celia's heart as she placed Faith into her mother's arms, and it laced with her tone as she replied, "I will see you back here in a month, then."

Maldia smiled an understanding smile at Celia's tone and visage. "You know I will probably see you before that at the palace."

Celia returned Maldia's smile. "Yes, you probably will. I have my own room there, but I hardly use it. I stay so busy here that I never have the time to stay the night. Maybe someday I will make time for Faith."

"We would like that," Maldia answered as she buckled Faith into a carrier and picked up her bag. She turned for the door, gazing over her shoulder and adding, "Farewell for now, Celia."

"Farewell for now," Celia replied as she gave a soft wave.

Maldia's smile brightened as she waved back and strolled out of the shop door. Celia watched as Maldia climbed into the metal pod before the shop. The pod door whooshed shut, and Celia saw Maldia securing Faith's carrier into the pod seat through the door's window.

A metal rod rose from the top of the pod, and when it had extended to its full height, a handle slid out from either side of the pole. The sapphire blue metallic-scaled dragon that waited beside the coach rose from a sitting position and shook itself like a wet dog. He extended his massive wings and gave a loud roar to the sky, signifying to any in the vicinity that he was taking off.

Puffs of cold billowed from the ice dragon's nostrils as it huffed and then rose into the sky above the metal pod holding Maldia and Faith. It hovered over the pod for a moment while it grasped the handles of the pole with its talons and then rose into the sky with the pod dangling by its strong feet.

Silver streaked across Celia's vision as she watched the metal pod soar across the sky toward the palace. Celia shuddered, a sigh escaping her throat as she stepped away from the window and sat at the table. She hated those silver pods that she referred to as death traps. She prayed silently that Maldia and Faith would reach the palace in safety.

Celia may be a seer, but there was much about the future that she did not know. Her sight was not set in stone. Things changed, people made different decisions, and situations did not appear as expected. Plus, Celia could not always see every detail of the future. There were times when Celia did not pay enough attention to catch things.

The strands of time weaved through Celia's mind faster than she could follow, changing with every minuscule difference that rippled through the pond of time and space. She could read these strands one at a time if she concentrated on the right one. However, the future could change in a fraction of a second, and Celia was more aware of that than anyone.

She cringed inwardly as she remembered the first reading she had done with Maldia. Sometimes, while Celia lay in bed and attempted to fall asleep, she could still feel the heat from the fires that had laid waste to the entire city of Solaris. She could still taste the smoke on the back of her tongue, and the smell of ash and sulfur still permeated her nostrils.

The chime signifying a customer sounded, breaking through Celia's thoughts. Celia dowsed the blasted memories from her mind and turned her attention back to reality. She put on her best smile as two figures she had never seen entered the shop, a young woman and man holding onto one another as young lovers might.

"We would like to know our future," the woman said as she smiled adoringly up into the young man's face.

"Certainly," Celia said in welcome, gesturing to the empty seats at the table. "Come in and sit. Let us see what the fates have in store for you."

Celia breathed in preparation as the young couple sauntered over to the table, holding onto one another as if they were afraid of being separated. Celia brushed all the thoughts and worries from her mind as she prepared to do a reading for these new clients.

Before clearing her mind in preparation, two things nagged at her subconscious thoughts…A crystal blue pair of baby eyes that held too much knowledge for such a tiny body, and a pair of black baby eyes that seemed to look inside Celia's soul.

Celia wondered which pair of eyes she would grow to love the most.

The sound of Ethan's cries awakened Raina, just as they had every morning since she had come to live at Celia's house…and every two or three hours during the night…and every two to three hours during the day.

It was draining, and if not for Celia's help, Raina would have died from exhaustion by now. The bassinet that Tenebris had bought for the baby still sat in Raina's room, making it easy to get to him in the middle of the night. But Celia would often come in before Raina could even get up and take Ethan to her bed.

Celia had discussed setting Ethan up in his own room when he started sleeping through the night, but Raina was not sure she would even be here that long. She hoped to find her sister. She refused to be a burden on Celia any longer than necessary.

She had called and checked in with Tanner shortly after settling in. Her mother was safe with Tanner, which lifted a tremendous weight from Raina's shoulders.

Her mother was safe, and Raina could stop worrying and concentrate on finding her sister with some help from her new friends.

Tenebris had visited frequently during the last month, and Raina was slowly growing attached to him. During one of his visits, after Raina had lived with Celia for a couple of weeks, he had gladly reported that the search for her had come to an end. Palace Asgorath guards had questioned the border patrol, asking where Raina had landed. The patrol officers had reported seeing her hobble onto a dragon's back and being flown over Lake Divere.

They told the palace guards that

the dragon returned a short time later without her. They did not believe the dragon had enough time to safely cross the lake and deposit her on the other shore. Therefore, they assumed the lady had fallen from the dragon to her death. It was a common occurrence when one rode a dragon over Lake Divere. It had happened to Celia's mother and father.

Raina had been horrified at the story Celia had told her, and her heart had softened for Tenebris when she discovered that he had adopted and raised Celia.

Raina searched her memory.

Had Tenebris left her side after he had deposited her on the ledge above the lava? That night's events were twisted into the memory of agonizing pain, but she remembered the momentary fear of being left alone and dying along with her child.

It had not happened, though. Tenebris had returned and helped deliver Ethan and then had brought Raina here. Had he flown back to the guard post to ensure the guards saw him and made the assumption that Raina had died? Had he given her a way out of the southern hemisphere by making it appear as if she were dead?

It sounded like something the soft-hearted Tenebris would do. If he was willing to take on a child to save her from being an unwanted orphan, he would make Raina look dead to hide her from Asgorath.

Ethan's cries grew louder, and Raina jerked herself into a sitting position. She had almost fallen asleep again as she lay pondering recent events, but the insistent sound of her baby fully awakened her.

She dragged herself from her bed and shuffled to the small bassinet a few feet away. She made soothing, cooing noises as she lifted the crying babe from the cradle and carried him to the rocking chair. Ethan's cries instantly ceased as she placed him on her breast, and Raina smiled down at her babe as he suckled his breakfast.

Or was it a midnight snack?

Raina did not know, but she let out a loud yawn as she rocked the eating baby.

The bedroom door opened just a crack, and Celia stuck her head inside. Raina had discouraged Celia from knocking the first week of her stay, insisting that this was Celia's home and that she had no reason to knock on her own doors.

Celia had insisted that it was a show of respect, to which Raina had responded that respect needed to be earned and not freely given. Celia had argued that point, but in the end, Raina had won the fight. Now,

Celia entered Raina's room whenever she pleased, and Raina accepted her presence without question.

"Is everything all right in here?" Celia asked in a quiet voice.

"Everything is fine. Ethan was hungry, and it took me a moment to get to him this time," Raina answered just as softly.

Raina raised her gaze to glance at Celia's head, still poking through the crack in the door.

She smiled at Celia's curious gaze and said, "Would you like to come in?"

Celia's eyes widened. "You don't mind?" She asked tentatively.

"Not at all," Raina answered.

Celia opened the door wider and stepped into the room. She crossed over to the bed and sat down, turning to face Raina, where she sat in the rocker with Ethan in her arms. He made contented wet smacking sounds as he fed, which made Raina chuckle lightly as she stared down at him. Celia chuckled as well as she settled herself onto the bed.

"So, have you found any information on your sister yet?" Celia asked Raina.

Raina glanced up from watching Ethan and looked at Celia thoughtfully. "I have not gotten to speak with my mother yet on the subject, and I have been hiding here, so I have not had the chance to ask anyone anything."

Celia nodded in understanding. "Well, now that the Palace is no longer searching for you, I hope you find something out soon."

"Me too," whispered Raina, lowering her eyes to the babe still suckling at her breast.

"In the meantime, what is your plan for staying here in the northern hemisphere?" Celia asked.

"Well," Raina answered. "I had not really thought about it. I guess my mind was so full of finding my sister that I did not think about anything else."

"Do you have any special skills or schooling that may help you find a job?"

Raina lifted her gaze to Celia's and shook her head.

Celia smiled softly and said, "I may be able to help in that aspect if you would be willing to learn."

Raina stared at Celia in stunned silence for a moment. She had expected condescending tones and judging looks, but Celia's visage and tone had been kind. How could Raina say no?

"I am always willing to learn new things," Raina responded. Her eyes brightened, and her head lifted a little further as she lifted little Ethan from her breast. He made tiny whimpering noises as Raina hoisted him onto her shoulder and patted his back firmly.

Celia smiled at the loud belch that came from little Ethan as she answered Raina. "I can find someone to start training you in about two weeks. I will arrange for a temporary nanny to help with little Ethan while you work, and you can even bring the nanny and Ethan with you."

"What kind of job would I be doing that I could bring my baby and nanny along?" Raina asked curiously.

Celia's smile never left her face as she answered, "You will be working with me in my shop."

Raina's eyes widened in wary surprise. "But, Celia, I am no seer! That kind of magic cannot be taught."

Celia laughed aloud and replied, "No, Raina, you misunderstand. I do not want you to tell fortunes. There are other things to running a shop besides just dealing out the merchandise."

Understanding flowed over Raina's face as she lifted Ethan onto her shoulder again when he refused to suckle the other breast. "Oh, I see. Like cleaning and stuff."

Celia nodded. "Yes, and other things."

Ethan released another belch, and Celia rose from the bed and reached for him. Raina handed the baby over to Celia, who laid him down into the bassinet and pulled out a dresser drawer. She pulled diapers and wet wipes from the drawer and then returned to the baby lying in the bassinet.

Celia proceeded to change Ethan's diaper as she spoke to Raina. "I would like to teach you how to run the monetary dealings of the shop. You would learn things like inventory, stocking and ordering supplies, running the register, and balancing the banking account. I want you to be my right-hand person, my assistant."

Raina looked doubtfully at Celia as she responded, "I don't know. That sounds like a lot of responsibility. It is probably awfully complicated."

Celia lifted the baby from the bassinet and examined her handiwork. Nodding her approval, she carried Ethan back to Raina and placed him in her arms.

Raina smiled in thanks as she placed the babe against the other breast once more. Ethan latched, and Raina frowned as she turned her attention back to Celia.

"I did not go very far in school. I dropped out early to make money and help my mother put food on the table."

An angry frown darkened Celia's face, and her tone came out low as she asked, "How old were you when you were forced to work?"

Raina's eyebrows rose. "Forced? I was not forced. I volunteered."

Celia's angry visage remained as she responded, "Raina, Tenebris told me what you did for work. You were a child. You did not know what you were volunteering for."

Raina dipped her head in shame as she said, "It is true that I did not know how difficult being a prostitute was until I experienced it for myself. However, even afterward, I continued. My mother tried encouraging me to stay in school, but I refused. I figured if she could endure that kind of work, I could too."

Celia's gaze softened, and she let out a sigh. "I am sorry, Raina. You should never have had to do that."

Raina glanced up at Celia with a sad smile. "Neither should my mother. Mom did not know what to do after my father died in the war. Her entire life had revolved around him, the new baby, and me. She had never worked, and her schooling was minimal. She did what she could when she was forced to take over our care alone. She did not have anyone to help her like…"

Raina's attention was pulled away as Ethan released his hold on her breast with a satisfied smack. Raina glanced down at the baby in her arms, and determination filled her soul. Raina smiled as she lifted Ethan to her shoulder to burp him for the last time.

She would do what she could for baby Ethan. Ethan let out a small burp, and Raina pulled him away from her shoulder and snuggled him into her arms, rocking back and forth softly.

"I understand," Celia whispered. "You are right. You and your mother deserved more, but it is not too late."

Celia was smiling when Raina met her gaze. "I know someone who would be an excellent teacher for you. Give yourself a chance, for Ethan."

Raina took a breath and said, "Okay. I will do it for Ethan."

"Good," Celia responded encouragingly. "And do it for yourself, too."

Raina smiled as she got up to place the sleeping Ethan into his bassinet, and Celia tiptoed from the room. Raina was still smiling as she climbed back into the bed, and her dreams were filled with a better future for herself and her son.

"What made you think that was a good idea?" Tenebris sneered at Celia after she had told him of her plan for Raina. He had come for one of his many frequent visits to check on Raina and the child.

Celia frowned in confusion. "What makes you think that it is not a good idea?" She shot back.

Tenebris paused. What could he say? Celia had no idea that Ethan was the demon dragon's chosen one, and Tenebris had no plans to tell her anytime soon. He was waiting to see how the hand played out before he showed that card.

"What if anyone finds out Raina ran away from Palace Asgorath?" Tenebris said. It was the only thing he could come up with quickly.

"How would they find out? You said that the Asgorath Palace thinks she is dead, so they are no longer looking for her." Celia narrowed her eyes, and Tenebris's heart sank to his feet. "Unless you know something that I don't."

Tenebris knew that look. She was thinking, sizing him up, and trying to use her divination to devise a solution as to why Tenebris was hesitant to let Raina out of the house. Tenebris wiped his mind and pictured a blank wall before Celia could pull anything from his brain.

It was not like it would do any good, anyway. Celia was a seer, not a psychic. He could picture a million blank walls, and Celia would still see something in his future. Celia did not get her information from people's minds like psychics.

Celia pulled information from the strands of time that lived inside her subconscious mind, her understanding of things, and her paying attention.

Tenebris swallowed nervously, hoping that Celia did not find out what he already knew.

Celia had told him that she had seen a different future for Faith. One of Celia's most recent readings with Faith had shown her Faith as a young woman, guiding all the dragons of Mikka through the newly healed lands with a demon dragon by her side. How long before Celia discovered the demon dragon by Faith's side was Ethan?

As far as Tenebris knew, Celia had not yet read Ethan. Tenebris was sure that when she did, she would find the truth for herself. Tenebris wanted to prevent that from happening as long as possible.

Tenebris had already put his signature into little Ethan to help Ethan control his powers when he came into them, but he had done it secretly without Celia's knowledge. It seemed to Tenebris that he was keeping a lot from Celia so that she would not learn about Ethan's heritage.

However, it could not be helped. He had his own reasons for keeping this secret from Celia, despite him having promised Raina that he would keep the secret for her benefit. He was also keeping things from Raina, but they would both find out what those things were soon enough.

Everyone would.

Soon, everyone would know who Tenebris was, the secret he had been hiding for so many years.

"Tenebris, what has gotten into you?" Celia asked loudly.

Tenebris shook himself mentally, pulling himself back from his thoughts, and fixed a blank stare on Celia. "Sorry, did you say something?"

Celia pinched the bridge of her nose between her thumb and forefinger in agitation. She sucked in a calming breath and then lowered her hand to the table where she sat with Tenebris.

"I was sure that you would be happy with this plan. I can see, however, that I was wrong. Why would you not want Raina to have the best chance possible?"

Tenebris deflated, slumping into his chair and lowering his gaze to the table before him. He sighed and responded, "I am just being overprotective. If she is discovered, then Asgorath will start asking questions about how she had made herself appear dead and made her way to Solaris. If they find out we helped her, it could start a war."

Celia straightened in her chair, her chin lifting in defiance as she said, "Do you think me stupid, Tenebris? Do you not think that I would not check for such outcomes? I have read the cards thoroughly, searching for any possibilities for future implications, and every reading has come out positive."

Tenebris's eyes shot up to Celia. "Yes, I have considered that, Celia. However, you, of all people, know that what you saw could change suddenly. One little decision in the opposite direction could set off a ripple in time that would change the entire planet's future. How can you be so certain?"

"True," Celia said matter-of-factly. "It is entirely possible that everything could change, but that is true for every decision that every person on this planet makes. Nothing is set in stone, so we must take chances. Even seers.

"How will Raina ever be able to move forward if she fears that every small thing will bring her a horrible future? How would anyone ever be able to move forward with that possibility hanging over their head?"

Tenebris huffed. "I suppose you have made your point."

Celia smiled triumphantly as she reached over the table to lay her hand on Tenebris's. "I will take care of her, Tenebris. You do not have to worry so much."

Tenebris returned her smile. "I know you will. I am just overly worried about her. There is just something about that woman that pulls at my heartstrings."

Celia chuckled as she drew her hand back away from him. "I have noticed."

Tenebris raised his eyebrows in surprise. "You have?"

Celia only nodded, still smiling.

Tenebris looked embarrassed as he responded, "I am thinking of asking her out on a date. Do you think she would agree?"

Celia shrugged. "I am not sure. She is focused on her son, her possible new career, and searching for her lost sister. She probably has not even considered that there could be love in her future."

"Love?" Tenebris questioned with a raised brow. "I care deeply for her, but I do not think I love her. I know I could love her if I let myself, which scares me."

"Why would that scare you?" Celia asked in amusement.

Tenebris was not amused. He gave Celia a serious look as he asked, "Why did you never marry Celia? You have had plenty of suitors, but you turned them all down. Why?"

Celia lowered her gaze and stared down at her hands that were folded on the tabletop. "It is impossible for a seer to have a healthy relationship, Tenebris. You know why."

Tenebris slapped the table lightly to get her attention. When Celia's eyes rose to his, he breathed and said, "Say it, Celia. Tell me why."

She blew out a breath and responded, "I do not want to become emotionally invested in someone only to 'see' them betray me in the future. It is painful enough for someone to have their heart broken without warning, but for someone like me…"

She trailed off briefly as a knowing look blazed into her irises before continuing, "It is pure torture. Watching someone betray me, knowing they could change the outcome by choosing a different path, and then watching as they do not choose that path…

"That would kill something inside me."

A pang of guilt shot through Tenebris as Celia stared into his face. She could never read his secret because of the spell they had placed over him to hold it, but it would soon come out. She would be like those who had no warning.

He knew it would hurt the people closest to him when he revealed his secret, but protecting the planet was more important than petty emotions.

He forced his gaze to remain neutral as he responded, "Betrayal hurts, no matter if you see it coming or not. Either way that is a chance we take if we want to try for love."

Celia shrugged her shoulders. "Exactly, and I am not willing to take that chance. I have love. I have you and now Raina and Ethan. I have Maldia and Faith as well. It may not be the love of my life, but my life is full. I am not such a hopeless romantic."

He flinched inwardly at Celia's words. The guilt filling Tenebris's soul grew ravenous, threatening to eat up all that he was. He almost confessed, almost spilled his guts and ruined everything, but he did not. Instead, he mentally pulled himself together, pulled on his concerned mask, and smiled at Celia.

"I am glad. I only ever want your happiness," he said happily as he rose from the table.

Celia rose as well. "I know. But what of your own happiness? I also want you to be happy, and if Raina is the one for you, then I say go for it."

Tenebris chuckled. "I will think about it. If I come up with the nerve to ask her out, you will be the first to know."

"I had better be," she said playfully.

Tenebris chuckled and walked around the table to pull Celia into a hug. He lingered, cherishing the feel of his adopted daughter in his arms. The time was closing in, and when it came, he would probably never hold her in his arms again.

She would hate him afterward and probably hate him for the rest of his life.

He kissed the top of her head before releasing her and said, "I will see you in two weeks. I must go to Asgorath and tend to a fairy that is coming into her powers. Please tell Raina I said goodbye. I'll see myself out."

Celia nodded and waved goodbye as Tenebris walked out of the dining room of Celia's house, through the living room and entryway, and out the door. He did not notice the figure huddled in the shadows beside the open dining room archway, holding a sleeping bundle in her arms.

Raina smiled as she watched Tenebris walk away, but the smile faded as she held Ethan close to her breast. She needed to focus on making a future for her son, and Tenebris would be a distraction.

She sighed as she turned and returned to her room, wondering what the hell she was going to do about Tenebris Fray.

CHAPTER 7: THE QUEEN OF LIGHT

Hestia stepped into the throne room of Solaris Palace, hitching up her pristine white robes as she walked across the polished marble floor. She approached the raised dais in the middle of the large room, her rubber-soled shoes padding silently as she walked.

The bright red symbol of a dragon curled into the shape of a circle with outstretched wings blazed brightly on the right side of Hestia's chest. It starkly contrasted against the white robes, as did the red sash she had tied around her waist.

As was tradition, Hestia's head was covered with a white gauzy fabric. The hair of a high priestess was sacred and therefore covered in the most holy places. The cloth covered her thick, wavy tresses, but the auburn color could still be seen through the sheer covering.

Tiamat's followers believed that the powers of the God and Goddess rode inside the head of the high priestess; thus, her hair was a conduit for that power. This was all speculation and symbolic. Hestia had never used her hair as a conduit for her power.

However, Hestia did not mind the head covering so much. It was comfortable, and it enhanced the sculpted features of her face. Most in the palace thought her beautiful, but Hestia was humble as well as traditional. She always wore her traditional clothing, whether it made her look beautiful or not.

But Hestia was beautiful. Her perfectly round eyes were a startling shade of turquoise. Her nose was straight and just the right size for her oval-shaped face. Her cheekbones were high, her lips full, and her chin perfectly curved. She moved with confident grace as she climbed the dais steps and then kneeled at the foot of the throne.

Today she was meeting with Queen Damaphur, the queen of the angel dragons and the last diamond dragon left on the planet Mikka. She was also the last of the original Drakaina family, descended from Echidna Drakaina, the first angel dragon queen.

The secured, impenetrable scroll room of Palace Solaris was full of different scrolls, and Hestia had read them all, including the scroll that listed Damaphur's familial lineage.

Echidna Drakaina had been the most powerful angel dragon of her time, and her lover, Typhon, was the most powerful demon dragon. Echidna fell in love with Typhon Gaian during a political meeting between the angels and demons. They mated and had a child, Maria.

Typhon returned to the demon court after the year-long political meeting and treaty signing, despite Echidna's pleading for him to stay. Typhon loved his daughter, but he was not in love with Echidna.

After his return, Typhon took another lover among the demon court, a demon called Galephria, and they had a son, Azriel. Typhon ended up falling for and marrying Galephria, which pissed Echidna off. She tried to kill Galephria while Galephria was carrying Typhon's third child, which started the Great War that split planet Mikka in half. Echidna took another lover during the war and had another daughter, Lucucia, Damaphur's mother.

Echidna and her first child, Maria, were killed in the war. Lucuia took the throne when Damaphur was young but was assassinated soon after, leaving the responsibility of ruling Solaris to young Damaphur.

During this time, the ancient Great Oracles wrote and recorded two scrolls, the angel scroll and the demon scroll. The scrolls predicted how the war would end.

According to the scrolls, the war was coming to its conclusion. The time of the chosen ones had started with the birth of Destiny Faith and another babe that had been born at the exact same time, in the land of the demon dragons.

Damaphur and Hestia had been waiting for information from their spies about the demon dragon's chosen one, but no news had been reported until that very morning. Hestia was here to report her findings to the queen.

Hestia tore herself from her thoughts as she looked up at the throne that sat imperially on the raised platform. Queen Damaphur sat majestically atop the throne.

Her tall, willowy body sat straight and rigid in the seat, her arms laid carefully on the tall armrests of the throne. Her hair was long and straight, and it shone with the color of the purest metallic silver. It flowed around her round face, and even though her gaze was stern, her features were soft and beautiful. Her icy lavender eyes were large and round, her nose straight and small, and her lips plump and shiny.

At the sight of Hestia kneeling at the bottom of the throne, a gentle expression came over her face. Damaphur's musical tones filled the room as she spoke.

"Hestia, why must you always kneel when you come before me?"

"It is a sign of respect, my queen," Hestia answered.

Damaphur scoffed. "Get up, Hestia. You know I hate it when you kneel. Sometimes, I think you do it on purpose to irritate me."

Damaphur had always favored Hestia since the day she was brought before her at the tender age of ten; Damaphur herself had only been sixteen and had just taken the throne. Damaphur's advisor, Sage, had brought Hestia before the young queen because he thought Damaphur needed a high priestess. Hestia vibrated with tenderness, love, and great power inside her tiny body. Damaphur had accepted Hestia as high priestess upon the advice of Sage, and Hestia had not let Damaphur down.

After only four years of training, Hestia became one of the most powerful, kind, and revered high priestesses of Solaris in such a short time. At only thirty-four years old, Hestia had held the seat of high priestess for twenty years. She was not the longest-serving high priestess, but she had taken on the role much younger than her predecessors.

Hestia chuckled as she rose. "I know you think that, but I mean no offense. It is quite the opposite, actually."

Damaphur rolled her eyes disbelievingly as she got up from her throne, standing to her full height as Hestia rose from the floor.

"Let us take our meeting to a more comfortable spot. This throne hurts my back," the queen said as she stood.

Damaphur leaned back slightly as she placed a hand on the small of her back and said, "Or maybe it is simply because I am getting old."

Hestia scoffed as she rose from her bow. "You are just barely forty," Hestia said. "Forty is not old."

The queen smiled wryly and responded, "Tell my aching body that."

Hestia laughed as she watched the queen's tall, willowy form walk gracefully from the dais. Hestia, accompanied by Damaphur's two guards, followed the queen as she made her way towards a private dining room that sat off the throne room, behind the dais and the throne. There was only one simple door leading into the tiny dining room. The room was simply furnished with a small table and six matching chairs.

Damaphur bade the guards wait outside the door since there was no other way into the small room other than that door, and they complied. They took up posts, one on each side of the doorway, and stood at attention as their sharp eyes swept around the throne room alertly.

Hestia chose a chair and sat down, and Damaphur chose the chair across from Hestia. The queen adjusted herself in the comfortably cushioned chair with raised arms and a high back and closed her eyes in satisfaction.

"This is much better," Damaphur said as she settled into the chair. She opened her eyes and focused her gaze on Hestia. "Now tell me, Hestia, how is the child?"

"The child fares well, my queen," Hestia answered. "And Maldia is an excellent mother. She has refused help from the handmaids and insists on doing it independently to the best of her ability."

Damaphur smiled proudly. "That is wonderful news. Nothing pleases me more than to hear this." She folded her hands together and rested them on the table.

Out of nowhere, a servant appeared at the side of the table. Hestia flinched violently as if something had struck her but recovered quickly. She had not even seen or heard the woman come into the room. Hestia's concentration and awareness of her surroundings were usually better than this.

Damaphur slightly frowned Hestia's way, but she made no comment. Instead, she looked at the servant and said, "Bring us coffee and bagels, please."

The servant gave a slight bow with only her head, then turned and left the room.

Damaphur turned back to Hestia and said, "You seem nervous. Is something wrong?"

Hestia let out a breath, almost a relieved sound, and answered, "No, ma'am. I am simply tired. It has been a long week. I have traveled with Chandra to visit the patrols at different border stations. Chandra's spies have reported that priests and guards from Palace Asgorath have visited them about the prince's young pregnant consort. She supposedly disappeared from the palace grounds. I do not believe she was simply another consort."

The queen's eyebrows shot up in curiosity. "Do you think it was her?"

"Yes, I do," Hestia said firmly.

"What happened to her?" Damaphur asked, her eyes widening in suspense.

Hestia cleared her throat and said, "Some of the guards say they saw her climb onto the back of a small dragon and disappear, going toward Lake Divere. When the dragon reappeared moments later, the woman was gone from its back.

"They believe she fell into the lake since the dragon did not have time to fly to the other side and deposit a pregnant woman before returning."

"That must have been very upsetting for Palace Asgorath," Damaphur commented. "Did the spies report on this?"

"Yes, they have. They have informed me that the palace thinks the woman is dead, and there has been much mourning and grief throughout the palace."

"That makes sense," Damaphur responded. "So, do you believe she fell into the lake?"

Hestia fidgeted in her seat, her nervousness growing as Damaphur's wise eyes watched. "No, majesty."

Silence fell. Hestia couldn't help but fidget under Damaphur's penetrating stare. She opened her mouth, closed it, and then opened it again. Damaphur frowned.

"Then why are you so nervous?" Damaphur asked. Her tone was gentle and uncondescending.

Hestia's face scrunched in dread as she said, "It is not good news, Damaphur."

Damaphur smiled sardonically and said, "No, I do not imagine it is, judging by your nervousness and twitching. But tell me anyway."

Hestia nodded, took a deep breath, and said, "I pulled the memories from the guard that said he saw the woman with the dragon."

Hestia paused as if trying to think of what to say next. She clasped her hands together firmly as the tension sang through her arms and into her shoulders.

Damaphur nodded encouragingly to Hestia, and Hestia squared her shoulders determinedly. "I saw the face of the woman Palace

Asgorath was searching for. I pulled the guard's memories of seeing the woman climb onto the dragon's back, and I saw the pain and struggle of her climb. She was in labor as she climbed onto the dragon's back.

"The dragon was Tenebris. I am sure of it. He took The woman to Celia. The spies said her name is Raina, but she is going by an alias. She and the babe fare well."

Damapher nodded as the finality of Hestia's story came crashing down on Damaphur's mind. The demon dragon's chosen one was here, not in Asgorath where he was supposed to be.

Damaphur had suspected all along that the chosen one was here. Damaphur had her own spies in place throughout Solaris. Her closest counselor and advisor, Sage, kept tabs on them for her.

Sage had reported to the queen the night that a mysterious lady and her newborn babe had come with Tenebris to Celia's home. One of her spies had witnessed Tenebris arriving with Raina and the baby and leaving alone.

It was easy to guess who this mysterious woman was. It was too much of a coincidence that this woman had shown up with a newborn the night Faith was born.

Then, there was the issue of Tenebris. He was a demon dragon, but Damaphur doubted that he would ever do anything to harm Solaris. He worked for both sides of the coin since he was the only one of his kind, but his adopted daughter, Celia, was a member of Queen Damaphur's court. Damaphur was sure that solidified Tenebris's loyalty to the angels.

So, why had Tenebris brought the demon dragon's chosen one here? The only answer Damaphur could come up with was that Tenebris was helping her somehow. Hestia had said that the chosen one had run away, so perhaps Tenebris had helped her do just that.

Maldia's voice cut through Damaphur's thoughts. "There's more, majesty."

Damaphur's eyebrows rose. "Oh?"

Hestia swallowed hard before continuing. "Maldia has told me that Celia has approached her discreetly about teaching someone some basic skills so that she can work for Celia in her shop.

"I did not tell Maldia about my suspicions. Instead, I asked Maldia if she knew who Celia wanted her to teach. Maldia said Celia did not tell her anything about the woman."

Hestia stopped speaking, but Damaphur did not respond right away. She sat motionless in her seat, taking in Hestia's words.

Damaphur took in two deep, cleansing breaths as she collected herself. "Did you tell Maldia or Celia that you suspect this woman is the one Asgorath is looking for?"

Hestia shook her head as she answered, "No, my queen. No one knows this but me and now you."

Damaphur nodded. "Good. Tell no one what you have shared with me this day. We will wait and see how this plays out."

Hestia turned a surprised look to Damaphur, her brows raised and her mouth slightly opened.

Damaphur, seeing the surprised distress on her high priestess's face, reached over the small table and patted Hestia's hand as she said, "Fear not, Hestia. If there is any danger coming, then Celia will warn us. Maldia is taking the babe for regular sessions, is she not?"

Hestia nodded quickly. "Yes, she has not missed a session yet."

"And the other babe is living in Celia's home, so if Celia gets any random readings from that child, she will let us know, I am sure."

"Yes, I am sure she would," Hestia consented.

"Then we are safe for now. I do not want to make any rash decisions here, Hestia. We cannot execute a woman and her baby simply because we fear her child.

"Besides, what kind of example would that be for little Faith? Would that not show that we do not believe in her as the chosen one and that we have no confidence in our goddess, Tiamat?"

Hestia hesitated for just a moment and then sighed in defeat. "You are right, as usual."

Damaphur patted Hestia's hand again before settling back into her seat. "We will watch the situation for now, and if the need arises for further action, we will deal with it."

Hestia did not respond and only nodded. The handmaid brought in the coffee and bagels just then, and they abandoned the conversation as the women enjoyed their breakfast. They chatted about other palace business as they ate, and by the time the meal was through, Hestia seemed more relaxed.

Damaphur was glad for that, but she was far from relaxed as Hestia bade goodbye to her and left the dining room. Damaphur sighed and slumped back into her chair as the handmaids cleaned the leftovers and dishes from the table. She watched them with wary eyes as they worked, her mind racing far away from what her eyes were seeing.

Damaphur wondered if Celia and Tenebris knew who Raina and her babe were or if they were just randomly helping someone? Damaphur knew that Tenebris had a reputation for bringing Celia strays, and Celia would always take them in. Is that what was happening?

If so, Celia would undoubtedly find out, eventually. She was a powerful seer, the most powerful in the northern hemisphere, and she would eventually read it in one of her many divining tools. Damaphur decided to set up a meeting with Celia before this happened. If she explained the situation to Celia and asked her to keep it quiet, she was sure that Celia would comply.

Tenebris was another story, and Damaphur wondered if Tenebris already knew the identity of the woman and child. And, if so, had he told Celia who she was? In any case, she would also set up a meeting with Tenebris.

The servants had stopped scurrying around in the dining room, and Damaphur realized with a start that they were gone. The dining room table was clean and gleaming, and the only thing on its surface was the vase of fresh-cut flowers in the center.

When Damaphur noticed the flowers, the sharp scents of wildflowers and roses hit her nostrils like a storm. The rose smell overpowered them all with its dark, rich scent, and Damaphur took in one more deep breath as she rolled the smells around in her mind.

Roses were her favorite.

Damaphur rose slowly from the table and turned to leave the room. Her guards were waiting for her just outside the door, as expected. She made her way out of the dining room and into the throne room, her guards falling in step behind her.

She was glad to see that the captain of her army and leader of her guard, Chandra, was waiting for her at the foot of her throne. Chandra stood tall and regal, despite not being in her usual warrior garb. At the moment, she was acting as a nanny and nurse to her friend Maldia, so she wore her customary white medical robes. The symbol of a large red dragon silhouette curled around in a circle and appliqued onto the right side of Chandra's chest, marked Chandra as an accomplished healer and set her apart from the holy women of the palace.

Chandra's full armor, adorned with gold and silver, and a red dragon silhouette on the chest plate made her an imposing figure as captain and head guard. She would also carry her shield that featured an angel with outstretched wings flying beside a gold dragon. This was Palace Solaris's symbol emblazoned on the Palace's flag.

Chandra's waist-length, straight hair hung free over her shoulders and down her back. It was the color of coffee with a small amount of cream, and it beautifully enhanced the bright green of her large, round eyes. Her face was serene, and her features soft. She had a little nose, a pouty mouth, wide lips, and sculpted cheekbones. Her triangular face ended with a small, pointed chin that enhanced the beautiful planes of her face.

She stood patiently, waiting for Damaphur, and Damaphur offered her a slight nod in greeting as she stepped onto the dais and sat on her throne.

Chandra bowed low at the waist, her hair sweeping down and brushing the floor, and then raised back up to face her queen. She swept her hair back around as she came back upright with a sweep of her arm and smoothed it down with her hand. The movement was automatic, but Damaphur always reveled at the gesture's grace.

"Greetings Chandra. Hestia tells me you have your hands full with Maldia and the babe." Damaphur's tone was slightly humorous as she greeted Chandra for the first time today.

Damaphur had enlisted Chandra to assist Maldia with the baby, considering Chandra's high healing skills and her existing close relationship with Maldia. But Damaphur still relied on Chandra as captain as well.

Chandra had supreme fighting skills with powerful defensive and offensive magic. She was talented at placing each guard in the perfect position according to their powers and strengths. She was efficient, loyal, and dependable, making Chandra indispensable to Damaphur.

No, Damaphur could not replace Chandra, and she would claim Chandra's services back as soon as she felt that Maldia no longer needed her.

"Maldia and the babe fares well, despite Maldia's stubbornness to take care of everything alone," Chandra responded, breaking through Damaphur's thoughts.

Damaphur chuckled. "Yes, I have heard of this. However, I think it is good that Maldia is dedicated enough to care for the babe on her own."

Chandra gave a slight bow with just her head as she responded, "Yes, you are right. It shows great loyalty and love for her child, which will be a great asset when the child grows to adulthood. It will make Faith a better person to have so much parental support and dedication."

Damaphur's bright smile widened at Chandra's words. "Exactly. I am happy that you understand."

"My understanding gives me the patience to deal with the situation," Chandra said, but she smiled and added, "And because I love Maldia so much."

Damaphur chuckled again, but her smile faded quickly with her following words. "I actually have a task for you, Chandra."

Chandra lowered her head and gazed at the floor respectably as she responded, "What would you have of me, my queen?"

"I need you to send word to Tenebris and Celia that I wish for a private meeting with them as soon as possible, but I want the meetings to be separate. Also, please tell Maldia that she has my blessing to teach the lady that lives with Celia."

Chandra's eyes shot up to the queen in surprise. "You know about that? I did not think Maldia had told you yet."

Damaphur's serious gaze never wavered as she answered, "I am queen, Chandra. I have eyes everywhere. However, I have not yet had the pleasure of meeting the lady."

Chandra harrumphed and crossed her arms as she said, "She is hardly a lady. She is polite enough but unrefined and uneducated, from what I hear. I do not understand why Celia insists on taking in these strays."

"Chandra," Damaphur said firmly, her tone chiding. "How can you say such a thing? You should understand better than anyone here how important is the kindness of others.

"It is not the lady's fault that she was born into poverty, yet she shows bravery by asking for help. She has a desire to learn and better herself. How can you deny someone such as this the help they need?"

Chandra's stiff stance relaxed, and her arms dropped to her sides. Her face and tone softened as she answered, "Well, when you put it like that, I suppose Celia is wise in that way, and I am just being a conceited ass."

Damaphur laughed aloud. "You are hardly that, but you are a bit judgmental sometimes."

Chandra's eyes shot up to the queen in surprise, but her visage relaxed as she noted the humorous twinkle in Damaphur's icy lavender eyes.

Chandra shrugged and said, "Yes, well, I will try to be more sympathetic, like Celia."

Damaphur shook her head and laughed. "Never change, Chandra. We are all unique and should never strive to be a copy of someone else. However, Celia is very wise with people and good at finding hidden talents. There are many in my kingdom that owe their success to her."

"So, you think it is good to have Maldia teach this lady to help Celia with her shop?" Chandra asked.

Damaphur nodded and responded, "Yes, I do. Tell Maldia that she carries my blessing and tell her I would like to meet this lady and her child. However, I would like to arrange my meetings with Tenebris and Celia first."

Chandra bowed her head and said, "Yes, my queen. I will search for Tenebris right away and then send word to Celia. I will let Maldia know that she can start teaching the woman."

"Good," Damaphur answered. "You may go."

Chandra gave one more curt bow, sweeping her hair back over her shoulders as she rose in that graceful gesture that Damaphur loved to watch. Chandra turned and strolled out of the throne room, leaving Damaphur alone, save for her four guards.

Four guards?

Had there not been only two guards stationed with her before?

Damaphur turned her head slowly toward the two additional guards, wondering why Chandra had added them to her watch. She opened her mouth to ask them their names but never got the chance. She never saw the mind blast coming that knocked her unconscious and faded her awareness into darkness.

CHAPTER 8: THE KING OF DARKNESS

Epialos stared out of the tower window solemnly. It had been four long weeks since the palace had received the news that the chosen one was dead, and there was much mourning throughout the land. It had outraged Epialos when he had heard the news, but his anger had soon turned to sorrow, just like the rest of his kingdom.

He had not eaten or slept in days and had only sips of water and Meade.

Mostly Meade.

He had hidden away in his tower where he could be alone and reflect on his thoughts. After four weeks of reflection, he still had not devised a single plan to rectify the situation.

The smoke and ash that had filled the sky over Asgorath Palace had dissipated, curling its way back over the land until it filled the sky over Lake Divere once more. The sun shone brightly over Asgorath, signifying the end of the time for the chosen one to come into the world. Epialos had lost his chosen one and lost his chance to put an end to this war.

At one time, he had thought he could end it by capturing the attention of the alluring queen Damaphur and making her his queen. She was the daughter of Lucuia, who was the daughter of his father's former lover. She had taken the throne after Lucuia had grown old and died, and Epialos had fallen for her at first sight. Damaphur would not give Epialos the time of day, however, deeming herself too good for the king of the demon dragons. The angel dragons had always always been arrogant and greedy, thinking themselves better than all others. If Damaphur only agreed to marry him and unite the angels and demons, they could bring peace to the land.

The sun streamed into the tower's window, and Epialos caught sight of his reflection as he stared out over the land. His skin was usually a healthy shade of gray, like a cloudy sky just before a storm. Now it was ashen gray like the old ashes of a fire, and there were blackish bags under his eyes from lack of sleep.

His red eyes, which usually resembled the purest of rubies, were closer to the color of dried-out apple skins. His black, shoulder-length hair was dry and frazzled, and the dullness of his typically glossy locks made his ashen skin look even ashier.

His normally straight, regal stance slumped in disappointment at the sight of his reflection, and he let out a tired sigh. Epialos was at a loss, and his lack of sleep was bringing him down physically and emotionally. He had tried for so long to bring peace back to the lands, but now it all seemed hopeless.

He turned away from the window and stared into the room at the imposing statue of the demon dragon God Bahamut, which took up the entire middle of the round room.

"Why have you forsaken us?" Epialos asked the statue, not expecting an answer. "Have you lifted your blessings away from us because of the crass actions of the evil ones that live in my land?"

He started pacing the room, tracking a circle around the statue's base with his hands clasped behind his back. He stalked around and around the image of his God as he spoke in low tones.

"I have been a good King to this land and have tried my best to rid us of evil. I have been a loyal disciple to you. My father, Typhon Gaia, was so loyal that he forsook his angel dragon lover and his daughter to return to you. He built this land so that we could worship you, free of the influence of Tiamat's greed and pride.

"Everyone knows that you, and not your sister Tiamat, were the kindest and most humble child of Gaia. Yet, here we are, your land forsaken and your people labeled as the scum of Mikka.

"Help me, Lord Bahamut. Guide me in your holy ways and show me how to make this right. Do not leave us to the machinations of the truly evil ones, whose slimy ways overrun my cities and drag our names through the mud. Do not leave us confined to the dark side of Mikka, alone and misunderstood. Darkness needs light to find peace and balance."

King Epialos stopped his pacing as he finished. He dropped to his knees in front of the stone Bahamut, bowing his head and resting it on the base of the giant statue. His shoulders shook as he wept, crying out his frustrations about his lost chosen one onto the cold stone of Bahamut's likeness.

The voice startled him when it entered his mind. It rang like a giant bell, clear and vibrant, through his scattered thoughts. The tone was like the softer thunder during a storm, deep and rumbling, and it trembled through Epialos's head with the force of a hurricane.

The warming power filled him with the voice, burning with the heat of a raging fire, yet it was a comforting burn and not painful. It was the soothing burn from sitting in front of a campfire, soaking in a hot bath, or the heat of naked skin in a lover's embrace.

The power of Bahamut raged through Epialos as Bahamut's words rang through Epialos's mind. "Do not despair, my son. The chosen one is not dead."

Epialos jerked his head from the stone base, raising surprised eyes up the statue's length to stare at the majestic dragon that towered toward the high ceiling.

"You spoke to me, my Lord?" He asked in a choked, surprised voice.

"I have not forsaken you, Epialos. Your grandson lives in the land of my sister, Goddess Tiamat. He is alive and well in the land of light." Bahamut's voice rang through Epialos's mind, booming and urgent, as Epialos kneeled on the cold stone floor of his tower.

A thrill of happiness shot through Epialos. The child was alive! He reveled in the glorious news while his mind whirled with plans to fetch his precious grandchild.

"Guide me, My Lord. Tell me how I can bring the child back," Epialos said reverently.

"The child must not leave its mother. The child must stay in Solaris."

"But, my lord, we could find another woman to serve as a nursemaid for the child. We do not need the mother." Epialos's eyes filled with anger at the thought that Raina had deceived him.

He had opened his home to her, given her the life of a princess, and she had run away with his grandchild still in her belly to those arrogant bitches. He would kill her with his bare hands when he got a hold of her.

"Calm your thoughts, servant," Bahamut boomed angrily. "Actions such as those in your head have deemed my children evil. You will show respect to the mother of your grandchild. Without her, he would not exist."

"But, my Lord, she has shown us no respect. She mocks us and thinks us evil, even as she runs to those who live in arrogance, greed, and pride," Epialos responded.

"She does not mock us, Epialos. She was simply afraid. This land is chaotic and dangerous, filled with the violence of those who have turned their backs on my teachings, and she was thinking of her child when she ran." Bahamut's tone had quieted to a rumbling bass. "Your own son, the child's father, is among those who think themselves above my laws. Raina was simply doing what was best for her son."

King Epialos thought about that for a moment. Had he not been complaining just moments ago about the disruptiveness of his subjects? Epialos could understand why one would consider the lands too evil and unruly to raise a child. He bowed his head reverently.

"I understand, Lord," He replied. "What would you have me do?"

"Do nothing now and tell no one that he lives. You will soon face a battle where you will fight alongside your enemies, but it will yield long-sought-after results. You will be reunited with your grandson after an absence, so do not mourn when you find him gone." The voice faded in Epialos's mind like the dying winds of a storm as he voiced his last words to Epialos. "The time for the chosen ones to heal the land is near. Follow your heart, my son."

"Yes, my Lord," Epialos said softly.

He stayed kneeling, head bowed, until he could no longer hear the rumbling voice inside his mind. He dared not raise his head until he could no longer feel the raging inferno of Bahamut's power inside his body. When all was quiet, and Epialos was alone inside his skin, he rose from his kneeling position and stalked back to the window of his tower.

He stared out the window over the land as he pondered on Bahamut's words, but the sorrow of loss had left his heart. The sun seemed warmer and cheerier as the last of its rays spilled in the window, lighting up the tower room in hues of burnt reds, oranges, and pinks. Happiness filled him as he gazed out at the mourning candles now lighting up in the windows of the various homes of Asgorath City.

They would not mourn much longer.

He caught his reflection in the window once more. His talk with his God, Bahamut, had done him a world of good. His black hair was shiny and soft-looking once more, the red of his eyes gleamed like rubies again, and his skin had regained its stormy luster.

His eyes were large, set back in a ruggedly handsome face, and the bags had disappeared from under them. His large nose was straight and strong, and his square chin and jaw set off his features nicely. There was no more slackness in his features. Gone was the slouch of miserableness as he straightened his stance, with his broad shoulders set back and his muscular chest puffed out.

All hope was not lost.

Epialos took a deep, cleansing breath as he turned from the window. He bowed slightly with his head as he passed Bahamut's statue. He moved to the door of the room that led to the winding staircase that wound down to the bottom of the high, round tower.

His step was livelier as he skipped down the winding stairs toward the door that led outside the tower and into the inner courtyard of Palace Asgorath. Two guards were permanently stationed at this door, and the guards changed depending on the time of day. There were only six guards on this guard duty, and Epialos knew them all and which ones would be on duty at this hour.

At least, he thought he knew, so he was confused when the two guards at the door were not the regulars for this time of day. He disregarded it with a shrug. Perhaps he had lost time brooding in his tower, and the lineup had changed.

Two guards came around from behind the tower, which did not worry Epialos either. His personal guards had been waiting for him to come down from the tower. He expected to see familiar faces as they approached since he knew all of his personal guards, but he had never seen these guards before.

Ever.

Had his captain hired more guards? And, if he had, why had he not informed Epialos? Sure, he had been in his tower, but surely his commander understood that he would not brood in his tower forever. He would have to speak to his captain when he next saw him.

The two unfamiliar guards took their places at Epialos's back and followed him as he moved through the inner courtyard.

He stopped at certain flowers, bending over to smell them and gaze upon their beauty as he always did when he walked through the courtyard. He sat on a bench before one of the larger fountains, staring into the cascading water as he enjoyed the leisurely calm he had not had in a long time.

The guards remained close to Epialos, standing at attention behind the bench as Epialos hummed happily to himself.

Epialos paid them no heed.

He regretted that decision moments later as he got up and made his way toward the grand doors that led into the throne room of his palace. He chastised himself for his carelessness as he felt a hand around his neck before reaching those doors. He cursed himself for his lack of attention as an acrid smell hit his nostrils from a cloth someone pressed over his nose and mouth.

The attack had been too sudden, and he had not been in a mindset to react quickly. He had been relaxed, at ease, and drowned out his surroundings in enjoying relaxed tranquility. He had no time to react or defend himself, and he fell easily into the trap he had not even known had been set.

The last thoughts that flitted through his mind before the darkness ate his reality were that he should have never let down his guard, but now it was too late.

I awoke in darkness, a darkness so complete that I was not sure if my eyes had even opened at all. I blinked a couple of times to be sure, and fear crept slowly into my body when I realized they were open. I tried not to panic, slow my breathing, and steady my rapidly beating heart so I could think.

I turned my attention to my sense of hearing, straining to hear anything in the surrounding blackness. The silence was deafening. The stillness of the dark was so complete that it left me with only the sound of my labored breathing and the heavy beating of my heart.

I needed to calm down and think, but my body refused to let go of the panic. I was drowning in the quiet darkness, and a scream built up inside my chest. I knew if I let it out that I would never stop screaming.

I calmed my breathing quickly, forcing the scream back into my gut. I forced myself to think, deciphering where I was and how I had gotten here.

I closed my eyes to fight the panic, tricking my mind into thinking that my closed lids caused the darkness. I breathed in and out slowly, forcing my mind into a tranquil state, and steadied my thoughts into something more calming.

I thought about my bed at home, imagining that I was there, tucked safely under my silk sheets. I imagined the ticking of my grand clock that echoed throughout my palace when the lights were all off, and everything was quiet.

I always fell asleep to the sound of that ticking, and imagining that sound now helped to calm my frayed nerves. It helped me ease the panic gripping my mind and scattering my thoughts into a frenzy of terror.

My head cleared with the calming of my breathing and the steadying of my heartbeat. I could better access my situation now, so I opened my eyes again.

Blackness still greeted my sight, but I could make out fuzzy silhouettes in the dark now that my eyes had adapted somewhat. I tried to sit up so I could search the room more conveniently, but something stopped me. I could only move my upper body slightly, and my arms and legs were pinned down. I tried to call upon my magic, but the familiar stirrings of prickling energy did not come to my call.

That familiar panicky feeling began to creep back into my chest, speeding my heartbeat and causing my breath to come in shallow, ragged gasps. I pulled at the bindings on my arms and legs, struggling to free them just as I tried to force the tingling energy to come to me. I heard chains clinking as I pulled and struggled, and a frightening thought entered my mind, spiking the terror inside me into a roaring storm.

If the person who had caught and bound me knew what I was, the chains were probably silver. Silver nullified the magic in a shifter's body, so I could not shift into my dragon form, or use my angel magic.

I would be completely and utterly helpless.

I took a deep breath, closing my eyes and chasing back the raging panic again. I calmed myself and reached deep inside my gut, searching for that energy that was my magic. I found it, coiled deep inside my core, still and unmoving. I tried calling it once again, but still, it did not respond to my call. It was as if it were in a deep sleep, suspended in that state and unable to break it.

I pulled in deep gulps of air into my starving lungs. I had not realized I had been holding my breath until that moment. I had been concentrating so hard on trying to awaken my magic that my breathing had ceased, and I had not even known it. I did know one thing for a certainty, however.

The chains were indeed silver, and I was absolutely screwed.

I tried not to let that rampaging panic seep back into my mind, but I could feel it stirring just outside the borders of my thoughts. I tried to ignore it, tried to think of another solution out of this conundrum, but that uneasiness played along my imagination like a snake hiding in the grass. It would sit, coiled and motionless until I discovered it or drew nearer to it, and then it would strike and it would be too late.

It messed with my concentration, and I simply could not think clearly.

Suddenly, a door opened, and light spilled into the room in a blinding fury. I squinted against that brightness, trying to raise a hand to protect my eyes. When my movement was thwarted by those blasted binding chains, the panic drew in nearer, causing my heart to pound and my breathing to speed up.

Gradually, my eyes adjusted, and I could see a cloaked figure standing in front of the open doorway, backlit by the bright light streaming in. My eyes widened at the familiarity of the figure, and my mouth dropped open in disbelief.

“Why?” I whispered, and my breathy voice was heavy with sorrow, disbelief, and terror.

“It is the only way,” The figure answered sorrowfully, the voice soft and breathy. “It is the only way to break the prophecy and right the wrong we have brought.”

“What do you mean? What wrong?” I asked calmly, trying to keep the shakiness out of my voice. Maybe if I could keep them talking, I could buy myself some time to escape this predicament.

“I am sorry. The entire planet is in danger, and we must save it. There is no other way.” The voice sounded tortured and broken.

The figure stepped further into the room, and I could see the light glinting off something it held in a gloved hand.

“For what it’s worth,” the voice said, shaky and filled with remorse. “You were a wonderful queen, and I will miss you.”

My eyes traveled to that shine, and they widened in horror at the sight of the sacrificial holy sword it carried, swinging it easily at its side. It raised the sword slowly, gripping it with both hands as the figure brought it up and over its head.

The figure came up beside the bed where I lay, helplessly bound in place, and I watched in terror as the blade came crashing down. I squeezed my eyes shut and braced for the bite of the sword.

"I am sorry, my queen. Great Oracles and Goddess, forgive me," The tortured voice whispered just before I felt the blade bite into my neck, a quick, sharp pain, and my entire world went black.

Celia sat straight up in the bed, gasping and clutching her neck frantically. A startled scream escaped her throat as the remnants of the dream floated away into the darkness of her bedroom.

A dream. It had only been a dream.

Or had it been a vision?

Celia did not know, but she knew that if it were a vision, it confirmed that her abilities were getting stronger and changing. It was not simply due to Faith's being the chosen one, as Maldia had suggested.

Celia had been inside the future body of Queen Damaphur herself, and the queen had been in deep trouble.

Celia replayed the vision in her mind, even though it caused her heart to race and her breathing to come in short, uneven gasps. She needed to do this, had to do this, because she needed to remember every detail, no matter how insignificant it seemed. Anything could be important enough to change the future strands and avoid this catastrophe.

She grabbed for the notebook and pen that she kept beside her bed. She recorded every detail she could remember from her dream/vision into the pages and then leaned back against the headboard in relief.

There, that was the best she could do.

She had recorded everything she could remember. Celia frowned at the pages in confusion. She did not understand how anyone could capture the queen, and she could not figure out who the figure was that had come into the room. She had not seen the person's face clearly, but the voice had sounded very familiar to Celia.

However, the queen had known who it was despite not being able to see clearly. The queen had felt betrayed when she looked upon the figure, so Celia assumed it was someone the queen trusted explicitly. Who could it be, though? Queen Damaphur had a small court, and Celia knew them all. But she could not think of who the cloaked figure could have been.

It was all a mystery to Celia, but she would warn the queen and tell her every detail she had written down. It was her job as palace seer to report all visions that had to do with the queen. Celia steadied herself and closed her eyes, meditating on the strands of the future that floated around in her mind. She chose the strand that signified Queen Damaphur, pulling it into her subconsciousness and holding it there.

She sat up and reached for the deck of divination cards she kept on her bedside table beside her notebook. She held the strand in her mind as she drew out a card on instinct. She turned the card over, and fear snaked through her veins as she looked upon the face of the Knight of Swords, the bringer of death.

She quickly rose from her bed and began to get dressed. She had to get to the palace and report her vision to the queen. She would need to call and reschedule her first appointment for the day, and she must hurry. Queen Damaphur's life was at stake.

She got dressed with as much speed as she could muster and then went to call the palace and ask them to send her a coach. It would be faster this way, even though Celia hated riding in the dragon-flown metal pods.

They were nothing but metal deathtraps.

What if the dragon dropped the pod while high in the air, or what if they ran into another dragon carrying another pod? The ride always left Celia full of irrational thoughts such as these, and it took several minutes to clear her head after landing.

Sitting on her living room sofa, Celia braced herself for the upcoming ride in the dangerous metal contraption as she dialed her first appointment. The call lasted only minutes, and then she was dialing the palace.

"Solaris Palace speaking. How may we make your day brighter?" came the soft voice.

It was Hestia's voice, and Celia smiled at the sound. It had been a long while since Celia had gotten to speak with her oldest friend.

"Hestia, it is so good to hear your voice after all this time," Celia said into the speaker of her portable phone.

"Celia!?" Hestia's voice breathed through the line, surprised and a little disbelieving.

"Yes," Celia answered with a chuckle. "It is me, friend."

Hestia seemed to recover because her voice was calm as she responded, "Well, it is certainly strange that you have picked this particular time to call."

Celia frowned in confusion. "Why is that?" She asked.

"Because," Hestia said, and her tone had an undercurrent of humor. "I was getting ready to call you, just at this moment. That is why I was so close to the phone."

Celia laughed out loud. "I was wondering why the secretary did not answer. I swear, I did not know you were getting ready to call me. It is just a coincidence."

"Mmm hmm," Hestia murmured in disbelief. "Tell me, my future reading friend, why have you called?"

Celia's laughter died, and her tone became serious as she answered, "I have called for a ride, and haste is of the utmost importance. I need to speak with the queen right away."

"I do not know if she has a spot in her schedule to meet with you today, but she has asked Chandra to schedule a meeting with you soon. That is why I was getting ready to call you. I told Chandra that I would get in touch with you and set up the meeting," Hestia said, and the humor had also left her tone.

Celia swallowed hard. "It must be now, Hestia. I had a vision." She stressed the word 'vision,' her voice lilting over the syllables.

"Oh," Hestia said, "when did you start having visions?

"When I first started reading Maldia," Celia answered, and her voice had dropped to nearly a whisper.

"Oh," Hestia said again, then paused for a heartbeat before she continued, "I will send a coach right away for you."

The line went dead.

Celia placed her phone next to her dream journal inside her purse. She gathered herself together and went out onto her front porch to await the coach. The coaches were fast, and Celia's house was situated right on the edge of Terrien, so she was very close to Solaris. It would not take long at all.

As predicted, Celia heard wings beating only minutes after sitting down in the chair on her front porch. She looked to the sky to see a jade-colored dragon soaring toward her house, holding a metal pod in its talons. The dragon slowed as it came closer and then hovered in the air before her house with the pod dangling from its claws.

The unmistakable small jade dragon caught Celia off guard. Tenebris carefully set the huge pod down, landed beside it, and waited for her to climb aboard.

Celia frowned. "Tenebris, you are too small to carry that pod with me inside."

Tenebris snorted indignantly and narrowed his golden dragon eyes in anger. Tendrils of electricity billowed from his nostrils, curling around his tiny dragon face.

Celia laughed at the look on his cute dragon face. She could not help it. Tenebris was cute as a dragon, and his temperament was more humorous than anything else. He did not have the evil appearance or arrogance of most demon dragons. The wicked-looking black horns on top of his head and the lack of metallic sheen in his scales were the only indications of his demon heritage. If the jade color of his scales had not been so matte and he had white horns instead of black, he would pass for an angel dragon.

Tenebris gave another indignant snort and gave a gesture toward the pod with one wing, gesturing for Celia to climb aboard. Celia's laughter died away. She stood frozen, looking at the pod with a hint of fear on her features.

Tenebris cocked his head and looked at Celia quizzically. The angry look was gone from his golden eyes as he approached Celia cautiously. He placed a wing gently on her shoulder and butted her forehead with his softly, causing Celia to look up at him with wide, chocolate-brown eyes. Celia took a breath and swallowed hard.

She did not want to get into that metal death trap, but she had no choice. She had to speak to the queen and quickly. Her visions were new to her, so she had no way of predicting when the vision would take place. For all Celia knew, her vision may come to be this very day, at this very second. She could not take the chance of waiting and her warning being too late.

Tenebris's golden dragon eyes were a comforting sight, and the soft touch of his scales against her forehead helped to calm her nerves. She was still frightened, but Tenebris's encouragement gave her the strength to pull herself together and step into the pod.

She strapped herself in securely as the door shut and trapped her inside. Celia's stomach lurched as the pod lifted off, and she fought to keep her quick breakfast of toast and coffee from making an unwelcome reappearance.

Finally, the pod moved in a more forward fashion, and the nausea eased as they moved through the sky. Celia concentrated on her future meeting with the queen as she rode, keeping her mind occupied.

Celia only hoped that she would be on time.

CHAPTER 9: THE MISSING KING AND

QUEEN

Raina found the note that Celia attached to the countertop in the kitchen. The handwriting was small and neat, with fancy little curls throughout. In the note, Celia told Raina where she had gone, how long she would be, and that Raina should go to the shop. Celia would meet her there later.

Raina's stomach quivered with nervousness. She had never opened the shop on her own. She had been with Celia several times when Celia had opened it, but Raina had never attempted the job herself.

Ethan's cries startled Raina from her thoughts and strengthened her resolve. She could do this. She had to do this for herself and her child. She had to prove that she could make it on her own. If she could not, what kind of example would that set for her son?

Raina drew in a deep, cleansing breath and gathered herself together. She got Ethan ready first, feeding him and changing his diaper before putting him into an outfit for the day. She smiled at the chubby baby in his tiny denim pants, baby blue t-shirt, and miniature jogging shoes. He resembled a baby doll with curly black hair, fair porcelain skin, and blue eyes. Raina wondered what color his eyes would be when the baby blueness wore away, but she suspected she already knew. She could see spots of red in the dulling blue of Ethan's eyes.

Black hair and red eyes with almost white skin.

It was an odd combination for a person, but Ethan was not a person. He was a demon dragon, and Raina believed he would be one of the kinder ones.

Like Doctor Ethan Tenebris Fray, Ethan's namesake.

Thoughts of Tenebris caused Raina's heart to skip happily. She had not seen him recently, which made her somewhat nervous. Especially since she had overheard the conversation between him and Celia during his last visit. He had been planning on asking Raina out on a date, and Raina had thought long and hard about what she would say if he asked her.

However, he had not visited since then, so she wondered why the hesitation?

Had he changed his mind?

She hoped not.

She could not get Tenebris from her mind. She constantly had naughty thoughts about the outrageously handsome dragon shifter. Her mind wandered to those thoughts now, imagining the sensation of his full lips pressed against hers, the roughness of his calloused fingers as they traced her delicate skin, and the softness of his dark hair running through her fingertips.

The scene ran through Raina's thoughts as she packed a diaper bag for Ethan. She packed extra diapers, wet wipes, and extra clothing into an over-the-shoulder bag as she daydreamed about Tenebris.

She laid Ethan in the bassinet and went into her bathroom, thinking about Tenebris's sexy smirk and sleek, muscular body. She pictured the grace of his movements as she imagined him stalking toward her in her mind's eye.

Her thoughts drifted to even naughtier things as she undressed, leaning against the wall for support. She pretended that Tenebris slowly undressed her as he kissed her everywhere.

She imagined his hands roving her entire body as her own hands did the same. She closed her eyes as she thought about the sensation of his fingers exploring her sensitive folds as her own fingers traveled to that spot. She envisioned Tenebris taking off his clothes and his naked body covering hers.

Her breathing quickened, her heart thudded in her chest, and her fingers worked faster as she imagined the feel of Tenebris's glorious shaft filling her. Her womanly walls quivered with sensation as her imagination ran wild.

She was close to bringing herself with thoughts of Tenebris having his way with her, and her fingers stroked her sensitive bud even faster. The sensation built to a crescendo as her walls throbbed with release, and she moaned softly as her orgasm ran through her.

She bent over the sink counter, clutching the sides to hold herself upright, allowing her breathing and heartbeat to slow to a normal pace before turning to the shower stall.

She had no clue how she would shower, put in her contact lenses, put on her wig, and apply her makeup with shaky hands and ravaged nerves, but she managed somehow.

By the time she was dressed and ready to walk out the door, she had worked herself into a frenzy of emotional turmoil. Her self-induced orgasm did nothing to ease her frustrations. She was still overheated with thoughts of Tenebris.

She was not expecting the subject of her thoughts to be standing just outside the door when she opened it.

It startled her so much that she let out a tiny scream and almost dropped the carrier holding baby Ethan. Tenebris's hand shot out and grabbed the carrier's handle, holding it until he was sure that Raina had recovered enough to hold it on her own.

Tenebris smirked and said, "I am very sorry I startled you, my lady."

Raina recovered quickly, giving Tenebris a small smile of gratitude as she pulled Ethan's carrier back into her grasp. She laughed nervously as she stepped out the door and closed it behind her, hoping her face did not show the mortification she felt.

Tenebris's eyes bore into hers as if he knew what she had been thinking and doing, and she could not help the blush that permeated her face.

"I just was not expecting anyone to be standing outside," Raina said, her voice wavering ever so slightly.

As she felt his heated gaze roam over her body, Raina was relieved that she had dressed up and taken the time to fix her hair and makeup.

She had tucked her natural, raven black hair into a blonde wig. She styled it back from her face but left the soft, fake tresses curling down her back almost to her waist.

The eyeshadow on her lids was mauve, complementing the sapphire color of her contact lenses and making her eyes appear to glow, while her full, pouty lips were painted with the same shade.

She had picked a cute, mauve sundress with dainty yellow flowers circling the waist. It hung just above her knees, billowing around her upper thighs as she walked. The strappy, yellow sandals matched the yellow flowers on the dress and accentuated her calves nicely.

"I think I like you as a blonde," Tenebris said in a low, growling voice that had nothing to do with anger and everything to do with desire.

Raina giggled in response as she lowered her head slightly, then raised only her eyes to him, staring at him through her thick, black lashes demurely.

His sapphire blue eyes sparkled in the sunlight as he gazed down upon Raina. Her eyes traced over the powerful lines of his face, his muscled jawline, and the rugged planes of his strong nose and chin. She admired the fullness of his kissable lips and the angle of his cheekbones that added to the handsomeness of his features.

Her eyes drew lower to his tan polo shirt and black dress slacks that fit his body as if they had been made for him alone. The tan shirt was tight enough to outline his toned chest and biceps, and the black slacks rode over his hips just right.

Raina smiled appreciatively at the sight of Tenebris as she raised her gaze back up to his face to find the heat in his eyes had risen to an inferno of desire. She smiled demurely into those fiery blue eyes.

Raina knew how to play this game.

"Did you need something, Tenebris?" Raina asked, quirking an eyebrow at him questioningly.

Tenebris seemed to shake himself mentally, flinching slightly and clearing his throat as he straightened himself.

There was a slight waver in his tone as he answered, "Umm, yes, actually. I was ordered to come fetch you and bring you to the palace. Celia is waiting for you there."

Raina frowned in confusion. "But she left me a note. She told me to open the shop for her and that she would meet me there later."

Tenebris shrugged. "Change of plans, I guess. I am only following orders."

Suddenly, Raina noticed the pod sitting in front of the house, the door open in preparation to receive its next passenger. She swallowed hard, turning her head to search for the dragon that would fly the pod with her, her child, and possibly Tenebris, inside.

"Where is the dragon?" Raina asked curiously when she found no sign of any dragon around the waiting pod.

Tenebris chuckled, spreading his arms wide and giving a slight bow. "At your service, my lady."

Raina's eyes widened. "You are going to fly the pod?"

Tenebris cocked an eyebrow and and asked in mock insult, "Why does that always surprise people?"

"Well, umm…it's just that…you are so…," Raina stammered, hesitating to finish what she was about to say. She did not want to offend him.

Tenebris chuckled again. "Go ahead, you can say it. I am too small to fly the pod."

Raina did not answer, but she gave a small apologetic smile and a shrug.

"You have flown on my back before, so you know I am stronger than my size allows one to believe. Trust me, Raina, I can fly the pod." Tenebris made a gesture, waving Raina toward the pod.

"It's Amelia, remember? Please, do not ruin my cover."

Tenebris gave a wry smirk. "Yes, of course. Thank you for reminding me, Lady Amelia."

He waved her toward the pod again with a formal bow and a smile. Raina rolled her eyes and stepped toward the pod. Tenebris followed close by her side and pushed a button that opened the pod door with a slight whooshing sound.

He pulled a nylon bag from the pod and stepped back to allow Raina to enter the pod. He took off his shoes and socks and placed them in the bag. He began to take off his shirt but paused at Raina's questioning stare.

"I do not want to ruin my clothes when I shift," he said with a small, heated smile. "I just bought this outfit."

"Then why did you even wear clothes in the first place?" She asked.

Tenebris's smile grew as he pulled off his shirt. His eyes never left hers as he folded his shirt and put it in the bag. Raina swallowed hard at the sight of his naked chest, but she never wavered as she continued to watch him hungrily.

He answered her question with another question. "Would you rather I have come to your door naked, then?"

Raina hesitated, and Tenebris turned to continue undressing as he said, "If you want to watch, you are more than welcome, or you can get in the pod if you do not want to see me naked."

Raina swallowed hard and started to turn and run into the open pod door, but she stopped. Tenebris was playing with her, and Raina knew how to play the game. Running like a coward was not how to play.

Raina smiled seductively, put as much heat as she could into her voice, and answered, "I have seen you naked before, Tenebris. I would not mind seeing it again now that I am in a condition to appreciate it."

Tenebris froze in the middle of unbuckling his pants. Tenebris's eyes flew around to meet Raina's contact-colored ones, and he felt his body responding to the heat emanating from her flirtatious gaze. He hesitated, wondering what her reaction would be when she saw the effect she had on him.

He swallowed hard and shrugged, thinking, 'What the hell,' turned, and dropped his pants. He pulled his legs out of them, bent down, and scooped them off the ground. Then he folded them and placed them in the nylon bag. His smile turned devious as he pulled down his underwear and revealed his hardness to her.

Raina's eyes drifted down to his groin, and Tenebris saw the blush creep up her neck and across her cheeks. He saw her throat work as she swallowed hard. Raina turned away toward the pod, and Tenebris thought he had won. But Raina placed the baby carrier with Ethan buckled in it inside the pod and turned back to Tenebris. Her eyes held the heat of a raging fire.

"Your dragon may be small, but other things certainly are not," Raina said huskily as she stared pointedly down at his nakedness.

Tenebris knew the game was growing dangerous, and now he knew that Raina knew how to play. However, Tenebris was much older and had been playing a lot longer. She would not win this one.

He strolled toward her, completely naked and with his bag in his hand, noting how she stiffened as he came ever closer. He smirked as he came right up to her, so close that his erection brushed against the hem of her short little sundress.

He tossed the bag into the pod as he leaned into her, letting the tip of his member slide into the space between her legs, brushing the sensitive skin of her inner thighs. He balanced his weight with his hands on either side of her head against the pod's side, effectively trapping her against the open pod door. She would either have to lean forward into him or turn and flee into the pod.

Raina stood her ground, and his breath blew softly across her lips as he whispered, "If you would like to test the size for yourself, then, by all means, be my guest. It would be easy to remove that tiny scrap of lace underneath that dress if you want me to."

He leaned even closer as if he would kiss her and paused, waiting to see her reaction. She turned her startled eyes up to his as her breath hitched, and then she turned and fled into the pod. Tenebris chuckled, the sound turning to a growling dragon chortle as he shifted into his dragon form mid-laugh.

Raina may know how to play the game, but Tenebris could play just as well as she could, and he had won this round.

It surprised Maldia when she spotted Celia and Hestia rushing up the hallway toward her. Maldia had Faith's baby carrier in one arm, her purse slung over the other shoulder, and a backpack-style diaper back on her back. She had been preparing to leave for Celia's shop to begin lessons with the mysterious Amelia.

Celia and Hestia stopped in front of Maldia, and Hestia placed a hand on Maldia's shoulder. The worry in her eyes sent a shiver up Maldia's spine.

"What is wrong?" Maldia asked as her eyes darted back and forth between the two women. "Has something happened?"

"Have you seen Queen Damaphur?" Hestia asked, gripping her shoulder gently.

Maldia's eyes widened. "No, not since yesterday. Has something happened to the queen?"

"We hope not," Celia answered, and Maldia's eyes widened even more at the urgency in Celia's tone. "I had a vision and have come to report it, but we cannot find Damaphur anywhere."

"You had another vision?" Maldia asked, her eyes still wide.

Celia only nodded. Maldia knew more than anyone of Celia's concerns about her growing powers, and Celia knew Maldia would understand the urgency. Maldia did not comment on it further and instead turned to the matter at hand.

"Have you looked in her private chambers and her private meeting room? I know she had a couple of private meetings set for today, but I would need to check with Chandra for the times. I cannot remember what she told me." Maldia had tried to keep the worry from her tone, but she knew she had failed. She had heard the waver in her voice as she had spoken.

"We have looked everywhere, including her regular meeting spots," Hestia answered in a defeated tone. "I do not know where else to look."

"Does the palace have a dungeon?" Celia asked, drawing surprised glances from Hestia and Maldia.

"We have no need of dungeons here," Hestia answered indignantly.

Celia huffed and placed her hands on her hips, staring Hestia down with a condescending look. "If that is true, where do you put someone who gets out of hand or breaks the queen's laws?"

"We deal with the rule breakers by banishing them from the palace or sending them to the jails in the city," Hestia replied, her tone still annoyed. "We do not lock people up here in the palace."

Celia continued to stare at Hestia, regarding her with a disbelieving stare. "You cannot expect me to believe that there are no holding cells in this palace," Celia said matter-of-factly.

Celia switched her gaze to Maldia, who fidgeted nervously under Celia's scrutiny. Her gaze flicked guiltily between Celia and Hestia as she set the baby carrier on the floor and dropped her purse beside it.

Maldia swallowed hard and said, "We have a place where we keep lawbreakers in the rehabilitation process. We have a few holding rooms for interrogation as well. It is not a prison per se, but a place where minor offense lawbreakers can be held until their sentences are served."

Hestia scoffed. "The rehabilitation quarters can hardly be called a dungeon, Maldia. They have suitable sleeping and eating quarters, plenty of entertainment rooms, and are cared for well until released."

Celia shook her head slowly. "No, I do not think the room in my vision was a bedroom or sleeping area. It definitely had a dungeon feel to it. Then again, I cannot be too sure since I did not get a good look at the room."

Celia pulled her purse around, digging in it, searching for her dream journal. She pulled the journal out and opened it to the pages of her notes from last night's vision. She scanned them carefully, reviewing the notes several times before closing the journal and placing it back in her purse.

"I guess it could have been a bedroom if you have a bedroom here with stone walls. They chained me…er, the queen…to a bed with silver chains, but it was completely dark. There were no windows in the room that I can remember. I guess that is why I associated it with a dungeon, because of the windowless darkness, the stone walls, and the chains." Celia ran her fingers nervously through her coarse black braids as she spoke.

Even now, the memory of the vision haunted her, causing her heart to speed up with the remembered terror. Hestia and Maldia glanced at each other warily. Celia caught the look, and foreboding chills radiated up her spine.

"You have thought of something," Celia said, making it a statement rather than a question.

Hestia nodded slowly. "Yes, there is one room in the palace with no windows and only one door. There is a bed with silver chains as well. That room was used in the war to interrogate prisoners, but since the war has eased to a few random battles that do not even come close to the palace anymore, the room has gone unused for quite some time."

"You can lock the room from the outside, and it is very dark when the lights are off," Maldia added.

"I thought you did not restrain people," Celia said indignantly, crossing her arms over her chest.

Hestia fixed Celia with her iron gaze as she answered, "As Maldia has stated, we have not used that room in years."

Celia huffed. "Fine, if you say so, but we have no time for this. Someone is trying to, or has already assassinated, the queen," Celia said frantically. "That is what my vision was about."

Maldia's face drained of all color.

Hestia only nodded, her features softening as she said firmly, "We have to get to that room."

Hestia turned and began striding down the hallway.

Celia turned a questioning look towards Maldia, but Maldia waved Celia off as she said, "I am not going. I dare not take baby Faith into a dangerous situation. I will find a handmaid to watch Faith and catch up with you later."

"I understand," Celia said. "Do not let anyone know yet that the queen is missing. Stall as long as you can. We do not want to incite a panic. Call Tenebris and tell him to pick Raina up at my house. I do not want her alone at the shop for too long, and I do not know how long we will be here."

Celia turned and followed Hestia down the hall, her words trailing down the hallway as she jogged to catch up.

"Don't worry," Maldia called after her. "I will do as you asked and catch up with you soon."

Celia caught up with Hestia, and the two women hurried down the corridor. Hestia led Celia down two more corridors that led off from the main one, down two flights of stairs, and finally down another small side corridor. That corridor ended at a small staircase that led into darkness so complete that Celia could not see the bottom of the stairs or the room below.

"What's down there?" Celia asked nervously as Hestia took the first few steps down.

Hestia looked up at Celia and answered, "There is a large, empty room directly at the bottom of the stairs with a heavy, locked iron door. Behind that door is a long hallway that leads to another locked door. Behind that door is the holding chamber."

Celia swallowed hard. "Are there lights down there?"

Hestia chuckled and answered, "Of course there are. Do not tell me you are afraid of the dark, Seer."

Celia glared at Hestia and answered, "No, but there are things inside of the dark that I would rather not tangle with."

Hestia's smile faded, and she nodded her head in understanding. "You have a point, but there are lights. Come, let us hurry."

Raina stepped nervously from the pod in front of the palace with Ethan's carrier in one hand and his diaper bag slung over the opposite shoulder. She had spent the short ride gaining back control of her tedious emotions that Tenebris's bold come on and her own wicked thoughts had shredded. However, Raina's nervousness turned to excitement when the pod was carried through the large main gates that opened into the palace's front courtyard.

The courtyard was huge, too much for Raina to take in as she soared atop it in the pod. She saw various plants and bushes surrounding a monumental stone fountain that Raina had gaped at in awe. She did not have the chance to see much more of the front courtyard before stepping out before the vast double doors of the main entrance of Palace Solaris.

Raina had not yet visited the palace, so the glistening white spires and towers of Palace Solaris captivated her. Raina had lived at Palace Asgorath for some time before she had run away, but Asgorath had been so much darker and foreboding. The towers of Asgorath had been black stone, dark red brick, and smoky tinted windows. The dim lighting and lack of color in Asgorath's corridors, hallways, and rooms made Raina feel gloomy, so she opted to spend her days in the courtyard.

The courtyard had also been depressing with its black roses, thorny bushes, and uncomfortable stone benches, but at least the sun had shone brightly. She had enjoyed seeing the clouds float across the blue sky and relished the sun's brightness and heat upon her skin.

Solaris was delightfully different. Solaris was brighter with its white stone towers and crystal-clear windows. The entryway Tenebris led her through was brightly lit and cheery with its light blue wallpaper and sparkling white marble floors.

The grand double staircase sat proudly pristine with its delicately curved wooden banisters and carpeted steps. Tenebris led Raina between the staircases to glass double doors that opened into an inner courtyard. The beauty of her surroundings completely flabbergasted Raina, bursting through her senses like the purest of rainbows. She paused just outside the door to look around the beautiful courtyard.

Various small gardens were scattered throughout the courtyard, featuring cushioned benches to sit and enjoy the sights. Wonderful reds, vibrant blues, and pastel pinks and purples lent bounties of color, and the strategic placement of the plants provided variety without being overwhelming.

Bird feeders and fountains flowing with crystal clear water were strategically arranged for beauty and to feed the birds that frequented the courtyard.

Many paths led through each garden, twisting and winding, to the courtyard's center, where they all met and became one large, circular path. A large stone and wooden gazebo sat in the center of the circle, twined with vines and surrounded by roses in a stunning display. Raina gazed longingly at the gazebo, wishing she had time to sit inside it and gaze out admiringly at the courtyard in all its stunning glory.

"Hurry along, Raina. We are almost to the entrance gate that will get us into the queen's quarters," Tenebris called to Raina over his shoulder.

Tenebris walked along the main path toward the gate, not bothering to veer off onto the other smaller garden paths. He knew something would probably tempt Raina, such as a particularly pretty flower. He could understand the fascination with Palace Solaris, especially for one who had only ever seen the dull colors of Palace Asgorath. While Palace Asgorath held a cold, unnatural beauty, Palace Solaris was warm and alive with vibrant colors that Palace Asgorath lacked.

Tenebris paused and turned back to check on Raina's progress, and his breath caught in his throat when he gazed upon the wonderment on Raina's sweet face. It was true that the disguise was sexy, but Tenebris preferred Raina's stunning beauty over any disguise. However, seeing the look of delighted astonishment at the garden's beauty, Tenebris thought twice about the disguise now.

Her lavender-shadowed eyes were wide with amazement as she took in the surrounding sights, accentuating the sapphire color of her contact lenses. Her lavender-painted lips were slightly parted, and a small smile played on the corners of that luscious mouth. Ringlets of curls from the blond wig, which had fallen from the half-ponytail style, framed her face and accentuated the delicate angles of her high cheekbones and soft jawline. The disguise gave Raina an angelic look that caused Tenebris's heart to flutter rapidly in his chest.

He had the strongest desire to wrap his powerful hands around her delicate waist, draw her to the front of his body, and passionately kiss her full, sensual lips. He wanted to lift that mauve sundress up to the flowered waistline and run his hands over the bare skin of her thighs. He longed to run kisses along the tender plains of her neck and down to her chest, taking his time to taste her skin and breathe in her warmth. His fingers itched to tear the wig from her head, allowing her raven tresses to fall down her back as he ran his fingers through the soft locks.

His body shuddered with the thoughts, and things began to harden that he did not want the guards to see. He shook himself mentally, trying to clear the images from his mind as he tried to control the growing heat in his pants.

He turned away from her and squeezed his eyes shut, but the image of her gazing in admiration around the courtyard was now forever burned into his brain. Tenebris took a deep, shaking breath to calm his body into submission before continuing along the path. He did not look back again until he had made it to the entrance gate to the palace's private quarters.

The two guards on either side of the gate glanced at Tenebris questioningly as he stopped before them to wait for Raina. He gestured towards Raina, who was still turning her head this way and that to gaze upon the large, flowering bushes that lined the path to the gate.

"She is with me. I will wait here for her," Tenebris told the guards.

Both guards glanced up at Raina and then back to Tenebris. The taller guard said, "Are you expected, Tenebris? Chandra has ordered us to keep everyone out except for those living in this wing and a few guests."

Tenebris nodded. "I was ordered to fetch Amelia and the babe and bring them here to Maldia."

The guard looked at the other guard and said, "Go and confirm his statement."

The other guard nodded and entered the gate, sure to close it behind him. He opened the large, double wooden doors of the palace and disappeared inside, closing the wooden doors behind him as well.

By the time the guard had returned, Raina had caught up with Tenebris and waited with him in front of the gate. They were chatting with the first guard as they waited. The conversation ended abruptly when the other guard exited the doors and stepped outside the gate.

"Maldia has confirmed that Tenebris and Lady Amelia may enter, and the child, of course," he said as he took back his post at the other side of the gate.

"Good. You and the lady enjoy your visit, Tenebris," the other guard said as he opened the gate for them.

Tenebris motioned Raina through in front of him and followed her closely. He opened the large wooden door and motioned her inside, following her through and closing the doors behind him.

They entered a small, enclosed foyer with another set of double wooden doors on the other side of the small space. Tenebris paused, turning toward Raina with a smirk.

"It looks as if you are moving up in the world. Are you going to forget me when you become best friends with the High Priestess in training?" he asked humorously.

Raina snickered and answered, "I don't think you would ever let me forget you, no matter who I am friends with."

"You got that right, my lady," Tenebris answered with a smirk still on his face. His smirk faded, and his look became serious as he placed a hand on Raina's shoulder and asked, "Are you ready to meet her?"

Raina took a deep breath and nodded as she said, "I guess this means that part of your promise will be fulfilled."

Tenebris's tone was soft as he answered, "Technically, I did not make the arrangements for you to meet the mother of the angel dragon's chosen one. That was all Celia's idea."

Raina smiled, but Tenebris saw the nervous tension still in her eyes as she responded, "I just hope she likes me and that I can learn what I need from her."

Tenebris smiled and squeezed Raina's shoulder comfortingly. "You will do fine, Ra…er…Amelia. I believe in you."

Raina had no time to respond or react to Tenebris's compliment before Tenebris turned and opened the double doors. Maldia was waiting for them just inside as they stepped into a small hallway leading to the palace's main living quarters. She stepped forward with a welcoming smile, and Baby Faith firmly held in her arms.

"Welcome, Amelia, to Palace Solaris. I am Sister Maldia, and this is baby Faith." Maldia walked up to Raina with her free hand extended in greeting.

Something about Sister Maldia set Raina instantly at ease. Maldia radiated calm openness so strongly that it made it seem like this woman would forever welcome Raina. Raina's gaze swept over the Sister's beautiful features; a round face framed by chocolate-brown curls, high cheekbones, a small nose, and full lips.

But it was the eyes that caught Raina's attention. Sister Maldia had the most beautiful eyes that were large and round and the prettiest shade of jade green. It closely resembled the color of Tenebris's dragon.

Raina was pulled from her contemplations by Tenebris clearing his throat loudly. Raina startled slightly and quickly took Sister Maldia's offered hand with her own free hand.

She tried to keep the nervous tremble out of her voice as she replied, "Nice to meet you, Sister Maldia. I am Amelia."

The name felt strange coming from her lips. Raina had never been a good liar. She only hoped that Maldia did not notice her guilt as she motioned toward the carrier she held in her other hand.

"This is Ethan," she said as she introduced her son, and she stared curiously at the bundle in Maldia's arms.

Maldia smiled as she cooed at Ethan, and Raina returned Maldia's smile when she heard an answering coo come from the carrier. Then, Faith cooed back, causing both women to laugh aloud.

Maldia moved forward, giving Raina a closer look at Faith. Looking at the child in Maldia's arms, Raina was sure her plan would work. She had been nervous about exposing her son to the other chosen one. What would happen if the prophecy came true and her son drew the child into darkness? What would she do if her child corrupted an innocent and destroyed the world? The guilt would consume her.

However, her nervousness vanished as she looked upon the angelic face of baby Faith. She could feel a sense of goodness and peace when she gazed at the child, and the sweet smile and rapidly waving chubby arms melted Raina's heart. How could anyone ever look at that face and think of anything but kindness and happiness?

If her son grew up with this child, then Raina was sure that Faith would lead her son into the light, just as the second part of the prophecy said. Raina smiled at the baby, and all the worries and fears for her son melted away.

She had done the right thing.

She had taken her son out of the darkness and brought him into the light, and now this child would lead her son down the right path to a life of kindness and peace.

Raina knew that she was where she was meant to be.

CHAPTER 10: THE PRISONER

Hestia lit the torches in the wall sconces at the bottom of the stairs. The room lit up in the firelight, but the light only reached half of the room. Celia stepped into the light, gazing around curiously at the empty room.

The walls were white stone, reflecting the firelight from the torches and casting shadows onto the concrete floors. The walls and floor were pristinely clean, but there were no furnishings. As Celia traversed further into the room, her footsteps echoed loudly, bouncing off the empty walls. She watched Hestia intently as Hestia searched along the wall for the next set of sconces.

Hestia found them and lit the torches, casting even more light into the massive room. The room was fully lit now, and Celia could see now that the room was indeed empty. Hestia lit two more torches on the wall on either side of a heavy-looking metal door.

The door was barred, and two massive metal locks held the bar in place. A chain was linked through the door handle, attaching it to a metal loop on the door frame. A massive metal lock connected the chain, preventing the door from opening even with the bar removed.

Celia's eyes widened at the excessive number of locks on the door, and she wondered what could be on the other side that warranted this much security.

"If these doors are still locked, and this is the only way into the room you speak of, then it is probably safe to assume that the queen, or anyone else for that matter, is not here." Celia's voice reflected the concern that she felt as it echoed off the walls of the empty room.

Hestia's face fell in defeat as she turned from her task of searching the pouch that she kept on her side for the key to the locks. "You are right to assume that Celia. But what if the person that took the queen has an accomplice? They could just as easily have replaced the locks on the door and are now waiting for a certain time to come and let the other person out. No one would be the wiser until we found the queen dead in that room."

Celia swallowed a lump that had formed in her throat, her heart pounding with fear and frustration. "Yes, I did not think of that. In my vision, I only saw one person with the queen, so I just assumed that the person acted alone."

"I could see where you would assume that, but if my theory is correct, we have the advantage of surprise and have them trapped down here."

Celia's blood froze in her veins. "What if it is the other way around, and we are trapped down here with them?"

Hestia scoffed. "Celia, you know how powerful my magic is. I doubt anyone is going to get the drop on me."

Celia said no more and just waited for Hestia to unlock the door. Once the door was unlocked, Hestia opened it carefully. The door hinges had been kept well-oiled because the door opened silently with only a slight whoosh.

The hallway beyond the door was just as black as the room had been, but the slightest shine of light came from a bend farther down the hall. Hestia glanced back toward Celia, and the look was enough.

Hestia whispered to Celia, "They must have a hand-held light because none of the torches are lit."

"We need to be careful," Celia whispered back. "This person could be dangerous."

"You stay behind me. If things get rough, I will protect you." Hestia gave Celia's shoulder a comforting pat and then turned toward the hallway.

Hestia extinguished the flame from the candle she had been using for light and to light the torches. Celia turned and carefully closed the heavy wooden door, casting the hallway into darkness again. Except for the faint light at the bend of the hallway beyond, the hallway was completely and utterly dark.

Celia placed a hand on Hestia's back, and Hestia stayed against the wall to guide her steps as she walked down the hallway toward the light. Their steps were careful and silent as they approached the bend.

When they reached the sharp turn, Hestia paused, putting her back to the wall. Celia followed Hestia's movements, putting her back to the wall also and dropping her hands to her sides. She could see faintly now since the light was brighter here.

Hestia peeked carefully around the corner, squinting her eyes against the sudden brightness of the hallway beyond the turn. The wall sconces had been lit in this part of the corridor, and Hestia could see a figure standing in front of the door at the end of the hallway. The door was still closed, and the cloaked and hooded figure stood in front of the doorway with its back to Hestia.

Hestia turned to Celia with a finger on her lips, gesturing that they should be silent. She pointed toward the corner, moving back to give Celia room to move up beside her. Celia moved forward, peeking around the corner much as Hestia had, and then jerked back around the corner with wide eyes. She looked startled at Hestia, who gave Celia the same look back.

"The figure I saw in my vision was wearing a cloak like that," Celia whispered low into Hestia's ear.

"Then we need to get there before whoever that is opens the door to that room," Hestia whispered back.

Celia gave a nod, her eyes filling with anticipation and fear. She took a deep, cleansing breath as Hestia disappeared around the corner, and Celia followed.

"Halt and turn around," Hestia called commandingly to the figure.

Celia stayed behind Hestia, watching the figure carefully as it turned around. The figure's hood was pulled down over its face, hiding its features. The cloak was large and billowy, shrouding its body in cloth so that Celia could not tell whether it was male or female.

"I must complete my task," the figure called back, and the voice was familiar to Celia.

"What task?" Hestia asked.

The figure did not answer Hestia. Instead, it raised a cloaked arm, a small, pale hand showing from the billowing sleeve, and pointed at Celia.

"Why are you here, seer? Palace business should be no concern of yours unless it involves the future or prophecy." The voice had dropped an octave, and the tone ran shivers up Celia's spine.

Celia swallowed and replied in a wavering voice, "I would ask you the same question, stranger. What are you doing here?"

The figure lowered its arm, and Celia could hear the anger in its voice when it responded, "Nothing is going on here that concerns you, seer."

Hestia jumped into the conversation. "The seer is here because she had a vision of the future, so this involves her. According to her vision, we must see into that room behind you."

The figure hesitated momentarily, then took a couple of steps forward and to the side. It swept its arm toward the door and said, "My apologies. By all means, then. Take a look inside. I know you have a key, High Priestess."

Celia and Hestia looked at each other with suspicion on their faces. Hestia gave a slight nod and started down the hallway. Celia followed closely but paused when she heard footsteps clacking down the hallway behind them.

Hestia also stopped and turned slowly, keeping the hooded figure in her peripherals, and Celia could see the slight fear in her gaze. Celia stared at the bend in the corridor and waited as the footsteps drew nearer, knowing and trusting that Hestia would keep the cloaked figure in her sight.

Celia listened intently, straining to determine how many footsteps she was hearing. There were definitely more than two, but Celia could not tell the exact number. It sounded like a small group moving steadily down the hallway toward their location.

Hestia gave Celia a gesture toward the figure and pointed at Celia, then made a gesture toward the bend in the corridor and pointed at herself. Celia understood and switched her attention toward the figure that stood motionless in front of the doorway at the end of the hall, seemingly unafraid of the approaching footsteps.

The footsteps drew closer. Celia kept her eyes on the figure, but it still stood motionless, focused on the spot where the noises were coming from. Why did the person not react? Were they not aware of the danger?

Then again, maybe the figure did not perceive the danger because there was no danger. Perhaps the figure knew who was coming and therefore was not afraid.

That thought made Celia even more nervous as she kept her eyes glued on the figure, trusting that Hestia would warn her if there was a threat. Hestia stayed silent, however, even as Celia heard the footsteps round the bend. Hestia stiffened but still said nothing.

The figure lifted its hands toward the hood, and Celia drew in a breath as the figure lifted the hood from its head and threw it back. As the figure revealed its face, a gasp of surprise escaped Celia's lips. Celia backed up until she could feel Hestia's back touch hers.

"What the hell is going on?" She whispered to Hestia, keeping her gaze locked on the light brown hair and serene face of Chandra, her emerald eyes shining in the torchlight. "Why is Chandra here?"

Chandra smiled at the surprise on Celia's face as she lowered her hood and revealed herself. However, it confused her when relief did not show on Celia's visage. She knew that Celia and Hestia had felt threatened since they did not know who she was, but she was sure they would be at ease when she revealed herself.

Furthermore, the queen's trusted guards should have eased the tension even more with their arrival, but the tension in the hallway skyrocketed when the guards came around the bend and revealed themselves.

"That is what I want to know," Hestia responded loudly. "What is the meaning of all of this? Why are you all here?"

"Chandra has requested our help with the prisoner," One of the guards answered, glancing back and forth between the women in confusion. "We left her here, locking the doors behind us so that Chandra would not be disturbed, and now we return to fetch her."

There were four guards, each one a trusted guard for the queen. They stood in a square formation with puzzled looks at the vehemence in Hestia's tone.

Chandra moved down the hallway toward Celia and Hestia, her hands held up in a gesture that she meant no harm. "Maybe I should explain," she said carefully.

Celia flinched slightly as Chandra drew near, but she held her ground. She pressed her back against Hestia's back as she answered, "Yes, I believe that would be helpful."

Chandra stopped just a few feet away from where Celia and Hestia stood. Hestia focused on the four guards, but Celia stood facing Chandra. Chandra's hair had frizzed around her face from being under the hood for so long. Her emerald eyes locked on Celia's dark brown ones, and she smiled comfortingly as she spoke softly.

"We have disturbing news that we have kept quiet so as not to incite panic. However, I believe that you need to know. I do not know what your vision was about, Seer, but if it is about this situation, then I beg you to keep this information quiet." Chandra paused and stepped closer.

"That is close enough," Celia said, raising her arm in a stopping gesture. Her tone was firm and commanding, belying the fear she felt creeping up into her gut.

Chandra stopped her advance. "Alright. I will not come any closer, but I do not understand why you fear me."

"According to the Seer's vision, we should not trust anyone wearing a hooded robe right now," Hestia answered, her attention still trained on the guards.

Chandra's eyes widened in surprise. "Tell me what you have seen, Celia."

Hestia turned slightly, keeping the guards in her peripheral vision, and answered, "You first. Tell us why you are here."

Chandra nodded slightly and replied, "The news is disturbing. I am afraid that Queen Damaphur is missing and has been all day. The prisoner I have in that room is a suspect in her kidnapping. We know him throughout the Palace, so I was shocked when I caught him trying to break into the scroll room.

"He was wearing this robe, trying to disguise himself. I took the robe and most of his clothing from him before locking him away. It is a common intimidation tactic.

"I wore the robe to hide my identity from him so I could interrogate him properly. I had just finished questioning him when you came down the hall."

Celia felt Hestia relax slightly, but Celia did not. She was still unsure of Chandra's motives, and until she saw what…or rather who… was in that room, it would not convince her that Chandra was telling the truth.

"We already knew that the queen was missing," Hestia said. "That is why we are down here. Celia's vision was of the queen chained to a bed in a dungeon-like room. This is the only room in the palace I could think of fitting that description. She also saw a cloaked figure with a sword, so we were wary of you. Celia says that the figure in her vision wore a cloak like yours."

Chandra's eyes widened, and a look of concern flooded her green eyes. Her skin paled, which was a feat since her skin was already a pale shade, causing the light sprinkling of freckles to stand out across her nose and high cheekbones.

"What else happened in your vision?" Chandra asked Celia.

Celia swallowed hard and answered, "The queen was assassinated, stabbed with the ancient sword that hangs in the room with the scroll."

Hestia jerked around toward Celia, anger growing in her Turquoise eyes as she spat, "So that must be why the prisoner was trying to break into the scroll room. He wanted to steal that sword."

Celia's breathing grew heavy as she responded, "Yes, that must be why. I just hope you caught him in time. What if he had already done the deed and was returning the sword?"

Chandra shook her head. "No, I found no weapons on him when I found him."

"Unless he had already returned the sword, and he was escaping the scroll room instead of trying to break in when you found him," Celia argued.

"There is no way that anyone could have broken into that scroll room," Hestia said.

Chandra quirked an eyebrow and said, "Given who I have in that room, I would argue that point."

Hestia did not argue. Instead, she turned to the guards and said, "Two of you, go see if the sword is missing or was disturbed in any way. The other two will stay and guard us."

The guards bowed in unison, and the two guards in the back moved off to see after the sword. The other two straightened and stayed where they were.

"Now," Hestia said, turning toward Chandra. "Let us see to that prisoner of yours. I am curious to find out who you have down there."

Chandra's smile was malicious as she turned and finished unlocking the door. "You will be surprised when you find out who it is."

Raina and Tenebris followed Maldia down the hallway and to the nursery door. Tenebris had taken the heavy carrier from Raina halfway down the hall, and Ethan slept soundly inside it. Maldia still carried baby Faith as she led Tenebris and Raina into the room, and

Raina's breath caught in her throat when she looked around the lavish nursery.

The prophecy had not been deceiving when it had said that the child of light would be born in a city of wealth and comfort. It was evident by the overstated nursery that Solaris was definitely a wealthy city.

The floors were done with lush, white carpeting, and the walls were plastered with pink and white striped wallpaper. The room's crown molding, baseboards, and casings were white wood and intricately designed. The flowing curtains that billowed from the window were gauzy white lace. Delicate pink bows held the curtains open, letting the sunshine into the room from outside.

The crib sat against the wall on the far side of the room, beside the window. A white, billowy sheer cloth hung from the ceiling and down over the crib, creating a loose canopy over the small bed. The cloth was swept to the side and tied with a pink ribbon, exposing a peek of the crib between the opening of the material. Raina could see the tiny pink and white checkered blanket with the lace trim inside the crib and the stuffed white bear in one corner.

A fancy rocking chair sat beside the crib, decorated with puffy pink and white checkered cushions. The cushions were held onto the rocker with ribbons and trimmed with the same lace that trimmed the tiny crib blanket. It looked comforting and inviting, and Raina longed to sit in it and rock Ethan in her arms.

The opposite corner across from the crib held a small toy chest overflowing with stuffed toys, baby dolls, and other toys that Faith was still too young to play with. A play mat sat on the floor in front of the toy chest, and a bookshelf overflowing with children's books sat beside the toy chest. The chest and the bookshelf were both pink trimmed with white ribbon decals.

"The nursery is so beautiful," Raina said softly.

Maldia smiled as she placed Faith in the crib and responded, "Thank you. I decorated it myself."

Raina's eyebrows rose in surprise. "You did all this?" She asked, and the surprise came out in her voice.

Maldia turned to Raina with narrowed eyes. "Why do you sound so surprised?"

Raina swallowed hard, and her voice shook with nervousness as she answered, "I...I mean no offense, Sister. It's just that I thought you would have servants that did things like this for you."

Maldia's eyes softened, and she chuckled lightly. "We have servants in the palace, and I actually have a personal servant, but I prefer to do things independently."

Raina smiled, her nervousness vanishing under Maldia's friendly gaze. "Me too," she responded as she returned Maldia's smile.

Raina heard Tenebris's soft laugh behind her. "You two are the most independent ladies I know, besides Celia, of course," he said.

He had been thrilled when he had discovered Maldia's stubbornness to care for Faith on her own. It had undoubtedly lain to rest the former anger he had held toward Maldia when he had thought her lazy and dependent on handmaids to care for her and the babe.

Maldia had explained the situation to Tenebris, and his anger had faded. Tradition was important, and he would never hold it against someone to follow tradition.

Maldia bowed her head toward Tenebris as she answered, "Why, thank you for the compliment, Tenebris."

Raina glanced over her shoulder at him as she said, "Yes, thank you."

Tenebris bowed low, sweeping one hand to the side as he answered, "It is my pleasure, ladies. I am only stating facts."

This made both ladies giggle delightedly.

Maldia gestured toward a door to the side of the toy chest, and Raina's gaze turned toward it.

"There is a travel bed in that closet that you can use for Ethan if you like," Maldia said as she walked over to the door.

Maldia opened the door and produced a folded contraption. Maldia unfolded the contraption with one simple movement into what resembled a bassinet. She placed it beside Faith's crib and returned to the closet. She pulled out a couple of tiny blankets and took them to the tiny bassinet, spreading them into the small bed.

"There, that should do it," she said, smiling over at Raina.

Tenebris sat Ethan's carrier down on the floor, and Raina let the diaper bag slide to the floor as she stooped over to unbuckle the straps that held Ethan in.

"Thank you," Raina said, smiling at Maldia as she lifted Ethan out of the carrier.

Raina was placing Ethan into the bed when a sharp knock sounded on the nursery door. Maldia swung around with a questioning look on her face.

"I wonder who that could be," she whispered as she moved toward the door.

Tenebris's arm shot out, grabbing Maldia by her arm as he said, "Wait. Do not answer the door without knowing who is on the other side. Celia told me what was happening when she called me to pick up Amelia. Under the circumstances, I think caution would be wise."

Maldia had stopped in mid-motion when Tenebris grabbed her, and now she stared at the door with mild fear. She glanced up into Tenebris's eyes in gratitude and nodded slowly.

Tenebris released her, and she called out, "Who is there?"

"It is your guards, Sister Maldia. We have some sort of commotion at the front gates."

Maldia looked at Tenebris in concern, and Raina looked back and forth between them in confusion.

"What is going on?" Raina asked softly.

Maldia glanced back toward Raina and answered, "It is palace business. It does not concern you, so do not worry. We will keep you safe."

Raina pulled Ethan back up into her arms. "I mean no disrespect, but if the situation was severe enough to warrant Celia sending for me, then don't you think I deserve to know?"

Tenebris cleared his throat and said to Maldia, "She has a point, Sister. Maybe she should know what is going on."

A loud knocking on the door interrupted the conversation. It was more forceful and louder than before, causing everyone in the room to flinch in surprise.

"I will be right with you, guards!" Maldia called to the still-closed door.

"Sister, I must insist that you let us in. We have received word from the guards stationed at the main gate. There is a group of Asgorath guards outside the gates. They say they are demanding the return of their king. They say if we do not return their king to them within the hour, they will storm the gates and invade the palace to look for him."

Maldia cast startled eyes toward Tenebris. "The king is missing along with the queen?"

Tenebris's eyes held never wavered as he answered, "It would appear so."

"Wait," interrupted Raina. "Are you telling me that the queen is missing?"

Maldia turned to Raina and answered, "Yes, she has been missing most of the day. Now, the king has gone missing as well. This keeps getting stranger and stranger."

Raina hugged Ethan closer to her chest as fear bubbled up from the pit of her stomach. She closed her eyes and took a deep breath to keep the panic at bay as she held her son close.

What could be happening that would cause the king and queen to go missing simultaneously? Where was Celia, and was she safe? What if the guards stormed the palace, and one of them recognized her?

These questions swirled around Raina's mind as she watched Maldia and Tenebris turn questioning eyes toward each other.

"What should we do?" Maldia asked him.

"I think you should address the Asgorath guards. I will come with you. They know me, so maybe they will listen to you with me by your side." Tenebris put a comforting hand on Maldia's shoulder.

Maldia nodded. "Yes, I should speak with them. This is part of what I am training for, after all. When the queen is unavailable, the high priestess can step in for her. Thank you for being here with me."

Tenebris removed his hand from Maldia's shoulder and bowed his head as he said, "I am happy to serve Palace Solaris, Sister. If I had it my way, I would stay here for good. But, alas, I am the only one of my kind, so I must serve both sides."

"I am grateful for that at this moment," Maldia said, and Tenebris nodded in agreement.

"Excuse me, Sister," Raina said timidly.

Maldia turned to her and smiled warmly. "Please, call me Maldia."

Raina returned Maldia's smile and said, "Maldia, I just wanted to ask where I should go while you talk to the guards."

Maldia frowned in confusion as she answered, "Why, you will come with us, of course. Where else would you go?"

Raina's heart beat furiously in her chest, and she turned panicked eyes toward Tenebris. He was the only one who knew who she truly was, and she knew he would guess the source of her panic.

What if one of the guards recognized her? What if they demanded her return or her death? There was no way she could go with Maldia and face the guards, and there was no way that she could explain the reason to Maldia. What was she going to do?

Tenebris stepped beside her, his concerned gaze turning to Maldia as he said, "Perhaps, Sister, Amelia should wait here with the babies.

It could be dangerous if the guards ignore your reasoning and decide to attack.”

Maldia glanced back and forth between Tenebris and Raina and then nodded her head in confirmation. “Yes, Tenebris, you are right. It may not be safe for Amelia and the babies to come.”

Raina breathed a sigh of relief as Tenebris’s hand dropped from her shoulder. She smiled at Maldia and responded, “Of course, I will stay here with the babies. I will guard Faith as if she were my own.”

Maldia smiled softly and said, “You will not be staying here. I want you to be in the safest part of the palace in case of an attack.”

Maldia turned toward Tenebris and said, “Please pack up the portable bed and bring it along. I will call for some handmaids to help us carry everything.”

“Where are you going to take them?” Tenebris asked in a worried tone.

“To the safest room in the palace,” Maldia answered with a mischievous grin. “I am taking them to the scroll room. Not even the entire king’s guard could penetrate that room.”

Tenebris breathed in a sigh of relief and gave Raina a comforting smile. Tenebris knew Maldia was right. It would take divine intervention to enter that room without multiple keys, passing the warding spells, and avoiding the traps. The only ones who had the keys and knew the spells to get in were the queen, Hestia, and Maldia. He knew that Raina and the babies would be safe in that room until the danger was over.

And there would be danger.

This was the day that he had been dreading all along. He knew that his betrayal would be revealed by the end of the day. He only hoped that Raina and Celia would see reason and forgive him.

As far as Palace Solaris went, they would have no choice but to overlook his deceit if they wanted to continue receiving his services. His place in both palaces was secure, but his place in Celia's and Raina’s hearts was not.

Hopefully, the danger would be over soon, and his two women would see the necessity of his actions. Hopefully, they would see that he had the best of intentions. Hopefully, they would see that he did it for the good of Planet Mikka.

Tenebris seemed to be putting a lot on hope lately.

CHAPTER 11: THE THIRD SCROLL

The tension in the hallway rose as Celia and Hestia stood at Chandra's back while she unlocked the door to the holding room. Chandra had not bothered to put the hood of the cloak back on. She knew that when the prisoner saw Celia and Hestia, he would probably guess who she was.

The locks were finally released, and Chandra pushed the heavy wooden door open with a loud creaking sound. The light from the hallway flooded into the room, illuminating a slight step-down that led into the room.

Celia first noticed the bare stone floors at the bottom of the step and the acrid smell that floated from the room. It smelled moldy and damp, like an old basement, and her nose wrinkled in disgust. The stone floor was shiny where the light hit as if it were wet, and Celia watched Chandra take a cautious step down into the room.

Chandra took a few more steps into the room, moving away from the hallway's light where it touched the darkness. Celia lost her for a second before the room was flooded with light, and Chandra blew out the match with which she had lit the torch.

Celia's gaze drifted around the room as her eyes adjusted to the sudden brightness, and she spotted the bed in the middle of the room. Except for a simple wooden chair at the foot of the bed where Chandra stood, there was nothing else in the small space.

The plain stone walls looked damp and cold, and there was not a single window in the room. It definitely looked like a dungeon, and it strongly resembled the room from Celia's vision.

However, the figure on the bed was not the queen, and Celia frowned at the thin-framed yet muscular man chained to the bed in confused shock. He was wearing nothing but a cloth tied around his waist to hide his nakedness, and Celia could see the cut of his muscles as they strained against the chains.

"What do you want now? I am not going to talk no matter what you do to me," Sage snarled.

Icy fingers crept up Celia's spine as she heard the harsh tone. Celia recognized that voice. It had been the voice in her vision. Celia was familiar with Sage as the queen's advisor, but Sage's voice was usually softer, smoother than the severe tone he spoke with now.

Celia's surprised gasp matched Hestia's as Hestia stepped into the room behind Celia and noticed Sage chained to the bed.

"He is the one. I recognize that voice, even though I couldn't see his face. In my vision, He killed the queen, and this is the room where I…er…the queen was held."

Hestia's gaze jerked to the platinum blond man chained to the bed, and her eyebrows raised as she asked in surprise, "Sage? Is this true? Were you planning to assassinate the queen?"

Sage struggled against the chains suddenly, rattling them loudly.

"Damn interfering seer! You're having visions now?" Sage shouted, causing all three women to jump in alarm at his loud tone.

Chandra collected herself quickly and turned to a spot on the wall next to the bed. She grabbed something black and snakelike hanging from the wall, lashing it out toward the man suddenly with a loud 'CRACK!' The movement was so sudden that Celia had no time to react.

"Hush and be still," Chandra demanded in a loud tone. She turned back toward Celia and asked, "Are you sure about that, Celia? Are you one hundred percent sure that this is the person you saw in your vision?"

Celia did not respond. She had brought her hand up to cover her mouth as it had dropped open in disbelief at the violence of Chandra's reaction to the man's shouts.

Celia only nodded, her eyes wide as she stared at Sage.

Chandra turned suddenly back to Sage. "You are the queen's most trusted advisor. How could you betray her this way?"

Celia flinched at Chandra's cold, calculating tone as she turned to Hestia, but Hestia's attention was on Chandra and the man. Hestia had not reacted to Chandra's treatment of the man.

Celia took a deep, calming breath, reining in her thoughts and emotions as she calmed her scrambled mind and put her thoughts in order. If the other two women could handle this situation calmly, then she could too.

"I had no choice," Sage answered, his tenuous tone belying the rage in his voice from earlier. "I messed up, so I must set the situation right."

"Oh, so now you want to talk?" Chandra asked as she wound the whip around her hand, stroking it like a beloved pet serpent.

"You will all know everything now. The seer will see to that, so I may as well tell you anyway," Sage said. He shot a vehement look toward Celia, but Chandra cracked the whip again, snapping his attention back to her.

"Fine, then talk and leave the seer alone. Perhaps I may let you live if you tell us what we need to know." Chandra spoke as if it were just another day, her tone void of emotion. However, the way she still stroked the whip in her hand was menacing.

Sage's smirk at Chandra's actions belied the wavering tone of his voice as he answered, "Alright, I'll tell you. I was supposed to have killed the babe soon after it was born, but I could not. I could not bring myself to kill a baby."

"And what about the queen?" Chandra asked, quirking her eyebrow in disbelief.

Sage stared at Chandra with his deep blue eyes. The muscles of his thin body strained against the chains as he responded, "I had to kill them both. The queen would not have been easy, but I could have done it. But I did not want to kill the baby. I suppose he will come now since I have failed."

"Who? Who will come?" Chandra asked.

Sage only smiled devilishly and said, "You will see. Perhaps I may convince him to spare you, Chandra."

Chandra exchanged confused looks with Celia and Hestia, but Sage continued, and they turned their attention back to him.

"He will be angry with me, though, so he may not spare anyone. He will have to finish it, which will make him angry. But we have no choice. We have to follow the instructions of the third scroll."

"There is no third scroll," Hestia said as she stepped closer to the bed, bringing her closer to Chandra. "If there were a third scroll, we would know about it."

"Of course, you do not know about it," Sage said with a derisive snort. "You will never get your hands on the scroll."

"Now I'm really confused," Chandra said. "We have no idea what you are talking about."

"Allow me to explain," said a smooth, male voice from the open door.

All three women spun around suddenly, casting confused glances at the man who stood in the doorway.

"You can relax, Sage," the man said dryly, flicking his hand casually toward Sage. "I'll take care of the ladies."

Sage immediately fell silent, and his body fell limp onto the dirty mattress. His lips were curled into a menacing, satisfied smile as his eyes closed in unconsciousness.

The three women stood frozen, staring in wide-eyed astonishment at the stranger leaning casually against the open-door frame. In their haste to question the prisoner and try to solve the mystery of their missing queen, the women had let their guards down.

They supposedly had two guards outside the room to guard their backs. The guards, however, were frozen in place where they stood. Chandra could see the sides of their bodies through the open door, but they stood as still as statues as if an invisible force held them there. They were not even breathing. Chandra took a hesitant step forward to check her guards, but Hestia quickly grabbed her arm.

Hestia eyed the large, dark-haired man that stood in the doorway suspiciously. He had a full beard the same color as his dark brown hair, a strong nose, and intense amber eyes that held Hestia's attention. He was wearing tight-fitting jeans, a long-sleeve t-shirt, and sneakers, all in black.

No weapons were visible on his person, but his imposing, muscled body and the way he stood towering over them gave the impression of a dangerous predator. The look he gave Hestia was undoubtedly predatory.

Her own Turquoise eyes widened with fear, even as she tried to hide behind a mask of calm façade. His sizeable upper chest and bulging biceps made Hestia nervous. If he meant them harm, there was no way any of them could fight him off physically unless they shifted. Hestia narrowed her eyes and assessed the situation.

This man was no shifter. Hestia could not detect dragon energy from him. Still, the small chamber did not have enough room for one dragon, let alone two, if Chandra shifted too. They would have to get past him into the hallway somehow to shift.

However, physical force was not Hestia's only weapon in her repertoire. She had enough magic to get past this man. Sure, he had put Sage out with a wave of his hand, but that was child's play. Hestia was sure she could beat him at magic, or at least that is what she initially thought.

Hestia released Chandra's arm and called upon her magic, feeling the prickling rush of heat fill her from her feet and rise to the top of her head. It spilled into her arms, hands, and fingers, filling her utterly and completely. She could feel the tendrils of the spell in the air that flowed from the man and spun around the two guards.

It was a spell of holding, freezing them in a space in time until they were released from their prison. She could feel the power of the spell radiating from the guards, indicating how powerful the man's magic was.

It was like a calm wind that breezed through the empty space between them, but it became like a hurricane when it hit Hestia's power. It was all Hestia could do to stay standing against the force of that power.

Hestia rose to her full height, straightening her shoulders and lifting her chin defiantly. She held her ground, refusing to succumb to the fear she felt climbing into her, mingling and swirling with the magic curling throughout her body.

She steadied herself, forcing her power to stand firm in the face of the stranger's magic. She was a mighty dragon high priestess who could shift and tear through this man if she had to, despite the lack of room. If she could not hold her own against a powerful stranger, she may as well retire here and now.

"Who are you?" She asked in a commanding tone, glad her voice did not waver.

The stranger smiled sardonically and answered, "I am Warren, the Grandmaster of the Wizard Spire. I wish I could say I am here on good terms, but that would be a lie. However, if you return my man to me, I may change my mind and leave you in peace."

Hestia swallowed hard. The Wizard Spire was a school of sorts. It housed and taught all manner of magical creatures. They were taught magic, hand-to-hand combat, weapons training, and more. However, the Spire had a reputation for producing spies and thieves, and many in Mikka believed you were cursed if they taught you.

Despite the rumors, most students that came from the Spire were very powerful, so the school did not lack students. On the contrary, Mikkans from all walks of life were lined up to apply for the school. The only thing about the Spire that was more well-known than the classes and its influential teachers was the Wizard Spire's leader, the Grandmaster.

The Grandmaster of the Wizard Spire had always been a sort of mystery. Almost everyone knew of him, but no one Hestia knew could say they knew him personally. Many did not even know what he truly looked like since he almost always wore a hooded robe in public, and it was rumored that he could change his appearance at will. He was respected, revered, and, more than anything else, feared.

Her voice was carefully controlled as she pierced the grandmaster with her most confident stare and asked, "What could Palace Solaris have possibly done to offend the Wizard Spire?"

Warren chuckled and said, "You have done nothing personally, High Priestess. It is simply a mission that we must complete to save Mikka. We must accept and complete the mission of our ancient scroll."

"So, you intend to murder Queen Damaphur and the chosen one?" Hestia asked, her tone a mix of surprise and anger.

Warren nodded, but his visage fell with remorse that belied his calm words. "Along with the king and the other chosen one, unless I can come up with another solution."

Celia stepped forward, moving within touching distance of Hestia, and replied, "So you have taken the queen."

Warren's steady look revealed nothing as he answered, "Not personally. I did arrange for it to be done. However," he paused and gestured behind the women at Sage. "You have the person who was supposed to handle the queen chained up there. Therefore, your queen should still be safe."

"Then where is Queen Damaphur if not with you?" Celia asked suspiciously.

Celia thought she saw a confused look pass across Warren's amber gaze, but he hid it quickly. His amber eyes filled with a darkness that sent shivers of dread down Celia's spine. The only indication that his look had changed was a slight flinching in the corners of his eyes.

"Are you saying that the queen is missing?" Warren asked calmly.

"Yes. She has been all day," Chandra said, her eyes narrowing in suspicion. "You do not have her, then?"

"No. You have captured my assassin. I simply came to release him and set his mistake right."

Warren's gaze remained steady, but Celia could hear a slight wavering in his tone that matched the almost imperceptive flinching of his amber eyes.

The three women glanced at each other in confusion, and Celia was the most confused. She had not seen this in her vision nor read it in her cards or crystal ball, and she knew nothing of a third scroll. Her great-grandmother was one of The Great Oracles, for Goddess's sake, so Celia should know if there was a third scroll. Especially since she had the tome that had all the prophetic scrolls recorded.

Celia knew that one insignificant gesture could change what she predicted. She usually saw all the futures in the strands inside her mind. These differed from the new visions she was having.

These were like multiple flashing pictures in her mind that would weave their way around her subconscious, allowing her glimpses of all the strands. She could pick one out specifically when she concentrated.

Her confused frown deepened when she realized no flashes or strands were floating in her brain right now. Celia's mind had not been utterly blank since before her powers had come into being. Where had the future strands gone? Why had her powers failed her now when she needed them the most?

"What have you done?" Celia whispered, her chocolate gaze piercing Warren's amber one.

Warren turned his attention to Celia, and she instantly regretted having his full attention on her. His eyes pierced Celia down to her very soul, and his gaze filled with heat as he raked his eyes up and down Celia's body.

"And who might you be, my dark beauty?" Warren asked, his tone filled with the inferno that blazed in his liquid gold eyes.

Celia swallowed hard, but her voice was louder and her tone steadier as she responded, "I am Celia, the palace seer, and I ask again, what have you done?"

Warren smirked. "I have done nothing yet, Celia."

Her name rolled off his tongue, causing Celia's nerves to quiver, and butterflies played in her stomach.

She shook off the sensation and asked, "Why can I not see you?"

Warren's smirk never left as he answered, "No one can see me unless I want them to."

Celia touched Hestia's arm, leaning close to her and whispering into her ear. "I cannot see the strands any longer. He has taken away my sight somehow."

"What have you done to our seer?" Hestia asked loudly, pulling Warren's attention back to her.

His smirk disappeared, and he narrowed his eyes at the High Priestess as he answered, "Nothing that will affect her permanently. And, who are you then?"

Hestia's stance seemed to grow even taller as she announced proudly, "I am the High Priestess of Palace Solaris."

"Well, well. The seer and the High Priestess. I am doubly honored," Warren said, but his tone was sarcastic. He turned his gaze to Chandra, who had been standing silently to the side throughout the entire conversation. "And you are?"

Chandra stepped up to Hestia's other side opposite Celia as she answered, "I am Chandra, Captain of the Guard."

Warren laughed aloud. "Well, I have found quite a trio. Whatever will the palace do if I take away the three of you?"

Celia's mind churned, scrambling for a solution. She had to think of something. She had to get out from under the influence of the grandmaster and check on her powers.

She checked again for the strands buried inside her mind, but they were gone. The back of her mind was a blank slate, as if time had never existed.

Fear curled through her as she concentrated on the buzzing energy that had always flowed through her system since her powers had awakened. It was a constant reminder that she had magic in her bones. She felt a spark of it light inside her gut, but the buzzing was gone. The magic was still there, but it was subdued somehow.

Chandra's voice cut into Celia's thoughts as Chandra spat, "What are you going to do, Grandmaster? We have done you no harm, nor do we know anything about a third scroll."

Warren's visage twisted in contemplation. "I am still thinking about it," he answered.

Celia's mind still raced, but one thought suddenly flew to the front of her mind. She stood up straighter, raising her chin defiantly as she spat out, "You said you would find another way."

Warren frowned. "What?"

Celia took a small step forward. "You said you wanted to find another way to avoid killing. Let us help you do that."

Warren's brows shot up in surprise, and his tone was disbelieving as he barked, "You help me?"

"Yes," Celia answered, her tone steady. "You tell us about this third scroll, and we will see if we can think of something that perhaps you have not."

Warren relaxed his stance and crossed his arms over his chest. His smooth, baritone voice was calming as he answered, "Fine. I will let you help me. Besides, I am curious to know what has happened to the queen since my assassin failed."

Hestia breathed a sigh of relief as the intense pressure of Warren's power eased, falling away from her like water receding from the shoreline. She relaxed her stance as well, reaching her hands out to either side of her to touch the other two women's hands.

The touch comforted her, and her nerves calmed even more when both women returned her touch, grasping each of Hestia's hands in one of their own.

Warren continued speaking. "I believe, ladies, that we must devise a plan to find the queen first."

"And I think we should start with you explaining what the hell this is about a third scroll." Hestia's voice was calm, which contradicted the churning in her gut.

The grandmaster leaned against the doorway as if he had no care in the world, crossing one foot over the other. "The third scroll is not technically a prophecy like the angel and demon scrolls. It is more of a warning vision from a powerful seer, warning of things that will come to pass if the prophecy comes true."

"It was one of the Great Oracles that had the vision, wasn't it?" Celia asked, her eyes full of curiosity.

Grandmaster Warren nodded with a curious look toward Celia. "Yes, it was. How could you possibly know that?"

Celia did not answer immediately, and Chandra spoke before Celia had a chance.

"Nevermind that," Chandra said, placing her free hand on her hip. "Are you going to tell us about the warning?"

"I was getting to that," Warren said irritably.

Warren stood back on both feet, coming up from the doorway with his arms still crossed. He stepped down into the room and moved closer to the women, and they backed up in unison closer to the bed where Sage still lay unconscious. They never let go of each other's hands.

The grandmaster's movements were not menacing at all. Still, his presence was intimidating, especially to Hestia, who felt that rush of power once more. However, it was not as strong as it had been minutes ago. This time, it was more of a caress of warmth than a storm of energy. It was a comforting warmth, but Hestia felt more fearful than comfortable.

She released her hold on Chandra and lifted her hand in a stopping gesture as she said imperiously, "Do not come any closer, Grandmaster."

Warren stopped his advance, but he did not back away. He stood where he had stopped, mere feet from where the women stood, but did not come closer.

He released his arms and let them fall loosely at his sides as he said calmly, "I already said that I no longer wish you harm. You are in no danger anymore."

Hestia did not lower her arm as she replied, "Why don't you just back off and finish your story, and then we will decide whether we believe you."

Warren sighed and raised his hands in defeat. He backed away and stepped up into the doorway once more. "Is this better?"

"It will be when you finish your story, Grandmaster," Hestia replied.

Hestia lowered her arm and grasped Chandra's hand once more.

"Fine," Warren replied in a defeated tone. The smirk faded from his face, and his look became serious as he continued, "As I said, the third scroll is not part of the prophecy but a recording of a vision from one of the Great Oracles. It outlines a mission to be carried out to prevent the destruction of the entire planet when the prophecy begins."

Celia frowned. "But that makes no sense. According to the prophecy, the planet will only be destroyed if the demon dragon's chosen one wins, and we do not intend to let that happen."

"And according to our scroll, the planet will be destroyed no matter which side wins," Warren answered.

Celia's frown intensified as she stared pointedly into Warren's amber eyes. "Are you completely sure that is what the words are? Have you had an expert read and analyze the scroll?"

Celia could see the Grandmaster visibly swallow before answering. "I have not."

"Then how do you know it is authentic and not some fake?" Celia asked defiantly. She straightened her shoulders and raised her chin proudly, continuing, "My ancestors recorded the scrolls, just in case something happened to them. I have no record of any recorded vision or third scroll."

Warren shot Celia a look that made her flinch slightly. "You are a descendant of The Great Oracles?"

Celia only nodded.

"Then you should know that The Oracles entrusted that particular scroll to our people and did not record it in the tomes. We are the protectors of the third scroll."

Celia's proud look vanished, and she fidgeted under Warren's gaze. "I was adopted. My parents died when I was young, so they never got the chance to teach me about my heritage."

Warren's curious eyes sobered at Celia's words. "Well, that explains why you did not know."

"But why would they separate them?" Celia asked, her voice almost a whisper.

"You would have to know the words of the scroll to know the answer to that question," Warren answered matter-of-factly. "Plus, you must know about the Spire and my people."

Celia swallowed hard. "And just who are your people?"

"My people are the protectors of the planet. The Wizard Spire is more than just a school. We are a secret organization of spies, assassins, and law keepers that were put together by The Great Oracles to protect the planet by any means necessary.

"The Oracles gave us the scrolls and every instruction to ensure the survival of Mikka. We keep a low profile and only step in when necessary. We pay attention to important prophecies and signs that could destroy or shift the balance of our planet. Unless it poses a direct threat to the planet, we do not intervene in the trivial day-to-day lives of the inhabitants of this planet or their conflicts and wars."

Chandra's angry voice interrupted Warren's as she let go of Maldia and stepped forward. "Nonsense. If that is true, then where was your organization when the planet was split in two?"

Warren's voice was brasher and livid as he answered, "We were created *because* the planet was split in two. We have been trying to set things right and keep the planet from being further destroyed since."

Celia also released Hestia, crossed her arms over her chest, and quirked a disbelieving eyebrow as she said, "Then all those rumors about the Wizard's Spire producing spies and assassins are true?"

Warren chuckled humorously before continuing to speak. "We are truthfully a school. We take in people we think will be an asset to our organization. The school is not just a front to hide our organization but a training center to train our members.

"We keep the details of our organization hidden because we were sworn to secrecy by the very ones that created us. The people who know about our organization are either part of our organization or have been sworn to secrecy. However, rumors are bound to happen. As long as they remain just rumors, I am happy to let them play out."

"I do not believe that my ancestors would create an organization of assassins," Celia scoffed.

"Sometimes killing is necessary to protect the planet," Warren answered matter-of-factly. "Would you not kill to protect your people and your cities?"

"Yes," Celia responded calmly, although she felt nothing close to calm. "Unfortunately, that happens in war."

"And we are trying to end the war," Warren said somberly.

"Your methods are barbaric," Chandra mumbled furiously.

Warren's eyes dimmed to a dark liquid gold as he replied, "We do not condone it, nor do I enjoy it. We only kill when completely and absolutely necessary. I am not evil, but I do what needs doing to protect the planet."

"There are some lines that should not be crossed, no matter the consequences," Celia said defiantly.

"Even at the cost of the entire planet?" Warren said, an eerie tone creeping into his words. "Why save one person's life when they will only die anyway, along with everyone else on the planet? Would not the sacrifice of one person, or in this case four, to save everyone else be the better solution?"

"I would find another way. There is always another way." Celia stepped forward, raising her chin defiantly as she spoke. "I would plead to the Devine to show me another way."

Warren's piercing gaze never left Celia as he responded, "I would expect no less from a seer descended from The Great Oracles. We had thought all the descendants dead. I am honored to know another."

"Enough of this," Hestia's irritated voice interjected. "We can stand and debate this all day, but there is no time. We need to find the queen if we can. We will discuss the rest after we find her."

The Grandmaster's gaze moved to Hestia, and his thick brows rose in surprise. "So, you trust me now?"

Hestia shook her head slowly as she answered, "Absolutely not, but we must take this one problem at a time. It will do no good to become overwhelmed and lose focus."

Warren's surprised gaze became humorous, and he chuckled before replying, "Very pragmatic. I am impressed, to say the least."

Hestia shot him an irritated look. "I did not become High Priestess on magic alone."

He chuckled once again and replied, "Obviously not. You three would do well in my ranks."

"We would never join you," Celia seethed.

Warren only smirked and responded, "Shall we temporarily join forces then? You said you would help me, after all."

Hestia pulled her energies back into herself. It had been a long moment since she had felt any magic coming from Warren, so she supposed he had also pulled his own back.

She gave a great sigh, slumped her shoulders in defeat, and said, "Fine, but if you try anything, I promise I will defend this palace and my friends through any means necessary. You do not want to underestimate me, Grandmaster."

He bowed respectfully as he responded, "Certainly not. I would not dream of it."

"You can start by releasing my guards," Chandra said as Warren rose from his low bow.

"Oh, yes. Sorry." Grandmaster Warren gave a sheepish shrug. "I had forgotten about them for a moment."

He turned and waved his hand toward the guards, and they both tumbled to the ground as if they were puppets that suddenly had their strings cut.

The sound of their armored bodies and hidden weapons (mostly knives and small swords) hitting the stone ground caused Celia to jump nervously.

Hestia gave a comforting squeeze of Celia's shoulder as Chandra stepped forward to the fallen guards. The guards recovered, dragging themselves into sitting positions and glancing around in confusion. Chandra's voice was loud and commanding as she shouted out to them.

"The next time you allow yourselves to be taken by a simple freezing spell, I will request a change of guards and you will be out of a job. My guards are supposed to handle magical attacks just as efficiently as physical ones."

At the sound of their Captain's tone, the guards gathered themselves quicker, coming to their knees to kneel respectfully as the closer of the two spoke deferentially.

"Captain, we have failed you. We did not even sense the spell before it took us. We deserve any punishment you see fit to give out."

Hestia glanced at Warren with narrowed eyes. Warren stood to one side of the doorway with a proud smirk, hidden from the guards. Hestia would have loved to wipe that smile from his evil, bearded face, but it would have to wait until they found the queen. Besides, she had felt his power and could not blame the guards for falling victim to it.

Chandra must have felt the same because she replied commandingly, "I will spare you punishment this time, but you all must train harder in the magic arena."

Both guards answered simultaneously, "As you wish, Captain."

"Come," Hestia said as she stepped forward, her voice softer and less commanding. "Let us go find our queen."

The guards rose in unison, coming to attention as if pulled by some unseen force. The guard in the back turned to take the lead, standing at attention far enough away from the door to allow sufficient room for them to file into the hallway. The other guard stood at attention on one side of the door, waiting for them to file out of the room so he could take up the rear.

Hestia moved first, nodding at Celia to follow her from the room. She tensed as she passed the Grandmaster, still hidden from the guards by the doorframe. She stopped by the guard waiting on the side of the door, leaving Celia standing close to Warren.

Celia gasped lightly as she felt Warren's hand brush her arm, and she jerked her head around to glare at him warningly. "Do not touch me," she hissed vehemently.

He held his hands up in a defensive stance, smirking as he replied, "Sorry, I did not mean to."

"The look on your face says otherwise," Celia shot back.

"Enough," Chandra said, glaring down into the room. "You two can squabble after we have found the queen."

"I apologize, Chandra," Celia mumbled as she ducked her head in embarrassment.

She had no other excuse for her behavior toward the Grandmaster other than he made her nervous. She could say she feared him, but that was not it. He had threatened to kill them, but her brain refused to believe he would actually do it. For some unknown reason, her mind did not equate this man to someone who would kill anyone in cold blood without reason.

Hestia's voice cut through Celia's thoughts as Hestia addressed the guards. "There is a man with us. He has safe passage if he stays with us and does not attempt to cause harm to anyone."

"Yes, Sister," replied the guards, and Hestia stepped through the doorway and into the hallway.

Celia followed Hestia, and Warren stepped out from the doorway, revealing himself to the guards. The guards remained unfazed as he emerged into the hallway. Still, Hestia could feel their tension as they escorted the party toward the empty, ominous room beyond.

"What of my spy?" Warren asked, passing Celia and Hestia as he came up beside Chandra.

"I will send another guard to give him food and water, but he will stay where he is for now," Chandra answered. He has been in our service for quite some time, trusted explicitly by our queen, and now we find that he has been a spy for some secret agency all along. He will no longer be so easily trusted, and he will have much explaining to do before he can be set free."

"That seems fair," Warren answered. "I will speak with the queen when we find her. Perhaps he can be a mediator for our alliance."

"We shall see," Chandra answered dryly, but her heart beat ferociously inside her chest.

With Maldia and Faith waiting in the nursery, she couldn't help but wonder about so many things. However, there was one question that dominated her thoughts.

Where was Queen Damaphur, and if she had been kidnapped, who had taken her?

Chandra silently hoped that they could find the queen alive and well.

CHAPTER 12: SETTING THINGS RIGHT

Raina took a deep, shuddering breath as she heard the scroll room door's locks click into place.

Tenebris had left with Maldia, leaving Raina alone in the massive room with the two babies asleep in the portable bed. Maldia had explained that if they locked her inside, no one other than herself, the queen, or the high priestess could enter the room. She would be safe inside the room.

Maldia had assured Raina that she would not be gone long, but Maldia had a handmaid prepare a box of supplies. Raina rummaged through the box curiously, coming across extra blankets, a play seat decorated in pink ribbons and white lace, another play seat decorated with a blue gingham pattern with blue ribbons, and a play mat with hanging toys, big enough for both babies to lie on.

Maldia had explained to Raina that she had some things stashed away for a boy because she had bought boy and girl things when she had been pregnant. She had been sure that her child would be a girl because of Celia's visions, but she had wanted to be prepared.

She had promised to give the boy items to Raina after this was over, but Raina had protested. She could not accept such extravagant gifts, but Maldia had shushed Raina's protests with a firm voice.

"I would prefer to give them to someone that would appreciate them rather than just give them to some stranger that may not need them at all and would take the gifts for granted," Maldia had said.

Raina stopped arguing after that and just graciously accepted the generous offer.

She would love and appreciate the items just as Maldia wanted her to.

If they got out of this mess.

In addition to the baby items, the box also held some bottles of water, a couple of sodas, bags of chips, and some healthy snack items for Raina. Maldia had also brought Faith's diaper bag, a stylish backpack-style bag in shades of pink and light gray.

The bag contained stuff for Faith, such as bottles of breast milk, wet wipes, diapers, and a few extra changes of clothes. Maldia had prepared her well in case she had to stay here for a while, but Raina hoped this would not be the case.

Raina stood up from searching the large box and glanced around the room. Her eyes widened as she saw the ornate decorations placed strategically around the room, the expensively framed paintings on the wall, and the antique-looking furniture she was afraid to sit on.

Maldia had instructed her not to touch anything, but she had not thought that included the furniture. However, upon inspection, she decided that if she sat down, she would sit on the floor. The floor was carpeted in white shag, so she was sure it would be soft enough for comfort.

Nothing in the room, however, impressed her more than the setup on the far wall that held the fireplace.

Two giant paintings hung on the wall on either side of the ornate fireplace, one hung high, and one hung low. The low painting on the right featured the most beautiful angel that Raina's eyes had ever seen.

Her long, flowing hair was raven black like Raina's own, and her startling blue eyes looked to the sky with a reverent gaze. She wore a white gown that flowed behind along with her hair, as if she were standing in the wind. Her arms were raised toward the sky as if she were reaching for someone or something.

Two feathered white wings rose from the angel's back, spread out so Raina could almost count each feather in each wing. The color was so pure white that it made the dress look pale in comparison but gave a stunningly startled contrast to the woman's raven hair.

It was a beautiful painting, and Raina gazed at it appreciatively for a moment before turning to the other painting.

The second painting, the one hanging high on the left side of the fireplace, featured a demon. He was dark and ferocious in appearance, but his face held a look of adoration that belied the fierceness of his features. His hair was a startling platinum white, contrasting sharply against his outspread wings' raven black feathers. He gazed downward lovingly with jade-colored eyes, reaching toward the ground as he hovered in the air.

Raina stared from one to the other of the paintings, admiring them both in turn, and finally, she realized the connection. If she could stack the demon painting on top of the angel painting, it would seem as if the angel and the demon were reaching for each other lovingly! It was a startling revelation, which made the paintings that much more striking than Raina had first thought them to be.

Finally, her gaze drifted to the decorations on the wall between the two paintings. The enormous fireplace seemed to stand out, even though it sank into the wall between the two paintings.

Above the mantel hung an ancient-looking sword inside of a glass case. Above the glass case hung an elaborately decorated cylindrical case that Raina could only guess held the angel scroll.

On top of the mantel sat two simple pillar candles on metal bases. One was black and sat on the side of the angel painting, while the white one sat closest to the demon painting.

The hearth was plain and unadorned save for a fireplace cover decorated with a pattern of white and black feathered wings. One wing was white, and the other black.

Raina liked the simple decoration, thinking that a more extravagant one would have taken away from the striking beauty of the paintings. She appreciated the room's design and wondered if there was any significance or a story behind the two paintings.

'*I will ask Maldia when she returns,*' Raina said to herself and then turned suddenly when she heard a whimper from the portable crib. She glanced over the side and down into the bed, breathing a sigh of relief as she saw that the two babies were still fast asleep. Raina thought one of them must have whimpered in their sleep as she watched Faith's hand twitch.

She heard the tiny whimper again and realized it was Faith because her hand twitched once more with her whimpers. Raina wondered if she was getting ready to awaken as she heard her whimpers and watched her tiny hand ball into a fist.

She started to reach down and pick up the baby girl, but a movement from her son stopped her. Her breath caught in her throat as she watched her son's hand reach out and touch the soft downy hair on Faith's head, almost as if Ethan were soothing her.

Faith's whimpers quieted instantly, and her hand relaxed, her fingers uncurling and opening. She lay quiet once more, breathing

even and steady in her peaceful sleep, with Ethan's hand softly
touching her head. Raina's son took in one of those deep baby
breaths, the ones they sometimes do in their sleep, and let his hand
relax again by his side.

Raina stood frozen by the bed. Surely it had only been a
coincidence that Ethan had touched Faith's head and that Faith had
quieted with his touch. Yes, it was definitely a coincidence, Raina
assured herself as she sank cross-legged onto the carpet beside the bed.

Newborns couldn't be aware of each other like that, but then again,
Ethan and Faith were not normal newborn babies. They were the
chosen ones, and Raina was sure their upbringing would be just as
unique as they were.

If they got through this day.

Maldia stood on the balcony overlooking the courtyard of Palace
Solaris. Tenebris stood beside her, looking down at the four angry
Asgorathian guards that had come demanding the return of their king.
Maldia had said nothing yet, waiting for the guards to speak first,
giving them a chance to tell their story.

"We have not seen the king all day," said one guard.

"The angel dragons are the only ones that would want to hurt our
king," said another guard.

"We know that you have him," said yet another.

Maldia stood through it all, a serene look on her face as the guards
called out insults and accusations one after the other. Tenebris
wondered if she would react when finally, she raised her arms and held
up her hands in a gesture for silence.

"Please, save your insults and accusations, gentlemen. I swear to
you that we do not have your king." Her tone was calm, but her voice
rang loud enough to be heard over the cacophony of the guards'
combined shouts.

The voices quieted, but the looks of accusation remained on their
faces as Maldia spoke. "I gave you a chance to speak first, to tell me

your story and help you come up with a solution. However, you have done nothing but hurl accusations my way."

"Stop stalling and give us back our king." The head guard sneered.

Maldia closed her eyes and took in a deep, calming breath. She would not allow herself to be insulted and give these crude men the satisfaction of a reaction from her.

She forced her features to remain calm, her breathing even and steady, and her voice clear and unwavering as she responded, "I have told you we do not have your king. Now, you all can leave us in peace, or you will have to deal with me."

"Oh, there are many ways I would love to 'deal' with you, princess," the guard said slyly, licking his lips and grinning leeringly.

Maldia finally allowed herself to become angry, her jade-green eyes darkening with malice as she stared menacingly at the leering guard. Her small hands balled into fists, and she could feel her energy coiling angrily around inside of her. It begged to be released, and Maldia was tempted to shift and cut through this obnoxious quartet of guards.

She knew her voice would be dark to match her eyes, like thunder from an ominously approaching storm. But Tenebris's voice cut through the enraged silence before she could reply.

"How dare you insult the lady in this way! She is not a princess. She is a holy woman. High Priestess in training, to be exact."

All four guards fell silent as they stared astonishingly up at Tenebris, who had stood silently by Maldia's side the entire time and then suddenly yelled at them angrily.

"King Epialos would be horrified at your behavior! It is behavior such as this that has given Asgorath an evil reputation. The king preaches that to his subjects daily, yet here you are, his own personal guard, acting this way!" Tenebris's voice had risen louder and louder as he spoke, so he was practically shouting by the time he had finished.

The guards bowed their heads in shame under Tenebris's scolding, and one guard even gave Maldia an apologetic glance. Maldia paid no heed to the guard's gaze, however. Her attention was on Tenebris and his unexpected wrath.

She had whipped her head around to him when he had begun speaking loudly, lividly, and now she stared at him as if he had sprouted a second head. She had never heard the gentle-natured Tenebris speak this way, even when he was annoyed with her, so it was quite a shock to hear him address the guards like this.

She looked at his face and gasped at the angry heat in his blue eyes. His straight black hair had fallen slightly into his face above his eyes, hiding his eyebrows that furrowed over his furious stare. His usually full lips thinned out over his teeth as he stared down at the guards in silent fury.

Maldia inched closer to Tenebris, placing a hand over his where it had a death grip on the railing of the banisters. He held on so tightly that Maldia could see his knuckles mottled with white. She patted his hand tentatively, causing him to flinch slightly and slide his eyes sideways to glance at her out of the corners of his eyes.

She smiled softly at him as she patted his hand, letting him see the care and concern for him in her eyes. Her voice was gentle as she spoke. "Thank you, Tenebris, for defending my honor. I assure you, however, that whatever these men say will not bother me."

Tenebris let out a long, loud breath as if he had been holding it in. "I am sorry if I overstepped my bounds, Sister. I should not have lost my temper."

"It is fine, Tenebris," Maldia responded, the soft smile never leaving her face.

Maldia saw the tension release from his shoulders and around his sapphire eyes, leaving his face softer and more handsome. He returned Maldia's smile and turned to face the guards serenely.

The guards stood silently, staring at the ground, shuffling their feet, or glancing around the courtyard. They were clearly trying to avert their attention away from the balcony. Maldia wondered if they were just as surprised as she was over Tenebris's outburst.

Maldia spoke into that silence, capturing the guards' attention once more. "As I have said, we do not have your king. We will be sure to send word if we hear anything about his whereabouts."

The head guard stepped tenaciously forward, gazing at the balcony and staring into Maldia's eyes. "The entire king's guard is on their way here. They will storm this palace if we do not deliver the king to them."

Maldia tried not to show any emotion, but the spike of fear that shot through her chest overwhelmed her steady control. She could see the look of shame and regret that crossed the guard's face as he spoke.

Tenebris's anger returned in an instant as he, once again, gripped the banisters and leaned forward as he spoke. "You did not think to check first before you acted? What kind of foolish guards are you?"

"Why should we give Solaris the benefit of the doubt? They think that they are better than us and that we are nothing. They will not even let demon dragons into their precious palace."

Maldia gave a derisive snort as she moved even closer to Tenebris. "Tenebris is a demon dragon, and he has free access to all parts of the palace. He even has his own quarters here in the palace. Furthermore, if your reasoning is correct, and we think of the demon dragons as nothing, then why in Mikka would we want to kidnap your king?"

"To start a war, of course," one guard yelled.

Maldia gave a humph sound and said, "We are already at war."

The guard pierced Maldia with a malicious stare. His voice dropped to a low, malevolent pitch as he said, "We have your queen. Give us our king, or you will never see her again."

Maldia barely had time to register the guard's words before the door to the balcony whooshed open. Tenebris jumped around to see who was coming onto the balcony behind them. Maldia, however, never moved other than a slight flinch, keeping her gaze glued to the guard standing in the courtyard below.

The guard met her steely gaze with his own furious stare, but Maldia could see the slight flinching of his eyes as they darted behind her. The anger in his gaze turned to uncertainty and fright, and Maldia turned to see who had scared the guard.

Hestia led the charge, followed by Celia, Chandra, and a tall, imposing man Maldia did not know. With a quick stride, he passed Hestia and made his way to the balcony railing. He looked down at the quartet of guards, his features darkening with anger and malice.

His brown hair curled just below his ears and mingled with the sideburns of his full beard. His amber eyes had turned a deep shade of molten gold in his fury as he stared down at the guards. Maldia moved back from the balcony, glancing at the stranger curiously as the guards shuffled nervously in the courtyard below.

The man's voice was dark as he boomed down into the courtyard. "What is the meaning of all of this?"

The guards instantly kneeled and bowed their heads in unison, and the head guard's voice held a modicum of fear as he said, "Lord Warren. We did not expect to see you here."

Hestia strolled forth, her hands on her hips and a disapproving look. "Do you have spies everywhere? I will find it difficult ever to trust anyone now."

The stranger chuckled low in his chest, but the sound was anything but humorous. It caused Maldia's heart to flutter slightly with fear, and she backed slowly toward Chandra and Celia, standing near the balcony door, never taking her eyes from the frightening man.

"Who is that?" Maldia whispered to Chandra when she had reached her side. Tenebris had followed Maldia's movements and now stood over Maldia, Chandra, and Celia's shoulders.

Tenebris answered before Chandra could, staring reverently toward the man as he did. "That is Grandmaster Warren, the leader of the Wizard's Spire."

Maldia's eyebrows shot up in surprise as she gazed at the broad shoulders and muscular back of the stranger before her. He exuded fear with his mere presence, and Maldia wondered why the Grandmaster of the Wizard's Spire was here at the palace. The voice of the head guard below caught Maldia's attention.

"Grandmaster, let me explain. We are only carrying out your orders," the guard said hesitantly. "There was a slight snag in our plans, which is why we are here at Palace Solaris."

Warren frowned, his thick brows furrowing over his intense amber gaze, as he asked, "What kind of snag have you encountered that would bring you here to Palace Solaris?"

The guard rolled back his shoulders and puffed out his chest as he answered, "I am taking care of the problem as we speak, Lord."

Warren simply responded in a sharp tone, "Explain!"

"I was the guard that helped take the queen. I was still holding her and awaiting orders, but they captured Sage before he could complete the job. However, it worked out in our favor.

"I received word from the planted guards at Palace Asgorath that someone abducted the king before we could apprehend him, so we were using the queen to negotiate for the king's return."

"I have the king, you idiot," Warren snapped, causing the guard to flinch. "I captured him myself after Sage failed to assassinate the queen. I told you all that I would investigate possible avenues not involving killing. You were all supposed to wait for my orders. I am aborting the mission until further notice. I need you to return the queen as soon as possible."

"But, my lord," the guard started, but Warren interrupted before he could speak further.

"Do you dare question my authority?" He asked, his tone low and treacherous.

The guard's visage showed a tiny spark of defiance, but he immediately kneeled and bowed his head. "No, my lord. I will carry out your will immediately."

"Be sure that you do. I will expect Queen Damaphur back here in the palace safe and unharmed. If I see one member of the king's army so much as sniff in the direction of this palace without his consent, I will see you exiled from the organization."

Warren paused, and from Hestia's vantage point at his side, she could see his amber eyes darken to an angry shade of chocolate brown. Each chilling word was enunciated through gritted teeth, causing the hairs to stand up on the back of Hestia's neck as Warren added ominously, "Do I make myself clear?"

The guard looked up at Warren. The defiance was gone from his features, replaced by defeated submission, as he responded, "Yes, Lord Warren."

Warren nodded in approval as he said, "Good. Now, go head off the army and bring me the queen."

The head guard shuffled slightly and, seeing the guard's hesitation, Warren stated loudly, "Go now before it is too late!"

The guard did not hesitate any longer. He jumped up from his kneeling position and gestured to the other guards to follow. They all obeyed without question, following the head guard across the courtyard toward the front gates of the palace.

As Warren watched them leave, he wondered what the hell he had just gotten himself into. He had come here fully intending to retrieve his assassin and discover what had gone wrong. Not only had they acted out of turn without his orders, but they were set on carrying out the killing without trying to find another way.

He knew that time was growing short, but that did not take away from the fact that his men had acted without his permission. He would have done the deed himself if he had to, so why had they jumped the gun?

Then, he found the trio of women in the room where his spy had been imprisoned and had spilled all his secrets. He could only assume it was because of Celia. He knew she would find out anyway, even though he had blocked her magic the minute he had felt what she was.

He had no idea, however, that she was descended from the Great Oracles. Now that Warren knew, he could see the resemblance, and it reminded him of the beloved three ladies he had lost long ago. It made his heart happy and sad at the same time.

He recalled Celia's words, 'I would find another way,' and smiled. He was counting on it and had just bet the planet on it. Warren wasn't worried.

He had seen the fierce determination of the three women as they sought to find their queen and protect their people. If anyone could help him find another way to save the planet, it would be these ladies.

When the last guard had exited through the gates, Warren turned to the people gathered on the balcony and breathed a sigh of relief. He looked around at all the faces staring at him, some in surprise, some in anger, and finally at Celia, whose face expressed approval and admiration.

The admiration surprised Warren. He had always been revered as the leader of The Wizard's Spire, but only those closest to him looked at him with honest admiration. Most of the planet considered him a mysterious danger that dared not be crossed.

But Celia hardly knew him.

As a seer, did Celia know something about Warren that very few others knew? Could this woman have the insight into his mind that others had never even dreamed of knowing, even though he had blocked her powers?

Sage had reported that Celia was powerful, and that her powers rivaled most seers. Sage had never told him she was descended from the Oracles, but then the subject had never come up. Warren's focus had stayed on the queen and the prophecy, so the palace seers were unimportant in his world. That was about to change, however.

The Great Oracles of the past were powerful enough to get around Warren's blocks. They could see a person's entire past, present, and future. Did Celia have these abilities? Had Celia already read him despite the magical block? Could she see his past and know that most of his furious maliciousness was a façade?

From the intense gaze she was sending his way now, he thought maybe she could. He imagined that Celia may just be able to see into his very soul, and surprisingly, he wanted her to.

CHAPTER 13: REVEALED SECRETS

Raina was pacing the scroll room impatiently when Tenebris finally came to fetch her and the two babies. She was about to bang on the door and demand someone release her, fearful that something had happened and she would be stuck in this room forever.

She did not know how much time had passed before she heard the blissful sound of the locks being turned, and her elation at seeing Tenebris step through the door could not be contained.

She flung herself at him before she could think about the repercussions of her actions, jumping into his outstretched arms just before she caught the look of joyous surprise on his handsome features. She wrapped her arms around his neck and pressed her body into his in an enthusiastic hug. She heard his delighted chuckle just before she realized what she had done, and she just as quickly released her hold on his neck and tried to step away.

She felt his arms wrap around her waist and hold tight for a moment before his hold loosened, and he reluctantly let her go. She could feel the blush creep into her already rosy cheeks as she stepped back.

Her voice trembled as she said, "I am so sorry for my reaction. I was so afraid that no one was coming for me that I overreacted when you came into the room."

A heated look came over his features, causing his sky blue eyes to sparkle as he responded, "If I had known I was going to get this type of reaction from you, I would have done my best to come sooner."

Raina's blush deepened as she averted her eyes from his passionate gaze.

Her breath came out in a rush as she stuttered, "I…that is…well…"
She huffed in frustration as she tried to gather her thoughts.

Tenebris only chuckled humorously as he reached out and grasped
her hand gently in his. "I did not mean to embarrass you, my lady.
Your greeting surprised me, is all."

"I was simply excited to see someone come through the door,"
Raina mumbled as she stared down at her toes.

Tenebris gently placed a finger under her chin, lifting her face
slowly. Raina forced her gaze up as her head rose, and a soft gasp
escaped her lips as she caught the heated look in Tenebris's eyes.

"Is that the only reason?" Tenebris asked softly, all humor gone
from his tone.

Raina swallowed hard, forcing the lump in her throat down. She
tried to smile tantalizingly, return that heated look, and put that
sexiness into her tone that she had used on so many clients in her past.
She was better than this, dammit!

She had been waiting forever for Tenebris to ask her out, and she
was growing rather impatient at his procrastination. This should have
made her bolder with her advances. She knew how to play this game,
so why was it that this man had her stumbling like some naïve virgin
on her wedding night?

She managed a small smile, although it was not half as alluring as
she would have liked it to be, and added some sultriness to her tone as
she replied, "Would you like there to be other reasons?"

Tenebris did not flinch at her return in the slightest. Instead, his
gaze became even more heated, and his voice dropped to a low tone.
He released her chin and stepped closer to her, so close that their
bodies almost touched as she gazed up at him with wide eyes.

"I would gladly accept any reason you have for touching me, my
lady," Tenebris said softly.

Raina stood straighter, some of her courage seeping back, and she
stepped closer to Tenebris. Her body pressed into his, her breasts
pushing against the lower part of his chest as she pulled herself to her
full height. She placed her hand on his biceps for balance and tiptoed
so that her face was almost level with his.

Tenebris's eyes grew wide with surprise as Raina half closed her
eyes seductively and said sultrily, "I would be happy to touch you
anytime you would like. All you must do is ask."

Tenebris's heart sped up inside his chest. He did not know what
had come over Raina at this moment, nor did he care. He should not

waste this opportunity, especially since his secret was about to be revealed, and she probably would not want him after that.

He lowered his face closer to hers, so close that their noses almost touched. She let out a soft sigh, and her breath brushed against his lips tantalizingly. His heart threatened to beat out of his chest as he watched her eyes close in anticipation of his kiss.

He was about to close the distance and press his lips to her waiting ones when the unlocked and de-trapped scroll room door was thrown open loudly. Raina's hasty retreat from Tenebris left her stumbling. Still, she quickly regained her balance and cleared her throat to mask any sign of her unease.

The disappointment was almost overwhelming for Tenebris, but he gathered himself much as Raina had and swiveled toward the sound. Hestia came striding through the now open door.

He leaned down and whispered to Raina before Hestia could notice. "We will continue this discussion later."

Tenebris smiled as Raina's eyes glittered with anticipation, and then he turned his attention back to Hestia.

"We have no time to delay," Hestia's stern voice rang through the room. "The queen will be back at any moment, and we must prepare to receive the king for this strange meeting."

Tenebris heard Raina's gasp of surprise, and he turned to see Raina standing by the portable bassinet where the babes still slept peacefully. Her contact-colored blue eyes filled with silent horror at the mention of the king.

"The king is coming here?" Raina asked, her voice trembling slightly.

Tenebris moved closer to Raina. He bent low and whispered into her ear. "Raina, given what has happened while you have been locked here in the throne room, I think it will be safe to reveal your secret now."

Raina's gaze darted back and forth between Tenebris and Hestia as she hissed in a whispered voice, "It is Amelia. You promised to keep my secret, Tenebris. You promised that you wouldn't tell them. You promised that my son would be safe."

"Your son will most definitely be safe," Hestia replied.

She had come close enough to hear the end of the conversation. Her tone was soft and kind, and she held her hands out in a calming gesture. Raina made no move to respond or back away. Her eyes held a curious look as she watched Hestia advance.

Hestia continued. "I already know that Ethan is the dark chosen one. You came here under suspicious conditions, so I investigated and discovered that you were the one Palace Asgorath was searching for.

"I had an audience with the queen and told her about you, but she decided not to do anything because you were trying to do better for yourself and your son."

Raina's eyes showed slight surprise as she asked in a low tone, "You knew who I was all along?"

Hestia chuckled and nodded, her eyes showing kindness and a bit of humor. "Of course we did, *Amelia.*"

Raina looked abashedly toward the ground, but she smiled at Hestia's attempt at humor. "It's Raina."

Hestia nodded and said, "Yes, we know. Palace Solaris is not as conceited as Palace Asgorath would have you think. Queen Damaphur did not want you to feel uncomfortable or unwelcome, so we were going to let you keep your secret and not alert you to our knowledge of you. However, considering the current circumstances, I suggest you come out of hiding."

"What happens if the king demands my return?" Raina asked nervously, casting a fearful glance toward Tenebris.

Hestia smiled, but it was a malicious smile, and her tone matched that smile. "Then, the king will have a fight on his hands."

Raina's eyebrows rose as she asked, "What has happened while I have been locked away here?"

Hestia's smile turned humorous, and she chuckled once more before answering, "You will have to come and see."

Raina's curiosity grew inside her chest. What had happened while she had been pacing inside this room? Her curiosity grew even more as she watched Hestia draw further into the room, pulling a pouch from the folds of her priestess robes as she walked.

Raina watched in fascination as she walked over to the fireplace. Hestia pulled the fireplace cover out from the hearth, and Raina gaped in awe as she realized it was not a fireplace cover. Instead, it was an elaborate stepping stool. The wings were the base of the stool, and Raina could see the small steps hidden inside the fireplace when Hestia turned the stool around.

Hestia stepped onto the stool and reached up toward the cylinder hanging in its glass case on the wall above the mantel. Raina expected to see Hestia open the glass case and lift the cylinder down. Instead, Hestia opened the case and turned the cylinder clockwise so that the cylinder hung in the case horizontally instead of vertically. Raina gasped in surprise, her eyes widening in astonishment as the angel paintings slid toward Hestia.

Hestia stepped down from the stool, turned it back, and placed it into the fireplace where it had been before. She had plenty of time to step away as the two paintings continued sliding toward each other.

The wall above the angel painting began to slide up into the ceiling, just as the wall below the demon painting started sliding into the floor. The paintings continued to slide toward one another until the top of the angel painting and the bottom of the demon painting aligned, hiding the fireplace.

The two paintings became one, and just as Raina had suspected, the angel looked longingly up toward the demon as they reached for each other. There was a loud *'click'* as the paintings joined, and the walls disappeared, revealing two hidden doorways on each side of the painting.

The doors looked metal with no knobs, but a heavy-looking wheel was set in the center of each door with a small keyhole underneath it. Hestia walked over to the door on the right. She turned the key from her pouch into the keyhole and turned it slightly.

Raina heard the tumblers in the lock settle just before Hestia began turning the wheel in the middle of the door. Hestia's grip tightened around the wheel as the grating sound of metal on metal filled the room. She sighed in relief as the final tumbler fell into place, and then Hestia stopped turning the wheel and pushed on the door.

She leaned her entire body into it and the door slowly opened with a whooshing sound. A cloud of dust blew out through the opening door, drifting and swirling into the room. Raina saw only darkness, and Hestia stepped into that darkness and disappeared.

Raina heard a series of noises coming from the open door. There were clicks and whirs, bangs and clacks, and even a semi-loud boom that made Raina flinch and look at Tenebris in concern. Tenebris seemed unmoved by it all, standing quietly and patiently beside Raina with a serene look on his features.

He glanced over at Raina as she looked his way, and he smiled a comforting smile as he said softly, "Do not worry. Hestia is simply dismantling the traps in the room."

"Traps?" Raina asked, her voice lilting with bewilderment.

Tenebris only shrugged and responded, "You did not think they would make it easy for anyone to steal the scroll, did you?"

"No, I guess not," Raina answered as she turned her attention back toward the open door.

She slid her gaze to the other door and asked, "What is behind the other door?"

Tenebris shrugged nonchalantly as he answered, "That is another storage for different types of scrolls. The scrolls in that room are even more guarded than the prophecy scrolls.

"Everyone knows what is written in the angel scroll, but the scrolls in the other room contain secrets about the Queen and other things. One would definitely not want to pick the wrong door.

"The one Hestia is in now contains a few traps that may hurt someone and deter them from wanting to take anything, but the traps in that other room..."

Tenebris's voice trailed off, and Raina swallowed hard at the implication.

However, she could not help but ask, "What happens if someone chooses the wrong door?"

Tenebris shot Raina a chilling look and answered, "It would be the last mistake they ever made."

Raina started to ask more questions about this elaborately guarded room, but her attention was stolen away by a few more loud clanks and clunks coming from the open door.

The noises finally subsided, and Raina could hear the hollow echo of footsteps. They stopped momentarily then started back up again, coming closer and closer toward the still-open door.

Finally, Hestia emerged from the open door, holding a small ancient-looking box. She sat the box on one of the small antique tables beside the antique chair Raina had been afraid to sit in. Hestia turned and closed the door but did not turn the wheel or relock it.

Instead, she turned and focused on the box she had carried out of the room. She pulled her pouch from her robes again, placing the key to the door inside and pulling another out. This key was smaller than the first large, brass skeleton key that had opened the metal door. This was minor, silver, and looked like any other door key.

Hestia gently placed the key inside the keyhole on the side of the box. She gave it a slight turn to one side, waited a split second, and then gave a larger turn to the opposite side. The lid to the box popped open with a low-sounding click, and Hestia lifted the lid all the way open.

She placed her hand inside the box and gently pulled the old parchment from the velvet lining inside the scroll's resting place. The scroll was the most ancient-looking thing that Raina had ever seen. She squirmed nervously as she watched Hestia handle it with ever-so-gentle movements.

Suddenly, Tenebris was at Hestia's side, holding a small open cylinder that looked as if it were made especially for the scroll in Hestia's hands. Raina had not even noticed that Tenebris had moved away from her side, but he had produced the cylinder from somewhere inside the room. Raina had been so fixated on watching Hestia handle the scroll that she had not noticed anything else around her.

Raina curiously watched to see if the small cylinder would fit the scroll as seamlessly as she thought. Sure enough, Hestia gently placed the scroll in the opened cylinder, and the scroll fit perfectly inside.

"Do you have the cylinder key?" He asked Hestia.

"Of course I do. These keys do not leave my person ever," Hestia answered.

Tenebris closed the cylinder gently and then turned a small knob on the side of the closed case. The slight clicking sound let Raina know the cylindrical case was now locked. Hestia would probably die before she let anyone have the key. Hestia placed the key to the box back into her pouch, put the pouch away in her robes, and then turned to Tenebris and reached out her hands.

Tenebris gently placed the cylinder in Hestia's waiting hands and closed the box. He turned to Hestia with a worried expression. "Are you completely sure about this, priestess?"

Hestia shrugged, her expression serene as she responded, "What other choice do we have? King Epialos has already sent for his scroll. We must help Lord Warren find a way to save Mikka."

"Lord Warren?" Raina asked. "Who is Lord Warren?"

Tenebris turned to Raina and smiled comfortingly as he spotted the concerned look on her face. "I will explain later. Do not worry, Raina. I will protect you and Ethan no matter what happens."

Hestia stepped up and placed her free hand on Raina's shoulder, her other hand still clinging to the cylinder that held the ancient angel dragon scroll.

"So will I, child. I swear by Palace Solaris that I will let no harm come to you while I still live and breathe."

Raina frowned in disbelief. "You do not even know me. Why would you defend me with your life?"

"I would defend any of my people with my life," Hestia said. "It is one of many vows I took when I became high priestess."

Raina's frown deepened, and she quirked a disbelieving eyebrow at Hestia.

Hestia chuckled at Raina's suspicious expression. "I am serious."

Tenebris came up behind Raina and placed a hand on her shoulder. "She is serious, Raina. Hestia is very protective of her people. If Hestia says you are one of hers, you are protected."

Raina stared at Hestia's unflinching gaze, watching as her eyes softened. The nervousness inside Raina faded slightly, and her suspicions dissipated slowly.

"Then I guess we better get going," Raina said as she pulled the wig from her head with a smile, shaking out her flowing, black tresses.

Tenebris's heart nearly stopped beating.

Hestia gave an approving nod and returned Raina's smile. She straightened and fussed with her robes, pulling a bigger pouch from its folds and placing the cylinder inside. She walked to the open door that led out of the scroll room, then turned back to wait on Raina and Tenebris.

"Just bring the diaper bags and leave the rest. I'll have someone come to clean the rest up and put it away," Hestia said.

Raina pulled a small case from Ethan's diaper bag, pulled out her contact lenses, and placed them into the case full of solution. She dropped the case back into the bag with the wig and then slung the bag over her shoulder.

She walked over to the bassinet to gather the babies. Tenebris had already gathered his namesake into his arms and had Faith's diaper bag slung over his shoulder.

Raina picked up Faith and said, "Thank you for your help."

Tenebris stared into Raina's emerald eyes, his heart returning to life with a vengeance. The mauve makeup was still intact, and the color made her green eyes stand out even more than it had the blue. Her black hair was frazzled from the wig, but it was still thick and shining as it hung over her shoulders and down her back.

"There's my Raina. I like you better that way," Tenebris said.

Raina smiled in gratitude as she glanced down at the sleeping babe in Tenebris's arms. The sight endeared Tenebris to Raina, almost as strongly as him calling her 'my Raina'. When all of this was over, Raina was going to give Tenebris a proper kiss for his efforts.

Sighing, Tenebris followed Raina as she turned to follow Hestia. The smile he had given Raina faded when her back was to him. He thought this may be the last time Raina entrusted Ethan to him.

When his secret was revealed, it may be the last time they welcomed him into the palace at all, unless he was there on business.

He was not worried about being banned altogether.

They needed him. He was indispensable, and he knew this. However, his easy comradery and the trust he had earned with these people would probably cease to exist.

He wondered if there was any way he could talk himself out of this situation. Would anyone listen or understand his reasons, or would he lose everyone he held dear?

Tenebris gave a defeated sigh as he followed the ladies down the hallway, heading toward the nursery to drop off the babes. Suddenly, Chandra was there, ushering them back toward the scroll room with a sweeping gesture.

"You must go back. Damaphur was brought back just moments ago, safe and unharmed, but she sent me to tell you that the babies must stay in the scroll room, where it is safe. She is sending maids this way to watch them."

Hestia stopped suddenly and turned. "Fine, let's get this over with so we can get to the meeting."

Tenebris felt Hestia's words deep in his heart. He was ready…ready to meet his fate…ready to find out if he would lose everyone he held dear…ready to get this damn secret off his chest.

Tenebris was ready…

Ready to get it over with once and for all.

CHAPTER 14: THE MEETING

The tension in the room was unbearable.

Queen Damaphur sat at the head of the table, with King Epialos sitting at the other end. Lord Warren sat on the king's right while Hestia sat on the queen's right. Maldia sat to the left of the queen, with Celia beside her. Tenebris and Raina sat in the middle on the right side of the queen, and Chandra sat across from them with Sage in shackles at her side.

Queen Damaphur glared angrily across the table at the king as she sat straight and regal. Her silver hair was put up into a braided bun on the top of her head. Her icy lavender eyes shone angrily as her hands rested on the table before her. She sat quietly, almost too quiet, as tension sang through her arms and into her shoulder, even as she tried to be intimidating.

It did not intimidate King Epialos. He glared at the queen as he sat with his bulging arms propped on the table, leaning slightly forward in his seat. His dark gray skin glowed with an eerie sheen, dulling the dark growth of a goatee that sprouted on his chin. His black hair was slicked back, and his angry red eyes blazed with all the fury of a bright sun.

Warren cleared his throat, glancing between both as he spoke.

"I am sorry for all the trouble today, your majesties. The Wizard Spire has existed since the planet was split in two, and its sole purpose has always been to protect the planet from further destruction."

"Ha!" King Epialos exclaimed sarcastically. "You have done an excellent job so far.

War and death abound on the entire planet. Is that your idea of protection? How is kidnapping us going to stop this war?"

Warren shook his head as he pinched the bridge of his nose between his thumb and forefinger. He sighed in frustration. "The Spire's job is not to be the middle man for your insignificant squabbles. We only protect the planet. The leaders' job is to protect their people and fight their battles."

The queen's eyes narrowed even more as she turned her furious gaze on Warren and responded, "Yet you had planned on taking out both leaders, leaving their people defenseless. What could you have hoped to accomplish by kidnapping the king and me?"

"As I have already said a thousand times, the answer to that question is in the third scroll," Warren said in a bored tone.

The queen scoffed. "And yet you have kept it hidden from us and everyone else. We did not even know it existed."

Warren carefully kept his features emotionless as his deep voice reverberated through the room. "And if you read it, you would understand why I kept it secret."

"And yet again, I ask!" exclaimed Epialos. "If the warning was detrimental to the planet's survival, why did you keep it a secret?"

Warren seemed unaffected by the king's anger as he replied, "And again, I say because the scroll's contents are sensitive and could be deadly if it fell into the wrong hands."

"Then why are you telling us now, and why did you abort the mission?" Queen Damaphur asked, her anger slowly draining away to be replaced with impatience.

Warren shifted positions in his chair and cleared his throat nervously. This was the part he was not looking forward to. He was not worried for his safety, especially since he had an army in the courtyard that would storm the palace with one yell from him.

Of course, no one in this room knew that.

His people were the masters of stealth and hiding.

No, his nervousness stemmed from what he was about to reveal. The mere reading of the third scroll would be enough to put everyone on their guard, but the other secret he had to tell would set everyone on their heels. He was not looking forward to their reactions or the repercussions. But it could not be helped.

He had promised Tenebris.

The queen cleared her throat loudly, pulling Warren from his thoughts. "Are you going to answer my questions or not?"

"I have already answered these questions and more," Warren said with a bored sigh.

"Then why did you drag us all here and release Epialos and me? You say you want to read us the scroll, but then you fear the consequences. You had better start explaining things more clearly before I really become angry."

Damaphur slammed her fist on the table, causing everyone in the room to jump or flinch in their seats.

Except for Epialos.

The king chuckled under his breath, catching Warren's attention. He glanced at the king out of the corner of his eye, watching inconspicuously as Epialos tried to hide his snicker behind his hand.

Damaphur's rant continued. "And do not think for one second that I do not know about your little army outside in my courtyard. I could have them squashed in a second if I wanted to, so you can tell us your secrets or go back to your Spire and leave us alone."

The king sputtered out a cough that sounded suspiciously like a chuckle. Warren slid another incognito glance toward Epialos, and what happened next had Warren reeling with confusion. The king smiled proudly at the queen. It was so quick, sudden, and hidden that Warren was unsure if he had actually seen it.

Before anyone else could see or hear anything, the king resumed his angry scowl, and no one had noticed the exchange except for Warren.

What in Mikka could that mean? Warren had always believed that the king and queen hated each other, but what Warren thought he had just seen told a different story.

This could drastically turn the tide if he played his cards right.

"Well," the king said gruffly, and Warren could tell he was still holding back laughter. "Are you going to tell us or leave?"

Warren quirked his eyebrow at the king and queen. "Fine. You want to know what the scroll says despite my warnings that you will not like it?"

Warren watched Damaphur closely, looking for any sign of fear on her face, but there was none. Instead, a determined look drifted onto her features as her lavender eyes pierced Warren with an intimidating stare.

"I think it is best that we know what it says. I want to know why I was kidnapped and almost murdered in cold blood." Damaphur's tone was low and dangerous, and Warren flinched inwardly at her words.

He showed no outward signs of his distress, however. He could not afford to look weak. He took a deep breath and reached over the arm of his chair. He grasped the briefcase that had been sitting on the floor beside him and hefted it up onto the table. It hit the table with a resounding thud, causing several at the table to flinch. He turned the small dials on the case's opening mechanism, entering the code that only he knew.

He pushed the button beside the keypad, and the lock opened with a pop. He opened the lid and lifted a cylinder from the briefcase. He sat it on the table carefully, then pulled the briefcase off the table and dropped it to the floor.

When he lifted his gaze to the surrounding people, he realized they were all looking at him in stunned suspense. Their gazes darted between him and the cylinder on the table.

"What?" Warren asked with a shrug. "I sent someone to fetch it while I was waiting for all of you."

"Yes, and they brought back an army," Damaphur added sarcastically.

Warren stood, hiding his chuckle as he spoke. "There it is, the third scroll. But I want both of your scrolls read first."

The queen stood, glancing down at Hestia as she asked, "Priestess, did you bring the scroll as I asked?"

"Yes, my queen," Hestia answered, bowing her head reverently as she brought the scroll up from under the table where it had been sitting in her lap. She placed it on the table in front of her.

"I sent for mine as well," Epialos said as he lifted a cylinder from his lap and showed it to the room. He sat it back into his lap with a bored expression.

"Celia should read them," Warren said, and he watched Celia's surprised eyes shoot up to meet his gaze.

"Why me?" she asked.

Warren smirked, glancing her way as he said, "Because out of everyone in this room, you have the most right to even hold the scrolls. You are a descendant of the Great Oracles themselves, the ones who initially protected the scrolls. It was they who started the Wizard Spire to protect the scroll that I hold."

Celia's eyes darkened in anger at Warren's words. She glared up at him from her place at the table and slowly stood to face him. Her hands were balled into fists at her side, and her voice was deep with ferocity.

"I am tired of hearing you say that!" she seethed. "I refuse to believe that my ancestors would have anything to do with you or your organization!"

Warren laughed, and Celia balked at the menacing sound, her eyes widening in surprised confusion as she stared at the grandmaster wizard. Warren's laughter died, and his face became serious once more.

He pierced Celia with his amber gaze, saying, "You do not even know us, so please be lax to judge us until you have read all three scrolls. We hoped you would be different once you learned the truth. We need the Oracles' wisdom and grace again, especially now."

"No, I would never join you," Celia whispered furiously as she stared into his eyes.

Warren sighed and ran a hand through his dark brown hair. He stroked his beard as he stood from his seat and stalked around the chairs toward Celia.

Chandra watched him suspiciously as he strode around her and the prisoner she still held at her side, but he ignored them and continued toward Celia. Sage smirked as he passed.

Celia shrank back from him as he approached her, but he grabbed her arm forcefully and pulled her to him roughly. She struggled in his steely grasp, to no avail.

"Your majesty, may I have a word with your seer in the hallway?" he asked the queen as his amber-brown eyes bore into Celia's dark brown ones.

Damaphur rose from her seat, a look of concern furrowing her brows as she answered, "What business do you have with Celia?"

Maldia also stood, placing a hand on Celia's shoulder and shooting Warren a dangerous look as she added, "You do not have to be so rough with her."

Celia gave Maldia a grateful look over her shoulder as she struggled in Warren's hold.

He leaned into her, placing his mouth right next to her ear, and whispered softly, "I promise I am not going to hurt you, love."

Celia stopped struggling and stood frozen, fighting the emotions Warren's touch had awakened in her body. The coarse hairs of his beard had tickled the side of her face, sending slivers of delight through her body. His soft breath on her ear as he whispered had heightened the feeling, and a slight tremble ran through her.

"Give me five minutes, please," the grandmaster said, loosening his hold on Celia's arm.

Celia stopped struggling and sighed in resignation. "Fine," she said through gritted teeth.

The queen nodded, Maldia's hand dropped from Celia's shoulder, and Warren led Celia from the room. He pulled her gently as his grip became less firm around her arm. Celia did not fight or struggle but allowed him to lead her into the hallway.

Once they had entered the hallway, Warren breathed a sigh of relief. He turned Celia to face him, pinning her up against the wall with the strength of his body. His hard body sank into her plush one, and electric bolts of desire shot through him.

He placed his hands on the wall on either side of her head to steady his suddenly weak body. He had always loved women with extra cushion, and Celia certainly had that.

Her ample bosom crushed against his rock-hard chest, and her small pouch of a stomach was pushed flat against his, creating a pillowy softness for his washboard abs to rest against.

He stared down into her black eyes, trying, and probably failing, to keep a stern expression on his face. He swallowed hard, hoping Celia did not notice the want and yearning that flowed through him and caused a particular part of his body to harden.

His hands pushed against the wall, lifting himself and putting some distance between his body and hers, never breaking eye contact with this enigmatic woman that had his blood boiling with need.

"Well," she snapped when he only stood and stared at her, towering over her as he trapped her against the wall. "Are you going to waste your entire five minutes by just staring a hole through me, or was there something that you wanted to say?"

Warren chuckled and shook his head. He looked into her black-brown eyes and said, "I took you from the room because I was afraid you would say something to give away my secrets. You seemed so angry when I said the Oracles were associated with us. But to everyone else besides you, Hestia, and Chandra, the Wizard Spire is a respectable school. There would be no reason for you to be upset over that.

"You three ladies are the only ones I have told about the secret organization of spies and assassins. The others do not need to know. You must be more careful, my little seer, or else you may find yourself on the wrong end of my blade."

Warren's tone had grown low and dark as he stared dangerously into Celia's face. His eyes darted across her features as he waited for her to say something.

Celia stood frozen in his gaze, and her eyes widened in fear. His words brought back memories, memories that Celia would soon rather forget. The image of the cloaked figure stalking into Celia's shop floated into her mind, causing Celia to cringe inwardly.

"If you continue on this path, you will only encounter death," The words of the cloaked woman rang through Celia's mind.

Fear coursed through Celia, and her voice trembled slightly as she responded, "I...I...I was not thinking. I am sorry."

Her apology stunned Warren, and he pushed off the wall, turned, and began to pace up and down the hallway. He had expected anger, indignation, or even humor. He had expected to play with her a bit. Despite his half-serious threat, he had not expected her to be frightened.

She had not been afraid when he threatened her or her friends before. Instead, she had been calm, collected, and wise. Maybe it was her friends' effect on her, and she faced him now alone.

He stroked his beard as he paced, a nervous gesture that he had adapted long ago to throw people from what he was really feeling. He made it look devious as if he were thinking of how he could torture his victims and make them suffer.

He realized what he was doing and stopped. He did not want Celia any more afraid of him than she already was. Instead, he placed his hands behind his back as he paced.

At this moment, all he could feel was confusion. Usually, he could handle people and manipulate them to his will. It was how he was taught, all that he knew, and he was good at it. But this woman had his mind reeling with all the different feelings and emotions he was not used to.

Celia must have misread his mood because she hesitantly stepped away from the wall and said, "Please, do not be angry with me. Let's just go back in the room. I promise I will be more careful with my words."

Warren immediately stopped pacing. He turned mid-stride and came back toward Celia. He stopped before her and instinctively raised his hand to cup her cheek. She flinched away from his touch. Warren took a deep breath of air and let it out slowly as he let his hand fall back to his side.

His tone was soothing as he said, "Celia, I am not mad at you. I only want you to understand the importance of keeping our organization a secret. I want you, of all people, to understand that since I hope to have you on my side someday."

Celia scoffed and replied, "I will never join you, and I still do not believe that my ancestors had anything to do with your Spire. My ancestors cared about this planet. They would never have condoned spies and assassins."

'*There she is,*' Warren thought to himself. This is the woman that Warren was hoping to draw out. Angry, sassy, determined to do the right thing. That was the woman that Warren wanted.

"Maybe spies and assassins were what the world needed to keep it safe, Celia. Sometimes, you must do bad things for the greater good." Warren's tone was still soft, but twinges of anger colored his words.

"No. I refuse to believe that." Celia crossed her arms over her chest as much as her large breasts would allow.

The movement lifted her cleavage, drawing Warren's gaze down to her chest. He quickly lifted his gaze but knew she had caught him looking at her cleavage. No matter. He could not have her that way. His life was all about The Spire. He had sworn off relationships a long time ago.

He could have her for a night but refused to think of Celia on that level. A woman like Celia was far better than a one-night stand. A woman like her needed a man that could handle her forever.

Unfortunately, that was not Warren, no matter how much he wanted her.

He leaned away from her, sighing and crossing his arms over his chest, mirroring Celia. "Do you still have the Oracle Diaries?" he asked in a derisive tone.

She jerked back with an offended look. "Of course I do. I have them hidden, and no one will ever find them."

"Good," Warren said sternly. "Read them if you do not believe me, and start from the beginning. They do not do any Oracle any good just sitting on a shelf."

Celia jerked in surprise. How could Warren have known that about the diaries? It was true that they had sat on a shelf in a secret room of Celia's home and that she had not read or touched them but only kept them safe. That had been her grandmother's instructions when Damaphur gave them and the note to her.

No one had told her that she was forbidden to read them. But Celia did not want to harm them or ruin them in any way by handling them. However, now Celia was curious to know what those pages contained.

She huffed in frustration and said, "Fine. I will read them when I have the time."

Warren nodded and said, "Good. But, in the meantime, keep your mouth shut about the organization. I would hate to have to kill you."

With that, Warren turned and strode back to the meeting room, leaving Celia gaping at his back as he disappeared into the door, shutting it firmly behind him. She did not see the smirk he carried on his full lips as he walked away.

Warren was just returning to his place at the table when Celia softly opened the door and slunk back to her spot. She cast nervous glances toward Warren as she sat back in her seat.

No one commented or asked questions, and Warren continued speaking as if he had never left the room. "As I said, we should read the demon scroll first, and Celia should read them."

Celia did not question Warren again. She simply stood and looked at King Epialos expectantly.

He produced the cylinder from his lap and laid it gently on the table. He opened the cylinder and brought out a scroll, yellowed with age and tied with an old, tattered string. He handed the scroll to Warren, who took it to Celia and handed it to her.

He smiled softly at her as he held the scroll out, looking deeply into her eyes. He gave her a slight nod of encouragement as her hand moved to reach for the scroll.

Celia swallowed as she nervously reached for the scroll, gently closing her hand over the delicate, aged paper. She returned Warren's nod before he turned and strode back to his seat beside the king. Her hands shook slightly as she gently untied the string and unrolled a tiny bit of the scroll.

The paper was unexpectedly more durable than Celia thought it would be. It was shockingly soft and pliant instead of dry and brittle, and she gently rolled it out on the table before her. She was startled when Hestia suddenly appeared beside her, handing her two lit candles secured in heavy brass candle holders for light.

Celia nodded in thanks and placed one candle holder at the top of the scroll and the other at the bottom, effectively casting light over the entire piece of the scroll she would be reading from.

Hestia returned to her seat.

Celia's eyes roamed around the room, readying herself for the reading. She caught everyone's eyes in turn; the queen, Maldia, then Hestia, down the table to Tenebris and Raina, up the other side to the king and Warren, and finally to her other side where Chandra sat with Sage.

Everyone sat in their seats and those that had been standing sat back down, shifting in their seats in suspense as they waited for Celia to begin.

Celia took a deep breath as she leaned down over the scroll and prepared to read the ancient words aloud, hoping against hope that she did not screw this up.

CHAPTER 15: THE READING OF

THE SCROLLS

Celia's voice was low and soft as she read, creating an ambiance in the room as if they had returned to those long passed days before the war.
Celia began to read…

Conceived by a worldly beauty who has known many a man…
Against all odds of pregnancy, the fetus will not be banned…
Born in smoke and ash, wrapped in a blanket of fire…
The child of darkness is born in a place most dire…
When the sun's light fades from the skies of the south…
Blotted out by the smoke from the great crater's mouth…
This is when the child will come.

He will rise in vengeance to rid the world of light…

Celia straightened after reading the demon scroll and looked around the table. Everyone had a bored expression, and Celia suspected that this was only one of many times they had heard the scrolls read. However, Warren had said that they needed to hear all the scrolls together, in order, for context.

"There, you see," King Epialos's voice thundered through the room. He gestured toward Raina and continued, "All prophesied in our scroll has already come to be. Her child is the chosen one, and she stole him from us."

Raina squirmed in her seat and scooted closer to Tenebris. Tenebris wrapped a protective arm around her shoulder as he glared at the king.

"No one is denying that her child is the chosen one," the queen retorted. "She did not steal anything. She is the child's mother, so she had every right to take him wherever she pleased. We have given her sanctuary here because she felt unsafe in your lands."

Epialos snorted indignantly. "Nonsense. She is most important to us and our cause. Why would we harm a hair on her head? We gave her status and a place in the palace; still, she ran from us."

"And just what is your cause, Epialos?" the queen asked.

"You know what our cause is, dear Damaphur," Epialos sneered, piercing the queen with his red-eyed gaze. "I have told you repeatedly that our cause is the same as yours, to rule the world together in harmony."

The queen returned Epialos's icy gaze with one of her own. "We never wished to rule the world, Epialos. We only want peace. Your mind and your lands have become tainted with this lust for power."

"Peace, you say?" the king boomed. "There is no peace in war, woman, and your so-called light dragons continue to slaughter my dark ones out of arrogance because you all think you are better than us. I would call that tainted. Light does not always equate to goodness, and darkness does not always mean evil."

Hestia stood, shooting Epialos an indignant look. "Do not speak to our queen in such a manner!" she yelled at him. "It is your evil dark ones that attempt to soil our lands with their treachery and evil doings. We only want what is best for our people."

Warren stood and moved closer to the queen's side of the table. "This is not the time to argue. We are here for the reading of the scrolls. We can fight later. We need to continue the reading instead of drifting off course."

Hestia sat back down in her seat. The king huffed and crossed his arms over his chest, and the queen smiled at Warren and nodded.

"You are right, grandmaster," she said politely. "Please, let us continue. I believe the angel scroll is next."

"Indeed, it is," Warren said as he moved back to his side of the table and sat back in his seat.

Given Warren's insistent that they read the scrolls, Celia expected to find something she had missed, but it read the same as it always had.

It was sort of disappointing to her.

No visions or flashes came to her, and she still could not feel the strands in that part of her mind where they usually coalesced and fed her subconscious information regularly.

Before coming into this room to start the meeting, she had excused herself for some quiet reflection in the room reserved for her in the palace. She had looked into her crystal, pulled cards, and even tossed her runes, which she had not done in a long time, to find some hint into the future.

Nothing.

It was as if her ability to see was blocked somehow.

Celia racked her brain, trying to think of when she first noticed her ability had faded. Her powers had been growing stronger and different for some time, but they had dulled after the last vision of the queen's death. Did the queen's kidnapping and almost death have something to do with her diminished abilities?

No, that was not it. She distinctly remembered searching the strands when she stepped into the palace to report to the queen. They had been there then. Celia's mind scrambled, going over each step, leading to finding Sage chained to the bed.

That could have done it. The shock of finding out Sage had been the traitor and the trauma of watching him be tortured for information could have sent Celia into a blocked state.

Now that she thought about it, Celia did not remember feeling the strands, and soon after that, she discovered them missing. That had to be it. That was when she first noticed the block.

She shook her head in frustration, pushing the thought aside for now. She did not have time for this. She had two more scrolls to read.

She picked up the spindle from the demon scroll's lower edge and began to roll the parchment up gently. As she did so, the silence in the room was deafening. She paused before rolling it all the way up when she had almost reached the top of the scroll. Her dark eyes scanned the faces at the table, and a feeling of icy dread washed over her.

Everyone was frozen.

Everyone except her.

She had not noticed the change while carefully handling the scroll other than the strange silence. Something moved in the periphery of her vision, and she gasped in fright and turned toward the movement. It was Warren.

Only, it was not Warren.

Warren sat frozen in his seat just as everyone else was, and yet he stood behind his own chair, resting his hands on the seat back, behind frozen Warren's head.

Celia opened her mouth to scream, but no sound came out. She tried to turn and run, but she was paralyzed with terror. She watched as Warren slowly walked toward her, his eyes deadened and hard, and that was where Celia saw the difference.

The Warren she knew, still sitting frozen in his seat, had eyes that burned right through her soul. When he looked at her, she could feel his heat and passion. Her thoughts flitted briefly to the hallway just moments ago, when he had pinned her up against the wall and looked at her with such longing in his eyes. Celia thought that he may have been trying to hide it, but she had seen the brief flickers of lust and heat in his amber eyes, and strangely, she had liked it.

Even as he had threatened her life, the tiny flickers of fear had been taken over by her lustful thoughts of the man as his eyes had burned into hers. His eyes held an inferno of passion that burned inside his soul and called to Celia on a level that she had yet to understand.

This Warren, the Warren that was stalking ever closer to her, was dead inside. Something had happened to him to make him hard and cold, and Celia wondered what it could have been. The fear in her heart began to subside, slowly replaced with compassion and sorrow for this Warren, who seemed to have given up a piece of his soul.

Celia swallowed hard as he approached her, but she was not afraid. He was not really looking at her at all but through her. She was having another vision. She began to suspect when she suddenly felt the strands fill her mind again when she first saw vision Warren enter the room.

Then she noticed the subtle difference between her vision of Warren and the other people sitting frozen in the room. The vision of Warren wavered, like the misty dew evaporating from the grass in the early morning sun, and his body was slightly incorporeal. It was so subtle that Celia would not have noticed it had she not noticed the flickering.

"What happened to you?" she heard herself whisper sorrowfully, but the sound had not come from her mouth.

It had come from behind her. She whipped around to find herself coming into the room.

Celia gasped at the vision of herself and the slight wavering of her own future body. She was more curious than frightened as she watched her vision unfold before her eyes.

"Get out of here, Celia, and leave me alone. I did what I had to do." Future Warren's voice was laced with fury as he stalked ever closer to Future Celia.

"You said we were going to find another way," Future Celia said, and her voice was smothered with emotion as if she had been crying before coming into the room. "Why? How could you have been so cruel? I could hear the screaming from the other side of the palace."

Future Warren dove for Future Celia, capturing her forearms in his strong hands and dragging her to his chest. Holding her close to him and staring into her eyes with his dead expression, he sucked in a breath and seethed his words into her face.

"The chosen children and the leaders had to die, or the planet would have been destroyed. It does not matter which side would have won. You read the scroll yourself, so you know I speak the truth. The cycle had to end, and it was up to me since none of my people had the guts to do the job."

Future Celia sobbed, choking out the words around her pain as she responded, "You said we would find another way. You didn't even give them a chance."

Future Warren shook her hard as he ground out, "You were there, Celia. You saw all the signs, so how can you deny it? The demon prophecy was coming true. Faith lost her way."

"She did not lose her way, you idiot!" Future Celia screamed, struggling against Future Warren's powerful grip. "She was just a teenager with a broken heart. She would have forgiven Ethan in time if you had just given her a chance! I saw it in a vision. I knew she would forgive him!"

Future Warren only shook Future Celia harder, and his voice went up an octave as he yelled back, "It would not have mattered! The damage was done! Ethan was about to return to Asgorath, and if he had left with that darkness in his heart, then there would not have been time for Faith to forgive him!"

They stood there for a moment, staring into each other's eyes and breathing hard. Future Warren's eyes softened slightly with regret and remorse as he bowed his head and broke his gaze from hers.

His voice was low as he stared at the floor and said in a choked voice, "It no longer matters, anyway. The damage is done. They are all dead. I only spared you. You will come with me to Spire Castle. Go get your things packed."

His voice broke as he added, "I tried to kill them all quickly, make it painless as possible, so no one suffered unnecessarily."

"Then why could I hear them screaming?" Celia asked with a choked sob.

"Because they put up a fight."

Future Celia broke down, sagging in Future Warren's firm grip and crying in agony and pain. The sound sent icy tendrils down Celia's spine as she watched her future self slide to her knees. Future Warren let her go and watched her fall to the floor.

Unremorsefully, he stepped around her prone figure and strode towards the door, never looking back as he left the room and slammed the door behind him. Celia's future self continued to cry out her pain and fury on her hands and knees.

Celia watched the scene play out with a tortured expression, hoping against hope that it would end. She could tell that these future versions of her and Warren were broken beyond repair because of what had been done, what had to be done. She was more determined than ever to ensure this future did not play out.

Suddenly, a wave of nausea hit Celia hard in the gut, and she doubled over, taking long, even breaths to keep herself from throwing up. She gripped the side of the table to keep herself from falling over as she waited for the nausea to fade. She kept her breathing deep and even, and her ears gave a little pop. Sound flooded her ears, a cacophony of voices and murmurs, chairs scraping the floor, and footsteps running toward her.

Celia raised her head slowly as the nausea dissipated, and she spotted Warren and Tenebris approaching her hurriedly. Maldia stood from her seat beside Celia with a worried look.

"What happened, Celia?" Warren asked as he continued to stalk toward her, a look of confusion in his amber eyes.

"Are you alright?" asked Maldia in a worried tone, placing a steadying hand on her shoulder.

Tenebris held no confusion, nor did he look overly worried. He reached her side first, pushing past Maldia and gripping Celia's forearm. He placed his other hand on her shoulder where Maldia's hand had been and helped her straighten up slowly.

"Are they becoming stronger?" Tenebris asked with concern.

Celia nodded, not bothering to ask how he had known that she was having visions. Maldia had probably told everyone since Celia had not instructed her to keep them secret.

Warren came up on her opposite side and took her other arm to give her extra support. Celia flinched at his touch, glancing up at him with narrowed eyes. Warren returned her gaze, the confusion growing across his features at her angry stare.

"Yes, I had a vision," Celia said between clenched teeth. Her fury grew in her chest as she pierced Warren with her icy stare.

She knew that this Warren was innocent. She knew that this Warren had not yet murdered her loved ones in cold blood, but she could not help the rage that overtook her when she looked at him.

Warren's gaze bore into hers, and emotions flew across their amber depths too fast for Celia to follow, but she saw them all. Confusion, anger, lust, and, most of all, concern flashed across his features as Celia glared at him mercilessly.

"You killed them," she seethed in a whispered tone. Only Warren and Tenebris heard her. "You did not even give them a chance."

Warren's eyes widened briefly, but then his face relaxed into an unreadable mask. Celia's eyes darted between his, her breathing rapid and her heartbeat unsteady in her chest.

She felt Tenebris stiffen and then pull her away from Warren. Tenebris turned her so that she fully faced him and firmly latched onto her other forearm so that he held her securely in his grasp. He glared at Warren over her head.

"She does not want you to touch her," Tenebris said to the grandmaster, his tone firm but not angry. "Her vision must have been about you."

"Obviously," Warren said derisively.

Celia took in a deep, calming breath and steadied herself.

"I am okay," she said to Tenebris. "You can let me go now."

Tenebris's gaze returned to hers, searching her features with a questioning look.

"Are you sure?" Tenebris asked in a troubled tone.

Celia did not respond aloud. She nodded and pulled away from Tenebris slowly, then turned to face Warren.

Maldia stood beside Warren, and Celia saw the questioning look in her jade-green eyes. Celia smiled reassuringly at her and gave her a slight nod. Seemingly satisfied that Celia was alright, Maldia returned to her place at the table, politely pushing past Tenebris to sit in her seat. Tenebris sighed loudly and moved around the queen toward his seat.

Celia's gaze remained fixed on Warren. She was breathing easier now, and her heartbeat had returned to normal. The anger was gone from her chocolate eyes, replaced with an eerie calmness that made Warren frown.

"What did you see?" he asked.

"I would rather not talk about it right now," Celia answered calmly.

Her eyes flicked quickly around the room, hoping he would get the hint as she continued, "We can talk about it later. Right now, I need to finish reading the scrolls."

Warren's jaw tensed, and his eyes narrowed, but he gave Celia a slight nod in understanding. They would discuss her vision later, in secrecy.

Celia turned away from Warren, and her gaze drifted to the end of the table where the queen sat. Damaphur caught Celia's eyes with her striking lavender stare as she stood from her seat.

"Celia, are you okay, child?" the queen asked worriedly.

"I am fine, my queen," Celia answered.

Damaphur scanned Celia up and down with her narrowed eyes before sitting back down in her seat. She turned to Hestia and gave her a slight nod. Hestia rose from her seat and took the cylindrical container that held the angel scroll in her hands. She opened the container with the key from the folds of her robes and carefully lifted out the scroll.

Warren stalked back to his chair as Hestia brought the scroll around the table to Celia. Celia finished rolling the demon scroll back up. She carefully tied it closed with the string and then returned the scroll to the king. She noticed Warren watching her every move out of the corner of her eye, but she ignored him as she walked back to her place at the table.

Hestia had the angel scroll unrolled and held open, and Celia helped her smooth out the scroll and place the spindles on the table. Hestia returned to her seat, and Celia closed her eyes for a moment, breathing deep and centering herself as she prepared to read.

Her tone was lighter, and her words clear as she read from the angel scroll…

*Conceived by the woman who knows not
the touch of a man…
The fetus is placed in her womb by the
goddess's own hand.
Born in wealth and comfort, wrapped in
a blanket of love…*

The child of light is born in the rich
lands above.

Her beacon shines forever bright in
the night skies of space...

So bright that the brightest moon
refuses to show its face.

This is when the child will come.

The child of darkness falls under her
mercy and is filled with light...

All the dragons that follow the dark
now refuse to fight...

Then the land will be lost to the dark
and forever belong to the light.

Celia took a breath when she had finished reading. She stood straight and leaned slightly backward to stretch the muscles in her back. She looked around the table at the faces staring back at her, and her shoulders tensed slightly. Was she going to have another vision?

Warren stood from his seat, and Celia breathed a sigh of relief when she spotted the movement. She turned her head to look at him as he walked toward her, circling around Chandra and the still-chained Sage at her side to reach Celia. He produced a larger cylinder from his inside jacket pocket and handed it to Celia.

"There, you see?" the queen's voice broke through the silence. "Our light one will stop the dark ones from fighting. She will bring peace and end the war."

"It says the darkness will die, Damaphur," the king answered, but his voice sounded tired instead of angry. "Our people will die, and your people have no remorse."

The queen snorted. "It does not say your people will die, Epialos. It says they will refuse to fight. Does that not sound like the end of a war and the beginning of peace?"

Epialos sighed as he responded, "It says the land will be lost to the dark and forever belong to the light. Light cannot exist without darkness, just as our darkness cannot exist without light, but you taint your light with arrogance and pride. Where is the balance?"

"Like your darkness is not tainted as well?" Damaphur shot back.

"You have more crime on your

side of the planet than we do. If you believe our light is tainted, so is your darkness, and more so than the light.”

“And statements like that just prove my point, Damaphur. Your arrogance is showing,” Epialos sneered.

“It is not arrogance, Epialos. It is simply a fact,” the queen shot back.

“We can argue this all day,” Warren interrupted loudly, pulling everyone’s attention from the argument. “Or we can listen to the last scroll. Maybe it will ease your minds and bring new insights into the prophecies.”

The Queen harrumphed, and the King sighed wearily, but neither of them commented any further. No one said anything else as Celia carefully rolled the angel scroll back up, tied it, placed it back into its cylinder, and handed it back to Hestia.

Warren helped Celia take the last scroll from its cylinder and unroll it onto the table. It was larger and harder to handle than the other two scrolls, so Celia was glad of the help. Warren helped with the heavy spindles, holding them in place while Celia smoothed out the scroll. He positioned the spindles accordingly, then paced back to his seat by the king. Celia watched him thoughtfully until he was back in his seat and then returned her attention to the last scroll.

She glanced around the table one last time before she started to read. Every eye was turned to her, and the bored look was wiped from their eyes. This scroll had never been read before, and everyone in the room was waiting in eager anticipation.

Celia was a bit excited herself, and her voice reflected her exhilaration as she read the last scroll.

*The shadows of a great war fall upon
the land, as told by the Great Grenadia’s
vision. This is what she saw in her own
words...*

“That is my great-great-grandmother,” Celia said, glancing up from the scroll. “This is her vision.”

Warren glanced at her and nodded. “Yes, it was. She was also the one who started our Spire.”

Warren gave her an ‘I-told-you-so’ look, but she turned away before Warren could see the anger in her eyes. She could not argue

190

this in front of everyone since Warren had warned her to be silent about the organization. However, it was becoming increasingly clear that Warren was telling the truth.

Her ancestors had started the Spire, no matter how much Celia wanted to deny it. Celia sighed and turned her attention to the queen.

"If this was truly Grenadia's vision, then we must heed it," Celia said. "You told me she was the greatest of the Oracles."

Damaphur gave Celia a nod as she said, "Yes, child, I remember. Please, continue the reading."

Celia bowed and said softly, "Yes, my queen," and then continued to read.

The star shines brightly in the night sky.
It lights up the night in the land of light
so intensely that the moon's light is
snuffed out.
The darkness is darker than ever before.
Smoke and ash blot out the light of
daytime in the land of darkness.
The time has come for the chosen ones to
heal the land, but Mikka will suffer their
wrath.
Keep your attention evermore focused on
the light and the dark.

If the darkness dies, the land will fall
under the rule of the angels. The land will
not be peaceful under their reign.
Hubris will fill the people's hearts, and
wars of pride will outbreak across the
planet.

Celia paused momentarily, clutching her racing heart and swaying in place as the memories of her first session with Maldia came rushing back to her mind. She had seen this when she experienced the vision in baby Faith's future body!

Clutching her chest, Celia remembered the feeling of betrayal that had penetrated her soul. She could still feel the pain radiating through her, smell the smoke from the burning planet, and hear the tortured scream that had torn from her throat when she realized what she had done.

"Celia," Warren's deep baritone voice broke through her thoughts. He was suddenly there, holding her steady with one hand on her elbow and the other on her back.

"Take deep breaths. I'm right here, and you are safe."

His soothing tone and calming words broke through the memories of that horrible vision, bringing Celia back to the present. She took a few deep, steadying breaths to calm her frayed nerves.

She glanced around the table with an apology on her tongue, but the faces that greeted her were encouraging, understanding, and kind. She smiled gratefully, knowing now that she was indeed among friends.

Her voice was steady and confident as she gathered herself and continued reading.

The land be further destroyed under their reign, and evil will fill the people's hearts. Wars of crime and deceit will outbreak across the planet.

The dark one will kill the light one out of anger and vengeance, but regret and guilt consume him. The longing inside his heart to have her again in his arms will awaken the light of love once more.
Nothing will survive when the dark one's anguish causes him to unleash his pain over the planet, destroying everyone and everything in his desire to have the light back at his side.
This is when Mikka will die.

Therefore, beware the fulfillment of the prophecy. No matter which side wins this war, the planet will die.
Light cannot exist without the dark, just as darkness cannot exist without the light.
The balance of the planet is the only thing that can heal it.
When the prophecy begins, the only path to true peace and healing is to bring balance.

We must banish the light one and the dark one from this life.
This is the only way to save the planet.
We must purge the light and dark leaders.

Celia finished reading and raised her gaze from the scroll. Her breathing had become ragged as her heart pounded ferociously inside her chest. The third scroll had not been what she had expected, and from the looks of all the faces at the table, they had not expected it, either.

Celia could not believe it. The king's words that he had spoken only moments ago rang in her ears. *'The light cannot live without darkness. Where is the balance?'*

The king had been right all along. He had been screaming for peace through world domination, begging the queen to rule by his side. The queen had been too conceited to hear it, thinking she and her people to be too good for Epialos and his dark ones.

Celia glanced at Epialos sitting straight and rigid in his seat, his face filled with weariness and strain. He was staring down the table at Damaphur with his hands curled into fists on the table, but there was no anger in his gaze. Only a defeated longing shone in the fiery depths of his red eyes.

Celia's gaze turned to Damaphur, who sat tall and regal at the other end of the table. She returned Epialos's stare with her icy lavender eyes with an almost apologetic look.

Did Celia imagine the remorse on the queen's features?

Celia turned back to the king as he stared at Damaphur, and she saw the hope flare in the ruby depths of his gaze. He opened his mouth as if ready to speak, but Damaphur's soft voice cut through the silence first.

"I suppose one could misconstrue my actions as conceited. I can see where you would think of me high up on my pedestal. Considering my mother's actions, I do not blame you for hating me."

Epialos's tone was steady as he answered, "I have never told you I hate you. I am constantly begging you to join me. Why would I want you to be my queen if I hated you?"

"For revenge, maybe? I don't know, Epialos. I only know that you should not judge me for the actions of my ancestors. Try to see my reasoning in a different light."

"What other reason could there possibly be for your rejection of me?" Epialos ran a hand through his dark hair. "I have never judged you for the actions of your mother."

Damaphur leaned forward slightly as she answered, "Did you ever consider that there are those that do. There are people on your side who would rather see me dead than join you. Do you not think that it is self-preservation that holds me back from you and not conceitedness?"

Epialos pierced Damaphur with a surprised stare. He frowned and took a deep breath before replying, "Do you not trust me to protect you? Not everyone wants to see you dead. My kingdom would be happy to see you by my side. The ones that wish you harm will be dealt with by my hand."

Her eyes narrowed as she replied, "I can protect myself if necessary. I do not need you to do so."

"Yes, I know you can," Epialos said, and Celia swore that she heard pride in his tone. "So, what is the problem? Why can you not give me a chance to be your king? We can rule the entire planet together."

Damaphur paused, considering how to put what she felt into words. Finally, she took a breath and said, "Your actions and words speak for themselves, Epialos. You are constantly spewing off about how you want to rule the world.

"What if I let you lure me into a sense of false security, and then you just stuff me in a dungeon somewhere to rot away while you enjoy your victory?"

The king's loud laugh surprised everyone at the table, and they all stared at him in stunned disbelief. "My dear, if I stuffed you in a dungeon, it would only be so I could use my whips and chains on you. In a good way, of course."

"So you just want to bend me to your will like some slave?" Damaphur seethed.

Epialos chuckled again and replied, "If you would rather tie me up instead, I would gladly play along."

Hestia, apparently having heard enough, stood suddenly. Her hair blew in an invisible wind, and angry sparks of magic flew from her arms and hands as she held them out by her sides. "How dare you speak to the queen in such a disrespectful manner!"

Epialos turned his humorous gaze toward Hestia and said, "High Priestess, this is not disrespectful. I say much worse when we do not have an audience; sometimes, my lady even enjoys it."

"I am not your lady," the queen said forcefully, but the anger in her tone did not match the embarrassed flush of her cheeks or the uncertainty in her icy gaze.

"But you could be if only you would give in," the king replied, and tiredness entered his voice once more. He sighed heavily and pinched the bridge of his nose between his fingers.

His glowing red eyes turned toward Warren, and he said, "This is why my people believe that Solaris is haughty and looks down their noses at us. I have made it no secret that I desire Damaphur, yet she refuses to give me the time of day. It is as if I am naught but dirt under her pretty little shoes, and she will not even give me a chance."

"I do not think that of you," came Damaphur's reply, and the softness and remorse in her tone had all eyes looking her way as she continued. "I have reasons for rejecting you, Epialos, but those are not it. I do not think you are beneath me at all. It is quite the opposite, actually."

A hopeful gleam lit across the king's face as he turned his attention back to the queen. "What do you mean, Damaphur?"

Damaphur's regal stance crumpled. She slumped in her seat, placing her elbows on the table and her head in her hands as if she had suffered a great defeat. Hestia sank back into her seat, casting a confused look at her queen.

Damaphur raised her eyes to Epialos and said quietly, "I keep you at arm's length because I am afraid. However, it is not your people that frighten me so…"

Damaphur stopped speaking suddenly, her mouth open as if she wanted to say more but could not form the words.

"Damaphur, you cannot be saying that you are afraid of me," Epialos said in a confused tone. "When have I ever given you a reason to fear me? I would never hurt you."

Damaphur hesitated in her response, so Epialos continued. "Damaphur, I know our ancestors did not get along so well, but I am trying to fix what they messed up. You ask me not to judge you based on their actions, and I ask the same of you."

Her face fell in defeat, and she shrugged her shoulders as she replied. "I am not afraid of you, Epialos. I am afraid of myself."

Confusion danced across Epialos's features.

Damaphur cast her eyes to the table before her as she continued, "I am afraid of the things I feel when I am near you. I am afraid that I will lose myself with you. I am afraid…"

Damaphur faltered, but a smile broke out across the king's face as he said, "You are afraid you will fall in love with me."

It was not a question, more like a statement, and to Celia's stunned surprise, Damaphur did not deny it. She sat slumped in her seat, still staring at the table, with a defeated look, and said nothing.

Epialos's smile faded as he regarded the silent queen for a moment. His visage turned remorseful as he sat back in his seat and stared at her across the table.

Finally, he took a deep breath and said, "Damaphur, we can take it as slow as you would like. I will relinquish all control until you learn to trust in me. All I am asking is that you try for the planet's sake if nothing else."

Damaphur lifted her gaze to the king with a hopeful gleam in her eye. "And you will speak with your people on this as well?"

Epialos nodded.

"You will agree to all my terms?"

Epialos chuckled. "Within reason. We can discuss it later, but for now, does this mean we have a truce?"

Her smile was not as wide as the king's, but she returned his smile as she said, "Fine. We will try it your way for now."

There were collective sighs and looks of relief around the table and some gasps of disbelief. Celia stared around at all the faces as the strands of the future suddenly fluttered excitedly inside her mind. Flashes of a restored Mikka and legions of happy demon and angel dragon faces coursed through her soul. She saw no sign of the vision she had before.

Warren stood, breaking Celia's concentration from the strands. Celia saw the relief on his features as he walked around the table to stand beside her. He leaned down and whispered into her ear, low enough for only her to hear.

"We have found another way."

Celia smiled up at him as he stood back straight, but his following words wiped her smile completely away.

"Well, it would seem that I may not have to complete my mission after all. Tenebris, you made the right decision to call me in on this and bring my attention to Celia. She is everything you said she would be.

"You have proven yourself a valuable member of the Spire."

CHAPTER 17: RING AROUND THE ROSES

The mood in the room shifted suddenly as everyone's gaze locked on Tenebris in surprised anger and betrayal. Tenebris tensed, returning everyone's icy stare with an apologetic one of his own. He sighed heavily and finally shifted his gaze to the table in front of him and waited for the angry voices to descend upon him.

This is what he had been waiting for and dreading for weeks now. Now, his betrayal was known to both sides. Now, he would either lose those closest to him, or they would listen to his explanations and forgive him.

Either way, it was time to face the music.

Tenebris had been a member of the Spire for quite some time now. He knew the secrets of the third scroll and what they must do to save the dying planet. He had not wanted to. Warren had not wanted to. No one had wanted to.

In fact, Tenebris had tried to prevent it by killing the dark one before this could all play out. He had tried to kill Raina before she even gave birth, but he had failed like the prisoner still sitting by Chandra's side. Sage could not bring himself to kill a pregnant woman, so Maldia was still alive. Sage could not kill the child either.

Tenebris slanted his eyes sideways toward Raina, where she sat silently beside him, and his bright blue eyes locked with her icy green ones. Behind the heat of her anger, he could detect a trace of sadness and hurt in the emerald depths of her gaze, and he lowered his eyes to the table once more. He could not bear to look her in the eyes as his guilt and shame burned through his soul.

No…not shame…guilt, yes, but not shame.

He could never feel shame for being a part of a guild whose only concern was protecting the planet and its people. Sometimes hard decisions needed to be made for the greater good of all. The Wizard's Spire cared for the planet and the people on it.

The silence became unbearable for Tenebris as he sat and waited for his world to come crashing down around him. What was only seconds seemed like hours as he waited for his fate. His gaze roamed the room nervously, and his eyes met Warren's amber stare.

Warren's look held a modicum of remorse and regret as he nodded encouragingly at Tenebris. Tenebris and he had known it was going to come to this. They had been planning this for years, and Tenebris had always intended to tell his secret when it was right.

Even so, there were still things they did not know.

They did not know that he had been the one to introduce Sage to the queen, telling her that he could be trusted and she should consider him for the adviser role. Sage had been a secret spy for the Spire, watching and waiting for the prophecies of the scroll to come.

Also, Tenebris had been the one to sneak in Spire guards, leaving a hole in security so Sage could take the queen. But Sage could not carry out the assassination, having grown attached to his queen during his years of service to her.

Tenebris had kept Warren updated on everything in Solaris and Asgorath since he had access to both palaces. When Sage had failed to carry out the mission, Tenebris had called Warren. And just in time, too, since the mission had started without Warren's go-ahead. Tenebris had insisted it was one of Warren's people that had given Sage the message to start.

Warren was still looking into that mess.

"How long have you been part of the Wizard's Spire?" Celia asked softly, her sorrow-filled voice breaking the monotonous silence and cutting off Warren's thoughts.

"I have been attending school since I was six before you were even born," Tenebris answered carefully. "Warren helped me develop and control my unusual gifts, and he put me in contact with the right people so I could use my gifts to help people."

Celia did not respond, and the anger in her chilly stare cut through Tenebris's heart.

"Well," the king interjected. "We cannot be angry about that. If not for Tenebris, many young ones would not have been able to control their magic so completely."

"Yes," the queen agreed. "Tenebris's magic benefits both sides, and there is none other like him on the planet. However, I am confused why you have kept this a secret from us, Tenebris."

The queen's knowing look pierced Tenebris, and Tenebris glanced away, thinking quickly for a response. However, Tenebris did not have to answer.

Warren, who still stood by Celia's chair, answered quickly as he stealthily threw a look at Tenebris to be silent. Tenebris complied, shifting his gaze again to the table before him.

"Most of my more treasured students are sworn to secrecy, your majesties," Warren said in his smooth, deep tone. "The secrecy is to protect the student more than the school. I still consider Tenebris a student, even though you consider him a doctor in your worlds."

"That did not answer my question," the queen replied sternly. Her eyes were still on Tenebris as she spoke, but Tenebris was still staring at the table.

He could feel the weight of the queen's disapproving gaze on him, causing his guilty conscience to intensify. It was all he could do not to break down and beg for forgiveness.

Warren did not flinch at the queen's tone, and his voice was confident and commanding as he replied, "The secrecy is paramount to the safety of my students because of their power. Guards protect you, my queen, and the security of your palace. It is the same for you, my king.

"What kind of security does one have if they are simple folk who cannot afford personal guards? My school provides that sort of protection for those that choose to come to me for sanctuary and learning. We have guards to protect the students while they are at the Spire, but who will protect them when they are not in school?

"Swearing them to the secrecy of the school and their powers is but one of my security measures to keep my students safe after they leave, either through graduation or to take a job as Tenebris has.

"He decided his magic would be better served by serving you both, which required him to leave the school. Therefore, I swore him to secrecy to protect his status at the school and to protect him. Does that explanation provide more insight for you, your majesties?"

Tenebris sighed with relief. That was quick thinking on Warren's part and a good and truthful explanation without delving into the whole truth. Hope filled his heart as he glanced up at the surrounding faces.

Raina's eyes had softened somewhat but still held a bitter hurt in their emerald depths. Celia stared at him thoughtfully, but the anger had vanished completely.

Well, that was something.

He did not know Chandra well, so her angry gaze did not matter much to him, but Sage gave him a knowing smirk as he sat by Chandra in his chains.

The king and queen regarded Tenebris with slight curiosity. However, the sternness in Damaphur's voice still reflected in her icy lavender eyes.

"Well, Tenebris," she said. "Is this true? Did you need to keep your secret for your own safety?"

Tenebris swallowed hard and ran a hand through his black hair before answering, "Yes, my queen."

"Can you explain?"

Tenebris took a breath as he thought about how to best explain the reason for the students' secrecy. He glanced at Warren, who nodded encouragingly. Tenebris decided that the best course of action would be to tell a bit of the truth without divulging the secrets of the secret organization behind the school, much as Warren had.

"Everyone in this room knows the reputation of the school. The Wizard's Spire is shrouded in mystery and is, therefore, misunderstood by many. People fear what they do not understand, and that fear makes them dangerous.

"There are students out there now that did not keep their secrets. Society shuns them, and even their own families want nothing to do with them. Those are the milder cases. Some were even hunted down and killed for fear that they would become dangerous. It makes it challenging to be a member of society and make a living when people discover you come from the Spire.

"Truthfully, would any of you have trusted me with your children had you known the Spire taught me? Would any of you have trusted me at all?"

Celia stood and entered the conversation, her dark brown eyes narrowed in anger. "I would have."

"You would not have even known me. The palace would not have employed me to help you develop your powers. Therefore I would not have been here to take custody of you and raise you," Tenebris answered gently.

Celia turned to Damaphur, who had lowered her gaze in thought. Celia frowned as Damaphur's eyes raised and connected with hers.

Damaphur's voice was low and remorseful as she said, "I am afraid he is right, Celia. When I learned of your ancestry and knew how powerful you would become, I automatically called Tenebris. He had a reputation for working with children of immense power, and he had helped the children of my people before.

"If he was known to have come from the Spire, I would never have trusted your safety and teaching to him. I would have taken custody of you myself before I trusted you to the Spire."

"Perhaps we have all been too judgmental toward the Spire and should not fault Tenebris for keeping such a secret," Epialos commented. "Just as we have been too judgmental about each other."

"That still does not forgive the fact that he called someone in to commit murder," Celia seethed.

Warren sighed and turned Celia gently to face him. He spoke loud enough for the entire room to hear him, but his gaze remained locked on Celia's face.

"Fine, you want to do this, then let's do this."

Celia frowned, but then understanding dawned on her, and she flinched. "I…I'm sorry. You don't have to …I will be quiet."

Warren was already shaking his head before Celia had finished her stuttering speech. "No, Celia, you are right."

She cocked an eyebrow in confusion. "Huh?"

"They need to know since they will probably find out eventually. I will tell them my secret and perhaps bring forgiveness for Tenebris."

Everyone looked to Warren in confusion as he released Celia and turned to face the room. His tone was loud and clear as he spoke.

"The Spire is partly a sanctuary and a school. However, that is not the only reason the Oracles created the Spire. The Oracles built the school, but what we teach is more than just how to develop and use magic. They built the school to train the members of the organization they created, which is what The Spire really is.

"The Wizard's Spire is a secret organization that protects Planet Mikka through any means possible. This may include spying and assassination, but only when absolutely necessary and only after much debate and study.

"I set Sage in place as a spy to watch for signs that the prophecies were coming true. Then, Tenebris would report to me, and Sage would assassinate the queen and the light's chosen one on my orders.

But he failed his mission by becoming too attached to the queen, and thankfully so.

"I had not given the order. I was still investigating other ways to carry out the mission without killing. So, when Tenebris called me after Sage failed, I had to come in personally to find out what the hell went wrong.

"I am not soft. I am the grandmaster and leader of the school, and I will do what needs to be done to protect the planet as I was sworn to do. But I always try to find another way. We study the prophecies thoroughly before coming to any decisions regarding taking lives. We try to find alternate solutions. Tenebris did not call me to complete the mission and kill. He called me in to find another way. He called me in to try to save you all because he cares for you immensely."

The royals sat silent, their gazes darting between Warren and Tenebris. Their faces were unreadable masks of normalcy, but Celia could feel the tension and anger in the room.

She was so filled with rage herself that it was hard for her to breathe. She turned to Tenebris, and Tenebris almost crumpled to the floor when he saw the hate on her face.

Her voice was harsh as she spat out, "you could have told me. I would have trusted you and kept your secret, maybe even helped, but now I will never trust you again."

She turned her back to Tenebris and stalked from the room. No one tried to stop her, but Warren sighed in disappointment as he turned to the scroll. He rolled it back up carefully and placed it back into its container.

Tenebris felt as if he would wither away and die at that moment, and the feeling only got worse when his gaze caught Raina's frigid stare. She said nothing and only pierced him with her icy gaze as she shook her head in disappointment.

He rose from his seat and made his way miserably to the doors that led out of the room. He felt the gaze of everyone in the room as he sloped across the floor, but he did not look back.

He knew this would happen when his secret was out, but it did not make it any easier to deal with. He had held on to a slim shard of hope that at least Celia would forgive him. Now that seemed impossible, and Tenebris did not know how to pick up the pieces and move ahead.

However, he had to try. He was still a member of the Wizard's Spire, and he had a planet to save.

CHAPTER 18: ASHES, ASHES

Celia paused in the hallway outside the conference room. She hesitated, wondering if she could get away with storming off and leaving. There was still much left to discuss, and she could not leave Raina and the baby behind. Besides, she had not gotten to visit with Faith yet.

"*Yes,*" she told herself. "*That is why I cannot leave. I must see Baby Faith first.*"

Celia took a calming breath and stepped back toward the double doors. She would stay, but she would not pay any attention to Tenebris.

She was about to turn the handle and open the door when a sound caught her attention from down the hall. The hallway ended at a sharp bend that turned left and headed straight, leading to the throne room. The noises had come from that direction. It sounded as if the entire queen's guard were unsuccessfully sneaking through the palace with their armor clanking even as they tried to be silent.

That thought led Celia to wonder where the guards that were supposed to have been guarding the door to the conference room were. They had not been here when she had stormed out, nor had they returned during her brooding.

Celia's blood ran cold as she looked up and down the empty hallway. Terrifying flashes of vision danced around her mind from the future strands, pulling her attention inward. Blood, gore, dead dragons lying everywhere, and the wounded screaming in agony tore through Celia's head as she stumbled blindly into the double doors, sagging against them in pain and fear.

Was she about to have another vision?

Celia did not know, but her head was splitting, and her body felt weak and shaky. Then suddenly, the flashes stopped, and the strands settled back into her subconscious mind, quiet and dormant as they were before.

Celia paused, leaning her full weight against the doors as she waited for the pounding in her temples to pass and her heartbeat to slow to a normal pace. Nausea hit her right after the visions stopped, and she doubled over against the door. Celia moaned in agony and dread.

She had to go back in now. She had to warn them about the coming slaughter. It had been the angel dragons that she had seen lying dead or dying all over the palace floors. The absence of the guards and the sounds coming from the throne room did not bode well.

Another loud clang sounded from down the hallway as if someone were flinging their armor across the room, then a dragon's roar tore through her ears. She grasped both sides of her head and screamed.

She had to get back inside. Celia had to warn them.

She pushed herself up from her bent position and slowly removed her hands from her ears. The dragon's roar had stopped, but she still heard the sounds of clanking armor. The guards must be fighting back, trying to protect the palace.

She thought there must be some magic at play if no one inside the room had heard the commotion yet. Surely, someone would have come out to check the noises if they had heard them.

Celia steadied herself and then pushed against the doors hard. She shoved them open and ran into Tenebris, who had just been about to go out the doors behind her. He caught her, folding her into his embrace to keep her from falling.

"Celia, you came back," he whispered to her, and her heart crumpled at the relief she heard in his tone.

However, there was no time for this or apologies that Celia could not even consider now. If her vision came true, if Tenebris was one of the dragons that had been dead in her vision, then none of what he had done in the past mattered here and now. He was her mentor and savior when the world rejected her, and she loved him despite his lies and hidden identity.

She squeezed him gently, returning his hug, and spoke reassuringly against his chest. "Tenebris, I will always love you no matter how angry I am at you. Please remember that, but we don't have time for this right now."

Tenebris pulled back, holding Celia by her shoulders and staring into her face. He took in her bloodshot eyes, her ragged breathing, and the wrinkle of worry between her eyes, and suddenly he knew that she had seen something bad.

Tenebris stiffened. "What did you see?"

Celia swallowed hard and blurted, "Death, pain, and it is happening now. I heard noises from the throne room, and the guards were gone from outside the door. There must be a noise-proof spell cast on this room because it is loud outside."

It was as if Celia had lit a fire in the center of the room. Chaos ensued, beginning with Queen Damaphur, as she shot up from her seat with an accusatory glare at Epialos.

"What have you done, you snake? Did you set all of this up to gain trust so you could infiltrate my palace?"

Epialos came out of his seat next, shoving to his feet and glaring daggers at the queen. "I have nothing to do with this. Maybe we should look at the stranger in the room. You said he had troops hidden in the courtyard."

The king and queen turned their attention to Warren, who was holding both hands up in defense with a worried look. "I have done nothing. You would both be dead now if this were my doing. However, we need to see what is happening in the throne room. It can't be good if they could slip past my guards."

Hestia stood and waved a hand in a dramatic gesture. "There, if there was a spell on this room, I have defused it."

Warren raised an eyebrow. "Very impressive, High Priestess. I could not have done better myself."

"If I find out it was you, Epialos," Damaphur seethed through gritted teeth.

Epialos cut her off. "It wasn't me, I swear it."

The deafening roar of a dragon shattered the sounds of arguing, and everyone in the room stiffened. Raina stood suddenly and ran for the door.

"The babies!" she exclaimed as she ran.

Tenebris released Celia and grabbed for Raina as she passed. He caught her by the wrist, jerking her around toward him as he said, "You cannot go out there!"

She rounded on him, using the momentum he had created to swing
her arm toward his face. Tenebris moved at the last second, and the
slap intended for his face caught him on the shoulder.

He recovered quickly, shaking her gently and saying, "Calm down
and think, Raina!"

"My son is out there!" she exclaimed as she struggled in his hold.

"Yes, and if you get yourself killed, then who will protect him? He
is safe in the throne room, remember?" Tenebris practically shouted.

Raina's struggles ceased, and she stared at Tenebris with wide,
worried eyes. During their exchange, Maldia rose from her place at
the table and approached them. She caught Raina's gaze and gave her
a comforting gesture with her hands.

"There are four guards stationed outside the room. I returned the
key to Hestia after I locked the babies and nursery maid inside. You
know how secure that room is. It is secure, even from dragons."

"This room is not as secure as the scroll room," the queen said as
she left her place at the table. "I suggest we all leave if we do not want
to be cornered here."

"That was probably the plan," Hestia said. "They probably
intended to trap us here after slaughtering everyone in the castle. It is
a good thing we had Celia to warn us."

"If we can stop them in the throne room, then perhaps they won't
get any further into the palace," Warren said.

"I will get us to the throne room," Epialos said as he moved to the
center of the room. "Everyone stand back."

"And why should I let you lead in my own palace?" Damaphur
asked, quirking an eyebrow disdainfully.

"Because whoever is attacking will hopefully be surprised by a
united force. I am not going to lead. I am going to partner with you.
Come, my queen, let us stop this useless bickering and defend your
palace. Perhaps someday you will return the favor for me in
Asgorath."

Epialos did not give Damaphur another chance to respond. Before
the queen could even open her mouth, Epialos's skin rippled with
power as bones shifted and remade themselves. Scales covered the
king's powerful body as his form grew larger. His neck elongated just
as his hands formed into talons that scraped against the marble floors
as he attempted to gain balance in his dragon form.

His glorious copper dragon rose over the entire room, his head
nearly touching the ceiling. Two great black horns graced each side of

his head, and spikes protruded from below his horns and down the sides of his face. Smaller spikes adorned the sides of his snout and framed his mouth, full of glittering white, razor-sharp teeth. His eyes glowed like rubies, and an icy wind blew from his nostrils as he shook his massive body.

His magnificent wings spread out behind him, stretching from one end of the room to the other. The wings of full-blooded dragons were leathery, with visible veins and sharp talons at the tips, whereas the wings of demon and angel dragons were feathered. Epialos's wings were covered with downy black feathers, as graceful and elegant as any pure demon's wings.

His tail curled across the floor behind him, sporting spikes from the top of his tail and down to almost the tip. The tip of the tail was barbed and sharp. One sting from his tail could kill with the toxin stored within, like the barbed tail of a demon.

He let out a mighty roar, shaking the furniture and vibrating the walls inside the room. He charged for the door with his horned head down, bashing the door open and roaring into the hallway.

"Do you have to tear up my palace?" Damaphur yelled up at the massive dragon.

His answering snuff sounded apologetic as he crept into the hallway. The talons of his feet clicked along the marble floor as he moved.

Damaphur did not shift.

Instead, she followed closely behind Epialos's massive form as they crept through the ruined meeting room door.

"I will stay in this form until I am needed to conserve energy," Damaphur explained.

Epialos snorted in answer.

Warren moved up beside Damaphur, Hestia and Maldia followed behind them, and Tenebris stayed with Raina and Celia. Chandra brought up the rear with Sage still in chains.

Nothing happened as they went down the hallway to the sharp bend. The tension increased once they turned the bend and headed toward the throne room. The sounds of battle had ceased, and silence greeted them from behind the closed doors.

Epialos's massive dragon form paused as they approached the throne room just before reaching the double doors. Warren, walking just behind Epialos's back talons beside Damaphur, stiffened and put his hand up to halt the rest of the party. Queen Damaphur stopped and turned questioning eyes to Warren.

Maldia and Hestia looked to their queen as they stopped, and Tenebris placed one hand on Celia and the other on Raina in a protective gesture. Chandra pulled on the chains that bound Sage, stopping him beside her.

He gave a questioning look around. His dark blue eyes narrowed, and he cocked his head to one side as if listening for something, his white hair swishing across his forehead with the movement. His slender form shifted as he looked around, and Chandra noticed the sleek lines of muscles twitching under the skin of his forearms as he strained against the chains.

Her eyes widened as Sage snapped his arms out to his side so suddenly and powerfully that the thick chains snapped in two. She started to protest and reached out to grab him as he bent down and pulled on the chains attached to each ankle, but Warren's words stopped her actions.

"He was never your prisoner, Lady Chandra. He could have gotten away any time he wanted."

Chandra swallowed hard, shooting Maldia a look with her eyebrows raised almost into her hairline. Maldia simply shrugged as she watched Sage pull apart the thick iron shackles that bound each ankle and toss them away. Sage stood straight and gazed down at Chandra with a satisfied smirk on his handsome face.

"I hear trouble coming, so I figured I would free myself to help if we have to fight."

"So, you're telling me that you endured my interrogations and could have gotten away all along?" Chandra asked in a whispered tone.

Sage shrugged with the smirk still plastered on his face. "If I had gotten away, I would not have been able to enjoy your company as long as I did."

He paused, his smirk becoming sultry and predatory as he added, "Besides, I liked how you handled the whip. Maybe we can do that again in a more friendly fashion, perhaps."

Chandra snarled and hissed at the insufferably sexy man in answer, and Sage chuckled devilishly as she turned away from him. He cocked his head again as the grin faded from his face, and his look became serious.

"Does anyone else hear that?" he asked.

The entire party strained to listen in the silent hallway. There was a slight sound seeping through the cracks of the closed double doors. It was the slightest scrape of metal on marble, as if someone were dragging something that was barely touching the floor.

Warren turned to the giant copper dragon in front of him and asked, "What about you, big guy? Do you hear anything?"

The dragon did not answer. He only nodded his massive head and gave a quiet snort.

"Maybe it is the guards," Damaphur said, keeping her voice low. "Maybe they have disposed of the intruders and are cleaning up the mess."

"Something is going on in there," Hestia said. "And we need to find out what it is."

"We could have our friend blow a powerful gust of wind into the room as a warning," Warren said, motioning to the dragon standing silently above the party.

"What if my guards are in there, cleaning up like I said?" Damaphur asked. "I do not want to harm my own guards."

"One gust of wind will not hurt anyone," Warren said, turning toward the door. "That's why it is called a warning."

Warren turned and looked at Epialos. "Ready, big guy?"

Epialos nodded.

Warren flung the doors open wide, and all hell broke loose.

A dragon roared, and fire shot from the open doorway. Warren ducked, barely dodging the stream of fire flowing into the hallway, and Epialos screamed out in pain.

The fire had struck the mighty dragon in his leg but blocked the fire from everyone else.

Damaphur gasped and ran forward to help Warren, but she paused suddenly. The stream of fire stopped, and she gazed through the doorway past the now non-existent double doors.

She stared into the open doorway that led into the throne room from the side of the raised dais where the throne sat. Damaphur's gaze swept around her throne room, and she counted no less than ten dragons wandering around alongside twenty or more soldiers. They all wore the black and red armor of the demon dragons.

The colossal space of the courtyard, foyer, and throne room was large enough for hundreds of shifted dragons. However, Damaphur's current position did not grant her a view of the main double doors that led to those spaces, so she could only imagine how many more dragons were wandering around that she could not see.

She cast an accusatory glance at the massive dragon, shaking his burning leg as if to shake off the pain, but Epialos did not seem to notice. Instead, the humongous dragon roared angrily into the throne room, shooting his breath magic toward the faces of two dragons standing in front of the ruined throne room doors.

The dragons seemed surprised that their king had fired on them, but they recovered quickly and roared into the rest of the room.

Tendrils of icy fear ran up Damaphur's back when she heard the screams of an army of dragons roaring back. Why were Epialos's own troops rallying against him? They must know it was him. There were not many copper demon dragons left. Why were they attacking?

But Epialos did not seem phased or confused in the least. His icy wind magic flew from his mouth, hitting the two roaring dragons in their faces as their cries of anger turned to cries of pain. The mighty gale knocked them backward, but they recovered quickly and retreated from the doorway.

Demon dragon soldiers began to pour forth, blocking the way into the throne room with the sheer number of their bodies. They advanced on the small party at the mighty dragon's feet. Epialos began to stomp, tearing soldiers up with his mighty talons and slowing the advance. Damaphur stepped back from Epialos, motioning for the others to give her some space, and shifted.

The splendid white scales of Damaphur's dragon spilled over her massive body, sparkling like diamonds in the sunlight that spilled into the hallway. Her white feathered wings uncurled from her colossal form as she stood, and her talons clicked on the marble floor as she tore at the soldiers around her feet.

They made a resplendent pair, and Celia stared at them in fascination. Celia was awestruck by the contrast between the coppery dragon with his black feathered wings and the shimmering white dragon with her white feathered wings. They were beautiful, lethal, and mesmerizing.

They worked as a team, switching positions accordingly. One would stomp and bite at the soldiers while the other breathed deathly breath magic into the throne room at the dragons. They effectively kept the soldiers from advancing on the others while keeping the dragon army contained in the throne room simultaneously.

The world began to spin suddenly, snapping Celia's attention from the dragon pair, and she groped the air for something to hold on to. She swayed in place and would have fallen had it not been for Tenebris, who still held her arm.

"Celia, what's wrong?" Tenebris exclaimed, dread coloring his tone.

Warren, who had recovered enough to stumble out of the way of the two fighting dragons, held out his arms and said, "Let me have her. I will protect her until the vision is done. You shift and help the king and queen."

Tenebris scoffed, glancing up at the pair hurling wind, fire, and ice into the throne room at the still-advancing army.

"Do you really think my tiny thunder dragon will do any more damage than those two can? Epialos's wind is lethal, and Damaphur possesses all the breath magics."

"You know you can hold your own," Warren said, reaching out for Celia. "Do not underestimate yourself, Tenebris. You are the only dragon shifter that has your talents with magic."

"Yes, but my unique abilities have nothing to do with my dragon's breath magic and fighting prowess."

"You hold your own in training, Tenebris. Hell, there is no time to argue this now. Give me the seer and join the battle."

Tenebris sighed and handed Celia's prone form to Warren. He turned to Raina and gently pulled his arm free. Raina stared at him with wide, fearful eyes.

"Don't worry, Raina. I will protect you," Tenebris said as he gave her a small, comforting smile.

Raina did not respond and only watched as Tenebris moved toward the fight, shifting into his tiny jade dragon. By the time he reached the king and queen, he had entirely shifted. Tenebris moved slightly back between the pair, so he intercepted the few soldiers that broke through the line of the two powerful dragons. He shot them down with his lightning as they broke through and released a few bolts into the throne room for good measure.

Celia was only half aware of the exchange. Her attention was focused internally as the vision gripped her in its paralyzing embrace. Her hands balled into fists as she watched the pictures of blood and death flash inside her head. Nothing was changing. Everything was the same. The future strands floated through her vision quickly, yet they all stayed the same.

Death, blood, destruction.

They flowed and moved so quickly that Celia could not tell one side from the other, so she did not know if they were winning or losing.

Warren held her close, keeping her upright as the vision rendered her helpless. Warren gasped in surprise as he noticed her eyes. They had turned completely white, no iris or pupil, just white orbs rolling around in her eye sockets.

"Celia?" Warren croaked out worriedly.

"Nothing's changing," Celia cried out. "I still see death but can't tell who is who."

"We must get to the scroll room," Raina cried out, her sobs mingling with the words.

Maldia patted her shoulder comfortingly. "We will get there, Raina."

"Come, Hestia," Maldia cried over the din of battle. "We must do our part to protect the palace and its inhabitants. We cannot just stand here and let the king and queen do all the work."

Hestia held her arms outstretched to her sides as Maldia came up beside her and did the same. They began to hum, their voices eerie yet strangely melodic, and their bodies began to glow with radiant white light.

The power built until the women glowed almost as bright as the sun, and everyone in the hallway had to shield their eyes or be blinded by it. The light throbbed once, twice, and then flew from the women and out into the throne room. The entire palace could hear the screams of pain as the light burned through the enemy forces.

The dragons began to tire, and throngs of soldiers pushed into the hallway as the tired dragons' efforts diminished. Chandra drew her sword from the sheath that was always strapped to her side. Warren drew forth a dagger from somewhere on his person and tossed it to Sage. Sage nodded his thanks, then joined Chandra's side as the soldiers broke through the dragon's defenses. Warren took a defensive stance beside Celia.

At least the dragons were still being held back by Epialos, Damaphur, and Tenebris. Blasts of wind, ice shards, and electric lightning bolts poured forth from their mouths as they held the line and kept the dragons back.

Five soldiers advanced on Hestia and Maldia, but Chandra and Sage were there to defend them while they worked their magic. Their bodies were building that glow again as they hummed the eerie tune. Chandra and Sage began swinging, blocking, and parrying with their sword and dagger, pushing the wall of soldiers back away from the holy women.

Warren moved away from the fighting, shielding Celia in his arms even as Raina clung to him in terror. He gently pushed Raina back behind him and pinned her against the wall with his body, shielding her from the fighting.

He turned with Celia in his arms and said to Raina, "Raina, focus on me, not them. Help me with Celia. Guard her so that I may help the others."

Warren's tone was calm but firm, and Raina gave him her attention with too-wide eyes. "I cannot fight. I could not protect her."

Warren narrowed his eyes at the mother of the chosen one. He could sense something in her but could not be sure what it was. It could be a backlash from her pregnancy. That was entirely possible since baby Ethan was only a couple of months old. But Warren did not think so. He would have to speak with Tenebris about possibly bringing out Raina's hidden power.

For now, however, there was no time to do anything but fight or protect. He would protect.

"Okay, Raina. I will stand here by you and Celia, but you must sit with her. I cannot fight and hold her. If the soldiers break through, I will need both hands free for my magic."

Raina only nodded, and Warren handed Celia over to her. The smaller lady had difficulty settling with Celia's more significant form. Still, she eventually had Celia comfortably leaning against the wall while Raina held her upright.

Warren turned to the battle at hand, standing before the two women. His power built inside him, flowing and churning through his entire body as he gathered it into his hands. His mind searched for the right spell. It had to be precise. There was no room for error.

The words came to him silently as he drew in the magic energy he would need to unleash the spell. He began to recite the words in his mind, not needing to speak them aloud, as most wizards did. This was part of what made Warren unique among the magic users.

Another part that made him unique was the range of his spells. Most wizards could cast spells on objects near them or from a distance if they could see their prey. But Warren could cast spells over vast distances whether he could see the subjects of his spell or not.

He only had to think about the general idea of the object of his spells. Right now, he focused on demon dragons and soldiers, leaving a space inside his mind to exclude Tenebris and the king.

He had almost completed the words and was preparing to unleash the spell when a soldier broke through the lines and came at him, sword raised and prepared to land a killing blow. He had no time to react, no time to move.

Celia screamed.

The sword struck and slashed, hitting the floor hard as it sliced completely through its target. The soldier brought the sword up with a victorious flourish, then frowned in confusion at the absence of blood on his blade.

With wide eyes, the soldier focused on the target he thought he had hit and killed. There was nothing there. The two women still huddled against the wall, watching him with weary eyes, but the spot where the wizard had stood was empty.

Warren chuckled darkly as he reappeared behind the soldier. He had to use his built-up energy for transportation, but it could not have been helped. He would not fall victim to a blade.

However, now he would have to rebuild his energy before completing the spell he had started before. But first, he would take care of the idiot who thought he could kill the leader of the Wizard's Spire.

The soldier turned when he heard Warren chuckle behind him, and Warren's sneering face greeted him. That was the soldier's last sight before a blade cut through his abdomen. He felt only a pinch of pain as the magical sword Warren had conjured sliced entirely through him, and the top half of his body fell to the floor as his soul dissipated into oblivion.

"Hold the line," Hestia ground out as she backed away from the advancing soldiers with Maldia beside her.

Chandra and Sage still fought vigorously, but the three dragons were failing. The dragons begin to break through the line with the soldiers.

Hestia shot a bolt of magic from her palm, striking down a small blue dragon that had slipped through. Maldia shot a bolt toward two soldiers that slithered by Chandra and Sage and were advancing on Warren.

"Thanks, sister," Warren called as he returned to his place in front of Celia and Raina. "Think you can cover me for a minute?"

"I'll do my best," Maldia called back. "There isn't room for us to shift, so we are doing what we can."

"You're doing great," Warren called encouragingly, turning his concentration back to building his energy.

Soldiers continued filling the hall as more broke through the line. Chandra and Sage began to be overwhelmed as soldiers flocked around them. Sage barely missed a blade that came dangerously close to cutting off his head but got a piercing stab in the gut for his efforts.

It did not go in deep, but it affected his ability to move and slowed his fighting.

Chandra dodged a blow that would have sliced through her abdomen only to receive a slash from behind that cut her from shoulder blade to shoulder blade. She screamed in pain and went down briefly before shooting to her feet and continuing the fight.

She was not head of the queen's guard for nothing.

However, she was slowed by the wound, and there was no room in the hallway for another dragon. She and Sage could not hold the soldiers back as effectively as before, and they began to succumb to their wounds.

As more and more soldiers slipped by the dragons and dodged around Sage and Chandra, they began to flank Maldia and Hestia. The sisters flung their magic out, hitting soldiers left and right, but their efforts became useless.

The soldiers pressed closer to Raina, who stood with Celia against the wall. Celia's eyes were still clouded as the strands of vision continued to rage through her.

Celia was having her own internal battle as she hurriedly picked through the strands. She discarded the ones that depicted only pain and death and tried to find one strand that would foretell victory.

It was not there.

Either it did not exist, or she had not found it yet, but Celia kept looking as she slumped helplessly against the wall, held up by Raina.

Raina gazed around at the battle helplessly, her emerald eyes wide and showing too much white. The queen's beautiful diamond scales were covered in soot and blood as she staggered on her feet, still shooting ice into the throne room in an effort to stay in the battle.

Epialos's massive copper dragon fared no better, but he was still shooting his breath magic through the slowly advancing dragon forces. The soldiers continued to pour through the door, slashing at the giant dragon's legs as they passed, but more than a few fell victim to Tenebris's lightning bolts as they came into view.

Tenebris's jade scales were also covered in blood, but most of the blood was splashes that came from cuts in the larger dragons' legs. Raina's heart pounded in her chest as one soldier came close to reaching Tenebris with his sword, but the bolt of lightning that Tenebris shot from his mouth rendered the soldier a useless, quivering mass on the floor by his feet.

Raina turned her attention to the two warriors behind Tenebris, swinging and slashing at the dozen or more soldiers surrounding them. Chandra wavered slightly on her feet, tired and exhausted at her continuing efforts to hold the soldiers back. Sage stood shoulder to shoulder with her, doing his best to support her weight while he himself continued to fight beside her.

Raina turned to Maldia and Hestia. Both sisters were now focused on the soldiers surrounding Warren as he stood a bit back from the fighting, his eyes closed in concentration. She watched helplessly as more soldiers continued to move toward Warren's position.

Finally, Raina's attention turned to the soldiers that were slowly advancing on her position. Raina stood helplessly, holding Celia against the wall.

"We have to do something," Raina whined helplessly to the oblivious Celia.

Celia's eyes were still glazed over.

"I have to do something," Raina said more forcefully.

She thought about her baby boy helplessly trapped in a room that no one could enter except Maldia, the queen, or Hestia. What would happen to her child if she and the rest were struck down right here in this hallway? Who would get the handmaid and the babies out then?

But what could Raina do? She did not possess any fighting skills, nor did she have any magic. She did not know any magic spells, and she was not strong at all.

What could she do?

Anger at her own uselessness bubbled inside her gut, coalescing and spinning violently until Raina feared she would throw up. Her heart pounded with rage as every muscle in her body tensed with the fury that radiated through her soul and heated her skin to an inferno.

The wrath built inside her with such ferocity that Raina could barely contain it. It came out in a long, ragged scream that filled the hallway and released such a bought of energy from Raina that her very blood froze in her veins.

Her scream of outraged fury became a scream of pain as her blood turned to ice inside her. She could faintly hear someone screaming her name, but the sound was so distant and drowned out by the pain coursing through her as she continued to freeze from the inside out.

The cold was more like fire as it burned through her, stealing her breath and stopping her heart from beating. Was she dying? For an instant, Raina believed she was. Then, just as suddenly as it had started, the freezing sensation stopped.

Her blood pumped through her once more, warm and alive. Her lungs unfroze, and she sucked in a deep, dragging breath as her heart beat again.

Nausea flowed through her, and dizziness caused her world to spin. Blackness ate at the corners of her vision as Raina wondered what was happening to her. She had no time to think about it before unconsciousness claimed her.

The darkness ate up everything as Raina's world faded away.

CHAPTER 20: CELIA'S VISION

There it was. The strand that Celia had been searching for, the one that gave them a slim chance of victory. She grasped at the strand, curling it into her conscious mind where she could investigate it and see what needed to be done.

She heard a scream of pain, but she ignored it. This was too important to be distracted. She released the strand into her mind and allowed the images to play out like a movie playing in her head. More screams of pain, but Celia kept concentrating on the strand.

Something pulled at her gut like an invisible hand was reaching inside her and pulling at her stomach. Celia felt as if she would retch, but she dared not open her eyes. Instead, she succumbed to the pulling sensation. She found herself being pulled into her own mind, into the starring role of yet another vision.

The rage was so cold. It flowed through my veins like ice, freezing my blood and seizing my muscles in a wintery embrace. It froze the breath in my lungs until I could do nothing but continue the scream. It hurt, but it was not unbearable. My scream of pain was more of a scream of surprise because I was not expecting the pain. I was not expecting any of this at all.

I could feel it. I could feel the energy coursing through me, swirling inside my stomach, being flung from me as I screamed out my fury into the hallway.

I could feel what it was doing and thought I could somehow control it. I knew it was freezing everyone it touched solid, creating frozen statues of interrupted movement throughout the hall. Maybe I could contain it enough to ensure that it only froze the soldiers and not the others, but I had no idea if it would work.

I could not control the range, the scope; I could not control how far out the magic went, freezing everything it touched. That was the thought that scared me. Would it reach and enter the scroll room? Would the magic I had not even known I possessed enter and freeze my son?

No.

I could not stop it, could not control it. I stood and screamed helplessly, unable to do anything until the magic drained from me and stopped its relentless assault on my senses.

Finally, I felt heat creep back into me, and the stream of energy dissipated as the last of it left me. My breathing was heavy and ragged as I felt myself slumping to the floor, but strong hands captured my shoulders and hauled me back to my feet.

"What have you done?" a deep voice thrummed through me, bringing me completely back to my senses.

I opened my eyes slowly to find Tenebris staring into my eyes, his piercing stare worried yet angry.

"I don't know what happened," I choked out on a sob.

"You never told me you possessed magic," Tenebris seethed. "And yet you are angry with me for keeping my secrets when you had your own secrets."

I hated how my voice trembled as I shouted, "I didn't know!"

"How could you not have noticed a power that strong?" Tenebris asked through clenched teeth.

He shook me, rattling my teeth and wrenching another sob from my throat, and then released me suddenly as he blew out a long, ragged breath. He turned away from me and ran a hand through his dark hair as I looked around the hallway at my destruction.

Everyone stood frozen. Despite my weak efforts to control who the magic froze, every person and dragon in the hallway were nothing more than icy statues.

"The damage extends out into the throne room," Tenebris said quietly, regarding me with an empathetic look that caused my heart to flutter with fear. "I don't know how much further it goes from there."

My heart hammered against the inside of my chest as my breath came in shallow, uneven gasps. I did not even think about the repercussions of my actions. I simply reacted. Without warning, I darted to the frozen Hestia, punching at the ice surrounding her body with my bare hands.

I punched at the spot on her skirt where her pouch hung, hitting the ice repeatedly until my skin split and blood poured from my knuckles. I ignored the pain, concentrating only on getting through that wall of ice that kept the key to the scroll room from my hands.

"Raina, stop," I heard Tenebris say, his tone rising with warning. "If you shatter the priestess, you will kill her."

I did not care. Tenebris tried to pull me away, but a scream of rage escaped me, and I struggled out of his hold. I kept hitting the ice, and a small hole opened. The key pouch was right there.

"Raina, no!" Tenebris cried in a panic.

I knew he would try to pull me away again, so I turned suddenly and pushed as hard as possible. My sudden movements surprised him, so he was not prepared for the force of my push. He flew backward onto his ass, sliding on the ice covering the floor.

I turned back to my work and started hitting again, punching the ice until the hole I had opened grew big enough for me to stick a hand inside. Then I realized that the blood on my hands had not all come from me. I was not just punching through the ice, but through Hestia. Blood poured from her side where I had punched a hole through it.

I started to get sick, my stomach churning with nausea at what I had done, but I had no time for regrets. The pouch was no longer surrounded by a layer of ice. The blood had melted the ice around the hole I had punched into the High Priestess's side.

Pushing back the nausea that roiled in my gut, I reached inside the pouch, rummaging around it until my fingers met something cold, hard, and metal. I grasped it and pulled it out, breathing a sigh of relief when I spotted the ring full of keys.

I ran.

Faster than I had ever run in my life.

And I never slipped on the ice.

My body moved over the ice as gracefully as a deer through the woods.

I ran through the throne room, dodging frozen dragons and soldiers, until I came to the door on the opposite side. The door was open, and frozen soldiers poured into the hall beyond. My heart thudded hard against my chest as I squeezed past their frozen bodies, the cold of the ice seeping into my veins. I could hear Tenebris's thundering footsteps behind me as he tried to keep up with me, but he kept slipping on the ice-covered marble.

I remembered the scroll room was down a hidden corridor off the main hallway. I knew the way to the hidden door but had forgotten how to open it. No matter. I would get there and figure it out.

I got to the hidden door without complication. Despite slipping and sliding on the icy palace floor, Tenebris stayed right behind me. So when we got to the doorway, I did not have to remember how to open it.

Tenebris did it for me.

When the hidden doorway slid open after Tenebris pulled the sconce down, I ran through the doorway and noticed I was still running over ice.

My heart fell to my feet. I had been hoping that the ice had ended here, somehow convinced that it had not come this far.

I was wrong.

The ice covered the scroll room door. I grasped the keys in my hand and searched for the keyhole. I felt Tenebris's heat at my back and heard him let out a moan of pure dread. He stepped around me, plucking the keys from my paralyzed hands.

"Stop, Raina, before you get yourself killed. Some traps and spells have to be dealt with first."

I let out a ragged sound of pure frustration and stomped my foot, but I did not argue. I simply gave up my spot at the door for him and watched as he waved his arms, spouting out words I did not know. There was a loud crack and a flash of light, and then Tenebris got to work on the door.

He used one of the larger keys to chip a hole in the ice around the keyhole, then switched to the key that fit the lock. He unlocked the room and opened the door.

I could hear my blood pounding in my ears as it coursed through my veins. My breathing was heavy and ragged as I stepped in the door, and my heart stopped cold when I heard the wretchedly despairing sound that came from Tenebris's throat.

I did not want to look.

I had to look.

What had I done?

The nursery maid appointed to watch over the babes stood in the middle of the room, holding Baby Faith in her arms. Her face was frozen with a look of horrible dread as she stared past me toward the door. I could tell that Faith had been crying by her frozen, twisted features. The frozen baby in the handmaiden's icy arms cut through my soul as I turned my attention to the portable crib on the other side of the room.

I did not want to look.

My feet were leaden as I forced them to move toward the silent crib that sat only feet from me. I knew what I would see, but I could not turn away. I knew the vision of my son frozen inside that bed would haunt me for the rest of my days, however short that might be, but I had to see what I had done.

I put one foot in front of the other, moving slowly until I stood beside the bassinet. I peered inside, and the most desolate sound my ears had ever beheld escaped my throat.

My son was not only frozen, but something had shattered him into bits. The icy confines of his prison had torn him apart, and the only thing left was icy chunks of body pieces scattered on the crib mattress.

A hand here, a tiny toe there, and one chunk that held a lock of black baby hair suspended in time. There wasn't even any blood.

The scream that tore out of my throat was the last sound I heard before my soul shattered and my consciousness floated into nothingness.

Celia gasped as she came back to herself. She could still feel the scream of agony lodged in her throat, and she used it to her advantage as she heard Raina's first screams.

"Tenebris!" Celia yelled loud enough for the entire palace to hear. "Shift, Tenebris, now!"

She saw Warren out of the corner of her eye as he struggled with two soldiers that had broken past Maldia and Hestia. Maldia struggled in the grasp of a soldier who was laughing cruelly as he tried to pull her shirt up. Hestia screamed with rage as she was held back by another soldier. The soldier holding her back screamed in pain suddenly and released Hestia, and Hestia smiled maliciously as his hands caught fire.

"Holy fire burns all!" Hestia screamed as she lunged at the soldier still struggling with Maldia. She jerked the man away from her protégé and flung him across the room. He caught fire as he stumbled away, screaming in agony as he watched the flames fly from Hestia's hands and into his face.

Celia's gaze shot to the space where Chandra and Sage had been fighting. Chandra had fallen, her red hair strewn across the floor, the red color blending with the blood that seeped from a gash across her side. Sage stood over her protectively, but he faced five soldiers alone with only a dagger for defense.

Ice began to creep along the floor toward the soldiers' feet. It spread slowly around them until it hit the bottoms of their combat boots, then it began to creep slowly up their legs.

Celia looked at the dragons. The two larger dragons staggered on their feet as they shot the last of their magic reserves into the throne room. Green smoke drifted out of the open doorway, floating toward Epialos.

A humongous grass-green dragon with black horns charged through the door, blowing another puff of poisonous smoke toward Damaphur. The dragon slipped on an icy patch and went down, and the ice began to freeze the green dragon to the ground.

Tenebris's jade green dragon shot an electric blast of cleansing toward the smoke, surrounding it and clearing it much as he had done on the ledge the day Ethan had been born. The poisonous smoke dissipated inside the sterile bubble of Tenebris's electricity.

Raina screamed again, grabbing Celia's attention away from the fight. She noticed the icy puffs of smoke billowing around Raina's hands, and her entire body trembled as if she was cold.

"Tenebris, get over here now!" Celia screamed, desperation raising her tone to a high-pitched squeal.

Tenebris turned sharply at Celia's call. He did not question. He just shifted and ran toward Celia but stumbled when he heard Hestia's desperate cry. He turned to see soldiers surrounding the two holy women.

He noticed the ice creeping up their bodies, freezing them in place. The ice drew near Hestia and Maldia, and the two women frantically tried to steer clear of the creeping ice while simultaneously dodging the soldiers, still trying to take them down.

Raina screamed again.

"Hurry before it's too late!" Celia cried. "You have to stamp her, take her magic, and help her control it before she freezes everything!"

Tenebris turned toward another cry of desperation to find Sage, backed against the wall with Chandra in his arms, staring toward the soldiers that had surrounded them before. Now, they stood motionless, frozen inside icy cages of death while the hoarfrost crept along the floor toward Sage.

Tenebris turned back to Celia with a confused look. Warren fought two soldiers that had come too close to Celia's spot, where she still huddled against the wall. The ice had not reached him yet, but it was precariously close.

Celia's eyes had returned to normal, wide and frightened, staring at Raina in terror. Raina was trembling violently and screaming in pain. Tenebris felt it then, the power freezing Raina's blood and building to a crescendo as Raina's screams of fury and pain tore from her throat.

Celia turned her gaze to Tenebris helplessly. "She didn't know she had magic before!"

Tenebris did not question how Celia knew this and did not doubt the validity of her words. He simply accepted what Celia said and turned his gaze to Raina.

Tenebris rushed to her and slammed his hand into her chest. He knew he would hurt her, but there was no time to be gentle. He threw his energy into her with the force of a hurricane, and Raina's screams stuttered into quick gasps of pain.

Her eyes fluttered into the back of her head, and her body jerked violently. Celia caught her before she could hit the ground and held Raina in place while Tenebris pressed his palm over her heart.

Tenebris coiled his energy through Raina, searching for the source of that growing build of magic until he found its center. Shining brilliantly, so long hidden inside Raina's core, the magic was so strong that Tenebris wondered if he could stamp it. He grasped at it, knowing that he would have to pull much of it into himself and not knowing how it would affect him.

He could end up frozen right where he stood.

However, there was no choice.

Tenebris could feel the power and knew that if it escaped further than it already had, it would destroy everything within Raina's range. Tenebris had no way of knowing how far her range was. It could be only the hall and throne room, or it could be the entire planet. Tenebris did not know, and he would not take a chance.

He pulled at the magic's core until he had most of it inside of him, pooling in his arms and torso. The cold was instantaneous, freezing his breath in his lungs and searing a blazing trail through his hardening veins. Raina's power was so cold that it burned.

Tenebris gasped, straining to hold onto himself and not give in to the cold. His eyes fluttered into the back of their sockets as his muscles began to succumb to the freeze.

"Tenebris!" he heard Celia cry out, her tone flooded with apprehension.

The sound of her voice, so concerned for him when he had thought she hated him, brought Tenebris back into himself. He grasped Raina's magic flowing through him, reining it in and coiling it into his gut. He flung his own energy into it, stamping his signature into the magic and claiming it as half his own.

It worked.

The magic melded with Tenebris's signature, and he could feel the control slipping into his hands. He could also feel Raina coming alive inside him as if he had taken a piece of her soul along with the magic.

Confusion rocked through him. That had never happened to him before. However, he pushed the thought aside as Raina came to, and her emotions began to reel with panic.

"Calm down, Raina. I'm here. I can help you." Tenebris kept his voice low and soothing as Raina slowly focused her brilliant emerald gaze on his.

She swallowed hard, causing her throat to bob up and down as she took in Tenebris's worried look.

"What's happening?" she asked confusedly. "Why are you pressing my chest? It hurts."

"I am helping you control your magic," Tenebris answered. He eased the pressure of his hand a bit since he had a good hold on the magic now.

"I am so sorry if I hurt you, love. But right now, you need to help me, Raina. Can you do that?"

Raina's confused frown deepened. "Help you…with my magic? What magic?"

"The magic that you did not know you had," Tenebris answered in a smooth, calm voice. "I have it inside me now. That's why I have to touch you. I have a piece of you inside me. Can you feel that piece of yourself now?"

Raina's features screwed up in concentration for a moment, and then she widened her eyes at Tenebris in disbelief.

"I feel it," she whispered in a shocked tone. "I feel it inside you."

"Good. I need you to focus on that, concentrate on the magic. We need to use it to take down the soldiers and dragons. I will help you control it."

Raina's eyes widened further as she stared into Tenebris's eyes. "I don't know what to do, but I feel it building. It's almost full."

Tenebris smiled comfortingly and responded, "For now, you do not have to do anything but release it. Just focus on the feel of all that magic and energy flowing out of you and into me, and I will control it for you. Can you do that? Can you work with me?"

Raina did not answer aloud and only nodded her head. Tenebris wasted no time. He pressed his palm firmly against her chest again and forced her magic, stamped with his signature, back into her.

She winced but did not cry out as the sensation invaded her core, snapping back into her like a rubber band. Then, she did cry out in surprise as she felt Tenebris take control of the freezing magic coursing through her.

"Now, Raina! Let go! Let it all go!" Tenebris called.

And she did.

She succumbed to the pull of his energy and the steadiness of his control as he wielded her own magic, pulling it from her and directing it. She could feel the steady hum of his energy coursing through her and her own magic coalescing with that energy. She could sense the magic responding to his unspoken commands, and she focused, feeling the power obeying his words that guided her magic.

The bite of the ice caused her to cry out in pain, and she heard an answering cry from Tenebris as he wielded the ice inside her. It only hurt for an instant, however, and then it coursed through her, freezing the breath in her lungs and the blood in her veins.

It tore through her and then out of her, and she could feel the focus and intent from Tenebris as he guided it around the hall, through the throne room, and out into the massive courtyard beyond. The magic froze enemy soldiers and dragons as it flowed harmlessly past their party and the palace soldiers fighting for Solaris.

When it was over, Raina felt drained and spent. She would have fallen if not for Celia's support and Tenebris's arms wrapping protectively around her and hauling her to his chest, supporting her weight as he held her close.

Raina closed her eyes, drifting into unconsciousness as the last of her magic faded. Tenebris held her, picking her up and cradling her like a baby.

Celia released a great, relieved breath as she locked gazes with Tenebris. His hazel eyes were questioning.

"I had another vision," Celia told him as she pulled herself from the wall and gestured to his naked form. "You need to find some clothes."

Tenebris chuckled. "You have seen me naked after a shift before."

"Yes, but I am sure Raina will not find it pleasant to be held by a naked shifter when she comes to," Celia said, adding, "especially not you."

Tenebris's heart fell at hearing that tone. The hope that had risen inside him that he and Celia would be okay, that she would forgive him for his secrecy and lies, died with her harsh words.

Later.

He could deal with that later.

Right now, he had to find somewhere safe for Raina, so she could sleep and recharge her energy. His attention shifted to the scene around him, and he noticed Celia also assessing the damage.

Hestia was helping Maldia to her feet as Warren handed Maldia his untorn shirt, glancing discreetly away as she put it on over her torn one. He kicked at a chunk of ice on the floor, no doubt the remnants of some enemy soldier.

Hestia and Maldia exchanged knowing looks, then turned and got to work healing everyone who had been injured.

Sage kneeled beside Chandra, who was sitting up with a cloth held firmly to the wound on her side. They sat among several soldiers' icy, shattered remains as Sage tried to tend her wounds.

"Hestia, heal me first so I can help you and Maldia with everyone else," Chandra said as she struggled to stay upright with Sage's help.

Hestia went to her side, laying glowing hands on Chandra's wound.

"Well," Warren said as he used the tip of his forefinger to tip over another icy soldier statue, sending it falling to the ground to shatter against the marble palace floor. "I was attempting to release a holding spell, but this is much more effective."

Damaphur, who had shifted back to her original form, been healed by Maldia, and was being helped into a robe by the still-nude Epialos, skewered Warren with her icy gaze.

"Do you know why demon soldiers and angel soldiers were attacking my palace?" she asked lividly.

Warren shrugged. "I have no idea. Ask Epialos. They were mostly demon dragons."

Epialos narrowed his red eyes at the Spire Master. "Do not try to blame this on me. Both ranks are full of your spies, and both sides were fighting against us."

Damaphur nodded thanks to Epialos as she tied her robe around her and then turned her attention back to Warren. "Epialos is right. Where are your soldiers that you had stationed in the courtyard? And don't try to deny that you had them stationed there. You are not the only one with spies and sentries watching everywhere."

Epialos turned to Damaphur, his shimmering silvery gray skin shining with the sweat from battle. His naked form rippled with muscles as he moved gracefully and bent down to whisper in her ear.

"Do you have spies in my palace, too?" he asked huskily. "Do they tell you that I dream of you every night?"

Epialos braced for the scathing remark he expected and was delightedly surprised by the seductive chuckle that escaped Damaphur's luscious mouth. She made no retort, no scathing comment, and only threw him a sly look over her shoulder.

Epialos turned quickly before the queen could see how she affected him and moved further down the hallway toward the meeting room. His bag still sat beside his chair that his people had brought to him for the meeting. It contained the scroll along with a change of clothing. He had known that he would probably be shifting into his dragon form to fly home after the meeting, and he had prepared for it.

"Wait," Tenebris called to him as he strolled toward the bend in the hallway. "Aren't you coming with us to find out what happened?"

"You can all catch me up later," Epialos called back. "I have clothing in the meeting room, and we can all meet there to discuss the situation."

"I have my own room here," Tenebris said. "I will take Raina there and get dressed."

Maldia came over and placed a hand on Tenebris's arm. "I will go with Hestia to fetch the babies. We will bring them back to the nursery. That is where Ethan will be when Raina wakes up."

Tenebris patted her hand on his arm as he responded, "Thanks for…well…for not being angry with me."

Maldia's eyes crinkled in the corners, and a slight smile played on her lips as she said, "Oh, I am furious with you. But you saved us all, so I will be courteous until I can find it in me to forgive you."

Tenebris chuckled. "That's all I can ask for."

Maldia removed her hand from his arm as Tenebris moved away and carried the still-unconscious Raina across the throne room and toward the main foyer, where the grand staircase led up to the private chambers, one of which belonged to Tenebris.

Tenebris wondered as he carried Raina up the stairs how long the queen would allow him to keep his own room here at the palace now that she knew of his secret.

He could not dwell on that now.

He needed to get Raina to safety, get dressed, and then find out what was happening in Palace Solaris.

CHAPTER 21: REBELS WITHOUT A CAUSE

The room was silent as the ice that still shrouded Palace Solaris as the king and queen, Hestia, Chandra, Sage, Celia, and Warren sat at the table in the meeting room. Everyone looked to Warren, who sat at the head of the table in Damaphur's usual spot. Warren sat with his elbows on the table, steepling his fingers against his chin.

Damaphur sat beside Epialos, the royals sharing the other end of the table as they gazed across the expanse to Warren. Chandra sat next to Sage on one side of the table in the seats they had occupied before, except this time, Sage sat free of chains. Hestia sat beside Celia on the queen's right side.

Tenebris had not returned with Raina, and Maldia was still seeing to the babies. They had been found unharmed and safe from attack in the scroll room. The handmaiden had reported that she had not even known an attack was happening since the scroll room was also soundproof.

Tenebris broke the silence. "Sage, tell us what you found out."

Sage stood, glancing around the table at each of them as he reported, "Apparently, there are groups of rebels parading about. They meet in groups in the north and the south, and they consist of all different species, mostly shifters. They found out somehow about the meeting today, and they stormed the palace with their largest group, overwhelming Warren's soldiers with pure numbers. They would have overwhelmed us had they not underestimated our abilities."

"Did you find the traitor that ratted us out?" Warren asked, his tone icy.

"Yes, Grandmaster. I already suspected who it was. He was the one that reported to me on your behalf, telling me to go ahead with the mission. He has been dealt with, and the rebels that did not shatter are all tucked safely away in the prisoner's quarters in the basement."

Warren shook his head in disappointment. "So, we have been betrayed, as well as the king and queen."

It was not a question, but Sage answered anyway. "Yes, it appears so. I will interrogate the prisoners later to find out who else from the Spire is in league with the rebels."

"And how did you find all this out? What methods do you use for your interrogation?" Damaphur asked Sage with raised brows. "We do not condone violence here. You know that, Sage."

Warren answered before Sage could. "It is his talent. Sage is an Adivino."

Epialos's eyebrows rose in surprise. "Is he now? I have not seen that species in quite some time. I thought they were extinct."

"I am the last of my kind," Sage said with a deep, respectful bow to the king.

"I am sorry," Damaphur said, and Celia could tell from her tone that she meant it. "I know how lonely it can be to be the last of your species."

Sage nodded in respect to the queen with a soft smile. "Yes, but I find it useful at times to be unique, don't you?"

Damaphur chuckled and replied, "Absolutely, I do."

"What is an Adivino?" Celia asked, cutting into the conversation.

Warren answered, "They are extremely rare, like Tenebris, except their power is to control minds instead of magic."

Celia shuddered. "So Sage can control people's minds? Then why didn't he just stop the rebels from attacking?"

Warren folded his arms over his chest and answered in a condescending tone, "Because minds can be very dangerous to work with. It takes a will of steel, tons of concentration, and plenty of patience to take over a mind, much less a hundred minds."

"So what? He took over one of the soldier's minds and pulled all the information from him?" Celia asked disbelievingly.

Warren smiled deviously. "Precisely. Why do you think he is my best spy?"

Celia shuddered again and commented no further.

"What do the rebels want?" Epialos asked, his red eyes flashing with anger.

"They are rebelling against your ruling," Sage answered before Warren could. He stood from his seat, glancing quickly toward Chandra before turning to face the king and queen.

"The rebels believe that the war has gone on long enough. They want peace, and they want the planet to be joined together as one once more. They no longer want the angels and demons to be divided."

"How ironic is that?" Hestia said with a snort. "We had been discussing how to do that very thing in the meeting that they interrupted."

Damaphur leaned forward as she asked, "What did they hope to accomplish by storming Palace Solaris?"

"They were planning to assassinate the queen and take over the palace. The rebels believe that if they get rid of the king and queen and place new leaders in their stead, then peace will reign on the planet," Sage said, casting a sarcastic, sidelong glance toward Warren. "The Spire betrayers told them of the scroll. They were acting on that."

"Imagine that," Warren said with a chuckle. "I should have let the rebels do my job for me."

The king grunted in outrage and stood from his seat just as the queen gave a squeak of protest and rose. Warren only laughed derisively, holding up his hands in a calming gesture.

"I am only kidding. Please sit back down."

The king sat down slowly, and Damaphur followed, but not before shooting Warren a hostile glance.

Warren seemed unfazed as he said, "However, now you see my point about the importance of secrecy. Those rebels were willing to assassinate you both to attain peace without thought. They did not even consider finding another solution or having the scrolls read by a seer who could translate the words correctly."

Warren paused to glance at Celia before continuing, "Just imagine what would happen if the general public knew about the warnings of the Great Oracles. Imagine how many more assassination attempts there would be."

"At least Grandmaster Warren tries to find all the angles before acting," Sage said. "Warren hates killing, especially women and babies. It is the only reason you are all alive right now."

"Fine, we concede your point," Epialos said in a defeated tone. "We will keep the secrets of the scrolls and your organization. Now, what do you propose we do about the prophecy and the rebels?"

"Well, it threw them off their game when they saw you fighting together. I believe I even saw some of them retreat when they saw Damaphur shift and stand beside Epialos."

Damaphur frowned. "What are you saying, Grandmaster?"

"I am saying," Warren said impatiently. "If you show a united front, the rebel forces may disperse. Hell, they might even come forward and help when they learn that you want the same things. An even better scenario would be you two joining actually works, and the war ends."

Epialos looked beside him to the queen, who sat regal and straight-backed beside him. "What do you say, your majesty? Can we put our differences aside and work together for a change?"

Damaphur stiffened out of habit, the former thoughts and emotions assailing her mind. Epialos was dangerous for Damaphur, and not in the way everyone assumed. Epialos was dangerous for Damaphur's heart. Was her heart worth more than her kingdom?

Her gaze slanted sideways, and she stared at Epialos out of the corner of her eye. His black hair hung down his forehead, covering his thick eyebrows. His ruby-red eyes gleamed with light, making Damaphur's heart flutter. The silvery sheen to his gray skin caused him to shine with some inner light, and the bulging muscles dancing under that skin caused the shine to shimmer as he moved.

The strong jawline gave an edge of ruggedness to the planes of his face, but the straight nose and full lips lent a bit of sensuality to his handsomeness. Damaphur sucked in a breath as she watched his tongue dart from his mouth and graze across his bottom lip. An automatic gesture, but Damaphur found her stomach fluttering with desire.

Could she do it? Could she maintain a relationship with Epialos to unite the North and South? She could, but she knew that she would lose her heart in the process. Could she trust Epialos to take care of her heart?

No.

She did not trust the demon king that much, but what other choice did she have? Her kingdom and her people were worth more to her than her heart.

She glanced around the table and met the steely gaze of Grandmaster Warren. She now knew how influential and far-reaching the Wizard's Spire was and the lengths its Grandmaster would go to save the planet. For that reason alone, Damaphur had better find a way to work with the king and protect her heart, or else the Grandmaster would find a way to get rid of them both.

"It is certainly better than the alternative," she thought as she stared into Warren's glowing amber eyes.

Tenebris sighed and ran a hand through his dark locks as he gazed down at Raina's black tresses strewn across his pillow. Her peaceful, sleeping face was turned toward him, and he watched as her eyelids fluttered in her sleep. The tiny shadows cast by her dark lashes atop her cherry-colored cheeks gave her an alluring look. Her luscious pink lips puckered, accentuating the dimple in her right cheek.

Tenebris stared down at her with longing. He would give anything to turn back the clock, find her in Asgorath, and take her from the streets himself. But alas, he did not have the gift of time travel.

No one did.

That he knew of.

He sighed once more and turned to his dresser to find clothes. He opened the top drawer for underwear and then froze with the drawer half open. The sound of Raina's breathing had changed, and Tenebris knew she was waking up.

He stiffened, not knowing what her reaction would be to awaken in his bed with him standing there naked. He swallowed hard and slowly turned to face her as he heard her breath hitch on a gasp.

Her shining emerald eyes were wide, filled with fear, and darting rapidly around the room. Her slender hand was clasped around her throat like she had swallowed something harsh. Her breasts rose and fell as her breathing sped up, and her heart beat so hard that Tenebris could hear it, thumping against her chest, with his enhanced dragon hearing.

Her eyes landed on his, and he stiffened even more as the emerald color of Raina's eyes darkened with anger.

"Where am I?" she rasped angrily, her voice rough and scratchy from screaming.

Tenebris swallowed hard. "You're in my room, in Palace Solaris. Do you not remember what happened before you passed out?"

Raina's eyes darted around the room as the nervous tension rose. "Where is Ethan?"

"Ethan is safe with Maldia," Tenebris answered and then asked again, "Do you remember what happened?"

Tenebris saw relief fill her eyes when she heard of Ethan's safety, but the anger stayed. Her gaze remained fixed on him, and his muscles tightened so forcefully that he trembled under her scrutiny.

"What did you do to me?" Raina asked, her voice still raspy.

Tenebris took in a deep breath and let it out slowly before answering. "I took over your magic. I stamped it with my signature so I could help you control it. This is what I do, Raina. This is my job."

The anger in her eyes leaked away, replaced by uncertainty and a bit of fear. Her throat bobbed as she swallowed and looked away from him, her cheeks turning pink with heat.

"Why are you still naked?" she asked, and Tenebris's tightness eased at the uncertainty in her tone.

He smiled rakishly as he answered, "I was just about to get dressed right before you awoke."

"Please, don't let me stop you," she said, hating that her voice trembled with every word.

Tenebris's smile grew. She still wanted him. He could hear it in her tone, see it in the twinkle in her emerald gaze, feel it in his soul…feel it…he could still feel her!

"Raina," he breathed out her name as her emotions swirled through his gut.

Her gaze flew to his. She asked again, whispering, "What did you do to me?"

Tenebris shook his head as he stepped closer and answered, "I did not do this. I don't know how or why this is happening. It has never happened before."

She held up a hand to ward him off as she responded, "Don't…don't come any closer."

"Raina," Tenebris said softly. "I am not going to hurt you."

Raina shot up, scooting to the edge of the bed and clutching the covers to her chest as she yelled, "You already have hurt me, Tenebris….I mean…I thought I knew you. I thought you had helped me like Celia has helped me, but you only did it for your own personal gain. You were going to kill me and my child!"

"But I didn't," Tenebris shot back, his voice raising an octave as he ranted. "I didn't because I felt something for you. From the moment I saw you, I felt it. I would never have been able to hurt you!"

"Lies! All lies! You are the same as any other man, conniving and scheming to get what you want! You are nothing but a liar!"

"I am not lying, Raina! Can you not feel it? Can you not feel me inside you like I feel you? I don't know how this happened or why, but can't you just try to feel me? Then you would know I am not lying about what I feel for you."

Tenebris's voice had gone low and deep by the time he had reached the end of his speech, and his tone was pleading. He took one more step toward her with his hand extended out to her in a silent plea.

Raina hissed and held her hand up in a stopping gesture. "No. I said don't come near me."

Tenebris stopped and closed his eyes, reaching into his center and down into that spot where a piece of Raina shone through the darkness of his soul. He could feel her pain, but beneath it all, he felt her desire for him. She wanted him to take her into his arms and kiss her senselessly, but her pain and anger toward him prevented her from asking.

"I can feel you, Raina," he whispered, keeping his eyes tightly shut. "Can't you feel me?"

Silence fell for a heartbeat as Tenebris poured out his soul to that bond he felt inside. He poured all the longing, all the want, and all the regret at keeping her and everyone he loved in the dark about his true nature. He poured it all in there, pushing it outwards toward Raina, begging her to feel what he felt and understand.

"I feel you," Raina whispered back.

"Then you know," Tenebris replied.

"Yes, I know."

There was a pause, and Tenebris almost opened his eyes. But before he could, Raina's soft voice filled the space between them.

"I know how sorry you are, how much you regret keeping things from everyone."

"Yes," Tenebris replied, barely a whisper. He heard the bed sheets rustling as Raina moved atop them, but he dared not open his eyes.

"I know how much you love Celia and want nothing but the best for her, and that is why you don't want her with Warren. You don't want her to have that kind of life where she must hide everything she is. You want her to continue working for Solaris, where she is free to make her own decisions."

"Yes," Tenebris whispered again, swallowing the lump that had formed in his throat.

The sound of Raina shifting on the bed had Tenebris wanting to open his eyes, but he was afraid of what he would see on her face.

"I know how much you hate what you have to do sometimes, but you will do it to protect the planet and those you love."

Tenebris only nodded this time, holding his eyes shut. He heard her shift again and wondered what she could be doing that required that much movement.

"I know how much you wanted me when you first saw me, how much you still want me, how much you wish you could just take me and steal me away from this life."

Tenebris nodded again as his whole body shuddered with the release of tension from his muscles. He heard the rustling of his sheets one more time.

"Open your eyes, Tenebris," Raina whispered.

Tenebris opened his eyes, and his entire world shifted when he saw what she had been doing on his bed.

CHAPTER 22: FIRE AND ICE

"**W**hat is taking Tenebris so long?" Celia asked as Damaphur announced they should take a break from deliberations to have dinner.

"I am sure he is just watching over Raina," Damaphur said with a comforting smile. "She would be frightened if she woke up alone."

"Yes, I guess you are right," Celia sighed. "I will go up and ask if he would like me to bring him a plate when dinner is ready."

"I am sure he would appreciate that," Damaphur said with a smile.

Celia did not care whether Tenebris would appreciate the gesture or not. She was still angry at him for keeping such enormous secrets from her. She understood his need for secrecy now that it had been explained. And she knew her life would have been much different without his influence. However, it would be hard for her to ever trust him again.

Celia thought back to the battle, the fear and dread she had felt at seeing her friends die, seeing Tenebris dead. She could not stay mad at him forever. She would have to forgive him eventually, but he would have to work at earning her trust back.

Not now, however. She wanted to be mad at him for a while longer, even though she knew it was childish of her. But he had hurt her, and she wanted him to hurt like she hurt. Childish or not, she was not ready to forgive him now.

She did need to speak with him alone, whether she was ready to forgive him or not.

She needed to ask Tenebris if he could stamp her with his signature like he had Raina. Celia's powers were changing, growing stronger,

and she did not know how to handle it. The visions were coming at
the most inopportune times, and Celia needed to learn how to control
them.

She would speak with him about that, ask him to stamp her with his
signature, and then she would deal with the rest later. She loved him,
and she always would. He had taken care of her when no one else
wanted her, so she was not about to abandon him now when he felt no
one wanted him. She would forgive him.

She just wanted him to suffer a bit longer first.

The ice flowed through Tenebris's veins, freezing him with a chill
so cold that it burned. He could feel her energy returning, her magic
restoring inside her core. She did not seem to be affected by it,
though.

She lay on his bed naked, her raven hair flowing out around her
head like some dark, avenging halo. Her emerald eyes flashed with a
sultry desire that had Tenebris's blood boiling to a molten heat,
melting the ice that flowed from Raina's magic.

Her breasts rose and fell with her breathing; the nipples peaked
from exposure. Tenebris's eyes roamed down the flat planes of her
stomach, dipped down to the dark sprinkling of hair that hid her
mound, and slid down her long shapely legs to her dainty feet and toes.

He swallowed hard as his gaze moved back up to her face, and his
member stiffened as she pouted her lips and said in a sultry tone,
"Well, what are you waiting for? Come and take what you want."

She didn't have to tell him twice.

He closed the distance between them and covered her naked body
with his own. Her arms went around his neck instantly, and her legs
went around his waist as his weight fell on top of her, pinning her
under him as she sank into the mattress.

He balanced his upper body on his elbows to grasp a handful of
those silky tresses and capture her mouth with his. He ravished her
with lips, teeth, and tongue. There was no gentleness, just savage, raw

heat from wanting her so much and the cold, new magic pumping through them both.

Fire and ice met in an unrestrained passion, gripping them both in its embrace. Heat pooled in his core as ice pumped through her veins, burning them both with a need so raw that there was no room for slow and gentle. He had already been hard for her before he collapsed on top of her, and her body had been wet for him before she had even undressed while his eyes had been closed.

She writhed underneath him, grinding herself against his hardness as her legs tightened around him. Tenebris abandoned the ravishing of her mouth to nip and kiss his way down her throat. Raina threw her head back, giving him full access to her neck and breasts as small moans escaped her.

The sound of her passionate little noises drew an answering growl of need from Tenebris as he moved his hips in time with hers, brushing his hardness against her as he positioned himself to enter her icy depths with his fiery member.

Raina breathed his name as he positioned his head at her entrance and bore down, barely piercing her opening before a loud banging on his bedroom door caused him to flinch and draw away from the icy heat of Raina's core.

A growl of disappointment and fury rang through the room as he rolled off the bed and came to his feet, and Raina cried out in protest.

"Ignore them, and maybe they'll go away," she whined as she held her arms out for Tenebris, gesturing for him to return to her arms.

"Tenebris, open the door! I know you're in there. I want to talk to you," Celia's tone was firm and loud, and Tenebris groaned in frustrated impatience.

"She will not go away unless I answer her," he said to Raina as he walked over to his dresser and began pulling open the drawers.

"Don't think you are off the hook with me, Tenebris," Raina said in a sultry tone as she rose from the bed and began searching the floor for her clothes. "We will continue this discussion later."

Tenebris turned in the middle of pulling on his pants and responded, "I look forward to it, Lady Raina."

"Tenebris, if you don't open this door…"

Tenebris interrupted her before she could say more. "I am coming, Celia. I'm getting dressed, dammit."

"You have had plenty of time to get dressed. What have you been doing…"

Her voice cut off abruptly for a heartbeat, and then she cursed. Her voice was lower, and her tone remorseful as she asked, "I interrupted something, didn't I?"

Tenebris had dressed and made it to the door. He opened it before answering, "Yes, you did."

Raina came up behind Tenebris, now fully dressed, with her hands on her hips. "Don't be an ass, Tenebris."

"Sorry," Celia mumbled under her breath, darting her gaze between Tenebris and Raina. "I wanted to come up and speak with Tenebris before dinner."

"Dinner? Is the meeting over so soon? What happened?" Tenebris asked.

"No, no," Celia answered. "We are just taking a break. There is still much to discuss."

"Catch us up," Tenebris said as he gestured for Celia to enter.

"Okay," Celia said uncertainly as she came into the room and sat on the edge of the bed, noticing how the blankets were pushed aside, and the sheets were disheveled.

"Are you sure?" Celia asked, gesturing toward the bed. "We can discuss this later."

Raina smiled as she came and sat beside Celia, patting her hand as Raina answered, "No, Celia. It's fine. Tenebris and I can finish our…um…discussion later."

"Yes," said Tenebris, shooting Raina a heated glance. "We will most certainly finish it."

Celia cleared her throat. "Okay then. I will catch you up on everything."

Celia told them about her vision first. She spared no detail, not even the part with the scroll room and the babies. Raina shuddered as she listened, thanking the Goddess that Tenebris had succeeded in reigning in her magic and helping her control the blast of icy destruction. Then a thought occurred to her, and she asked her question after Celia had finished speaking.

"I wonder why Tenebris did not get caught in my uncontrolled blast like everyone else in your vision?"

Tenebris shrugged. "I am immune to most elemental magic, which is yet another of my odd abilities. Immunity is not unique to me, but it is extremely rare. I am more concerned about what went wrong with the signature stamp. It has never failed me before."

Celia's frown deepened. "But it did not fail. What do you mean?"

"When Tenebris took control of my magic," Raina answered. "Something caused him to feel not only my magic but my emotions as well, and vice versa."

Celia's brows shot up. "You mean you can feel Tenebris's emotions?"

Raina nodded and said, "Yep, and I can read his thoughts too when he opens his mind to me. He can do the same with me."

Celia stared in open-mouthed disbelief momentarily before turning to Raina with a smirk. "I was all set to be the understanding stepdaughter, but now I'm just jealous. I would love to pick his brain."

Celia smiled and winked at Raina, causing her to laugh as she responded, "Trust me, it isn't pretty up there."

"Hey!" Tenebris exclaimed in mock indignation, and both women laughed.

Celia's laughter died as she turned to Tenebris and asked, "Seriously, what do you think happened with the stamp?"

Tenebris shrugged. "The only thing I can think of that differs from any other magic I have stamped is the age of the magic bearer. I work with kids. Raina is the first adult I have stamped."

"If that is the case, the effect will disappear when you remove your signature, right?" Celia asked.

Tenebris nodded and answered, "In theory, yes."

"And if it doesn't go away?" Raina asked.

Tenebris gave her a look that was a mixture of defiance and desire as he answered, "Then we will have to learn to live with each other. I am certainly up for the challenge."

Raina rolled her eyes. "I guess I won't have a choice, will I?"

Her tone was humorous, and she gave Tenebris a wink before turning back to Celia. "Tell us about the meeting, Celia."

"I will, but first, I would like to speak more on this subject," Celia said, then turned to Tenebris. "That was why I wanted to come up here and speak with you. I wanted to ask if you would stamp my magic with your signature like you did Raina's."

Tenebris raised his eyebrows in surprise. "Why would you want me to do that?"

"Tenebris, I know you have noticed how my magic is changing. You were busy fighting, so perhaps you didn't see, but my visions rendered me powerless in the middle of the fight. I need better control than that before something horrible happens."

Tenebris's amber gaze lit with understanding as he replied, "So that is why you went limp in my arms. Warren took you so I could go help with the fight."

Celia shrugged. "Which is yet another reason. I do not want to be responsible for someone else being rendered useless just because I am.

"I need to learn how to control that and see the vision while being fully aware. You know, like how I can see the threads, sort through them, and see what they show me without losing my grip on reality.

"Also, I may have accidentally brought on the vision myself. I was searching the strands, trying to find one that would lead to our victory so I could tell everyone which path to take, and that is when the vision took me.

"I would like to learn to control that as well. It would be helpful to see visions when I needed to and not when the vision decided to take me. I want control over my power, not the other way around."

Tenebris nodded. "I agree. If your magic is growing more powerful, you must learn to control it. When do you want to do this?"

Celia shifted uneasily on the bed as she answered, "Well, I am not so sure now. I would ask you to do it immediately, but maybe we should wait until we see how it affects Raina."

Tenebris frowned. "Are you sure? What if the visions get you into trouble again?"

Celia opened her mouth to answer but was interrupted by Tenebris's bedroom door flying open. It slammed against the wall so forcefully that Celia thought it would be flung off its hinges.

Everyone's eyes flew toward the sound to find Warren standing in the doorway. His massive presence radiated anger as he stalked into the room. Celia's heart thundered at the furious glare he shot her way. His amber eyes darkened to molten gold, his hands clenched into fists at his side, and his muscular chest rose and fell rapidly with every fuming breath.

"Let him stamp you, Celia," Warren seethed. "They could have killed you out there, and I was taken out of the fight because I had to protect you."

Celia shot to her feet, raising her chin in defiance. "Were you listening to our conversation outside the door?"

"So what if I was?" Warren shot back. "At least it prevented you from making a big mistake and possibly getting me killed in the future."

Celia's hands clenched into fists at her sides as she seethed in fury. "No one asked you to save me. You could have just left me."

Dread shot through every nerve in her body as the large Grandmaster stalked ever closer to her, but she would not give him the satisfaction of seeing her fear.

She stood her ground as he seethed into her face, "I would never do that, Celia. I would die first. Now, let Tenebris stamp you."

"Who do you think you are? You can't tell me what to do," Celia shot back. He leaned into her even closer, his face mere inches from hers.

She stood with the backs of her knees touching the bed, staring at him in defiant anger.

"I am the Grandmaster…," Warren started, but Celia did not allow him to finish.

"You are not my grandmaster," she interrupted furiously. "I am not a member of your fucking secret society."

Tenebris coughed, which sounded suspiciously like a disguised laugh, as he grabbed Raina's hand and pulled her away from the faced-off couple.

"Come, Raina. Let us leave these two alone before we get caught in the crossfire," Tenebris said as he led her to the door.

"Good idea," Warren said through gritted teeth, never losing eye contact with Celia. "I need to teach my seer better manners."

Tenebris stopped at the open door and turned back with a worried frown. "With all due respect, Grandmaster, if something happens to Celia, we will have a problem."

Warren turned his furious stare on Tenebris, but Tenebris caught the slight tilt of his lip and cleverly hidden wink as he responded, "Go, Tenebris, but do not go far. She will be getting that stamp."

Tenebris paused, opened his mouth to say something, but only gave a respectful nod before pulling Raina through the door and shutting it behind them.

Warren turned back to Celia, but Celia spoke before Warren could.

"I am not your seer," she said in a low, seething tone.

Warren moved even closer to her, so close that her breasts were mere inches from touching his upper stomach, forcing her to raise her head to look at him.

"You will be," Warren drawled, almost whispering. "One way or another, I will make you mine."

Celia could not move back. The backs of her knees were pressed against the mattress, effectively trapping Celia between the bed and the Grandmaster. She would have to shove him back physically if she wanted to escape his presence.

Her throat bobbed as she swallowed her fear at his nearness. The fire swimming through her veins and heat coursing through her center told Celia that it was not only fear that had Warren's nearness causing her heart to pound and her breathing to quicken.

She took a deep breath and tamped down her swelling emotions as she glowered at Warren and said, "I will never be yours."

Warren chuckled darkly as he reached up and grasped Celia's chin between his thumb and forefinger. Celia flinched at his touch, but Warren's hold was surprisingly gentle.

His hot breath fanned across her large lips as he said softly, "We shall see, won't we?"

Celia was about to respond and jerk back from his touch, but Warren moved so quickly that Celia had no time to react. His lips were on hers, and Celia was so stunned with shock and desire that she could not do anything but sink into the sensation of Warren's kiss.

The taste of the Grandmaster's lips sent coils of desire flowing through Celia's core. Her breath hitched at the electricity shooting through her veins and the surprising softness of his beard grazing her nose. He released his hold on her chin to trail his hand around to the back of her head, and his other arm snaked around her waist.

He pulled her closer to his body, crushing her softness against his muscled form. Celia's center pulsed with need as Warren deepened the kiss, thrusting his tongue into her mouth, tasting her heat and desire.

Warren was frozen in the moment. He had not even meant to kiss her, but his body had instinctively reacted. One moment, he was staring into those nearly black eyes that seemed to see straight into his soul, thinking how lovely it would be to throw her onto that bed and pound himself into her thick lusciousness. The next moment, he was grasping her chin, bending down as he breathed in her spicy scent, and then his mouth was on hers.

Her succulently sweet lips filled Warren with her taste, shooting an icy wave of want through his veins. Her soft gasp drove him into ecstasy, and he wrapped his arm around her ample waist to pull her closer. The taste and scent of her drove him mad with the need to be inside of her, and he felt his member harden against her softness.

Celia gasped as she felt him harden against her, and the sudden urge to have that hardness fill her scared her. She wanted him with an intensity so strong that it broke her away from the lust-filled haze she had fallen into when his lips had touched hers. She stiffened in Warren's embrace, raising her hands to push at his chest.

Warren felt Celia's resistance, her muscles stiffening and her hands pushing against his body. What was he doing? Had he not admonished himself recently against getting close to the seer? He could endanger his entire organization if he did not control himself.

He released her suddenly, his body growing icy cold without her heat pressed against him. His breathing was ragged, and his heart threatened to beat out of his chest. He closed his eyes for a moment, gathering his shredded self-control. When he opened them, Celia's dark gaze met his, and he narrowed his eyes.

"Get the stamp, Celia. No more arguments," he said, his tone firm yet soft. He took a deep breath, turned, and left the room before Celia could answer, slamming the door behind him.

CHAPTER 23: THE BEGINNING OF

THE END

Celia stared at the closed door for a long time, trying to regain control of her shattered emotions. She could not believe that he had kissed her, and she could not believe that she had kissed him back. Celia could not fathom why her self-control was non-existent when Warren was around.

She heard Warren's words floating around in her mind. *"One way or another, I will make you mine."*

She was dangerously close to giving in to the Grandmaster in any way he would have her. The intensity of her desire for him scared her, but she could no longer deny it. She wanted him.

He was also right, as much as she hated to admit it. She needed to let Tenebris stamp her with his signature as soon as possible. She could not afford to lose control of her magic. The Palace depended on her, along with so many others that came to Celia regularly for readings. She could not let everyone down.

Celia took a deep breath and was about to search for Tenebris when he came striding through the door. He looked at Celia questioningly as he strode toward her.

"Are you alright?" he asked. He reached for her, grasping her shoulders and looking her up and down with concern.

Celia shook him off but smiled comfortingly. "I am fine. Warren is right, though. I cannot afford to lose control again."

Tenebris chuckled. "You handle Warren better than anyone I have seen.

Are you sure you don't want to join us if not for anything more than to control the Grandmaster?"

Celia shot Tenebris a glare that only made Tenebris chuckle again and shake his head.

"Seriously, Celia, just think about it. Listen to him and really consider what he says. I never wanted you mixed up in all this. That was another reason I kept you in the dark. But, now I know you can handle yourself against Warren, and I believe this organization would benefit from having a seer like you."

With a defeated tone, Celia blew a frustrated breath and answered, "There is too much to consider, Tenebris. I am loyal to my queen. I have friends here. I have my own place and my shop…"

"Alright, alright," Tenebris interrupted. "We can talk about it later."

Celia smiled with relief and said, "Good. For now, though, I really think you need to stamp my magic, if only until you can help me determine what's wrong with it."

"I can do that," Tenebris said, returning her smile. "And I can do it gently. I had to force it with Raina, and I don't like doing that."

"What do you want me to do?" Celia asked.

Tenebris nodded toward the bed. "Lie down and relax. Just close your eyes and clear your mind."

Celia did as Tenebris said, taking a deep calming breath and clearing her mind of all thoughts. She closed her eyes, blocking out the sight of Tenebris leaning over her with a comforting smile. It startled her when she felt his hand cover her chest over her heart.

"Relax," Tenebris said. "It doesn't hurt unless I have to force it."

Celia swallowed and took another calming breath, relaxing her tensed muscles and sinking into the soft mattress. Tenebris's hand pressed more firmly against her chest, and she felt heat radiating from the touch. It filled her chest, ran down her arms and torso, and spread through her legs.

The heat changed to tingling as it swirled around in her body and then traveled back up to her chest. It coalesced around where Tenebris's hand still rested atop her chest. The tingling sensation pulled out of her suddenly, shooting up into Tenebris's hand and leaving Celia feeling cold and empty.

A small sob escaped Celia's throat at the intense loneliness and hopelessness she felt without her magic inside her. Is this how people without magic felt all the time? How could they deal with it? Celia opened her mouth, ready to beg Tenebris to stop, when the power snapped back into her so suddenly that her body jerked with the force.

It had not hurt. It simply crashed back into her like a wave crashing onto the shore of a beach, and then settled back into her core where her power lived. It felt different now somehow, warmer, more alive than before.

Curiously, she poked at it, pulled it forth, and played with it. It seemed different, yet it was the same. The future strands still played through her head, silently streaming through the possibilities, waiting for their chance to show Celia what they knew. The energy still coalesced in her core, ready to assist if Celia needed to pull a card and determine its meaning or sit and stare at pictures in her crystal ball.

It all still seemed normal, yet something had changed. Celia could not tell what it was, but she felt it. She opened her eyes to find Tenebris smiling above her.

"How do you feel?" he asked.

Celia frowned. "The same, yet different, if that makes sense."

Tenebris nodded. "It does. That's normal. You will feel the difference if I take over your magic and help you use it."

"Let's just hope that doesn't happen in the near future," Celia said as she sat up.

"I agree," said Tenebris. "It isn't fun to take control of someone else's magic in the middle of a vicious battle."

"You did fine with Raina," Celia said. She swung her legs over the side of the bed and began to stand up but sat back down suddenly as a wave of dizziness hit her.

"Woah, take it easy," Tenebris said as he reached out a hand to steady her. "You may want to just sit for a minute before trying to move about."

Celia placed a hand over her eyes, willing the spinning to stop as she leaned back against the headboard of the bed. "What the hell was that?"

"It's your magic," Tenebris explained. "It will just take it a moment to settle back in, that's all."

Celia sat still, waiting for the bought of dizziness to subside. Tenebris's hand was a comforting weight on her shoulder. After a moment, Tenebris released Celia's shoulder and carefully sat on the bed at Celia's feet.

"I have never done that before, what I did with Raina," Tenebris said, his voice strained as if he didn't want to say the words. "I just acted out of instinct without even thinking about it. I heard her screaming, heard you shouting for me to take her magic. Hell, I didn't even know she had any magic."

"Neither did I," Celia said as she slowly, oh so slowly, sat back up on the side of the bed. "I'm just glad the vision released me in time to stop what I saw."

Tenebris's eyes were tortured when Celia opened her eyes again and stared into his. "I saw it too. When I took your magic, I saw the remnants of the last vision floating around in your head."

Celia touched his cheek gently with her hand. "Oh, Tenebris. I'm sorry you had to see that."

"What if it doesn't next time?" Tenebris said, his tone matching the look in his eyes.

"What?" Celia asked confusedly.

"What if the vision doesn't release you in time to stop what it shows you?"

"Then you will be there to help me come out of it," Celia said softly. "That's the entire reason we did this. You have part control of my magic now."

Tenebris did not answer and only stared at Celia with an arduous expression. Celia sighed at the doubt in Tenebris's eyes. She squeezed her eyes shut for a second and opened them again. Her gaze softened as she looked upon the person who had raised her, taught her everything she knew, and helped her grasp control of her magic when it first manifested.

He stood there staring at her with his bright blue gaze, his look sad and tortured. Celia could feel the remorse and regret radiating from him as he slowly got up from the foot of the bed.

"I think we should go downstairs and join everyone for dinner," Tenebris said. He moved closer to Celia and held out a hand to help her from the bed.

"I'm still furious with you, Tenebris," Celia said, but her tone was soft. "It will be hard for me to trust you again, but I love you."

Tenebris smiled, but it did not reach his eyes. "I love you, too, Celia."

"And I forgive you," she added.

This time, the smile reached his eyes as Celia took Tenebris's offered hand, allowed him to help her from the bed, and together they went downstairs to dinner.

They left Damaphur alone with Epialos as everyone went to clean up and prepare for dinner. She rose from her seat and made to leave for the door, but Epialos stood and blocked her way. He stared down at her with his ruby eyes aglow.

"Are you going to stop resisting me now?" he asked, his voice a low, husky whisper.

Damaphur returned his sultry gaze with an icy one of her own. "Is that what you think I have been doing all this time?"

"Is it not?" Epialos returned with a cocky quirk of one eyebrow.

"No," Damaphur said firmly, without an inch of humor in her tone. "There was a reason behind my hesitation."

"Oh, yes," Epialos said as he moved closer to the queen, closing the distance between them. "You are afraid that my people will not accept you. I heard your speech, Damaphur, and I told you that I will give them no choice."

"I'm not talking about that part," Damaphur said softly as she held his gaze.

The king's smug look vanished. "Damaphur…"

Her name was a whisper on his tongue as his red eyes flared with a light Damaphur had never seen before. She swallowed hard as he leaned closer, but she did not back down or flinch away.

"Did you ever stop to think that your fear is moot because I am already in love with you?"

His breath brushed against her lips as he continued to speak, sending sparks of electric desire coursing through her.

"Did you ever consider that I tease you mercilessly because I want you so badly?"

His hands grasped either side of her face as she leaned into him. Her heart danced with every word he uttered.

"Don't you know that you complete me? Don't you understand that you are the light in my darkness?"

He closed the distance faster than Damaphur could react, and his mouth was suddenly on hers. She did not flinch or pull away. Instead, her arms snaked around his waist as she pulled herself closer, accepting his kiss as her body begged for more. A seductive growl issued from his mouth as he cradled her face in his large hands and deepened the kiss.

She opened to him, flicking her tongue against his as it snaked inside her mouth, and the growl trailing from Epialos's throat deepened to a husky moan of pleasure. An answering moan of desire coalesced with the sound of his as Damaphur pressed herself more firmly against Epialos's rock-hard body. His hands left her face to travel down her neck, across her shoulders, down her arms, and finally around her waist.

He lifted the queen up with only his hands, and she let go of his waist to wrap her arms around his neck while she wrapped her legs around his waist.

Epialos began carrying her toward the door and only broke the kiss long enough to ask, "Where?"

"The small door on the left, right before the bend in the hallway," she answered against his lips. "It's my private office."

He said no more as he recaptured her lips with his, carrying her as he kissed her down the hallway and toward the door. Suspiciously, there were no guards, and no one disturbed them as they slid inside the door, and Epialos locked it behind them.

Sage and Chandra stepped around from behind the bend in the hallway, smiling knowingly. Sage nudged Chandra teasingly with an elbow.

"You owe me fifty pense," he said humorously. "I knew I should have raised the stakes."

Chandra scoffed. "Hold that bet. We still have to see if the queen takes you back as her advisor. If she doesn't, then we are even."

Sage raised an eyebrow as he said, "And just what will you do with me if the queen does not take me back?"

Chandra turned to look at Sage, raking her eyes up and down his body. His tall, thin frame was deceiving under the clothing he now wore, just as it had always been when he had been Damaphur's most trusted advisor.

His clothes had hidden the muscle tone Chandra had discovered underneath when she stripped him of his clothing in the dungeon room. She had always admired the contrast of his white hair against the dark gold of his skin and the way his deep blue eyes stood out against the light and dark contrast. She had often scanned the delicate features of his angelic face and thought him too handsome for words.

Now, she knew his body's cut and toned muscles and thought sexy instead of handsome.

Sage noticed her hesitation in answering his question and how her eyes scanned his features. He smirked as her eyes returned to his face, giving her a wink to let her know that he had noticed her appraisal of him.

"Like what you see, captain?" he asked swaggeringly.

Chandra's tone matched his as she replied, "Throw you in the dungeon again and whip you until you beg for mercy."

Sage jerked back in surprised confusion. "What?"

Chandra chuckled. "You asked what I would do with you if Damaphur did not take you back. That is what I would do."

Sage's visage became hungry and dark as he responded, "Then let us hope that she doesn't take me back."

Chandra's tone was husky as she said, "How about a preview?"

Sage's growl filled the hallway before he answered, "Find guards to cover the king and queen, and then take me to the dungeon."

Chandra smiled seductively and said, "Only if I get to handle the whip first."

Sage chuckled. "Baby, you can handle the whip all you want."

Damaphur's skin felt as if it were on fire as Epialos trailed kisses down her body. It had not taken long for her to lose her clothing after Epialos had swept everything off the top of Damaphur's desk and laid her down on its surface. He had taken his time with the exploration of her body, though.

He had ravished her mouth with teeth and tongue until her breathing came in panting breaths, and her heart raced in her chest. Coils of desire and longing swam through her veins as Epialos's kisses trailed down her face, lingering on the sensitive spot under her ear. His hands swept up her sides and stopped teasingly close beside her exposed breasts.

Damaphur's back arched as her body begged for more, which Epialos gladly gave. His kisses moved down to the tops of her breasts, and his hands came around to cup them in his palms. He massaged the pillowy mounds, teasing the nipple between his thumb and forefinger as he suckled, licked, and nibbled along her skin.

The burning need inside her raged, threatening to burn her to ash. Epialos caught one of her nipples with his lips and sucked, drawing the nipple into his mouth, where he gently bit down and flicked it with his tongue. Damaphur gasped and cried out with longing as she writhed under Epialos's touch, the burning inside her veins bursting into a raging inferno.

He trailed his hands down her side, returning once more to her hips as his mouth followed, trailing kisses down her stomach and lower. The inferno raged, threatening to turn Damaphur into a molten heap of ash on top of her desk.
Heat pooled in her center, causing her walls to throb with the need to be filled

by him as his mouth played along the top of her naval.

"Please," Damaphur pleaded, her voice a ragged whisper.

"Patience, love," Epialos said. "I have waited so very long to worship your body. Allow me to do so slowly."

"I don't know if I can stand it," Damaphur said breathlessly.

"I promise you will like it, love," he responded as he kissed past her navel over the sprinkling of hair hiding her womanly secrets.

His breath rolled along her skin, and she felt the heat of it flow through her veins. The sensation fanned the flames of her desire even higher. She writhed and moaned as the pleasure took her to places she had never dreamed possible. She had lovers in her past, but none had dipped into her very soul as Epialos seemed to be doing now.

He dragged his tongue ever so slowly from the bottom of her folds to the top. He paused at the top, penetrating her folds with his tongue and swirling it around the sensitive bud above her opening. Damaphur cried out in passion and want as he ravaged her with his mouth, licking and flicking with tongue and teeth.

Epialos's stiff member throbbed with need, but he pushed the sensation down. The taste of her sweetness and the heat from her center fanning his face had him ready to go at any moment. However, he had waited too long to worship his queen and would have her screaming his name before he was finished.

He wanted to continue tasting her, but he could tell she was close by how she writhed for him, and her gasps and pants told him she could not take much more. He took one more taste before pulling away, and her moan of protest brought a satisfied smirk to his wet lips.

Epialos rose from his kneeling position, parting her legs and wrapping them around his waist as stood. He covered her body with his own and ravaged her mouth with his, still wet and from her juices. He let her taste how sweet she was as he nipped and bit her lips. He slid a hand between her thighs as his fingertips brushed along her folds, still wet from his mouth.

Damaphur cried out and pushed against his fingers, begging them to enter her and cool that burning need that threatened to burn her to ashes. His fingers slipped between her folds, finding that sensitive bud and swirling a finger around it, teasing and taunting. Bolts of sensation shot through Damaphur's walls as a building wave of pressure gathered in her core. Her insides throbbed as he slipped another finger into her wet center.

Damaphur writhed as her walls throbbed around Epialos's fingers while he continued to play with her, feeling her slick wetness on his skin. His own burning coursed through him, threatening to spill out of his hardened member, but still he held back. He continued to torture her with his fingers as he used his other hand to unfasten his pants and free his hardened shaft.

He played with her, swirling his thumb over that bud as he thrust his fingers in and out of her fiery core. He could feel her walls throbbing around his fingers and knew she was close. He could tell by her writhing, her ragged, uneven breathing, and the soft moans that escaped her swollen, kiss-ravaged lips that she would orgasm at any minute.

He pulled his fingers from her, eliciting a whimper of protest as her back arched pleadingly. He chuckled as he stood again, pulling his pants down his legs and kicking them away. He grasped her hips and pulled her close to him so that the head of his shaft brushed against her hot, wet entrance.

"Tell me you are mine," Epialos rasped as he brushed the head of his member against her center teasingly.

Damaphur whimpered and moved her hips, attempting to take him into her. Epialos simply grasped her hips tighter and moved back a bit, taking the touch of his hardness away from her.

"Tell me," he insisted.

"Not fair," Damaphur rasped breathlessly.

"I don't fight fair," Epialos said, pushing his head against her again. "Tell me. Let me hear you say it."

"I am yours," Damaphur rasped longingly.

Epialos pushed against her, and his head pierced her opening slightly.

"Say my name," he commanded. "Say my name when you say it."

"I am yours, Epialos," she whimpered, pushing against him as her core throbbed with need.

He allowed the push, sinking just the head into her hot depths as she cried ecstatically at the sensation.

"One more time, love," Epialos choked out, his tone rough and husky with need.

"I am yours, my king," she said, her tone filled with desire so strong that Epialos almost orgasmed.

He recovered by pulling out of her, and she cried out.

"Please, Epialos. I am yours. Take me. Take me, my king," Damaphur begged as she writhed beneath him, and Epialos could take it no longer.

"As you wish, my queen," he rasped as he pushed himself into her fully, skin meeting skin as he buried himself into her.

He ground himself against her as he covered her again with his body. She lifted her hips and tightened her legs around him as he pulled out slightly and then shoved himself back into her.

She held on tight as he rode her, the sensation of his stiff shaft thrusting in and out of her causing that building wave of pleasure to crash through her. Her walls throbbed as the orgasm took her, and she screamed his name to the heavens. She writhed and thrashed underneath him, raking her nails down his back as she rode her orgasm.

The sound of her screaming his name, the sensation of his member pounding into her throbbing hot core, and the sting of her nails scraping down his back brought Epialos's orgasm crashing through his soul. The pleasure ripped through him as his screams coalesced with hers in the small room, and he shoved himself deep into her one last time.

Their combined orgasms built, rising to a crescendo of building energy and magic. Their skin shone with it, his a dim aura of purple passion and hers a blinding halo of white-hot desire. The glows swirled together into a dazzling dance of light and emotion, so powerful that the lights in the room buzzed with energy.

The pleasure was so intense that Damaphur swore she felt the desk shake underneath her, but she didn't care. She was lost in the feel of Epialos pulsing inside her, his seed filling her with every throb of his massive member.

Epialos swore that he saw the building energies of their passion fly out of the office window and shoot into the sky beyond. Still, he paid it no heed as the sensation of Damaphur's hot walls pulsing around his shaft engulfed his very soul. He emptied himself inside her with every pulse of her tight walls.

When it was over, he pulled out of her, picked her up off the desk, and sank to the floor with her in his arms. He lay on the lush carpet of the office, tucking her close to his side as he waited for his heart to stop trying to pound its way out of his chest.

They lay in each other's arms on the floor, and Damaphur swore that the ground was still shaking. However, she paid it no mind as she cuddled into Epialos's hard body and relearned how to breathe.

They lay like that for what seemed like an eternity. Damaphur's eyes grew heavy as Epialos's steady breathing lulled her into a half-sleep state. She was still conscious, still aware, but her body felt limp and useless.

She was sure Epialos had fallen asleep judging from the stillness of his body and the deep, even breathing. She was content to lay in his arms and let him sleep, but the ground tremored again, catching her attention.

It was small at first but then rose to a steady shaking. Frowning, Damaphur shook Epialos gently. She heard his breath catch and knew he was awake.

"Do you feel that?" she asked, her voice scratchy from screaming.

"You mean the trembling?" Epialos responded sleepily.

"Yes," Damaphur answered. "What is that?"

"Earth-shattering sex," Epialos answered humorously.

Damaphur chuckled, but her tone was firm as she said, "Be serious for a moment. Something might be wrong."

Epialos was about to respond but was interrupted by a pounding on the office door.

"Your majesties, forgive my interruption, but this is an emergency," Hestia's voice rang through the door, fraught with concern and perhaps a bit of fear.

Curious, Damaphur got to her feet and searched the room for her discarded clothing as Epialos did the same.

"Give us a moment, Hestia," Damaphur yelled at the still-closed door.

"Please hurry, my queen. There is little time," Hestia shouted.

Epialos frowned at the worry in Hestia's tone and yelled, "Hestia, what is the emergency. Tell us while we get dressed."

"While you what?" Hestia asked, her voice lilting.

Epialos chuckled, and Damaphur shot him an irritated look as she pulled her dress back on. Epialos's gray skin sparkled in the sunlight coming in through the office window as he looked around for his shirt, catching Damaphur's attention.

She stared smugly at his bare chest, his muscles rippling under his radiant skin. She thought how thrilled she was that she was now free to touch that incredible body anytime she wished.

Epialos caught her watching him, noticed the half smile on her luscious lips, and gave a seductive growl as he stalked toward her.

"That look on your face," he drawled huskily. "It makes me want to throw you over that desk again."

"Majesties, we are running out of time!" Hestia's tone was panicked and hurried.

Damaphur shook her head to clear it and turned for the door. "Later," she said, casting a seductive smile at Epialos over her shoulder.

Damaphur opened the door, and Hestia practically tumbled in as if she had been leaning on the office door.

"Queen Damaphur," Hestia said as she regained her balance and gave Damaphur a quick bow.

Damaphur glanced curiously over Hestia's shoulder when she noticed Sage and Chandra behind her.

Her eyes widened in surprise when she noticed Sage was standing at attention and scanning the hallway, completely nude from the waist up. There were fresh welts along the skin of his back and nail marks down his arms.

The queen's gaze flew suspiciously to Chandra, who was also scanning the hallway, standing back to back with Sage. Her hair was mussed and swept back over her shoulders, and her clothing was wrinkled and out of place as if thrown on hurriedly.

Damaphur was sure she looked no better, but she still gave a knowing smile as her eyes darted between Chandra and Sage.

Hestia cleared her throat and said, "Queen, there is a disturbance at the border that requires your immediate attention."

Epialos moved closer to Damaphur's back, peering out the door over Damaphur's shoulder. "What is it, Hestia?"

Hestia's gaze flicked to Epialos. "Actually, this concerns you as well."

Damaphur huffed in exasperation. "Spit it out, Hestia," she said impatiently.

Hestia swallowed hard and said, "The lake is drying up, and the fissure separating the planet is closing."

"What?" Epialos bellowed.

Damaphur just stared wide-eyed and did not move.

Hestia flinched at Epialos's loud tone.

Sage broke from his stance and approached the door, leaving Chandra to guard the hallway alone. He nudged Hestia aside and looked to Epialos as he said, "The guards sent a dragon messenger. The shifter reported that a massively huge bright ball of light came out of nowhere. Some guards said it looked like the sun had fallen from the sky. It shot into Lake Divere, creating a giant explosion on the east side, where it is mostly wasteland.

"The lava began to burn to ash and float away with the ash clouds, and then the fissure started to close up. They say the ground is actually moving! There are hordes of people at the borders, and the guards are having difficulty keeping the people away from the closing crevice."

"Chandra," the king said commandingly, catching the captain's attention.

She swung around and instantly went to attention. She gave Epialos the full weight of her expectant stare, the stare she usually gave the queen when Damaphur gave her orders.

"Take a unit of your soldiers to the border to help with crowd control. Sage, go with her. Warren told me that you can hold your own in a fight."

"Yes, sir," Chandra answered and turned to Sage.

"Yes, sir. I have her back," Sage answered, then added, "as soon as I get my clothes."

Epialos smirked, but his tone remained firm as he said, "Well, get to it then, and be quick about it."

Sage bowed respectfully, turned, and marched away with Chandra on his heels. Damaphur marveled at the smoothness in which Epialos took charge of her people, and they had actually listened. She watched Epialos in amazement as he took her arm and led her to the throne room, calling for Hestia to gather everyone to the throne room.

He just took charge and rolled with it without any hesitation. He was in control, confident, and everyone moved when he said to move.

He held her arm gently as he led her to her throne room. He guided her up the dais and held her hand as she sat on her throne. He brought her hand to his lips, kissing it firmly before bowing to her and taking his place by her side.

Standing by her right side.

Damaphur decided that her decision to be his queen would be a good one.

Chandra had never seen anything like it in her life. Throngs of people crowded around the border gate, yelling profanities at the guards. They were trying to push their way to the front of the line or screaming at the people on the other side of the rapidly closing lake.

The other shore of the lake loomed ever closer, and the ash cloud was greatly diminished from the last time Chandra had been this close to the border. She could see the crowds on the other shore and Asgorath soldiers trying to control them from swarming the border.

Chandra shouted orders to the troops she had brought, ordering them to help control the ever-pressing crowd. They had to get them pushed back before the Lake closed completely, or they would have a massive fight on their hands.

Then, Chandra noticed something strange. She began straining to hear the individual voices over the cacophony of shouts coming from the crowd. She noticed that the shouts were not angry shouts or threats of violence but excited shouts of welcome and happiness.

Frowning, Chandra turned her attention to the sky.

Dragons of all kinds and colors swarmed the air over their heads, roaring into the sky as they flew in and out of the diminishing ash clouds above the lake. They shot their magic harmlessly into the air as they dipped and dove through the smoke and ash, sending streaks of fire and ice over the land.

It was almost as if they were all celebrating.

And maybe they were, Chandra realized as she watched the revelry. None of them were attacking. They simply flew around each other, touching wings occasionally or lightly brushing against each other as they flew. It was as if they were playing a fun game of aerial tag.

"What are your orders, captain?" Sage asked as he came up beside Chandra.

Chandra stood and watched in fascination. The two shores of the lake were so close together now that an athletic person could leap across with some effort. The ground still rumbled and shook as the two pieces of planet Mikka continued to merge together. Steam rose above the shrinking crack in the ground as the lava dried up, but the thick smoke and ash were no more.

The people shouted in celebration, joy, and mirth as they tried to push past the guards. Some were trying to get to the people drawing closer to the other shore. Others were waiting for the crack to close so they could swarm unhindered to the other side.

Screams of "sister" and "mother" assaulted Chandra's ears as she watched recognition light up in many an eye. She saw more than one face drenched in happy tears as they gazed at the crowd on the other shore.

"Captain," came Sage's voice in a more forceful tone, dragging Chandra from her captivated stupor. "What are your orders, Chandra?"

"Let them go," Chandra said, her voice barely a whisper.

"What?" Sage asked in disbelief.

"Let them go," Chandra said, raising her voice to a normal pitch. "They are not fighting, Sage. Just look at them."

Sage turned his attention to the assertive crowd and frowned. After a moment, his eyes held the same strange enthrallment that Chandra had held a moment before.

"By the God and Goddess, you're right," he said, his voice a mix of disbelief and relief. "Everyone looks happy that the lake is closing."

Chandra nodded. "Yes, but this still presents a problem."

Sage frowned as he scratched his head. He looked out over the celebrating crowd with confusion in his sapphire eyes. He ran a hand through his platinum hair as he blew out a breath.

"What kind of problem could a cheerful crowd be?" he asked confusedly.

Chandra smiled and answered, "It's not the crowd I'm worried about. You can tell the guards to let them all pass, and they can handle the individual fights that may or may not occur."

Sage nodded, but his visage was still confused. "Then what kind of problem are you speaking of?"

Chandra smirked and answered, "I was just wondering which palace we are all going to live in when Damaphur and Epialos finally get married."

The confusion drained away from Sage's face as he chuckled and turned toward the guard post.

Quietly, he replied, "That, my dear, is an excellent question."

ORIGINS OF SAGE

Palace Solaris was buzzing with excitement when Chandra and Sage returned. The Sisters of Echidna and the Brothers of Typhon were holding a special, last-minute ceremony in the palace temple, Temple Tiamat, for the king and queen, to congratulate them on their union.

The Brothers of Typhon scrambled to make last-minute preparations while Hestia barked orders to her congregation of Sisters. Chandra's guards were scrambling to ensure everyone, including the king and queen, were guarded. The handmaids, housemaids, and servants scrambled to fulfill everyone's orders.

It was total chaos.

Celia and Tenebris approached Chandra as she and Sage entered the throne room from the main entrance. Tenebris had a worried expression, and Celia was wringing her hands, anxiety written all over her face.

"Celia, what's wrong?" Chandra asked.

The fact that Chandra asked without Celia saying a word told Celia all she needed to know. She was stressing out, and it was written all over her face. Of course, she was only just coming to terms with these cursed visions she was having. Had it not been for Tenebris having just stamped her with his imprint, then this particular vision would probably have done Celia in. As it were, Tenebris had taken control and helped Celia ride through the vision.

Unfortunately for Tenebris, he had taken the

ride with her and had seen what Celia had seen. Celia glanced over her shoulder where Tenebris followed close behind, and she could tell by the look on his face that her vision had also stressed him.

"I just had another vision right before you two came back," Celia announced as she stopped before Chandra and Sage. "The queen had just dismissed everyone from the dinner table when this creepy feeling came over me. It scared me so badly that I went to my room in the Palace, which I hardly ever sleep in, and laid down for a bit.

"When I returned to the throne room, all hell had broken loose with the feast preparations. I was about to return to my room when the vision hit me. Thank goodness that Tenebris was there to help because it was hard-hitting."

Celia finished explaining and took a large swig of water from the bottle she had been carrying.

Chandra raised her brows in worry and asked, "What did you see, Celia?"

Celia huffed. "I would rather only have to say it once rather than relive it repeatedly. That is why I am trying to gather everyone involved and have them meet me in the conference room. Can you wait for me there?"

Chandra nodded, "I can do that. Is there anyone you want me to help you find?"

"No, not you, but do you possibly know where Warren is, Sage?"

Sage shook his head. "Last time I saw him was right after the battle with the rebels."

"We can help find him," Chandra offered, but Celia shook her head again.

"No, if everyone is running around trying to find everyone else, we will never get together. I think it would be better if you went to the conference room and waited while I go find everyone. Tenebris is already there."

Sage grabbed Chandra's hand and began to lead her toward the conference room as he responded, "we can do that. If anyone else shows up in the conference room, I will tell them to wait there."

"Yes, and I will check in periodically," Celia called back as she turned toward the door that led to the other rooms of the palace.

Chandra glanced up toward the empty dais as she passed it and wondered if the queen and king were already there. One Sister in her pristine white robes and habit brushed against Chandra, muttering an apology as she hurried past.

Chandra smiled comfortingly to signify that she accepted the apology, but the Sister did not even acknowledge that she noticed. Sage pulled on Chandra's hand, hurrying her along, and Chandra allowed Sage to lead her from the throne room.

Once they were out in the hallway, Chandra pulled her hand from Sage's and spat, "I can walk on my own, you know."

Sage chuckled as Chandra pulled away from him, but he let her go without a response. He knew how to handle women, and he knew that he would have to take his time with this one. He had almost had her before.

They had some fun earlier in Chandra's room with her whip and chains, but Hestia had interrupted them before they had gotten too far. There was something about Chandra that got his libido buzzing; it wasn't just the whip and chains. He had wanted her from the first time he had laid eyes on her.

He was a glutton for pain and commanding women, and Chandra certainly fit that bill, but it was more than that. He had noticed her fire before he knew about her commanding presence or her talent with a whip.

Sage slowed, allowing Chandra to pass so he could watch as she walked down the hallway. She glared at him menacingly, albeit playfully, as she passed, narrowing those sparkling emerald eyes he could get lost in if he allowed himself to. She brushed her luxurious, coffee-with-cream-colored hair over her shoulder with a defiant gesture as she stalked ahead of him. His fingers itched to run them through that silken mass of brown waves.

Sage's sapphire eyes raked over her hourglass figure, taking in the way her voluptuous hips swayed gracefully as her long legs glided along each step. He thought about having those curvy legs wrapped around his waist as he sank himself into her, and had to shake his head to get rid of the thoughts before he grew too large for his pants.

He thanked the God and Goddess that he had put on a long jacket after he had lost his original shirt and jacket after their make-out session. He pulled his jacket closed and buttoned it to the bottom, which hung low enough over his pants to hide the bulge that naughty thoughts of Chandra had raised.

They entered the conference room, and it surprised Sage that Chandra and he were the only ones there.

"Didn't Celia say that Tenebris was in here?" Sage asked.

With a frown on her lovely, triangular face, Chandra turned to him and answered, "Yes, she did. I wonder where he is."

Sage shrugged with a cocky smirk as he stalked closer to Chandra and said, "I guess it's just you and me for now."

Chandra's emerald eyes narrowed. "Don't get any ideas. You are still a traitor in my eyes, even if the queen does pardon you. I was not done with your punishment."

Sage raised his eyebrows at Chandra's boldness. The bossier she was toward him, the more she turned him on. He wondered how much worse she would 'punish' him if he were naughty.

He cleared his throat before responding, "I would never betray my master, so I am not a traitor."

"You were going to assassinate your master. How can you say…"

Sage cut off Chandra's words.

"The queen is not my master; she is only a queen. My master is Grandmaster Warren."

Chandra lifted her chin in defiance as she spat, "but the queen is everyone's master. That's what a queen is."

Sage stalked closer to Chandra, stopping only inches in front of her. He lowered his voice to almost a whisper and put a menacing pitch to his tone as he replied, "the queen nor the king does not hold sway over the Spire or its members. We are an entity of our own. We respect the rulers of the lands as the rulers they are, but the members of the Spire only answer to the Grandmaster. He is our ruler."

Sage could tell he was pissing off the feisty general by how she balled her hands into fists at her side. The furious look on her face made her bright green eyes sparkle, and her reddening skin caused her cute freckles to stand out in contrast.

She was beautiful when she was angry, and it excited him to think what she would do to him when she finally let loose with her whip.

He moved even closer to her, so close that the tips of her armored boots almost touched the tips of his combat boots, but she did not flinch away.

Instead, she raised her chin even further and seethed, "how can you say that? How can you say they do not lead you when your schools are on their lands?"

"Our schools might be located on their lands, but our main establishment is not. The buildings in Terrien and Asgorath are just what they say they are…they are schools. Our real power center, the primary hub for our members, is not on claimed land."

Chandra narrowed her eyes, leveling her piercing emerald gaze on Sage as she said mockingly, "so you have a secret hide-out where all your assassins and spies are located?"

Sage threw his head back and laughed, causing Chandra to flinch slightly. He was still chuckling when he replied, "you watch too many movies."

"Well," Chandra said with a scoff. "That is what it sounded like you were saying. How else would you describe it then?"

Sage's visage sobered as his laughter died away. He gave Chandra a serious look as he replied, "When the Oracles were alive, they had to hide away from the world. Too many people wanted them dead, so they built a home in a hidden location that no one had ever explored. It was uncharted land, unclaimed and wild, and it became the location of the original Spire.

This facility is yet another reason for the Spire members' secrecy. Warren would be furious if he knew I was even speaking of it. Many ancient artifacts are hidden there, as well as an extensive library that dates back to before the Great War. They have been well preserved in our library.

The library also contains tomes and scrolls that possess the power to ignite wars if they fall into the wrong hands, and only the Oracles and Spire members have had the privilege to read many of the books. Most of the books of power were destroyed in the war, but we have the few remaining ones left.

The anger in Chandra's visage melted away, and understanding dawned in their emerald depths. "Wow. There are treasure hunters and conspiracy theorists out there that would kill for the artifacts alone, much less the information contained in the library."

Sage nodded. "Exactly."

Sage watched Chandra's throat bob as she swallowed hard. He stiffened as he waited for her reaction to see if she would betray his shaky trust. He would not read her unless invited to. It was rude, and he would never betray her trust that way. Especially since he was putting his trust in her.

He had not even meant to tell her any of that. The information had poured out of his mouth before he could stop it. He did not know why he had so easily confided in this woman. He barely knew her. He wanted her, sure, but to trust her in such a capacity was a new concept for him.

Sage never trusted anybody, especially given what he was. Adivinos did not trust anyone unless they read them, and even then, some could hide their thoughts and resist mind control.

So, it was not surprising that Sage found himself out of sorts after such an outpouring of faith, which is what he blamed for his next stupid move.

Chandra gazed into his eyes with such trust and understanding as she said, "I understand now why all the secrecy. It doesn't excuse your actions, but I understand. Your secret is safe with me, and I won't tell Warren you told me."

Sage breathed out a sigh of relief. Her words sank in and called to his soul, beckoning him to give in and tell her everything. The trust in her eyes elicited an emotion from him that was foreign to his heart, an almost irresistible need to give himself to her completely.

A fierce protectiveness and need to shelter this treasure from the world rose inside him. He knew she could handle herself, so the emotion made no sense. But there it was, called from the depths of his blackened soul by those piercing emerald eyes.

Sage's gaze flicked to Chandra's luscious lips, watching as she sucked the bottom part into her mouth and chewed nervously. Sage sucked in a breath as an overwhelming need to take her mouth with his own overtook him. He wanted to suck that bottom lip into his mouth, and he did just that before he could stop himself. He didn't even want the whips and chains anymore. Just the feel of his mouth over hers was enough.

He grabbed her face gently between his hands, pulling that succulent mouth up to his and claiming it as his own. Chandra let out a startled cry, letting go of her bottom lip and allowing Sage to suck it into his mouth. He licked, sucked, and gently nipped that succulent morsel as he guided Chandra toward the wall and kissed her thoroughly.

Chandra moved with him, gripping his hips with her tiny hands for balance. The touch sent spirals of desire coiling through his groin, causing his erection to grow as he feasted on her sweet mouth. Suddenly, he felt her body stop and realized that her back had hit the wall. He released her face and placed both hands on the wall above and on either side of her head.

He deepened the kiss as he pressed his body into hers and growled with anticipation when she did not resist. Her mouth opened to his probing tongue, and he swept inside her mouth, exploring her deliciousness.

The need to be inside her filled him, overwhelming his senses and blocking out any rational thought. He pressed against her more firmly, grinding his hardness against the softness of her lower stomach. It would be so easy to enter her from here. She was just tall enough that all she had to do was wrap one of those long legs around him, and then he could sink his hardness into her moist depths.

The thought elicited a predatory growl from his throat, and Chandra answered with a moan of ecstasy that vibrated against Sage's mouth. Tendrils of delight snaked through his body, and he released her mouth to plant kisses down the side of her face and neck. He licked the sensitive spot under her ear and delighted in the soft moan that caused her warm breath to blow across his own ear.

The pulse in her neck throbbed in time with her heartbeat, drawing Sage's attention to that location. He kissed his way to that spot, licking over the heat that radiated from it. He felt Chandra's body tremble as he pressed his lips to that pulse and sucked lightly.

Chandra's head went back as her body arched into his, pressing her soft breasts against his muscled chest. His fingers dug against the stone wall in an effort to keep himself from grabbing her roughly and crushing her to him. His body shook with the struggle to keep himself from biting into her flesh and letting her warm, delicious blood flow into his mouth as he sank his member into her fiery depths.

Chandra whispered his name softly, desire causing the sound to come out husky. It sounded almost like a plea.

"Sage…please."

The sound jerked him out of his trance, a trance he had thought he had mastered. Chandra had almost caused him to lose his tentative control.

Sage was only part Adivino. The other half of him, the monstrous half, was locked away deep inside. It had taken him years to tame that part of himself, and it had been years since that part had come out.

Thanks to Warren and his mastery teachings, he no longer needed a steady diet of fresh blood. Now, Sage could live off regular food and a diet of animal blood since he had embraced his Adivino side.

No one knew what Sage was except Warren and Tenebris, and they had kept his secret. Adivinos were an endangered race, with him being the last, but the other side of him was thought to be extinct.

Sage was the last of his kind of both species. His mother was Adivino, and Sage was the last since his mother had died long ago.

But Sage's father…

He was a monster, tamed by his mother, but a monster nonetheless. The others, including his father, had been hunted and killed out of fear, and rightly so. They had been vicious monsters that feasted on others without care or remorse. They took what they wanted by force, often leaving the victim dead and drained of blood.

Or eaten completely if attacked by a shifted vampire dragon.

Sage was the last vampire dragon.

Warren had raised Sage after Sage's mother had given him up to the Spire. Sage's mother had been a member of the Spire before she had fallen for the vampire. She had a long affair with the vampire shifter and was estranged from the Spire for years.

Then, his father had been killed by vampire hunters, and his mother had sought help from the Spire. Warren had forgiven her, especially when he found out she was pregnant. However, she did not want to rejoin the ranks, so she left her newborn son in Warren's care and disappeared.

She was found later when Sage was just a babe, murdered in a seedy hotel in a trashy city of the Southern Hemisphere.

Warren raised Sage as if he were his own and taught Sage to control his hunger and lust. He had taught Sage discipline, respect, kindness, and compassion. He had taken Sage to Tenebris as a baby, and Tenebris had stamped Sage. When Sage came into his powers, Tenebris had helped Sage control his magic and take mastery over his shifts.

Thanks to those two, Sage was not like the others of his kind.

He had more control over himself than this.

Sage released his hold on Chandra's neck and pushed himself off the wall. He turned away from her and began pacing back and forth along the marbled floor of the conference room. He ran a shaky hand through his white hair as he blew out a frustrated breath.

"Sage?"

Chandra's worried tone made him stop and turn to her. Guilt pierced his soul when he saw the hurt and confusion in her emerald gaze.

"I'm sorry, Chandra," he whispered. "I…I…" His stuttering ceased as he gave Chandra a tortured look.

He took a deep breath and tried once more. "I got carried away."

"It's fine," Chandra said. "I liked it."

Sage ran a hand through his white hair again, then turned and walked toward the door. He paused after opening the door and threw her a glance over his shoulder.

"I'm going to see if I can find Tenebris," he said before leaving the room and shutting the door softly behind him.

Chandra stood and watched him leave the room, wrapping her arms around herself as her body shook with the coldness that his absence left in its wake. Her confusion consumed her as she wondered what on Mikka had caused him to react that way.

Her confusion grew as she thought about how much he had enjoyed letting her use the whip on him. Of course, she enjoyed it as well. She liked getting a bit kinky in her love play.

He had been the one to initiate the kiss, and then he had turned away from her when it became heated. However, the most confusing thing was why she had let it bother her. She had always been casual with her lovers in the past, and rejection had never bothered her before because she didn't care.

Sex was just entertainment for her, especially with bondage and rough play. So, what was it about this one that had her lusting after his touches like some love-starved slave? He was alluring and handsome, Chandra admitted to herself, but she had been around charming males before.

What was it about Sage?

Chandra did not know, but she knew that she wanted to find out and would enjoy it very much.

Especially if he allowed her to keep handling the whip.

CHAPTER 26: VISIONS, SCRIBES, AND SCROLLS, OH MY!

Celia entered the room shortly after Sage had left, followed by Tenebris, Warren, Hestia, Maldia, and Raina. The king and queen were not in sight.

"Where is Sage?" Celia asked after glancing around the room questioningly.

Chandra's face reddened as she cleared her throat and answered, "He said he was going to find Tenebris."

Warren cast her a suspicious look and responded, "I thought Celia asked you two to wait here."

Chandra shrugged. "She did. It's not my fault if he chose not to listen."

Warren cursed as he turned to the door. "I'll go find him."

"No need," Sage's voice rang out as he strolled through the open door with the king and queen on his heels.

"I may not have found Tenebris, but I found the royals," he quipped with a smirk and gesture behind him.

"What is this about?" asked the king as he entered the room.

Celia stepped forward, clasping her hands together in front of her in a nervous gesture as she said, "I called this meeting because I have had another vision."

Warren raised an eyebrow. "How did you control it this time?"

Celia narrowed her gaze on the Grandmaster. "I got the stamp from Tenebris. He helped me control it."

Warren turned his attention to Tenebris, who nodded in affirmation.

He turned to Celia and asked, "What did you see?"

Celia gestured toward the table. "I think we should all sit down, and I will tell you."

Warren turned to Sage. "You know where I keep my things in Terrien Spire?"

Sage nodded and answered, "Yes, master."

"I need my quill, a vial of my good ink, and an empty parchment," Warren said to Sage and then turned to the rest of the room. "I must record the prophecies of Celia, the Great Oracle of our time. Therefore, I request that you wait until I gain the proper equipment."

"I am no Great Oracle," Celia said. "I cannot even control my visions."

Warren scoffed. "Your great-grandmother was over sixty before she began to have her visions. It took her years to control hers. The Great Oracles did not become so 'Great' until well into their seventies. Do not sell yourself short, Celia."

Celia's eyes widened. "I did not know that."

"Well, now you do. Will you give me time to gather my things?"

Celia looked worried as she replied, "I do not know if we have the time."

The queen entered the conversation. "If I may interrupt, Grandmaster, I have some ink, parchment, and a very nice quill here at the palace. Perhaps my scribe can record Celia's words, and then you can copy it to the parchment of your choice later."

"That'll do," Warren said with an approving nod. "Call your scribe then."

Sage chuckled as he walked toward the door. He glanced over his shoulder as he left the room and said, "I will be back momentarily with my things."

Warren raised his brows at the queen. "Sage is your scribe *and* adviser?"

Damaphur smiled softly as she shrugged and answered, "He is, yes. I joined the two jobs into one. I don't like having such a large court, so I cut corners where I can."

Warren's brow remained raised as he asked, "Does this mean you will pardon him?"

Damaphur's smile vanished, and her lavender eyes hardened. She pushed a strand of her shining silver hair back from her face as she answered, "I have not made up my mind yet, but he will do for now. He is an outstanding scribe."

Chandra watched the conversation unfold. Her heart had leaped with hope when Damaphur had suggested Sage record the prophecy that Celia was about to give, but it sank now at Damaphur's visage and tone. Chandra did not think the queen would pardon Sage easily, if at all.

Chandra did not understand her attraction to Sage nor her desire to have the queen's pardon for him. She especially did not understand why she had allowed him to kiss and handle her as he had done, but she had. The memory of his kiss still burned upon her lips.

"How long is this going to take?" Raina asked, jerking Chandra from her inner reverie. "I was just about to go to the nursery to collect Ethan for lunch."

Raina had sat down at the table while everyone had been talking, and she sat there now as she asked her question to the group standing around in front of her.

Maldia walked around the table and sat down beside Raina, patting her hand comfortingly. "I sent a handmaiden to give the babies lunch. After this, we can take them for a walk in the courtyard if you would like."

Raina smiled in gratitude at her new friend. "That would be lovely, thank you."

Chandra smiled at the exchange as she sat down at a seat in front of her, across from the two women. She was glad that Maldia had made a new friend, and she liked Raina. Maldia would need friends that had children now that she was also a mother. Chandra wondered what it would be like for her to be a mother.

She had never thought of it before now.

Her mother had given her away when she had only been a babe, but the parents who had raised her were wonderful. If a mother who had not even given birth to her could be so great, then how much greater would Chandra be with her own child?

Chandra knew the answer to that question.

She would be fantastic. She would never give her child away, always be there for them, and strive to be the best parent a child could have.

When she was ready.

She was not desperate enough for a child to have one randomly, just because her best friend had one now. When she had a child, it would be with someone she was going to spend the rest of her life with, and it would be at a point when she had the time to dedicate to raising it.

"And then after the walk," Maldia said as Chandra pulled herself from her thoughts again. "We can take them to the pond to play in the water. It is a beautiful day for it."

"I will assign you a couple of guards to watch over you two and the babes," Chandra said, suddenly nervous for the babies' safety.

"Oh, Chandra, do you really think it is necessary? We will be in the confines of the inner courtyard," Maldia complained. "We will not go into the main courtyard where the rebels were."

Chandra frowned. Her voice was firm as she replied, "The rebels broke into the sanctuary of the throne room. What makes you think they could not have entered the courtyard if they had wanted to?"

Maldia turned her attention to Chandra with a scrutinizing look in her jade eyes. "Chandra, are you feeling extra protective because of the palace invasion, or do you honestly feel that we need to have guards in the sanctuary of our own home?"

Chandra thought about that for a minute. She could not explain the sudden, overwhelming feeling of protection that had washed over her when the women had talked about taking the babes outside. Perhaps it was due to the invasion that had her nerves on edge, or maybe some deep inner sense. Chandra did not know, but she could not ignore her intuition when it came to her people's safety.

"I do not know for sure," Chandra answered honestly. "But it would make me feel better if you had protection."

Maldia quirked an eyebrow at her friend.

"All right, fine," she relented. "We will take some guards of your choosing with us."

Chandra blew out a relieved breath and nodded in gratitude. "I will find two guards for you as soon as this meeting ends."

Raina had watched the exchange with curious eyes, and now her voice cut into the conversation. "Maldia, are you sure it will be safe? Perhaps we should wait until the excitement of the invasion is over."

"We can never be completely sure that anything is safe," Maldia said in a wise tone. "But if we shut ourselves off from life every time something happens, then we will never live."

Chandra chuckled and said, "When did you become the philosopher?"

Maldia smiled and shrugged. "I can think of smart things to say occasionally."

The three women laughed, catching the attention of the rest of the group that still stood in a huddle, carrying on their own conversation.

The queen smiled at their laughter as she broke from the group and walked toward her seat at the table.

"It is nice to find you getting along with Raina and making her feel welcome," Damaphur said as she sat in her chair. "I hope that Raina will be here at the palace more often. I find that I like the babies around."

Raina smiled shyly and dipped her gaze to the table as she answered, "That is overly kind of you, my queen. I would like that very much."

Epialos came around, standing behind the queen's chair and placing a hand on her shoulder lovingly. "I hope you will also come with us to Asgorath when we visit there. I would like to be in my grandson's life."

"Visit there?" Hestia said, joining the conversation. "Does this mean you will be living here?"

Damaphur and Epialos exchanged knowing glances, and Damaphur answered, "Epialos has given me total control until I am sure I can trust him explicitly."

Hestia's eyes held a relieved look. "That is wonderful news…well…that you will not be leaving Solaris, I mean."

Epialos chuckled. "In the future, I would like to build a new home for us in the middle of our kingdoms. I want us united, but I want my queen to trust me first."

"Very pragmatic," Hestia said, nodding approvingly.

Raina's fearful, emerald gaze pierced the king's ruby-red eyes. Her voice shook as she cut in, "I fear what your son might do to me if I ever go back to Asgorath, especially since I ran away with his child."

Chandra noticed the frown on Maldia's face as she scooted closer to Raina and placed a protective hand over hers. Chandra nodded in approval.

"I will appoint you your own personal bodyguards if you prefer," Chandra said, shooting the king a bold look as if daring him to object. "They will go with you wherever you go and protect you with their life."

The king did not object. Instead, he turned hopeful eyes to Raina, who sat considering Chandra's words.

After a moment, Raina cleared her throat and said, "I do not need full-time bodyguards, but I will not mind taking one with me if I visit Asgorath. I hope that does not offend you, my king."

The king smiled softly at Raina and answered, "No, Raina. That does not offend me. I would prefer it, actually. I want you to feel safe in my home so that you will want to visit often."

Damaphur smiled at the exchange and nodded her head approvingly. She was about to join in the conversation when the door to the conference room opened, and Sage came strolling in.

He had an armload of supplies. Parchment, a quill box, a vial of ink, and a box of things that Chandra eyed curiously. She smiled at the sight, noting how smart the sensual Sage looked carrying paper and pen.

He caught her eye as he walked around the table and set his load down to the right of the king's seat. He gave her a sexy smirk as he sat in his seat, then turned his attention to organizing his stuff. When he had his stuff ready, Sage looked to Celia, who stood beside Tenebris, whispering with him quietly.

"I am ready to record your prophecy, Great Oracle," Sage said, respectfully bowing his head.

Celia frowned at the gesture but said nothing. Instead, she walked over to the table to sit, but Epialos stopped her with his words.

"Celia, given the seriousness of the situation, I feel it best that you sit at the head of the table in my spot. I will stand here behind the queen."

Celia's eyes widened in surprise. "I do not deserve such reverence, Majesty."

"If you are becoming one of the Great Oracles, then you certainly deserve reverence," Damaphur answered for the king.

Celia sighed as she moved to the head of the table and said, "As you wish, your majesties."

Chandra watched the exchange and noticed Warren's broad, proud smile as he sat beside Sage, who fussed with the quill and ink vial. Chandra's eyes drifted to the now open box beside the parchment paper stack. She saw two wooden dowels, some thick, gunky liquid in a metal container, and a cylindrical metal vessel.

Frowning in confusion, she watched Sage smooth the parchment onto the table. He pulled a brush from the bottom of the box and dipped it into the gunk. Carefully, he brushed it onto the bottom of the parchment and then pressed the top of another piece of parchment onto it.

He smoothed the second piece of parchment, pressing where he had attached it to the first piece until the pieces stuck together and became one long piece. Sage glanced up from his work to see Chandra staring at him in confusion.

He smiled at her confused face and said, "Would you like to know what I am doing?"

Chandra nodded as she watched Sage repeat the process with the gunk, making the parchment even longer.

"I am making a scroll," Sage said, then he smoothed the entire piece of parchment he had made onto the table.

Chandra watched, her eyes widening in fascination as Sage made a slit in one of the wooden dowels. He attached the top of the first piece of parchment to the dowel by sliding the edge into the slit and using more of the sticky gunk to hold it in place.

Finally, Sage rolled a quarter of the first piece onto the wooden bar to secure it to the dowel. He made a flourishing gesture with his hands and smiled at Chandra.

"Tada," he said in a sing-song voice.

Chandra giggled.

Sage prepared to write, picking up the quill and dipping the metal tip into the ink. He primed the quill by writing a few practice lines until the ink began to run smoothly from the tip. He rolled the parchment onto the dowel until the practice lines were hidden. Then he nodded at Celia to indicate that he was ready to record her words.

A sense of foreboding suddenly washed over Chandra, and she remembered that feeling. It was the same feeling that had washed over her when the women had talked about taking the babies out for a walk. Frowning, Chandra pushed the feeling aside. What on Mikka was going on with her?

Shaking her head to clear it, Chandra forced her attention to the head of the table where Celia was about to reveal her prophecy.

The lights streaming in from the windows dulled as clouds covered the sun, causing the room to suddenly go darker. Chandra shuddered as the foreboding feeling grew stronger with the dimming light. Silence fell upon the room as Celia stood at the head of the table and closed her eyes.

Chills of apprehension ran down Chandra's spine as she leaned forward in anticipation. The dullness and silence in the room became a weight in Chandra's mind, filling her chest with a heaviness that made it hard to breathe. What was it that had Chandra ready to jump out of her skin? It probably had something to do with the ambiance of the darkened room.

Then, Chandra noticed the object of her discomfort. Chandra shuddered as she saw the glow around Celia's body. Celia's power filled her so completely that it spilled out of her in a bright aura of light. Thunder rumbled in the sky, and lightning lit up the darkened room.

The sound of rain pelted against the windows as Celia slowly opened her eyes, and Chandra gasped at the sight. Celia's eyes were glowing an iridescent gold color. The sight of Celia with her powers activated sent ominous sparks of fear coursing through Chandra, even as she tried to ignore the feeling.

Was this causing Chandra's discomfort? She had never seen the Seer in her full power before. Could that have something to do with this sinister feeling smothering Chandra?

Celia's voice did not help as she spoke in a deep, drawling tone, causing the tiny hairs on the back of Chandra's neck to stand on end. She shook off the feeling and sat back in her seat as the words of Celia's prophecy filled the darkened silence. The vibrating rumble of thunder sounded just before Sage began to write…

*This is an account of the prophecy of the
Great Oracle, Celia;
Recorded by Sage the Scribe on this day of
Ehud, Tajik 22, 200 A.G.W.
These are Celia's exact words…*

*The land is newly healed and ready to
welcome peace. The war is over, the leaders
are joined, and the rebels have been subdued.*

*Something isn't right, though. Someone is
crying while everyone else is celebrating. No,
not someone… many people are mourning.*

*I can't see who they are, but their cries fill
the halls of Palace Solaris. I run through the
halls, searching for the crying and mourning
voices, but no one seems to know I am there.*

They are asking about missing people, asking
if anyone knows where they are.   They are yelling
at each other and blaming each other for what
happened.

Now I am outside in an unfamiliar land.   I
have never seen this land before.   There is an
enormous castle, larger than either Solaris or
Asgorath.   The people here are not celebrating,
but they are not mourning either.
They are preparing for a new prophecy.   It
must be written and must begin.

The new prophecy is this...

The dark and light. The five dragons
Banished to the town of mountains in the East
to avoid destruction and death.

The queen of pride will wed the king of justice,
and peace will abound in the North and South.

The lady of the moon will seduce the child of
the dark, but his confession will break the moon's
heart,

In the city of mountains, an Army of the
South will fall, and in the Palace of the South,
stars will fall from the sky.
When this comes to pass, the broken heart will
unleash the beast and destruction reigns.
The banished ones will bring forth the return
of pure dragons, angels, and demons to fight the
great beast.
The harbinger of war will burn, and the Dark
King will be slain, but the forces will rise and slay
the moon in the East, putting an end to the moon's
reign.

CHAPTER 27: THIS IS HOW THE WORLD ENDS; NOT WITH A BANG, BUT A WHISPER

Celia slumped as the last words of the prophecy left her mouth, and Warren was suddenly there to catch her. Tenebris still sat in his seat, a look of concentration on his features.

His brow was furrowed, his eyes closed, and sweat trickled down onto his closed lids. His breathing was heavy as if he had been running a marathon even though he had not even left his chair at the table.

Celia straightened slowly with Warren's help and shot a thankful look Tenebris's way.

"That was easier this time, with your help," she told Tenebris.

Tenebris opened his eyes slowly and responded breathlessly, in a sarcastic tone, "I'm glad it was easy for you."

Celia stiffened, and her eyes narrowed, but then Celia saw the smile tugging at the corners of Tenebris's lips.

"You're incorrigible," Celia said jokingly.

Her smile quickly faded at the queen's following words.

"Celia, do you know what the words of your prophecy mean?"

Celia had been wondering the same thing. Just because she had spoken the words did not mean she knew their meaning. Much of what she had seen and heard during her vision was confusing and fuzzy.

This had not been a vision that she usually had. Instead of being in the front row for the action in someone else's body, she had been in her own body. However, it had been more like a dream where one observes what is happening instead of being part of it. Some of what she had seen made no sense, so she had no idea what it meant.

She did, however, know how to answer the queen's question. "I do not know what the words of my prophecy mean yet, nor do I understand what I saw in my vision. I must consult my crystals and cards, meditate, and commune with my Goddess to get the answers."

"How long will that take?" Epialos asked.

"That is a question for the Goddess. It depends on when she decides to give me the true sight," Celia answered.

"What is the true sight?" Raina asked.

"It is a gift from the Goddess. It means seeing the truth in the prophecy and translating it into words we can understand."

Celia was about to sit down after a brief pause, but then other questions began to roll in.

"What does it mean about the dark and light being banished? I thought they had been restored." Raina asked.

"Is that the reason for the mourning in Palace Solaris?" Maldia asked. "Will the dark and light be imbalanced again?"

Chandra's heart raced as she added, "I can attest to the land being healed. That is where Sage and I went, and we saw it for ourselves. We saw the people celebrating and getting along. We saw the beginnings of peace."

"I am inquisitive about the part where it says the queen and I will be married," Epialos said as he eyed the queen lustfully.

Damaphur scoffed. "How do you know it is speaking of us? It could mean anything. These prophecies are very obscure sometimes. It could mean the king and queen of a private home, as in the owners of the home, for all we know."

"It also said that the king of the dark would be slain. Is it the same king that marries the queen of pride?" asked Hestia.

The questions continued until all their voices were raised into a cacophony that filled the conference room and echoed off the stone walls.

Tenebris had recovered from helping Celia control her powers and was now breathing normally. He held his hands up in a stopping gesture and yelled over the crowd, "Please, everyone, let's lower our voices and speak one at a time. We are overwhelming the seer."

That had been putting it mildly. Celia's varied emotions definitely overwhelmed her, but it had nothing to do with the noise. She was tired from the toll on her body, irritated by her lack of knowledge of the new prophecy, and nervous that everyone would think of her as a failure for having no information about her vision.

"Maybe we should check on the babies and return later," Maldia suggested. She gave Raina a knowing look, gesturing for her to follow suit.

Raina stood from her seat. "Yes, that sounds like a good idea."

"I will go with you two," Chandra said as she rose from her seat as well. "I have not yet planned for you to have a personal guard, so I will go guard you."

"I think we should all go to give Celia some time to collect herself," Damaphur said as she stood.

"That is an excellent idea," Epialos said, turning to the queen before adding, "Why don't you show me around the palace's inner courtyard? I want to see those beautiful gardens everyone always tells me about."

Damaphur turned to him with a smile and linked her arm through his. "I cannot believe I have never shown them to you before."

Epialos chuckled as he led her toward the door. "We always spend our time fighting, not speaking of gardens and flowers."

"Well, it is high time we change that," Damaphur said just before they left the room.

Chandra, Raina, and Maldia gave each other knowing looks before shaking their heads and following them out, laughing all the way. Hestia followed as well, but she was not laughing. Instead, she kept shooting angry looks at the back of Epialos's head.

Sage began to collect his things silently, but his lips twitched as he watched Hestia glaring at the back of the king's head.

Warren chuckled. "It's good to see them finally getting along," he said to no one in particular.

Tenebris answered, "Yes, it is. I wonder if it had anything to do with Lake Divere closing up."

"You know it did," Sage said. "According to the last prophecy, it will heal the land when the leaders are purged and new leaders are put in their place. I would say that Epialos purged Damaphur rather well in her office."

Warren laughed aloud at Sage's pun as he said between snickers, "It makes sense. They are leading together instead of fighting, so they are new leaders in a manner of speaking."

"You are right; it does make sense," Tenebris said. "Now, however, we have a new prophecy to adapt and figure out."

"I remember a wise woman asking me if I had consulted an expert on the last prophecy," Warren said, smiling at Celia. "We will hold a celebration to close out the era of the previous prophecy and welcome in the new. I will definitely be inviting my expert to translate the new prophecy."

"When and where would this ceremony take place?" Celia asked curiously.

"We can discuss that later," Warren answered, his tone growing serious. "For now, you need to rest so you can be better prepared to translate the prophecy and receive any new visions the Goddess may send your way."

Celia nodded as she lowered herself into her seat. "I wouldn't mind a good bath and some sleep."

"I will just return these supplies to my room. Tenebris, can you help me so I don't have to carry everything alone this time?" Sage asked as he hefted the box and carried it toward the door.

"I'll be right behind you," Tenebris said.

He gave Celia a light peck on her cheek before grabbing the rest of the supplies and following Sage.

Warren came over to sit beside Celia.

"Would you like me to draw your bath?" he asked, giving her a seductive smirk.

Celia rolled her eyes. "I can turn on the water. It isn't that hard."

Warren chuckled and shook his head. "What will it take to convince you to join the Spire?"

"Well, you certainly won't be able to seduce me into it," Celia said with a humorous smirk.

Warren's gaze turned serious as he scooted closer to Celia. His voice dropped to a whisper as he said huskily, "I would want to seduce you either way, my lovely Celia."

She pierced him with a disbelieving stare with her dark brown eyes as she said, "I know what I am and what I am not, and lovely I am not."

Warren frowned, and Celia thought she saw anger in his amber eyes as he turned in his seat to look at her full-on. "Who told you that you are not lovely, Celia? I will hunt them down and tear out their tongue."

Celia chortled, but her laughter faded when Warren did not join her. She gave him a questioning look and asked, "Seriously? You would really do that?"

Warren's gaze did not slip as he asked, "Don't I look serious? I would never let anyone say that you were not beautiful."

Celia frowned. "I tell myself that every time I look in the mirror. No one else has to tell me."

It was Warren's turn to frown, his dark brows drawing down over his eyes as he said, "Then you must not see what I see."

Celia shook her head in denial, saying, "I see hair that is too frizzy and a nose that is too big for my face. I have huge lips, hips that could take down a small house, and a large stomach. And let us not forget the darkness of my coffee-colored skin."

Warren's eyes narrowed as he leaned in, bending his enormous frame over the arm of the chairs to place his face close to hers. His amber eyes darkened seductively as he spoke in a husky tone.

"I see hair that accentuates the beautiful features of your gorgeous face. Everything on that face is a perfect size. Lips that are perfect for feasting on, juicy and delectable.

"Those hips that are not delicate, like a woman's hips should be. I am not afraid of breaking them when I grip them tightly in my hands while I fuck you hard.

"I know the softness of your flesh on your bones will feel wonderful pressed against my hardness. Much better than sharp bones protruding through thin skin against my muscles, the way they do on those stick-figure girls that everyone thinks are perfect.

"And let us not forget the silky softness of that sweet, dark skin. The thought of running my tongue over every inch of it makes me want to cum in my pants."

By the time Warren had finished, Celia's eyes had gone wide, her breathing erratic, and her heart thumped against the inside of her ribcage. Warren had moved closer and closer while he had spoken, and now his face was so close to hers that their noses almost touched.

Celia swallowed hard and ran her tongue nervously over her lips. She noticed the passionate glint in Warren's amber gaze grow darker and ravenous as he watched her mouth.

Did he really see her that way?

Celia's center heated as she thought about Warren's mouth on hers as he gripped her hips like he said he wanted to while he…gulp…fucked her hard. She thought about the sensation of her softness pressed against his hardness while he did that, and her insides quivered with longing. She thought about the sensual feeling of

Warren's tongue running over every inch of her, pausing between her legs to…

She had to stop. She had to shove the thoughts away before she melted away right there in her seat.

"I want you, Celia. Never think otherwise," Warren said, his voice dark and sultry.

Celia did not know what to say. She wanted him too, if she was being honest. She wanted him with an intensity that she had never felt before. But she could never have him.

Reading of a betrayal or scrying it inside a glass ball was one thing, but now that her powers were growing…

Well, she did not want to see an actual vision of Warren betraying her or breaking her. She had already suffered that once, even though that vision had been averted. It had still hurt, and she had been angry at him afterward, even though it had not really happened.

No, she could never give herself to this Grandmaster. If she did, her feelings would grow so deep that she would never find her way back. Then, if he hurt her, she may not survive it.

Warren's intense gaze pierced Celia as she stared into his amber, gold-flecked eyes. She took a deep breath and turned away, rising from her seat to leave the room. Warren's firm hand gripped her wrist, pulling her around to face him as he stood.

"Don't turn away from me, Celia. I know you want me as much as I want you. There's no need to deny it any longer."

He gave another gentle pull on her arm, but she pulled back, pulling her arm from his grip as she shook her head.

"No, Warren. There can never be anything between us, and I am too loyal to Damaphur for me to work for the Spire. Please, just let me go."

Celia saw the momentary flash of hurt spark in Warren's eyes and felt a pang of guilt, but she ignored it and pushed on. She could not fall victim to Warren's charms.

He sighed as he let her go and dropped his hands to his sides. "Fine, Celia. Have it your way for now. I will have you someday, one way or another."

"You just don't give up, do you?" Celia said admonishingly.

Warren smirked. "No, I do not, and I am stubborn to boot."

Celia shook her head and turned to leave when the door was flung open, and a panicked Hestia entered the room.

"Oh, what now?" Celia asked in frustration.

Hestia stopped before Celia with fear and worry etched all over her features. "Remember the first of your vision when you said Palace Solaris was mourning because of a loss?"

Celia's heart stopped beating for a split second, and her breath froze. "Yes," she squeaked.

"Well, I left Maldia, Raina, and Chandra at the nursery and then checked on my congregation. I wanted to ensure they had everything ready for the celebration tonight."

Hestia took a breath as she paused to see if she had Celia's attention. Celia nodded without responding, so Hestia went on.

"I stationed two guards in front of the nursery room doors. When I returned, the guards had not moved. They said that no one had left the room, and no one had entered, but when I went in to check on the babies and the women, no one was in the room."

Celia began to tremble, and her voice was shaky as she asked, "Hestia, what are you saying?"

"I am saying," Hestia said as she nervously fussed, straightening her robes. "Raina, Maldia, Chandra, and the babies have all gone missing."

Celia choked out a gasping sob as she shook her head repeatedly.

"There's only one person I know of that has the people and the means to kidnap people right under other people's noses," Hestia said accusingly.

Her eyes darted to Celia, then behind Celia, then back to Celia as they widened in confused horror. Celia frowned as she watched Hestia's muddled gaze drift back to where Celia had left Warren standing alone.

Celia followed Hestia's gaze and gasped.

"There is no possible way," Celia whispered as she stared at the spot where Warren should have been.

He had disappeared without a trace.

"Where is Sage and Tenebris?" Hestia asked.

"Tenebris helped Sage take Sage's stuff back to his room," Celia answered, still staring at the spot Warren had disappeared from.

"I'll go find them and return here. Do not go anywhere," Hestia said, and Celia nodded.

Confused, Celia sat back down in the seat she had just left, placing a hand beside her where Warren had sat only moments ago. A heaviness consumed her heart as tears welled in her eyes.

Had Warren really disappeared? Celia knew he could transport, but where had he gone and why?

Those thoughts and more ran through her mind as her eyes grew strangely heavy, and a weariness that Celia had never before felt came over her. It was suddenly challenging to keep her eyes open. Her vision grew fuzzy, and she could have sworn she saw Warren's face just before her eyes closed, and the world grew dark around her.

Hestia never found Tenebris or Sage. When Hestia finally made her way back to the conference room, Celia was gone as well. Queen Damaphur heavily mourned the loss of her people, and Epialos was overwrought over losing his grandchild yet again. The king and queen organized search parties, sending them out to every corner of the castle and all throughout the lands.

They looked all over the palace, the grounds, the city, and more. For days and days, they looked everywhere they possibly could. They scanned the northern and southern regions as far as their reach would extend, checked every inch of both Spires, scourged every city on both hemispheres and even scouted certain houses.

Their searches came up empty…

Nothing…

It was as if they had vanished into thin air and had never even existed.

They remembered the words of the prophecy that predicted the mourning in the palace. They thought maybe they could find some clue in the prophecy but could not find Sage's supplies to consult the recorded words.

Epialos remembered something about mountain cities, so Epialos ordered that all mountains be searched as safely as possible. They sent teams and teams of dragons and foot soldiers, but they came up empty.

They found nothing.

Epialos and Damaphur could do no more to find the missing members of Palace Solaris, and they mourned their lost people. The palace mourned while Mikka cheered.

During that time, Mikka began to celebrate peace and the newly united king and queen of the planet. Many began to speculate how long it would be before they married and which palace they would pick as their permanent home.

The rebels disbanded, and some even joined the king or queen's army. Most went home to their families, feeling more confident that Mikka would be safe enough for their children in the future.

Celebrations, parties, and balls were held throughout Mikka in the north and the south, except for Palace Solaris, where mourning and sadness reigned.

The once bright palace fell into gloominess, and even the flowers seemed to wither; their colors diminished to dullness. Palace Solaris began to look more like Palace Asgorath as time went on.

Their world had ended…not with a bang, but with a whisper.

Just as predicted by The Missing Great Oracle, Celia Fray.

THE FOLLOWING SHORT IS BONUS MATERIAL THAT WILL BE HELPFUL FOR BOOK TWO:

COMING OUT IN JULY 2024

****Cover art © Rebecca Jose ****

Cover Art Subject to Change

Angels, Demons, and Dragons

A BRIEF HISTORY OF THE SPECIES

Written by: Dorian Vasgar in the year 200 A.G.W.*

Information was gathered from the Spire Library in Solaris, the Spire Library in Asgorath, and live interviews with Celia, the Palace Solaris seer and keeper of the ancient B.G.W.** scrolls. An escorted tour through Solaris Palace Library also provided some information. Grandmaster Warren was not available for an interview.

DRAGONS

Dragons are beasts that have magic breaths. Dragons possess seven types of magic breath, which will be discussed later.

There are two types of dragons: Draconians and Wyrms.

Draconians have bodies like a giant dog with scales. They are usually smaller than Wyrms and have smaller horns and shorter necks. Their heads are large, with short snouts and tiny horn buds sticking out on their nostrils. They have wings, leather, and bat-like with talons along the tips, and they usually live in high mountain caves. They have four legs with talons for feet and a super-strong tail that can break stone.

The Wyrms have slimmer, serpent-like bodies with long necks. They have spines along their bodies with great horns on their huge, elongated heads. They have four legs with a super strong tail like their winged brethren, but they have no wings and are bound to the earth. They can burrow through any surface with their talons and usually live underground.

Both dragon species are super intelligent and can speak their own language, primarily noises, growls, and high-pitched squeaks. They can also speak common languages and interact with most species.

DRACONIANS

The Draconia royal dragons have two forms, beastial (their dragon forms) and bipedal (a humanoid form).

The bipedal forms have scales that run over the torso area and down the arms and legs, and their eyes glow when they use their magic. If a Draconia conceives and bears children in bipedal form, their children will be the same. If they conceive in beastial form, they will lay eggs. The hatchlings will all be beastials and not able to shift.

Beastials can also breed with each other, laying and hatching eggs and producing more beastials. Beastials cannot produce royals with bipedal forms.

DRACONIA ROYALS IN BATTLE ARMOR AND HELMS

WYRMS

The Wyrms only have one form, but the royals of the Wyrm species have a stripe of soft fur that runs from the backs of their massive heads to the tip of their strong tails. The fur is colored according to the magic they wield.

WYRM

WYRM ROYAL

DRAGON MAGIC BREATH

The magic breaths are as follows: Fire, Ice, Wind, Lightning, Poison, Acid, and Smog. The dragon's magic depends on their parents or the royal that conceived them. Royals that are conceived are usually stronger than their hatched brethren.

~Wyrms only have two types of magic; Fire and/or Ice. The royal Wyrms have both, while the normal Wyrms only possess one or the other.

~Draconians have all magics, some rarer than others, and some can even possess all seven magic abilities simultaneously. The magic and what kind of magic they can produce are listed as follows:

☺The diamond-colored dragons possess all types of magic at once and are the rarest of all dragons. Diamond dragons produce beastials that can have any breath magic. Still, they do not possess all at once as their bipedal counterparts do. Some of the stronger ones can produce two, or even three, breath magics, but no bestial diamond dragon has ever had more than that.

It is extremely hard for the royals to reproduce and even more challenging for them to fertilize eggs in bestial form. Even when royals do conceive, it is even more difficult for them to carry the babies to term.

Pregnant royals are very protected, and beastials carrying fertile eggs are also. The eggs are well protected until hatched too.

☺The wind dragons are the second rarest. They are silver, gold, or copper in color, otherwise known as metallic dragons. They produce beastials with the same magic.

Wind dragons have a difficult time fertilizing their eggs, so their beastials are even rarer than their royals. The royals do not conceive frequently, so when they do, they are protected until they give birth.

☺Acid dragons are the same as wind dragons on the rarity scale. They are dull yellow, like the color of a dandelion, and are often confused for gold wind dragons.

They have no trouble fertilizing eggs or conceiving, but raising an acid dragon to full term is problematic. Because of their developing acidic saliva and blood, young acid dragons tend to accidentally melt themselves. Care must be taken to neutralize the acid in their saliva and blood by feeding them regular rounds of ginger anise tea. It is hard to find and even harder to get dragon babies to drink due to its foul taste.

They develop the ability to control the acid levels in their bodies during adolescence without drinking the tea. Still, acid dragons do not live long since their magic dwindles with age, and it becomes harder to maintain control.

Electric dragons are orange or jade green in color. They are rare in bipedal form, so the electric royals are highly guarded. The green ones are sometimes confused for poison dragons. Still, the color can be easily distinguished by determining whether it is shiny or matte. Electric dragons are matte in color.

It is tough for lightning dragons to conceive in bipedal form, so royals are rare. They can lay eggs and create beastials just fine, but most electric royals mate in bipedal form to try to conceive more royals.

Poison dragons are not common, but not as rare as wind or lightning. These shiny, grass-green dragons can conceive bi-pedal royals if they monitor the fetus closely and feed the mother anti-venom once a month, but it is challenging for the females to hatch their eggs. The eggs tend to not hatch because the babies poison their environment inside the eggs and die.

For these reasons, poison royals are much more common than poison beastials. Poison beastials are highly sought for defense, but don't piss them off!

Smog dragons are as rare as poison dragons. Black in color, these dragons can conceive royals or hatch beastials with no problems, but they tend to be anti-social, even among their own kind. Most smog dragons tend to keep to themselves and enjoy being alone.

☾Ice dragons are common, and the most common of Draconians.

They are light blue to medium blue in color and are mostly beastial; however, there have been a few icy royals in the diamond dragon's court. Ice kings and queens are rare. Tiamat was the only Ice queen that ruled, and she created the first ice court. She was one of three ever to exist that actually ruled a court.

☾Fire dragons are common, and the most common of the Wyrms.

Fire dragons are primarily red, though there have been some fire dragons that were black and were mistaken for smog dragons. The difference is the eyes. Black fire dragons have red eyes even in bipedal form, while smog dragons have blue or green eyes.
Like ice dragons, the fire dragons are mostly beastial, but some royals were members of the wind dragon's court. Bahamut Gaian was the only fire dragon king who created a fire court and ruled over it, earning him his God status.

DRAGONS DURING THE WAR

The Draconians paired with the angels or demons during the war, depending on the species. The pairing was as follows…
The diamond court sided with the angels.
The wind court sided with the angels.
The lightning court sided with the angels.
The poison court sided with the demons.
The smog court sided with the demons.
The ice court sided with the angels.
The fire court sided with the demons.
The Wyrms sided with the demons no matter what court they belonged to, creating a division between Draconian and Wyrm dragons that still exist today. If any pure dragons existed today, they would undoubtedly still hold onto that division.

ANGELS

Angels are humanoid creatures that possess great power and magic. They have great, white, feathered wings, and their skin has an ethereal glow that could blind an average person if it glows too brightly. Their magic is powered by their emotion; if they are happy, their magic is gentle and their glow is dim, but if they are angry, their magic is destructive and could burn the world.

Angels lived in a massive glass palace on top of the highest mountain. The mountain was said to be so high that one could not see the top with the naked eye from the ground.

The palace could only be reached by flying up to it, and most creatures (even ones with wings) ran out of air or froze to death before they rose high enough to even see the palace, much less enter it.

The angels were the only ones who could reach the palace. Visitors could reach the palace by being in touching vicinity of an angel. The angel would fly the visitor up safely. Once in the palace, the climate was controlled magically, and visitors could wander freely on palace grounds without touching the angel that brought them.

It is said that when the last angel fell in the Great War, the palace shattered, and the pieces dissipated into thin air. No one knows what happened to the mountain, but some say it disappeared with the shards of glass.

Enoch was the first angel to take a dragon lover. He was in love with the Royal Draconian, Tiamat Drakaina, the only Ice queen in existence at the time.

She ruled over the ice court during the war and swore her allegiance to Enoch, giving him her body as well. She was prideful, conceited, and coveted only the best and wealthiest things. Only the beautiful and prideful were allowed in her court.

Tiamat and Enoch had a child while Tiamat was in bipedal form. She was the first child that was part angel and part dragon. She became the first angel dragon queen when she took the throne after her parents were killed in the war. She took her mother's last name, starting the family name of the angel dragons that would carry down to Damaphur's reign.

The lineage of the angel dragons:

1) Tiamat Drakaina- first queen and now Goddess of the angel dragons.

Tiamat was the last pure dragon queen, but the angel dragons still consider her the first queen since she is the mother of the first angel dragon. In addition, the angel dragons consider Tiamat their Goddess. The Sisters of Tiamat and Brothers of Enoch worship her as their Goddess and Holy Mother of all angel dragons.

2) Echidna Drakaina- the first angel dragon queen.

Echidna fell in love with the first demon dragon, Typhon Gaian, and they had a child, Maria. Typhon took another lover, a demon called Galephria, and had a son, Azriel. Typhon ended up marrying his demon lover, which pissed Echidna off. She tried to kill Galephria while Galephria was carrying Typhon's third child, which started the Great War that split planet Mikka in half.

2) Lucuia Drakaina – Damaphur's mother and second angel dragon queen.

Echidna took another lover during the war and had another daughter, Lucuia. Her first child, Maria, disappeared and was believed to have been killed in the war. Lucuia took the throne after her mother was killed by assassins, and she assassinated the demon's queen to avenge her mother and step-sister.

4) Damaphur Drakaina- the current angel dragon queen.

Angels are almost extinct, and the ones left have lost most of their magic because their wings were cut off during the war. They now live like regular non-magic people, and most hide what they used to be.

DEMONS

Demons are humanoid creatures with great power and magic. They are as powerful as the angels, but their magic is different. Their magic is fueled by logic, so the wiser the demon, the more powerful their magic.

Demons have very dark skin of various colors, the most powerful being the black demons and the least powerful being the common red demons. They have massive horns growing from their heads, except for the fertile females, who have smaller horns.

Demons lived in a vast underground city called Asgorath, which is where the demon dragons got their name for their capital city. Asgorath could only be reached by a massive underground tunnel that stretched for miles before finally diving down into the deepest recesses of the earth, almost to the fiery center core. Demons and certain dragons were the only creatures able to access the city unless protected by a demon's magic. Any who tried to reach the city without the protection of a demon fell dead from heat exhaustion before reaching the city.

It is said that when the last demon fell in the Great War, the fiery lake of the city rose and broke Mikka apart, which is where Lake Divere came from. It is believed that demons possess the magic to send the lake back down and heal the planet, but unfortunately, demons are extinct.

Lilith was the first demon to take a dragon lover. She was in love with the Draconian Bahamut Gaian, the king of the fire dragons and the only fire dragon king in existence. He created his court and swore his allegiance to the beautiful Lilith. His fire dragons followed.

Bahamut was kind, loyal, and deeply respected Lilith and her cause to unite angels and demons into one powerful, unbiased unit. Bahamut married Lilith, and he became the first dragon king to have a pure demon as his queen.

Bahamut impregnated Lilith in bipedal form, and she had a child, Typhon, the first demon dragon.

The lineage of the Demon Dragons:

1) Bahamut Gaian– the first king of the fire dragons and now God of the demon dragons.

He was promoted to God status by The Brothers of Typhon and the Sisters of Lilith. They worship him as their God since he is the father of the first demon dragon. Lilith is considered the Holy Mother.

2) Typhon Gaian – son of Bahamut and Lilith.

Typhon had three children. His daughter, Maria, was born to him by his angel dragon lover, Echidna. However, he did not love Echidna and left the angel's court. He returned to his own court, the demon court, with his father Bahamut and took a demon lover, Galephria. He married his demon lover Galephria after she bore his first son, Azriel. While Galephria was pregnant with his third child, Epialos, Typhon defended her against his former lover, Echidna, which started the Great War.

He took the throne after Bahamut and Lilith went into hiding when Lake Divere rose from Asgorath and split the planet in half.

3) Azriel Gaian – First son of Typhon and Typhon's demon wife, Galephria.

He ruled after his father was killed in the war, but his reign was short-lived. It is believed that Lucuia, Echidna's second daughter by another lover, assassinated Azriel when she took the throne after Typhon was killed in the war. However, Azriel did not die and instead went into hiding with the help of his younger brother, Epialos.

4) Epialos Gaian – Third child of Typhon.

He took over the throne after Azriel was supposedly assassinated. He still protects his brother, his brother's bride, Tatiana, and his aging mother, Galephria. Epialos sent them into hiding soon after taking the throne to protect them from Lucuia's wrath.

Lucuia grew old and passed, leaving the throne to her only living daughter and heir, Damaphur. Epialos never took a lover because he was secretly in love with Damaphur. After Lucuia's passing,

Epialos no longer hid the fact and tried to woo the queen every chance he got.

Demons are almost extinct, and those left have lost their wings and magic during the great war. Like the angels, most demons hide what they used to be and live like ordinary, non-magic people.

The end

THIS CONCLUDES OUR SHORT DEPICTION OF ANGELS, DRAGONS, AND DEMONS. FOR MORE INFORMATION ON THE GREAT WAR AND THE PROPHECIES, CONSULT THE SOLARIS PALACE SEER, CELIA.

YOU MAY ALSO SPEAK WITH THE GRANDMASTER OF THE WIZARD'S SPIRE, WARREN, ABOUT INFORMATION ON THE ANGEL, DEMON, AND DRAGON LINEAGES WHEN AND IF HE IS AVAILABLE.

THE LIBRARIES OF PALACE SOLARIS AND PALACE ASGORATH CONTAIN SOME EDUCATIONAL INFORMATION ON THESE SUBJECTS, BUT PUBLIC ADMISSION IS LIMITED.

THE SPIRE LIBRARIES ON BOTH HEMISPHERES ARE VAST AND CONTAIN PLENTIFUL INFORMATION ON THESE SUBJECTS. PUBLIC ADMISSION IS ALWAYS WELCOME WITH AN ESCORT.

A.G.W. – After the Great War
**B.G.W. – Before the Great War*

FREE DOWNLOAD!

ABOUT THE AUTHOR

Rebecca Jose lives in a small town in the heart of Kentucky. She has three grown kids, a multitude of "adopted" kids, six grandkids, four dogs, and a parrot. She enjoys her job at a local historical sight in Harrodsburg, Kentucky.

When she is not working at her job or at home on the computer, she enjoys her time with her husband, grandkids, and the rest of her family. Her dream is to create many stories for many readers, and she hopes that people will enjoy her stories for years to come.

THANK YOU FOR READING AND FOR BEING A FAN...

REBECCA JOSE XOXO

If you enjoyed this story, please write a review and post it to your favorite reading site. Tell others about Rebecca Jose and her stories, so that they may be able to enjoy them as well.

FOR NOTIFICATIONS FROM AMAZON ON NEW RELEASES AND OTHER INFORMATION, FOLLOW REBECCA JOSE ON AMAZON AUTHORS

https://www.amazon.com/stores/author/B08M5H Z1JS

TO RECEIVE UPDATES ON NEW RELEASES AND MORE IN YOUR EMAIL OR TO SIGN UP FOR HER NEWSLETTER, VISIT HER WEBSITE

http://mymeshara.wixsite.com/nethersouls

<u>**FOLLOW HER ON SOCIAL MEDIA FOR PR BOX GIVEAWAYS AND OTHER SPECIAL PRIZES FROM REBECCA JOSE...**</u>

TIKTOK...https://www.tiktok.com/@REBECCAJOSE4080

FACEBOOK...https://www.facebook.com/rebecca.maggard.79

TWITTER...https://twitter.com/Rebeccajose8

INSTAGRAM...https://www.instagram.com/mymeshara/

GOODREADS...https://www.goodreads.com/author/show/21408581.Rebecca_Jose